GOLDEN SERPENT

MARK **ABERNETHY**
GOLDEN SERPENT

ARENA
ALLEN&UNWIN

This edition published in 2008
First published in 2007

Arena Books, an imprint of
Allen & Unwin
83 Alexander Street
Crows Nest NSW 2065
Australia
Phone: (61 2) 8425 0100
Fax: (61 2) 9906 2218
Email: info@allenandunwin.com
Web: www.allenandunwin.com

National Library of Australia
Cataloguing-in-Publication entry:

   Abernethy, Mark, 1964– .
   Golden serpent.

   ISBN 978 1 74175 506 0 (pbk.).

   I. Title.

   A823.4

Set in 12.5/15.5 pt Joanna MT by Midland Typesetters, Australia
Printed in Australia by McPherson's Printing Group

10 9 8 7 6 5 4 3

PROLOGUE

Zamboanga City, southern Philippines, June 2002

John Sawtell sopped gravy with a bread roll and kept one eye on the Cubs–Yankees game. Catering grunts cleared out bain-maries and wet-mopped the service area while the late eaters dragged it out in the demountable cafeteria, avoiding the thirty-six degree heat of early evening. The officers' mess was almost empty except for two white guys in clean woodland-cam fatigues sitting three tables away.

Sawtell kept his eyes on the pitcher's wind-up and away from the white guys – secondees dropped in from Langley with bullshit ranks. Sawtell's US Army rank of captain was real. Yet here he was, spending whole days in meetings with these blue-eyed boys. He'd now heard enough about paradigm shifts and 'the big picture' to last him a lifetime.

Most of Sawtell's Special Forces Green Berets were working-class men who needed solid leadership, not weasel words. Sawtell heard what his men had to say about some of the intelligence briefings, especially from the guy they called 'Pencil Neck'. He glanced across the mess and chuckled: everyone on an army base got a name, whether they liked it or not, and Pencil Neck's was a good fit.

Pencil Neck had lectured the men on the cultural sensitivities of the Muslim Filipinos. But Sawtell's men were fresh from Kandahar, and they didn't much care about which way to point a Muslim's ass when you buried him.

Sawtell wiped his mouth with a paper napkin, took a draw of iced water, kept his eyes on the game.

The analogue clock above the chow line said it was 8.43 pm local. He threw the napkin on his plate and walked into the blistering evening heat.

The black carpet of the Sulu Sea sparkled through palm trees as Sawtell came off the concrete parade ground and entered the Command Centre. The air-con was like a wall coming out of the windless humidity. He ran a hand over his stubbly head, felt the damp of perspiration. An MP looked up briefly, but didn't react. The real anti-terror work was done on the perimeter, from bullet-proof glass cages, pop-up bollards and a mean-as-hell MP detail trained at Fort Bragg.

He moved down the narrow hallway, the floor flimsy beneath his size 13s. From this demountable, perched in an old schoolyard above the city of Zamboanga, the United States controlled the South-East Asian end of its War on Terror, codename: Operation Enduring Freedom.

For six months US military advisers had supported the Philippine Army Scouts and their Navy commandos, the SWAGs. It was a joint operation, so the locals clung to their own name, Balikatan 02-1, but the result was the same: hunt tangos, catch tangos, put tangos out of business.

Sawtell's Alpha company had already been involved in two full-blown battles in their first four months in Zamboanga. He'd lost two men. He didn't feel like an adviser – he felt like a commander in a war zone.

As Sawtell made his way down the trailer towards his office, a Signals corporal called Davis emerged from a room filled with computer screens.

'Something just in, sir,' said Davis, then turned back into his room. Sawtell followed, stooping his footballer's frame to look at Davis's screen.

Davis pointed to a secure memo from CINCPAC in Hawaii, dated two minutes earlier. The header on the memo was a bar of letters and numerals. They gave Sawtell the order to chase and catch or kill 'Number One'.

Sawtell read it again. 'Shit!'

'Number One' was code for the most dangerous man in South-East Asia, Abu Sabaya, the senior terrorist in the Abu Sayyaf organisation. Sabaya — born Aldam Tilao — was responsible for hundreds of kidnappings, bombings, assassinations, executions, massacres and extortion rackets around the southern Philippines and Malaysia.

One attempt to free eleven foreign hostages from Sabaya's stronghold on Basilan Island had led to a forty-two-hour gunfight between Sawtell's Alpha company and the rebels. Two weeks earlier, Sawtell's Berets and Philippine Army Scouts had stormed the terrorists in the jungle boonies behind Sibuco. Sabaya got away, but not before killing most of his hostages.

Sawtell rubbed his jaw as he stared at the screen. Sabaya looked like a movie star and enjoyed enormous loyalty from the local villagers. He was almost impossible to track, and if he'd been pinpointed, they'd got incredibly lucky. Either way, Sawtell's boys would want a shot at this.

'Get CINCPAC, tell them "confirm",' said Sawtell, turning towards the door.

Davis turned. 'Sir, there's more. We've got eyes.'

Sawtell followed Davis's finger to a larger screen. It was black with bright green lines on it. 'Sir, we had an AWACS in the air when the memo came through,' said Davis sheepishly. 'I took the liberty of asking them to give us a lock.'

'On his boat?'

'Umm, no, sir.'

Sawtell didn't like coy. 'What is this, Twenty Questions?'

'Sir, the AWACS has eyes on a pizza box.'

Sawtell gave Davis a quick look, then focused back on the screen. 'Show me.'

Davis pointed his pen at a cigar shape. 'That's Sibuco Bay, sir. It's real time. And that thing moving — that's Number One's pizza order.'

'Are they on the water?'

3

'Roger that. Slower craft, just started moving, perhaps to Number One.'

Sawtell stared at the screen. If Sabaya was anywhere near that boat, he'd bail pronto if he heard one hint of helo engine. They'd do this by sea.

'Print it,' said Sawtell, nodding at the memo, 'then get it to the locals asap.'

As Sawtell moved away he almost crashed headlong into the CIA white boys rushing in, obviously tipped off through their own channels.

'Be ready in five,' said Sawtell as he passed them. 'Only one of you though. And come loaded – this is for real.'

Pencil Neck tried to take control.

'Captain, where's the colonel?'

'Don't know, but give him my regards when you find him.'

Colonel Dave Henson couldn't make a decision without making seven phone calls. Which was a shame, since Colonel Henson was technically in charge of Enduring Freedom.

Sawtell moved through the centre of the white guys and said to the staff sergeant at the desk, 'Give me a five-minute call on Alpha and Bravo. Green for Go.'

As he pushed through the demountable's front door and into the tropical heat Sawtell saw Davis fly out of a side door and head to the Filipino area of the compound. The locals would get to lead the op – as politics dictated – but the Berets would be there every step of the way.

Abu Sabaya! thought Sawtell to himself, the adrenaline now racing. *Abu fucking Sabaya!*

The Philippine Navy SWAGs were waiting at the fenced-off military annexe of Port Zamboanga when the Green Berets' Humvee convoy arrived. Floodlights lit the huge wharf apron and the hangars. Sawtell issued orders for the sergeants to load the boat, then he made for the first Navy vessel, a forty-foot open-deck powerboat painted in matt olive. It was filled with camo-flashed Philippine special forces dressed in black fatigues – the SWAGs. Sawtell guessed there were twenty of them. They looked well-armed with their customised Colt M16 A2s and flash grenades on their webbings.

One of them stood abruptly and jumped onto the dock. Lieutenant-Colonel Miguel Arroy, Sawtell's counterpart. They greeted each other informally, as Special Forces etiquette required.

Arroy's eyes flashed. He'd lost three men in the bungled raid on Sabaya's Sibuco camp two weeks before and his men wanted payback.

'We still live?' he asked, pointing to Sawtell's throat mic.

Sawtell nodded. He'd been taking updates from the AWACS during the ride from Camp Enduring Freedom and the airborne surveillance people still had a lock on the pizza.

'By the book, Mig,' said Sawtell. 'Your boys get first chop.'

Within minutes the two-boat flotilla was ready to move out. The boats' configuration meant the soldiers sat back to back down the centre, with a skipper at the rear.

The SWAGs glistened in the southern Philippine heat. It didn't matter how advanced the materials, full battle kit in the tropics was a walking sauna. The Berets wore kevlar helmets and matt-black jumpsuits. Their flashings were boot-blacked along with their M4 assault rifles. Men went through their rituals – rubbing crucifixes, checking their weapons for load, playing with neckerchiefs worn since Kandahar, play-punching each other. Some closed their eyes, others sang to themselves. Several vomited quietly over the gunwale.

The only thing that wasn't happening was movement. As Sawtell and Arroy went through a mission brief, the Americans' radio system came in with a direct patch through to Colonel Henson, who was in Jakarta.

Sawtell took the call, unable to believe what he was hearing. Henson wanted the mission put on hold till some intelligence guy could be flown into Zamboanga.

'I hate to do this to you, John,' came the high nasal sound of Henson's voice, 'but my hands are tied on this one – you know how it is.'

'Sir,' said Sawtell, doing his best to conceal his frustration in front of his men, 'we've already got intel on board . . .'

'I know, John.'

A drop of sweat trickled down Sawtell's upper lip, onto his teeth. 'We've got eyes and we're good to go, sir.'

'Jesus, Johnny,' said Henson, using the name only Sawtell's football buddies dared call him. 'You think I didn't tell them that?'

Sawtell knew Henson hadn't told the brass anything like that.

'Thing is, CINCPAC wants this intelligence guy in the boat, so he's in the boat. Got that, Captain?'

Sawtell stamped his leg, and sweat dripped into his right boot. He looked over to see Arroy staring at him.

'I got him timed for ten minutes,' said Henson. 'And Johnny – he's one of the good guys, okay? He's Australian.'

The Australian arrived early – but he might as well have been seven hours late by the time the Black Hawk had blasted in over the harbour, dropped its human cargo on the two-hundred-year-old quay and taken off into the night.

Sandy-blond and pale-eyed, the Australian was about six foot and built but not worked on. He was all arms and legs but a smooth mover. He wore dark blue overalls, special forces boots and a black Adidas baseball cap pulled low. A black Cordura sports bag was slung over his shoulder.

The Aussie didn't offer a name or his hand when Sawtell and Arroy greeted him. Sawtell pointed to the back of his boat and the Australian simply moved to his seat next to Pencil Neck.

The outboard engines fired up and Sawtell watched the CIA honky offer a handshake. The Australian ignored it.

The troop boats cast off, the revs came up from the triple Yamahas. Sawtell landed in the back of the boat with a thump and they moved into Zamboanga Harbour. Sawtell saw an airborne plug of tobacco come dangerously close to their visitor and he gave his men a look. He fished a kevlar helmet from the kit box under the transom and offered it to the Australian, who shook his head dismissively.

'Chief, stop the boat,' said Sawtell.

The sergeant at the helm looked back in disbelief, and then cut the revs. The boat lost way, fumes washed across the humidity. All eyes turned to the back of the boat. Sawtell looked into the Australian's pale blue eyes, then threw the helmet into the spook's lap. The Australian put the helmet on.

Sawtell gave the 'go' sign.

The revs came up and the boat lurched into the darkness.

At nine pm the two troop boats exited Zamboanga at fifty-one knots and turned hard right – north towards Sibuco and the most dangerous man in South-East Asia.

CHAPTER 1

Western Queensland, November 2006

There were seven of them. Six Australian SAS and one Aussie spook on a line of Honda trail bikes slipping through the outback night.

The lime-green GPS instrument on Mac's bike read 2.49 am, putting the posse ten clicks from the target.

A voice crackled through the headset in Mac's military helmet. 'Keep with your mark, Mac.' The voice belonged to Warrant Officer Ward, the troop leader who was right behind him. 'You're doing fine, mate.'

Alan McQueen was doing far from fine. Other special forces had hangars filled with military toys that whisked people like Mac all over the world. In, out and back in time for a cold beer. The Aussie SAS used motorbikes, which did the job but were hard on the arse and thighs. Mac still wasn't used to riding with lights killed and no night vision. And even with a full moon and clear night, the terrain of western Queensland was not suited to amateur riders.

Mac stayed in third, focused on the guy in front through the spray of dust. He eyed the digital compass beside the GPS and spoke through his throat mic. 'Wardie, time to go west.'

The SAS man acknowledged, and the posse swung out of the channel.

Thirty minutes later a sand dune loomed two hundred feet above them. They idled to the foot of the black giant.

Mac came to a halt, flipped the stand and almost fell off the bike. Ward walked up. 'Well, we got you here, mate. Your mission now,' he said, dispatching a trooper called Foxy up the dune.

Mac squinted at Ward through pale eyes. He never knew when some of these blokes were taking the piss. At six foot, Mac was the bigger man but he wouldn't want to get in a blue with the soldier. Ward had the classic special forces build: heavily muscled and athletic. Mac had seen what the SAS boys could do when they got annoyed and he was glad to be playing on the same team.

Stretching his fingers under black leather gloves, Mac dusted off his blue overalls and replaced his helmet with an old black cap. The tops of his thighs felt like he'd gone three rounds of kickboxing.

He unzipped his black backpack and checked the contents with eyes and fingers. No one used a flashlight. In the pack was a silenced Heckler & Koch P9S handgun, an M16 A2 assault rifle and two devices the size of casino poker chips – 'tags' that guided an air-mounted missile. Nothing fancy, but it all worked.

The SAS troopers were dressed in black urban fatigues, with variations of scarfing. It was ten degrees Celsius in the desert and a couple of the soldiers wore field jackets. They cammed their faces, checked weapons.

Ward brought the boys in close and Mac knelt in front of them. Their headsets crackled: Foxy giving the all-clear from the top of the dune.

The bike engines pinged as they cooled, troopers pulling in closer as Mac outlined the turkey shoot.

Mac lay on the cold sand at the top of the dune. He thought about how his original idea of intelligence work – debonair chat at cocktail parties – had been stymied by someone's decision that he'd be useful in a paramilitary role. That was history, and so was his intel career. He'd done his bit, taken his shot. This would be his last assignment before getting out for good. Tomorrow was the next step; tomorrow meant Sydney and a step closer to having a fiancée rather than just a girlfriend.

He looked out over the endless outback. Thirty miles further west and it turned into the Simpson Desert. Here, below them, there were still channels and clumps of spinifex punctuating the ground.

Ward lay beside him, binos to his eyes. They did a traditional sweep.

'What are we looking for, Macca?' asked Ward.

'Stand-by for a cammo tarp, some sort of covering.'

'You kidding?' muttered Ward. 'Not exactly using spotties here, mate.'

'Plan B – find the perimeter,' said Mac. 'They'd have at least two blokes on the wall.'

The group scanned the desert darkness for the next ten minutes. It was boring, mentally draining work.

Then one of the troopers saw something.

Ward moved down, followed by Mac. They lay on either side of the SAS trooper, who kept his head still and talked softly. 'My eleven o'clock. Two fingers below the horizon. I saw a puff of smoke. Could be a ciggie.'

Mac peered through his Leicas. Found the sentry. 'Out-fucking-standing,' he muttered.

The sentry was well-hidden in a hollow one hundred and fifty metres from the dune, sitting against a rock in a dark pea jacket and khaki pants. On his lap was what looked like a Heckler & Koch MP5 machine pistol, the kind used by counter-terrorism forces. One hell of a thing. Mac had once seen a demo of what an MP5 on full auto could do to a cow carcass. He didn't eat a hamburger for three whole days.

The guard dragged on a cigarette and let out another plume of smoke. A light breeze carried it south.

'Got him?' asked Mac.

'Roger that,' said Ward. 'See that round his neck?'

Mac looked again. 'Yep.'

'Night vision,' said Ward. 'They've got some toys.'

The camp was fifty metres behind the sentry, built in a channel with tarps running for about eighty metres north–south, and cammo webbing over the tarps. No way to see it from the air, unless someone was looking for it. It was a terrorist training camp, the kind of structure usually found in Libya or Afghanistan.

11

It appeared that food and power were at one end of the camp, sleeping at the other, operations and stores in the centre. There were a couple of rough timber latrines to the east of the camp, not far from where the sentry was sitting.

Mac reckoned the camp would hold up to thirty men, and if his snitch in Jakarta wasn't telling him pork pies, one of them was Ali Samrazi – an Indonesian double agent who had dropped from the radar eigtheen months ago and had reappeared with a mob called Moro Jihad. Moro Jihad was a middle-class outfit that focused its activities on economic and maritime terror. If you could drive up the price of shipping through the Malacca Straits and South China Sea by even five per cent, you were eating into the Western world's profit margins. The modern tangos could read spreadsheets as well as al-Qaeda propaganda.

'Wardie, can you find the other sentries? I need to know where they are,' said Mac.

Ward had already found them; they were in a triangle arrangement around the camp.

'Any ideas?' asked Mac.

Ward took his eyes away from the binos. 'No worries. There's three sentries but they're not overlapped. We take out Mr Ashtray and the others won't know about it. It's a free run to the try line.'

The group slid down through the spinifex, gathering behind a rock at the base of the dune. Mac's adrenaline was pumping, his breath short. He looked back up the dune to where Foxy was hidden in the scrub.

Ward tapped his G-Shock and held up both hands.

Mac nodded. Ten minutes to knock the sentries out, then the mission would begin.

Ward gave thumbs-up and went south with one man while a trooper named Jones took two troopers north. Manistas – a tough western Sydney kid they called Manny – remained with Mac. Manny was about five-nine and powerful but lithe. Like a stuntman or a gymnast. As an added bonus, he spoke Farsi, Bahasa Indonesian and some other languages favoured by tangos. That's why he was with Mac.

They got on their bellies and crawled. The advance was slow and painful. The earth of the Australian outback looks like red talc from a distance, but get amongst it and it's filled with gravel, rocks and insects.

Mac followed the SAS trooper into a channel where they could stand in a crouch and they followed the dry bed slightly to the north and around a bend for forty metres. That brought them north-east of the sentry. Manny stopped as they heard the low hum of what was probably a power generator in the camp.

Manny leaned on the wall of the channel, stuck his scarfed head up slowly, pulled back, nodded at Mac. Then he checked his M4, looked down the sights at the ground.

Mac unholstered the Heckler, checked for load, checked for safety. With the suppressor screwed on, the handgun was more than twice its normal length. He found a smaller creek bed that fed into the channel and crawled into it on his elbows, the Heckler in his right hand. The creek bed was perfect: shallow enough to be able to keep eyes on Mr Ashtray but deep enough to move undetected through the dark. He moved quickly, his breath coming dry and shallow.

Mac was just about to take another look at the countdown on his watch when he realised he was face to face with what looked like an eastern brown snake. He froze, watching as the diamond head and darting tongue came out from behind the scrub which was half a foot from his face. The snake moved out into the creek bed, its black eyes like onyx, its body glistening in the moonlight.

Mac backed up across the sand, gulping hard. The venom from a brown snake wouldn't necessarily kill you, but twelve hours of delirium was not Mac's ideal platform for a mission. The snake's gaze was steady, the tongue glowing as it flicked. Mac kept reversing through the dust, trying not to breathe on the thing for fear of annoying it.

As the snake focused on him, Mac fought the panic urge.

The snake raised its head, lifted a whole section of itself off the ground.

Mac back-pedalled like a politician.

The snake pulled its head back on its body, ready to strike. Mac had no choice but to roll sideways out of the shallow depression, into the open. He rolled onto his stomach, looked up at the sentry who was now only twenty metres away. Mac was close enough to smell his Marlboros.

The snake kept coming, Mac could see it slithering fast across the ground. He rolled again and the sentry raised his head. Panicking now, Mac steadied himself on the rocky ground, took a cup-and-saucer grip on the Heckler, aimed it at the sentry and squeezed. The gun spat – the round missed.

Now the sentry was off his perch, MP5 in his hands. Clueless, but alert. The snake didn't stop. Mac looked down and fired at the animal, but only grazed it. The snake was as confused as the guard who was now walking towards him.

The snake finally made a move, came in fast and struck at Mac's Hi-Tec boot. As the fangs sank into the black rubber sole, Mac prayed they wouldn't hit flesh.

The sentry was fifteen metres away and carrying a weapon that could cut a man to ribbons. A couple more steps and he would see Mac. The sentry put his free hand to the night vision goggles and lifted them.

Shit!

Mac had to drop the guy.

He forced his eyes away from the snake and aimed again: two shots in succession. They sounded like a man spitting grapefruit pips.

One shot hit the sentry in the chest. His eyes went wide, his legs folded. Mac should have been on his feet and halfway to the sentry by now, but he turned back immediately to the snake, kicking his legs like a child. He muttered, a clear sign he was on the verge of doing something really stupid.

Pointing the elongated Heckler at the snake on his foot, Mac heard a voice in his head say he'd probably shoot his foot, and what a joke that would make him in Townsville's SAS barracks for the next six months.

Before he could do it, a knife glinted in the moonlight and the snake's head was severed.

Manny held the snake's head and neck in his hand, then he chucked it aside, and put his Ka-bar back in its webbing scabbard.

Mac gave thumbs-up and turned, his breathing still fast and his heart racing.

He was way, *way* too old for this shit.

The sentry was down, but no one was coming out of the camp for a nosey-poke. Lucky break.

Mac checked his G-Shock – three minutes and twenty seconds to sentry deadline.

The two crawled across the ground to the sentry, whose eyes were still open. He lay on his side gasping for air, blood erupting from his mouth spasmodically and splashing on his MP5. Mac pushed his face into the dirt and tapped him behind the ear.

Manny bent over the sentry, pulled his jacket collar back, looking for something. Mac reloaded the Heckler, panting with adrenaline. Took the M16 off his back, checked for load and slung it. Then he moved towards the camp in a crouch, Manny at his four o'clock.

They got to the building and squatted in the shadows. Manny pushed a tarp aside and they looked in: there was a solid wall under it. A prefab building covered in tarps.

Mac grabbed a tag from the right breast pocket of his ovies. Peeling the adhesive protector off its back, he stuck it to the plastic wall, pushing the button in the middle of it. A tiny red LED blinked. Armed.

They moved south, along the wall and inside the canvas covering. The hum of the generators grew louder. They got to the south end of the camp, the generator now screeching in their ears. Manny tested the door, it opened and they moved inside to a strong smell of diesel. The engineer's night-light bathed the warm room in a soft red glow. There was a large yellow engine, mounted on skids on the concrete slab, the black letters CAT painted on it. Otherwise the room was deserted.

Manny pointed to another door.

The next room was three times larger. Filled with barrels, stores, boxes. Mac and Manny moved among them: there was food and water, guns and ammo. There was avgas and there was a stack of wooden boxes with MALAYSIAN OPTICAL COMPANY stamped on their sides. Mac lifted the lid on one, saw three Stinger SAM rocket launchers sitting inside, cradled in wood shavings.

Sweat ran down Mac's neck, soaked the back of his ovies. At the north end of the storage area was a door to what looked like a cool room. There was a digital combination lock on the handle.

Manny pulled a strip of wax paper from his front pocket, peeling the paper apart to reveal a line of dark red putty. Pushing the red putty around the door handle in a horseshoe shape, Manny squeezed it to make sure it was properly stuck against the lock, then pulled a mini detonator from another pocket. He looked at Mac, flashed both hands three times. A thirty-second fuse.

Mac moved back into the power room. Manny joined him five seconds later. The din of the generator room made the explosion sound more like a pop.

The cool room door was now hanging open, artificial coldness mixing with the acrid stench of plastic explosive. It was inky black inside. Manny cracked a light bar and the scene lit up dull green. This was the acid test: either Mac's snitches had it right or the whole thing had been a fuck-up.

The far wall of the cool room was stacked with green plastic suitcases with built-in handles. His snitches had been spot-on. Cases like that only held one thing: HMX, one of the most powerful non-nuclear explosives ever produced. It was made in tiny, government-controlled quantities in Germany and the United States, for military use only. Every batch was numbered, every case was signed for. It very rarely left a military base once it had been escorted there. You couldn't buy it.

Each of the cases contained five small bricks of HMX, and a single brick was powerful enough to do more than just put a hole in an aircraft carrier – it could break its back. Governments around the world had a hard enough time dealing with the effects of C4, the plastique favoured by suicide bombers. HMX had five times the expansion rate of C4. A piece the size of a five-cent coin was enough to split a bus like a watermelon.

And Mac was looking at twelve cases of the stuff, stacked against the wall of a terrorist camp in the middle of the Queensland outback. What a pretty mess that would make at Port of Brisbane container terminal.

He had an idea – it would only take a couple of minutes.

Mac and Manny moved to the north end of the structure where the camp management would be dormed.

Mac had briefed Manny on the target: a thirty-eight-year-old Javanese male, average build, average height, no facial hair, good teeth.

Manny had said, 'Thanks for narrowing it down, champ.'

The north end of the camp had what Mac assumed was a guardhouse. It stuck out from the main structure like a nose. He'd have preferred that the SAS take it from here, since they were the storming experts. Mac preferred stealthing. But the target had to be right first time. He didn't want the troopers hauling arse out of the camp with the wrong bloke. They might not get a second bite.

Manny stuck his head around the north end of the camp, made a hand gesture to the other SAS troopers who had taken out their sentries and were now waiting on the other side of the camp. All clear.

Then Mac stood back, let Manny do his thing on the guardhouse door. The trooper slung his M4 and pulled out his suppressed handgun. He walked into the darkness of the canvas canopy and knocked on the door. Mac's heart thumped, his ears roared with adrenaline, his breath rasped.

Manny said something conversational in Bahasa. Now Mac realised what Manny had been looking for on the sentry – a name-tag.

The door opened, everything relaxed and comfortable, revealing dim light and laughter coming from an Indonesian game show on satellite TV. Manny walked forward, head still, shoulders relaxed. His handgun spat seven times. A matter-of-fact professional. Mac took his four o'clock, less relaxed. He held his Heckler ready as he entered the guardhouse, but Manny had done the job. Three young Indons slumped in white plastic chairs. A fourth lay dead on the ground, dressed only in a white singlet and boxers.

Mac swung right, Manny swung left. Area secured.

The TV blasted raucous laughter, it was good cover. The corridor leading from the guardhouse remained silent. Mac waited for a couple of seconds to be sure. Nothing.

They moved into the right-hand leg of the corridor. It was dark and smelled of sweat. The floor swayed under their feet as they moved down the narrow enclosure. It was flimsy, a cheap hire out of Darwin to Arafura Explorations Pty Ltd. Mac had seen the invoice.

His breathing was in the panic range again and he could feel his baseball cap getting wet around the edges. A drop of sweat hit his eyelid.

There was a door on the right but Mac ignored it. They walked further into darkness and away from the light of the TV. Manny moved like a cat behind him and Mac liked that. He hated working with mouth-breathers and leadfoots. You want to walk like a klutz? Join the fire brigade.

Mac kept going till he reached the final door. It faced north. He was guessing an important visitor would be closest to Mecca. He stood at the door, listened. Manny pulled out a steel tube the length of a small flashlight. It was a stunner, a sort of mini cattle prod. Mac pulled his own out from his side leg pocket, put his gloved hand on the aluminium door handle, pushed down real slow, then pushed it open. There was one steel-frame bed against a wall, beneath a window. One person in it, snoring.

He pushed his head in further, saw another bed, someone in it.

The room was dark. Mac knew he didn't have long. People sense things and wake up.

He lingered just long enough to see what he was looking for. The snorer had a moustache. That meant the other guy was Ali Samrazi. This was confirmed almost immediately when the bloke sat up in bed, looking at Mac like he'd seen a ghost. Mac moved forward, Heckler levelled. He sensed Manny move in behind him.

'Ali – it's me, mate. Richard. Richard Davis.'

Ali Samrazi's eyes were wide with fear. He scrabbled for something on the bedside table. Mac got there just as Samrazi put his hand on a Beretta handgun. As Mac broke the little guy's wrist, Samrazi fired the gun.

The shot cracked like a cannon. Ali screamed and his gun fell to the floor.

Fuck!

Two seconds of silence, then the sound of voices started up and down the camp. Mac stabbed his stunner into Samrazi's chest and pressed the switch. Samrazi's chest heaved like a horse had kicked him. Eyes rolled, he went limp. Behind Mac, Manny had pacified the other sleeper.

Mac duct-taped Samrazi's wrists and ankles, broke a couple of caps of Xanax into the Indon's mouth. Manny came over, threw Samrazi into a fireman's lift.

Mac pulled down his M16, checked for load – a nervous habit. Exchanges of fire had started up outside the camp. Ward's men laying down diversionary fire, hopefully pulling the camp's inmates away from the north dorm.

He looked through the door. The lights were on down the length of the corridor. Doors were opening, young Indons or Malays appearing. Some were armed. They were confused, even comical, in three am hair styles.

Mac pulled his head back in.

Manny already had his M4 slung at hip height and Samrazi over his left shoulder. He nodded at Mac.

As they pushed into the corridor, Mac kept left and started firing. The tangos didn't know what was happening. Most were dead before they hit the floor. Manny was on Mac's four o'clock, more accurate with one hand than Mac was on a range.

They moved towards the guardhouse, squinting hard as their eyes adjusted to the lights.

Gunfire continued from the western side of the camp. They raised the pace, moved past the game show host and jogged out into the desert.

'Mate, get this bloke to Foxy,' said Mac. 'Keep him alive. I'll give the guys a hand.'

Manny gave thumbs-up and march-jogged the way the special forces do.

The radio silence had broken and bursts of adrenaline-powered commands flew across the airwaves.

Mac circled around the north end of the camp building, his ovies drenched in sweat. He poked his head round the corner, watched it unfold: four SAS blokes in a half-moon, three in the classic kneeling marksman pose, the other in the prone position. They laid down three-shot bursts of fire at the trainees who were firing wildly into the desert. Tracer rounds glowed white, but tangos kept falling. An RPG came whistling out of the canvas but flew over the SAS boys and into the great beyond. They were wankers, thought Mac, but well-equipped wankers. Their basic issue seemed to be MP5s; he could hear their signature sound.

One group of tangos, still in their underwear, had got in behind a white LandCruiser parked between the camp and the SAS. Three of the boys fired around the truck. One bought it in the shoulder, a hideous thwack that twisted the kid into a standing contortion before he dropped to the dust, staring at the clear night sky. The others looked at him briefly, then one of the tangos opened the rear door of the Cruiser and pulled out a box while the windows and tyres were being shot out. He threw the box on the ground, pulled out an RPG. The air whistled with lead. He took a shot in the ankle. He leaned against the Cruiser, his foot dangling by skin. Mac watched him pull the RPG onto his shoulder, and then turn on one leg. One tough kid. He moved along the bonnet of the Cruiser, prepping to fire. Mac aimed up, shot him in the floating ribs with a three-shot burst.

The other two shooters turned and Mac took them down.

Mac's new firing angle allowed the SAS boys to race in. They took the western side of the LandCruiser, keeping the fire-rate constant. One of them lobbed a flash grenade at whoever was left.

The dust and smoke cleared as insults and shouts came from inside the building. Mac sparked the radio mic. 'Wardie, let's get out while the going's good.'

Ward didn't want to know. 'We've still got tangos in there, Mac – I reckon fifteen, twenty of the bastards.'

Ward was talking into his mic but hadn't taken his eyes from the sights of his M4. 'Gimme five, Macca – we've got these cunts.'

Mac didn't want to hang around. 'Snatch completed, mate, time to roll.'

There was a pause. The kind of thing that always happened when the soldiers realised the intel dude was pulling rank. Again. Joint missions required loads of trust between military and spooks. But when it came down to it, the soldiers – SAS, SEALs, Green Berets – found it almost impossible to walk away from a bunch of tangos who were shooting. It wasn't in their nature or their training.

'Roger that . . . sir,' replied Wardie. Almost snide.

The clear-out proceeded without trouble. They RV'd at the top of the dune where Manny had already hogtied Samrazi and bundled him onto the carrier rack of his bike.

The camp was silent but, looking back, Mac could see figures stalking around the north end. He watched as Ward switched frequency. Saw him morse something with the manual radio trigger.

They moved down the dune, packed their stuff, got on their bikes. The adrenaline eased and Mac vomited quietly into the dirt. His overalls were wet down the back. He put on a field jacket and helmet. The SAS lads did the same.

Foxy led them out. Seven minutes later Mac heard the F-111s roar in from RAAF Base Darwin. They stopped their bikes and behind them, over the horizon, the air boiled up twenty or thirty storeys into the sky, flashing orange, white, red and then orange again. The ground shook slightly, and the group turned east again for the helo pick-up.

Samrazi would sing, Mac was sure of that, and the Australian government would own a pile of free HMX that Mac and Manny had buried in the desert.

CHAPTER 2

Mac watched the Dean of History and wondered how much of this chat was Davidson's doing, how much a testament to his own genius. The fact that the dean referred to him as being from Foreign Affairs put the odds heavily in favour of it being a gift from Tony Davidson, Mac's recently retired boss.

Mac had flown in from Townsville that morning on an Air Force flight after a day sleeping and debriefing. Today's mission: find a solid civilian job, ease himself into the straight world without anyone noticing, and have a legitimate life to offer Diane.

Going civvie was harder than throwing on a tweed jacket and pulling the degree out of a drawer. It meant decisions about things he hadn't had to consider before during his adult life. Things like getting a mortgage, selecting a phone company, getting the gas turned on. Things you learn by living straight. Things a woman expected from a man if she was going to get even halfway serious with him.

Mac hadn't owned a car since university but he'd owned six or seven identities. There was going to be a learning curve.

He exhaled, made his shoulders go soft.

The dean loaded a briar pipe. 'Old habit,' he chuckled.

'Go for your life,' said Mac.

The view from the dean's office in the old Quadrangle building of the University of Sydney looked over a sloping lawn, across one-hundred-and-fifty-year-old fig trees and down on to the city. It felt like a stronghold.

The dean smiled, pushed a stapled set of papers across the wooden desk. 'An adjunct position isn't much. Sort of a contracted attachment. But it'll get you on board and we can take it from there, hmm?'

Mac wanted to throw himself on the old bastard, weep with appreciation. But he stayed calm. 'Sounds good to me, Jim.'

The dean pushed back against his desk with his right foot, put the pipe in his mouth.

'I've assigned you to Derek Parmenter,' said the dean. 'He can brief you on curriculum before the summer break. You can sit in on a few lectures and you should be fine for a February start.'

Mac had met Parmenter and didn't like him much. But he'd be lecturing and tutoring postgrad students on Australian foreign policy in South-East Asia. The gig was an 'institute' rather than a faculty, and that suited Mac. He couldn't complain.

'Just look it over, it's all the basic guff,' said the dean, nodding at the offer. 'Then sign it and get it back to me by Monday, okay?'

Mac grabbed the letter and looked gratefully at the dean, who pretended to puff on his pipe as he gazed out the window. 'Can't even smoke a pipe these days,' he said, smiling at something far away. 'Times have changed, Alan – you know that, don't you?'

Mac had been pegged for paramilitary duties almost the minute he joined the Australian Secret Intelligence Service from university. He'd played rugby in Queensland and he guessed that to a desk jockey in Canberra he'd looked the part. He couldn't recall any huge desire for the military direction.

So they'd shipped him to the United Kingdom and into the loving arms of the Royal Marines and their infamous commando training in Devon. He was part of an intake of other British and Commonwealth intel recruits sent for a crash course in elite soldiering.

For seven months he was 'hardened' as only the Royal Marines believe a man can be hardened. It was brutal. Straight out of an honours degree in history, suddenly Mac was getting his head shaved in the quartermaster's yard at Lympstone Barracks. The early days were still a blur. He remembered the fights, the cold, the hunger. He remembered purple-faced men with Geordie accents screaming, 'You silly-looking cunt.'

The Marines built you up physically and then taunted you psychologically. The airborne course was a good example. High-altitude, low-opening jumps weren't that bad if you'd trained properly. The killer was the three am test: getting pulled out of a warm bed – 'wakey-wakey, hands off snakey' – to go HALO jumping in the dark.

Mac went on to the Special Boat Service course, which involved a survival route in the Borneo jungle. The course, known in British military circles simply as 'Brunei', entailed hunger, thirst, loneliness, confusion, trench foot, fatigue, malaria, deadly wildlife and madness. There were swarms of mosquitoes so aggressive he'd been bitten on the inside of his throat.

There was one guy Mac particularly remembered: Lane, the Canadian. Though Mac's height, Lane was a bulging gym bunny and a black belt in something. Lane had never missed an opportunity to behave like a wanker, bringing new meaning to the concept of self-belief.

In Brunei, Lane's macho act fell apart in spectacular fashion. On the SBS survival section – the last test in a six-month course – the candidates were placed in four-man teams. Three days into the hike Lane lost it – dehydrated, fatigued, disoriented and completely spooked by the Borneo wildlife that included spiders the size of dinner plates. Lane's breaking point came when the Malaysian candidate in their team caught a fat snake one afternoon and prepared it as an early dinner. They were so hungry that three of them seized on the snake meat, but not Lane. He was finished. The martial artist was in an advanced stage of mental collapse by the time he took a seat by the river and started babbling.

Mac couldn't even get him to stand – all the bloke could do was cry.

Mac finished Brunei with a small piece of his psyche gone forever. When the successful candidates were all out of hospital, they were called out to the parade ground in searing tropical heat. Five instructors walked the line, ritually roughing the hair of their successful candidates and muttering reluctant praise. Non-violent physical contact was too much for some of the guys.

Mac kept it tight, looked the chief instructor, Mark 'Banger' Jordan, in the eye. He'd completed, and he was out. But he'd be a Royal Marine forever.

Mac walked down from the university knoll and north-east towards Chinatown. Happy. Sydney in early summer was all jacaranda blossoms and the smell of frangipani buds. He had a letter of offer in his pocket and a lunch date with Diane.

Diane Ellison had lured him from his single status about six months before. They'd met at an Aussie trade function in Jakarta where he'd introduced himself as Richard Davis, a sales executive from Southern Scholastic Books. It was a lie he hadn't yet undone.

Mac had been instantly taken with her. She was beautiful and smart, blue-eyed, blonde, tall and curvy. The daughter of a British diplomat, she worked as an IT maven for a global outfit. She was based in Sydney but her beat covered Jakarta, Manila, KL and Singapore, and her father let her stay in the British compound when she visited Jakarta.

They'd hooked up again in Sydney, as Mac had found more reasons to fly down from Jakkers. Things had become serious. It wasn't just the sex, which was great, but all the close-in stuff that Mac had kept in a psychological vault for fifteen years. She laughed hard when something was funny but was razor-sharp with men who tried to talk down to her. She was also witty, especially after a couple of wines. Mac really liked that.

It had turned into love.

And she had no idea what Mac did for a living.

That's where the university job came in. A chance to slip out the back way of his current life and reappear like a regular citizen with regular prospects. The kind of thing civvie women demanded.

She was worth it, thought Mac, patting the lump in his pocket. As the dean had said, *Times have changed*.

As Mac strode past the University of Technology he looked across the six-lane road at a Credit Union building covered in mirror glass. He gave it a sideways glance. It was an old habit: use any reflective surfaces to see who was following. He saw himself and reckoned he didn't look bad for a thirty-seven-year-old with some hard miles on the clock. But as he turned back to the footpath something caught his attention.

Mac had once spent a secondment with Shin Bet – Israel's internal intelligence service – learning the part-art, part-science of psychogenic gait analysis. For eight-hour shifts he strolled in front of one-way glass at Ben-Gurion Airport, sat in front of monitors at Haifa's central railway station and walked the public concourses of the infamous bus interchange in Jerusalem. Between the Shin Bet officers, most of whom were women, and the classes at the academy, Mac learned the psychogenic truth that acting natural is more conspicuous than just being naturally nervous. Things happened to your body when you consciously tried to correct nervousness. You tensed down the front of your pelvis, for example, which resulted in a lifting of the heels as you walked.

The bloke behind him now had that overacted coolness. Mac reckoned him as twenty-five, Anglo. He was dressed like a student with a red backpack, navy T-shirt and runners. He had a medium build, was six foot and professionally exercised. He looked the part, thought Mac, and the bare head was at least a start since only amateurs wore hats on a tail. They made you a walking, breathing beacon.

He checked the time: twenty minutes before lunch with Diane. Mac looked ahead, saw the pedestrian lights across Harris Street holding on red and a bunch of people waiting for the light to go green across the busy intersection. He slowed, stopped and looked intently in the window of a big university bookstore, keeping his peripheral sight on a circle to his left. He wanted his stalker to pass.

He didn't.

Game on.

Making as if to move towards the pedestrian crossing, Mac saw the traffic lights turn to amber. He stopped, turned back to the bookstore, an academic catching sight of something. Then he counted down ten seconds to himself, not looking at the crossing at all. The kid would be getting jumpy, probably also having to feign interest in Windows XP boxes or a book on economics by Samuelson.

Mac heard the squawking of the green pedestrian signal and

waited until he heard it stop. *Seven thousand, eight thousand, nine thousand* . . .
He counted it down slowly then stood straight and started towards
the crossing. The crowds had crossed and a few people were building
up again on the kerb as the light flashed red. He had fifteen metres
to make the crossing. He accelerated and made the distance in four
strides. Horns sounded and cars edged forward as Mac ran across the
four lanes.

He made the east side of the street and slowed to a walk, panting
slightly as he slipped into the cool of a crowded convenience shop.
At the newspaper rack he turned and waited. He could see the kid
across the road, rubber-necking like a tourist worried he wouldn't
see another kangaroo.

Mac needed to make sure any backup broke cover too. He picked
up a banana from a display tray and moved back into the swirl of the
shop, positioning himself behind two customers. On the other side
of Broadway, a middle-aged tenderfoot had his hands in his pockets,
whistling at the sky. Mac thought he knew that face. It was ludicrous.

He guessed the backup had made him, so the tail would hang
back. Mac bought the banana, left the shop and kept walking with
the lunch-hour pedestrians along Broadway as it swept around left
towards the broad boulevard of George Street. In front of him the
panorama of Sydney's theatre district opened up. Mac was certain that
the backup guy would now have stepped in as the main tail. His mind
spun with the possibilities. They both looked Aussie. Service? ASIO?

Two blocks down the slope of George Street Mac came to an
old hotel bar on his left, with several identical glass-door entrances
spaced about ten metres apart. He sped up, doubling his walking
speed through the foot traffic. As he reached the last glass door on the
corner he turned left without stopping and pushed straight through
into the pub.

It was dim inside. No one looked up from the horseracing on
the bar TVs as Mac moved through the gloom and a door marked
BISTRO. He kept moving through the cool of the air-con, into the
pokies parlour, with scores of slot machines whirring. Against the far
wall was a glass door that led back onto the street.

He took off his jacket, put his left arm on the top of a pokie
machine and looked at it intently, while keeping an eye on the door

under his left armpit. Almost immediately the backup passed the door, stressed and sweating. Perfect.

Mac was straight out the door and into Mr Backup's shadow. He was hoping that by removing his jacket he'd lose the tail who was probably behind Backup. Suits not only change your colour – they change your shape.

Mac blended into the pace of the street and followed Backup, who was dressed in pressed blue jeans, riding boots and a windbreaker – way too hot for the weather and a sign that the bloke was probably armed.

Mac watched him slow, fade to his left at the door Mac had disappeared through forty seconds before. Mac was closing so quickly that by the time Backup moved through the inward-swinging door, Mac was right behind him. He moved into the small of the guy's back and pushed the banana in hard, steering the portly bloke towards an empty bench table that looked out on the street.

'Keep your hands open and where I can see them, mate,' he hissed.

Backup did as he was told.

'And make that a schooner of New, you bludging bastard.'

Backup hit the table and turned. His florid face glowed. He smiled.

'Jesus Christ, Macca. Sorry, mate.'

Rod Scott was an old colleague from the Service who was once expected to rise through the ranks, do a lot of lunching in Jakarta and KL. He was at least ten years older than Mac and had been assigned to the young Alan McQueen during the first Iraq War. And here he was tailing friendlies in Sydney.

Mac shook his head, threw the banana on the table. 'Mate, what are you doing in the field?'

Scott's face dropped and Mac instantly regretted his cattiness.

'Fuck it, Mac. You want that beer?'

The door flew open. Mac had been waiting for it. The young crew-cut tailer came through in exactly the pose Mac had expected: right hand under his left armpit and into his backpack.

Scott stepped in. 'It's okay, mate,' he said, holding the youngster's arm. 'I'll see you back at the car in thirty. Right?'

The youngster slowed his breathing and looked from Mac to Scott as the punters in the pub went back to their racing. He was confused as he made for the door.

'And mate,' muttered Scott, 'stay off the air on this, all right?'

The youngster nodded and left, giving Mac a sneer.

Mac winked.

Scott brought two beers back to the stand-up table.

Mac worried at his watch. 'Better make it snappy, mate. Only got a couple of minutes.' The tension had gone out of the air – Scott hadn't been tailing Mac, as such, just having a look at his movements before moving in for a chat.

Scott's eyes lost their professional hardness as he sipped his beer. 'Sorry about this bullshit, Mac. Tobin's got something for you. Urgent. He wants to talk.'

Mac felt the bottom fall out of his day. Greg Tobin was the Asia-Pacific director at the Service. He headed a territory that spread from New Delhi across to Tokyo and down to Jakarta. Tobin had taken over from Tony Davidson four weeks earlier in what had been one of the most unpopular successions in Service memory. Even in a profession staffed by sneaky little shits, Tobin was the alpha shit. He was the new breed: slick, expensive suits and armed with an MBA. Not high on fieldwork experience but great at getting promoted. Tobin had not acknowledged Mac's transition agreement, which meant he might pretend it didn't exist.

'I'm on the way out, Scotty.' Mac eyed the beer but decided against it. He didn't want Diane thinking he was on the piss with the boys. 'Thirtieth of January and I'm gone, right?'

Scott nodded, not meeting Mac's eye. 'Look, mate –'

'No. You look. I've done it all by the book, I've done it totally the way Davidson and the department wanted it.' Mac felt his anger coming up and he breathed deep. He could see Scotty was scared. 'I've even landed a straight job. This Sydney Uni gig is Davidson's doing. Look at me,' said Mac, holding his arms out, looking down at his charcoal suit and black office shoes.

Mac realised he'd been yelling slightly and he calmed it. 'Christ, Scotty, why didn't someone just call?'

Mac already knew the answer to that one. Getting into the spy trade was the easy part. Surviving the debriefings, departmental threats and surveillance on your way out was another thing. Intel operatives never really left the life.

Mac had been where Scotty was now back in '02. A financial operative named Kleinwitz had tendered his resignation. The official reason: he'd fallen in love with a local bird during a posting in Manila. Problem was, Kleinwitz was simultaneously applying to the Australian Trade Commission. Mac was in Manila at the time and was thrown the debrief.

He didn't like it. Kleinwitz just didn't vibe in love. His file had no trail of love affairs – no wife, no girlfriends, no interoffice bedwork, no whoring. His colleagues had him as a professional robot. The girlfriend was news to them.

Kleinwitz didn't drink, smoke or gamble and his music tastes ran to Phil Collins – the ninety-nine per cent giveaway that this boy was no bounder. His induction file revealed a wave of girls, women and men paid to lure Kleinwitz into bed during his first posting in KL. Standard procedure with new recruits. The accounting major hadn't blinked. Mac recognised the name of one of the contractors paid to seduce the geeky young Australian at the embassy. If that bird couldn't make Kleinwitz giggle, then something wasn't right.

Mac had run a two-week tail on the bloke. Yes, there was a bird – a dancer from Angeles City. She was clean. But a bit more digging and intel from the Australian Federal Police turned up her brother, a hoodlum named Miggy Morales. Miggy ran nightclubs, Miggy ran bare-knuckle fights and, most interestingly, Miggy ran brothels where the bait was prepubescent boys. Mac reckoned Kleinwitz was being blackmailed into joining Trade. And where there was blackmail there was a rival intelligence outfit – probably the Chinese – getting an advantage it shouldn't have.

Mac had cornered Kleinwitz in a basement room at Southern Scholastic Books. Helping out were two officers from the Service, Nguyen and Kritikos, along with the AFP's intelligence liaison officer, Jenny Toohey.

Mac started hard, accusing bug-eyed Kleinwitz of being a rock spider. Accused him of being blackmailed by Miggy Morales and his sister. Mac told Kleinwitz that as far as he was concerned, the Mindanao Forest Products infiltration had gone pear-shaped because he was doubling. Kleinwitz was integral – as the accountant, he had constructed the whole financial scenario. And a local asset had died.

Kleinwitz stayed calm until Mac pulled out the black and whites of Kleinwitz on a bed with a couple of Miggy's boys, who did not look to be enjoying the experience. Mac threw them on the bolted table top and watched impassively as Kleinwitz squirmed in his chair, the blood rushing into his face. Kleinwitz took another look at the pics and smirked. Jenny Toohey – standing five-ten and a former Australian Universities basketballer – took a step forward and landed a straight right in his teeth.

Canberra dispatched its I-team, a shady group made up of seconded cops, soldiers and intelligence types whose job was completing 'sensitive disengagements from Commonwealth employment'.

So Mac knew this part of the game. Didn't like it, but he knew it.

'When and where?' he asked Rod Scott.

CHAPTER 3

She rose as Mac walked into the Happy Dragon.

Diane.

The Chinatown lunch crowd turned as one. She was wearing a sleeveless black linen knee-length dress, her honey-blonde hair falling to her bare, tanned shoulders. Mac's heart rate bumped up a couple of notches.

'Hi Richard,' she purred, quietly cross at his lateness. 'How did it go at the university?'

'No worries. Yeah,' said Mac, greeting her clumsily, a bit distracted. They leaned in and he kissed Diane's hair rather than her cheek. Her kiss landed on his cheek, where it always did. Diane had a wet kiss – a kiss you still felt on your face two minutes later.

He sat heavily and babbled about the uni job until he ran out of puff. There wasn't much else to say. He'd been offered the job and he was going to take it.

Diane smiled at him and raised her glass in a toast. 'To Richard the Brainiac.'

He tried to get with the spirit, have a laugh. But wine splashed out of Mac's glass when he tried to drink. He could feel himself losing it. All that embassy life had given Diane a knowingness about life and men, and sometimes Mac felt she was looking straight through him. As if he would always be the small-town Queensland boy – a ton of energy but no class.

Mac knew how to track, snatch and dispatch people. He could interview, interrogate and inveigle. He could manipulate perceptions with deceptive scenarios. But he had no idea how civvie relationships actually worked. He was used to cops and customs girls, embassy staffers, assistant military attachés, trade mission officers – the classic embassy-colony types. All of them work-obsessed, slightly worthy and deeply embedded in the politics of bureaucracy.

In the last few weeks his professional demeanour had been falling apart as Diane came closer to the centre of his life and a new part of himself tried to emerge. She made fun of office politics and jockeying for favour, and made it clear that the best thing about her job in IT was that she was largely her own boss. Diane thought men in suits were boring and the women who loved them were even worse. She was hilarious and had the vaguely piratical air of a rebellious person born to privilege. And Mac loved her for it, an indulgence he couldn't really afford.

The situation was ridiculous: Diane thought he was a textbook sales executive called Richard who spent a lot of time in South-East Asia. How long did you keep that up when you had feelings for a girl?

In the Service they'd have said his nerves were going, that he was choking.

Mac made a joke about the heat in the restaurant, and calmed himself by acting the part of a composed person. Diane twirled the stem of her wineglass between thumb and forefinger. She leaned on her left hand and focused on him. 'Are you avoiding me, Mr Genius?'

Mac realised he'd sat down opposite her. Diane liked him to sit adjacent to her, so she could hold his hand under the table. The first time it happened, at a restaurant in Jakarta, Mac had blushed.

Now Diane raised her hand imperceptibly at the maitre d' and three men descended on their table. Mac never liked this sort of carry-on. Diane gave a slight wink to the maitre d' as he bowed, and asked him to change the setting for 'Mister Richard'.

The Chinatown lunchers smiled as Mac stood and waited for the setting to be changed. One bloke nodded at him with a silly grin, until his wife gave him The Look.

When he sat down again, Diane grabbed his hand and put it on her lap. He tried to avoid her eyes. He took a peek. She was smiling, blue eyes sparkling.

He was way, way gone on this bird.

Mac found a small park under the southern approach to the Sydney Harbour Bridge as Japanese newlyweds hammered for their photographer.

The lunch had not gone well. Mac couldn't get his mind off what Tobin might want, and so close to his retirement. Diane had wanted to talk about something. Mac knew it was relationship stuff, an 'us' chat – the future. He couldn't do it and made sure she couldn't take things in that direction. Then he'd claimed an urgent meeting and done a runner.

He felt like he was tearing himself apart, four or five ways at once.

Mac took another look at the wedding party. He couldn't look at a camera without thinking about surveillance; couldn't look at a groom and his bride without wondering where their backup was and thinking, *Is it a snatch or a hit?*

He couldn't do it anymore, couldn't live two or three lives, operating under three names, working for bullshit companies, travelling on false passports, inducing weak people to be even weaker by betraying something they shouldn't. Couldn't pull missions and not even speak about them with colleagues.

He couldn't shoot up a terrorist camp in the outback and then schmooze the Dean of History two days later. Couldn't break up a street detail and then go to lunch with the woman he loved like nothing was wrong.

It was all wrong.

No one in his world really had the nerves for what they did. To establish trust and then suddenly become the blackmailer, the torturer or the executioner to those who believed in you was not a question of nerves. It was about shutting off a part of yourself – a part that Mac had shut down to get through the Royal Marines and SBS.

Diane had opened him up, and now there was no going back. He was out.

He pulled his mobile phone from his suit pocket and turned it on. He assumed it was bugged. He thought about saying something smart into the back of it, but he didn't.

Play it cool – be the straight guy.

The messages icon came up and he dialled in to the voicemail. The first message was from Diane, wanting to know why he was late for lunch. The second started with *Richard, I really wanted for us to talk at lunch . . .* and ended with *. . . I'll send the books I borrowed over to the office. Perhaps I could get my keys . . .*

Mac approached the back entrance to Southern Scholastic Books with Scotty two steps behind. They walked through the fluoro-lit open-plan office space, past 'secretaries' and 'sales people' who were mostly on phones or working screens. ASIS was supposed to have a foreign-only brief, but if you ran around Asia with a card from an Australian company, you needed an office in Sydney.

A group of Malays in a fishbowl meeting room turned and looked as he walked past. He smiled, gave thumbs-up, and walked into a large corner office reserved for the visiting brass. Greg Tobin looked up. Three men in dark suits sat on a sofa.

Tobin came at him like a campaigning politician, the confidence shining from his perfect teeth. He hadn't changed since his glory days at the University of Queensland in Brisbane. He was still tall, tanned and athletic with perfect black hair, clipped close and pushed back. Although he had a large jawbone he still managed to look as sleek as a seal. Errol Flynn without the mo. A good-looking man used to having things happen his way.

'G'day mate,' he said heartily. Mac shook his hand and watched Tobin spin on a heel and walk back to a large dark desk. He smelled of success, like freshly mown grass.

'Have a seat, mate,' said Tobin as he leaned back in a leather chair. 'Just on my way up to Tokyo and thought we might have a chat, huh?'

Mac took a chair and scoped the three men on the sofa to his right. They stared back at him. Two of the men he didn't know. The third he recognised: David Urquhart, who smiled briefly without warmth before turning away.

Mac didn't like it.

Urquhart and Mac had endured boarding school and uni together. They'd played footy, sunk beers and chased girls. But Urquhart was of a different tribe to Mac. He was one of those blokes who always moved in the slipstream of power and didn't pretend he was anything other than the manager of his own upwardly mobile fortunes. He'd begged Mac many times to make more of his UQ background and burrow further into the power structure of Australian intelligence – a part of the Commonwealth bureaucracy that had been heavily influenced by UQ graduates over the years. But Mac wasn't up for it. Didn't have the ticker for the toadie routine.

'So, Al, you're leaving us?' said Tobin, breaking into Mac's thoughts.

Mac nodded.

'But according to my debrief, we have a few months more of your expertise available to us, right?' asked Tobin.

Mac said nothing. He had a velvet box in his suit jacket that would have to go back to the jeweller, he had a job offer from Sydney Uni that was suddenly looking very shaky and he had a transition agreement with Tobin's predecessor which he assumed was about to be ripped up in front of his face.

Davidson had said, *Bring in Samrazi then take a break till you leave.*

Urquhart wouldn't meet Mac's eyes and Scotty moved his feet awkwardly in the doorway. Not a good sign. Scotty was embarrassed.

'Good, good,' murmured Tobin, then held out his hand to one of the flunkeys on the sofa, a Commonwealth bodyguard by the look of him. The bodyguard reached into a black document case and came out with a file. He was meat-fingered and slow. Tobin almost clicked his fingers.

The file was a standard manila folder, with plastic binders along the top. Tobin opened it and looked at Mac, closed it and half threw, half slid it across the desk. Mac had to get out of his chair to pick it up. Tobin creaked back in his leather chair, put a shiny black shoe on the desk and settled his fingers in the cathedral position.

'Her name's Judith Hannah,' said Tobin, looking down at his two-hundred-dollar tie as Mac opened the file. 'Smart, pretty, going places. So God knows what she's doing with us, eh boys?'

Tobin's little gang laughed in that lifeless way of the politically astute.

Mac opened the file and eyed a black and white photo of an attractive blonde in her twenties.

'What's she done?' asked Mac.

'Don't know,' said Tobin. 'But we'd like to find out.'

Mac turned to the final page of Judith Hannah's file. Her last posting was the Australian Embassy in Jakarta, her cover was 'business development officer' at Southern Scholastic Books. Mac couldn't remember meeting her.

'She detained?'

Tobin shook his head. 'She's gone, mate.'

Mac looked up. 'Where?'

'Gone from the embassy, gone from the compound. Seems to be on the run.'

Mac looked at the sidekicks for a clue. They deadpanned.

He looked back to Tobin. 'From what?'

'Like I said – we need to find that out.'

'From me? Where're the Feds?'

Tobin squinted at him. 'Can't do that, mate. There's no crime, we have no complaint. Besides, the AFP already have a bigger network than us in Asia. Why give 'em a free kick, eh boys?'

The sidekicks nodded their agreement.

Mac had what they called an S-2 classification, which meant the Minister for Foreign Affairs had authorised him to carry and use weapons in the conduct of his duties. Because of the way the Service was structured, only a handful of colleagues knew of this secret status. But Tobin knew, and sending him to find a girl recruit was like using a cold chisel to fix a Swiss watch. What this was really about was the special access the AFP had gained to the Department of the Prime Minister and Cabinet during the tenure of the current government, at the expense of intelligence outfits like ASIS. This was about empires.

'What about I-team?' asked Mac.

'Steady on, old man! I said we didn't know what she's done.' Tobin laughed, then pretended to be collecting himself. 'That's why I need someone to just slide in there, have a chat and get things sorted. The I-team?! Shit, mate – fair dinkum!'

Mac ignored Tobin's song and dance. 'No one in Jakkers can do this?'

Tobin gave him a smile that said, *Grow up*.

Mac exhaled through his teeth, looked at the ceiling. Fuck!

Tobin changed his tone, fixed Mac with a stare. 'Mate, I need you on a plane tonight.'

CHAPTER 4

Mac was forty-two thousand feet over north Queensland when he pulled Judith Hannah's file from his briefcase. He was in business class on the late-afternoon Qantas flight to Jakarta. Executives were sprinkled around the upstairs deck of the 747. Still in his interview suit, Mac sat alone by the window.

Judith Hannah had a first-class honours degree in law from the University of Sydney and an MA in history from the same place. Mac ran his finger down her bio: Protestant. Perfect credentials for the Foreign Service. But she had applied to ASIS and she was accepted on the first go. Must have had a calling or something.

Many people didn't realise that ASIS was part of the Ministry of Foreign Affairs. Its operatives belonged to the same Commonwealth stable as the diplomats and were identical employment conditions and pay scales. The real difference was that ASIS officers had individual contracts with the Director-General which made it easier to sack and isolate them. But they all operated out of Australian embassies and consulates. In the parlance of diplomats, they were part of the same mission.

If you really wanted to go places in the public service, you applied for a place in the elites of Treasury or the Foreign Service. That's how you'd get to graduate to PMC – the Department of Prime Minister and Cabinet – where all the real glory happened for ambitious public servants.

If you wanted to get to PMC, you didn't generally set out to be a spook.

Mac worked through the pages. Judith Hannah had joined ASIS straight out of university in '01, then trained in Canberra. She'd had deployments in London, DC, LA, Manila and Jakarta. The Jakkers posting told Mac that Hannah was being groomed for interesting things. Jakarta was to the Australian intelligence community what DC was to the diplomats: where the action was; where the Americans and Chinese collided on a full-time basis within the enigmatic context of Indonesia – the world's largest Muslim nation and one which had never fully committed to the US–Australian view of the world. Jakarta was the centre of the Western world's counter-terrorism activity and Judith Hannah had been given a shot at it just two years into her ASIS career.

He kept flipping. It seemed to be a largely uncensored file, a rare thing in intelligence circles, where someone was always trying to exert their right to keep information secret from someone else. There were performance reports with the expected conclusions: Hannah was a fast learner, earned people's trust quickly and had very good ad hoc negotiation skills. A cool cucumber.

There was a list of her specialist rotations: decryption with the British, maritime with the Indonesians, Sinology at the Australian National University, transnational finance with AUSTRAC, field craft and interrogation in Canberra, telecommunications units in Singapore and counter-terrorist secondments to Langley and Tel Aviv. It was a full file. The Service had done well. Mac found what he wanted down the back. Every ASIS officer operated in a team known as a 'desk', a sort of specialty they were expected to develop during their career. There were desks for whatever it was that affected Australian interests, so there was an Indonesia Desk, an America Desk and so on. But a desk team was not confined to the embassy posting. You could be deployed in Singapore, but if you were on the China Desk, you were working with other officers who were in Jakarta, KL, Manila, DC and Beijing. You'd probably have overlaps with AFP, Australian Customs and

Austrade – the Australian trade legation. And if you happened to be on the China Desk or the Terrorism Desk, you would almost certainly be working in some capacity with the CIA and Indonesia's BIN and BAIS, and probably Mossad and MI6.

Mac sipped on his Pellegrino and allowed his thoughts to wash over him. He was trying to see the scenario of this bird and her story. Because Judith Hannah, according to her file, worked on the China Desk.

Too good to be true.

Certainly too good to be missing.

The steward led Mac to a meeting room in the intelligence section of the Australian Embassy and asked if he wanted anything.

'Coffee, thanks, champ.'

It was past nine pm local time and after two checkpoints of physical search and biometrics Mac was back in a place he knew well. He felt like shit: needed a shave and a fresh shirt. It was muggy and hot in Jakkers and he wished he'd made better use of the Brut 33 when he'd had the chance.

Mac paused at the threshold of the meeting room out of habit. Jakarta was a mean town for people in his profession, and even in the lockdown of the Aussie Embassy, he wanted to scope the room. There were four men around a large timber table. Mac knew two: his Service colleague, Anton Garvey, and a US Army Special Forces captain called John Sawtell.

Anton Garvey stood from his place at the head of the table and walked around to Mac.

'G'day, mate,' said Garvey, big face lighting up. 'How was the flight?'

'Piece of piss,' smiled Mac, 'once you get used to the shit food, bad air, crap service and the fact you're only ever a split second away from disaster.'

Garvey laughed. He was a solid, bull-like guy with big arms and a deep tan that included his totally bald head. He dressed in the spook uniform for Asia: polo shirt, khaki chinos and a pair of boat shoes. He'd done a lot of jobs with Mac and they liked each other. Now that Garvey was moving into management, Mac wondered if the relationship would change.

'Mate, glad you could make it at such short notice.' Garvey gestured to a chair. 'Dave briefed me on the assignment; sorry about all the rush.'

Mac's mind raced: Garvey had been briefed by Urquhart, not Tobin? So Garvey was answering to the political liaison arm of the Service, not the operational. Puzzled, he threw his briefcase on the table and eased into leather.

'Quick introductions. You know Charlie from Manila?' Garvey indicated a dead-eyed guy in his early forties who looked like a tired businessman. He had short, greasy salt 'n' pepper hair and slack jowls that rattled around his long face. Mac knew him by reputation: Charles Dunphy, who last time Mac had checked was overseeing the Service's China Desk. Dunphy inclined his head in greeting, a veteran of meetings that took place in bugged rooms.

On the other side of the table, Garvey introduced Philip Mason, CIA. Mason could have been anywhere from forty-two to fifty-five, a round-faced Anglo male, shortish, out of condition, navy blue suit, cotton Oxford shirt, no tie but collars buttoned down. Mac had him figured as a luncher. Mason leaned across the table, went for the firm handshake. Mac took it, smiled. Watched the guy wince.

Only office guys tried the gorilla grip.

The fourth guy, Mac knew: Captain John Sawtell, US Army Special Forces – counter-terrorism. He was based out of Zamboanga City in Mindanao. Neither of them made an attempt to shake hands. They nodded.

'G'day, Captain.'

'Evening, sir.'

Sawtell was dressed in grey sweats and Nike runners. There was nothing to suggest his rank or job, except the haircut and the worked physique. No one would mistake this bloke for a luncher.

Mac's stomach churned. Sawtell's presence meant Mac was going into the field again, and he wouldn't be directing the operation from a hotel room. They wouldn't fly a major-leaguer like Sawtell all the way from Zam to find a missing girl, just as they wouldn't bring Mac up from Sydney. Sawtell was a hardened counter-terrorism soldier whose command was called US Army Special Forces, but was better known to the world as the Green Berets.

'So, Garvs, we're looking for a wayward girl,' said Mac, keeping it civil while he boiled inside, 'and you bring in the cavalry. Must be some girl.'

Sawtell smirked and Mac clocked that he wasn't in the loop either.

The suits all stared. Too many years of having their every thought bugged to let loose even a hint of off-message communication.

'Look, Mac,' said Garvey, smiling nervously, getting into reasonable-guy mode, 'you were probably told one thing in Sydney . . .'

'Damn right.'

'And now you walk in here and things have changed a little.'

'Spare me, Anton. Since when did you need the Green Berets to find a girl recruit?' said Mac, reaching for the water jug, his head buzzing slightly. It had been a long day and he was hungry and tired. His mind was still competing for space on the Hannah and Diane front. One bird goes walkabout; another dumps him via voicemail. Somewhere in there was also a worry that the Sydney Uni job was a trick, like Lucy and Charlie Brown's football.

Garvey cleared his throat. 'Okay, mate, I don't know the whole story either,' he lied. 'We're just the Indians, right?'

Mac caught Sawtell raising an eyebrow. Maybe a black American reacting to the racial bit, or maybe just a special forces hard-head with no fuse for this crap.

Mac wasn't up for this shit either. His mind was in overdrive: why was Sawtell here? Why was Hannah so important? And why was an Agency guy in the meeting?

Mac eyeballed Charles Dunphy. The intel lifer's face was expressionless.

Looking at Garvey, Mac said, 'Okay, mate, spell it out.'

Garvey's face hardened as he adjusted himself forward and rested his forearms on the Australian hardwood table. 'Mac, we have a problem with this Hannah bird. She's missing but the word we're getting is that she's on the lam with an American.'

Mac shrugged.

'Ah, yep,' continued Garvey. 'It's not so much *an* American, but which one . . .'

Mason pitched in. 'One of ours, I'm afraid, Mr McQueen. Peter Garrison – he's Agency.'

No one said anything for what seemed like ten seconds.

Garrison was a problem.

And so was the fact that Dave Urquhart had briefed Garvey on the missing girl. Urquhart was intel liaison with the Prime Minister's office. He wasn't operations.

It had turned political. A snake picnic.

In Mac's Royal Marines days, the handful of intel people who got through the initial training found themselves in a world of revelation. The Royal Marines were probably the foremost trainers of intelligence people required to do paramilitary work. And foremost among them was Banger Jordan, an NCO who was not technically running the section but was the person who had a lasting impact on the candidates.

On their final day of training, Jordan took the candidates out to a pub and told them how it really was. 'The most dangerous animal you'll ever face,' said Banger, 'is an office guy who wants a bigger office.'

Mac had never forgotten that. Not a week of his career had gone by when Banger's words weren't vindicated in either small ways or large.

The crap that had just gone down in the embassy was a classic office-guy shit-blizzard where ambitious pen-pushers jacked up some mad adventure to please the political masters. An adventure where the bad guy gets nailed and the girl is saved. Always so clean on a whiteboard but incredibly dangerous for the people who carry it out.

Mac seethed about it as he walked along the largely deserted streets of the expat district of south Jakarta. Police 4x4s and military escort cars cruised the oversized boulevard. There were no sidewalk vendors or hawkers in this part of town. No local lads on Honda scooters crawling the kerbs offering foreigners special deals at the local whorehouse. If those guys showed up they'd be treated as if they had a bagful of C4 over their shoulder. The only locals on the street around here wore their embassy photo ID around their necks on lanyards – an international sign in the brown and black world that said 'don't shoot'.

In a strip of Western-style shops not far from the Aussie compound, Mac found a red and white illuminated sign that said BAVARIA LAGERHAUS. He walked past it to the corner. Turned left and kept walking. He stopped after twenty paces, turned and waited. Nothing. No cars, no people.

He walked back to the corner, paused. Head out, head in. Looked around. Walked to the Lagerhaus, pushed through the swinging doors into the air-con darkness. A polka band played in a corner and European backpackers dressed like dairy maids carried large glass beer steins to tables. Germanic tack hung low.

Mac went to the end of the bar nearest the wall, leaned on it, ordered a Becks and made himself inconspicuous. He had showered and was wearing jeans and a polo shirt. His suit was back in the compound motel room, along with his dodgy phone. He felt tired yet jacked-up on adrenaline, his mind racing in an exhausted body. He wanted out, he wanted respectable, he wanted Diane. He wanted to fly into a foreign city once in his life and not have to remember if he was Richard Davis or Thomas Winton, depending on whether he was coming into Jakarta via KL or Singers.

The drink arrived, the bierfrau gave him a smile. He gave her the wink, then positioned himself so that a corridor in the corner that led to the toilets was in his peripheral vision.

The clientele were expat. It was after eleven pm and most of them were bombed drunk. Lonely, overworked, overpaid whiteys stuck in a part of the world that was never going to accept them. Somehow the zero-taxation and cheap servants just didn't cut it. He saw himself as lucky – a bloke with a woman. Then he checked that. He had *had* a woman. Now he had some running to do to get her back.

Halfway through his beer, Mac saw a Javanese man emerge from the lavatory corridor. He was early forties, full head of hair and very thickly built through the neck, chest and arms. An orange tropical shirt hung loose, covering what Mac knew to be a chromed Desert Eagle .45. Saba's bodyguard.

The man cocked his head slightly at Mac and turned away, scanning the room with casual menace.

Mac left his beer at the bar, walked to the corridor. The bodyguard let him go past and followed him down the hallway. They stopped in front of a door at the end. The bodyguard moved in front of Mac, unlocked the door from a key chain, pushed through and waited for Mac to enter.

The room was an office, large and cool. There was a wide oak desk at one end, a bank of screens along the wall and a white leather sofa suite set up around a low coffee table in the middle of the room. The place belonged to a man called Saba. He was ex-BAKIN, Indonesian intelligence from the Suharto days. Now he ran a bar which doubled as a safehouse. All spies had safehouses where they kept spare guns, unofficial mobile phones, contraband passports and emergency Amex cards in bogus names. It was no reflection on the Service, it was just that spies needed to work untriangulated at times.

Mac never paid Saba. He owed him 'favours', and so far, the ex-BAKIN man had only wanted the occasional file and some telecom logs. But that would change.

The bodyguard patted Mac for weapons. Felt him for wires. Scraped his fingernails over the area just behind the ears and under the hair, looking for the tick-sized flesh-coloured transmitters that were now being used.

Mac put his arms down. The bodyguard moved to a door on the opposite wall. Opened it, gestured.

John Sawtell walked in, still in grey sweats. He was built like a brick, yet athletic. Mac remembered a detail from the file: Sawtell had played for Army as a running back. Mac wasn't sure how that translated to the rugby codes but it was probably a position requiring high correlations of speed and power. Sawtell was built. And he moved smooth.

The bodyguard saw himself out.

The two men looked at one another. Sawtell broke the silence. 'The fuck was that shit?'

Mac chuckled, took a seat on the sofa. Sawtell sat opposite in an armchair. 'That was a mutual secondment,' said Mac. 'That's what that shit was.'

'Can we speak English, McQueen?'

Mac spelled it out: the Australian intelligence apparatus had statutory sanctions on performing paramilitary work. The US intelligence community had similar laws making it illegal for them to conduct assassinations. It suited both DC and Canberra to 'mutually second' agents from one another's intelligence operations to do certain things for one another that the politicians back home would crucify their own nationals for. Certain things that you may not want the military implicated in. Politicians and intel people called it 'deniability'.

'So you get to tap this Garrison dude?' snarled Sawtell, not convinced. 'And some Agency dickhead gets to do a job for the Australians? That it?'

Mac shrugged. 'I don't have many more answers than you, mate. I was told to be in Jakarta this evening to hunt down a missing girl. Now we have Peter Garrison pissing into the tent.'

'You what?'

'I assume he's going to be a nuisance.'

Sawtell was up, moving to a water jug on the coffee table. Mac nodded, Sawtell poured two glasses, handed one to Mac.

'So excuse my ignorance,' said the American as he settled into the chair, 'but who the fuck's Garrison?'

Mac had a choice: clam up and play it tight, or let the American in on the joke. The smart way was to say nothing. Military guys with snippets of information could go off and actually start thinking for themselves. Not always a good idea. But Mac spilled. After all, that's why he'd called Sawtell here, away from the full-time listening posts at the embassy. 'Peter Garrison is a rogue CIA man. Very smart, very dangerous.'

Sawtell paused, looked at Mac, neck muscles flexing. 'And you know this, but the Agency doesn't?'

'Sure they know,' shrugged Mac. 'But he's been useful, I guess.'

Sawtell looked away. Mac could see he was disgusted with the whole spook thing.

'Look,' said Mac, 'he was stationed for a long time in northern Pakistan and then northern Burma. He's pulled a lot of real freaky stuff. He's been on our radar for years. Now he's in Jakkers and he's with one of ours.'

'Freaky? Like what?'

'Remember the bombing of that Pakistani police compound in '03? CNN ran with it as "The Taliban still strong in northern Pakistan"?'

'Sure.'

'It wasn't a truck bomb, champ – it was US Navy Hornets. An air strike.'

Sawtell cocked an eye at the Australian, like he was challenging that version of events.

'You've called in strikes?' asked Mac.

Sawtell nodded.

'There were more codes, grids and passwords than *The Da Vinci Code*, right?'

Sawtell nodded. Looked away slightly.

'We knew who called it in about two hours after the air-to-grounds painted the joint – about an hour after the Agency told their stooges at CNN that it was a Taliban truck bomb.'

Sawtell's nostrils flared. 'Why?'

'The Pakistanis were finally pulling their fingers out and shutting down the heroin-for-arms trade.'

'Was Garrison part of it?'

'Sure, and more than just Garrison – remember, the Agency kept him on the leash. They sent him to Burma after the fireworks.'

Mac watched the soldier's jaw muscles bulge. Your average special forces guy lived in fear of a friendly-fire incident since it was one of those things you could never train for, couldn't control. The idea of some slippery pen-pusher calling in friendly fire on purpose was the kind of thing that made soldiers talk about calling in their own personal head-shot.

Mac didn't want Sawtell distracted. He just wanted him to know the calibre of the person they were hunting.

'So where does the girl fit in?' asked the soldier, finally breathing out.

'Don't know,' lied Mac. He looked at his civvie watch. 'Gotta go, mate – we're on a plane at five.'

Sawtell stood and turned for the door he'd come through, then stopped and fixed Mac with an X-ray look. 'That was some shit in Sibuco, huh?'

Mac's heart sank. He wasn't close enough to touch wood. He hated talking about missions where someone carked it. 'Yeah, those are some boys you got there.'

'They call you the Pizza Man, by the way,' Sawtell winked. 'Just thought I'd warn you.'

The street was even quieter now than an hour ago. It was almost midnight and Mac sauntered the three blocks to the Aussie residential compound. He concentrated on relaxing from his feet to his head, breathing hibiscus fumes deep and slow and trying to concentrate on pleasant things.

But he couldn't clear his mind. Sawtell had asked, 'Where does the girl fit in?'

The file on Garrison said he'd been seen with Chinese agents. In Jakarta. He was believed to be fronting at least two identities in Chinese intelligence's preferred banking domicile of the Cook Islands.

Now Garrison had inveigled himself into the Australian China Desk, the Hannah bird was missing and their last known sighting was a place Mac had vowed to never visit again.

The morning flight was landing them in Sulawesi – land of a thousand nightmares.

CHAPTER 5

Frank McQueen left nothing but shadow in his wake: rugby league star, North Queensland's top detective and veteran of the Vietnam War. When cattle-stealing season came around, all the young detectives put up their hands for Frank's expeditions into the interior. Mac grew up poring over the newspapers with his sister Virginia, looking for the inevitable photograph of their dad dragging a couple of ringbarked bumpkins into the lock-up.

When Mac won a sports scholarship to Nudgee College in Brisbane, Frank gulped down some big ones. That was until he realised that the pride of Queensland Catholic education preferred rugby over rugby league. Frank regularly captained Country Police in their annual rugby league stoush with the Brisbane Cops and Frank didn't like the idea of his son going to Nudgee to play a sport he declared was only for 'wankers or ponies'.

Mac spent his privileged education smarting under the sneers of his father. Even making Queensland Schoolboys in his senior year couldn't turn it. Everything hinged on Mac going into the Queensland cops and getting an armchair ride through the Ds as Frank's Son.

The day he phoned his mother and told her he'd taken a job with a textbook company, his mum actually groaned. He didn't tell her he was going to be a spook. Wasn't allowed. Didn't know that the fib he told her would be a lifelong habit.

Frank got on the line, asked Mac a couple of questions and figured it pretty quick. 'Don't tell me, this place is in Canberra and Jakarta, right?' Frank upgraded his insult about rugby players. 'Intel people,' said Frank, who was infantry in Vietnam, 'are wankers and ponies.'

Which was what Mac was thinking about as he strode in a crowd across the sticky hot tarmac of Makassar's Hasanuddin Airport, carrying a black suit bag over his shoulder, a black wheelie bag trailing behind. In order to get the salesman cover going he wore a short-sleeved beige safari suit, Italian brown woven shoes and a pair of Porsche sunnies. His thin blond hair was gelled straight back and he had a thick gold chain at his neck. The tan was real but it could easily pass for one of those indoor jobs. It was the salesman look he affected for travelling as Richard Davis from Southern Scholastic Books.

If Frank saw his son like this, Mac's cover would be secure. Frank would ignore him. Stone cold motherless.

Just after ten in the morning and the pilot had warned them that it was already thirty-eight degrees at the airport. To the south, massive cloud formations rose thousands of storeys into the air – black, blue and purple and staring down over the tropical sauna of southern Sulawesi. There was no wind: the very air strained under the weight of what Mac reckoned was ninety-eight per cent humidity.

Mac glanced back at the Lion Air 737 cooling its wings behind him. Garuda was a nest of spies and informers during Suharto's era, and no one in the intelligence community had trusted it since. Still, the Lion flight was comfortable, unlike what Sawtell and his boys would be going through: Jakarta to Balikpapan by helo and then a C-130 flight into Watampone across the peninsula from Makassar. It would look like a military milk run. No flags, no Chinese nosey-pokes.

The cabbie who drove him to the Pantai Gapura was understanding about Mac's requests for a few detours here and there. There was no tail, but that didn't mean there wouldn't be. He got the room he wanted at the Pantai, 521, overlooking the pool bar. There were no balconies looking down on his room and there was only one other door on the floor. He checked with reception: no bookings in 522.

He threw his suitcase on the bed and opened it: a few loose clothes and samples. The samples were real: history, geography and mathematics high school textbooks in Bahasa. He took a blue Nokia from the bag and made a call to a number in Canberra which was routed through Singapore and into the government/military secured section of the Telstra cellular system in Australia. He confirmed arrival and good health with his weekly logs.

Shortly before midday he opened the sliding doors onto the patio and clocked the sprawling resort with bungalows scattered amidst stands of old palms and saltwater pools. Nothing untoward, just screaming Malaysian kids in the pool and nagging parents trying to get them to swim in the shallow end.

Mac rubbed his eyes. He was tired, needed sleep. In two days he'd RV with Sawtell's team and he'd need a lot of energy in the saddlebags.

Mac re-entered the room, locked the balcony door and swept the main bugging points: phone, TV, coffee table, under the bed, mattress, the lamps.

Nothing.

He found a box of matches and tested the mirrors for two-way vision. They looked okay but naked flame was not foolproof.

Running the shower hard he positioned himself behind the main door, where he could also see out to the patio. If the Chinese or Indons wanted to move on him, they'd do it while he was showering. Most business hotels in Indonesia were bugged, some of them for video. If he'd missed a comms point, this should flush them out.

He waited five, seven, ten minutes.

Steam wafted into the room.

Nothing.

Ringing down to reception, he complained that the bed was broken. Told the girl he was going out for an hour and wanted it fixed before he returned.

He hung up before the receptionist could confirm and let himself into the corridor. Shutting the door he moved to the other end of the landing area, beyond the elevator doors and behind a planter box of indoor palms. He stood still, casual and humming to himself. Just some halfwit Anglo with a game of pocket billiards going on.

Five minutes. Ten minutes.

At fifteen minutes Mac moved back to the room. If management were in on something, they would have had a spook up the stairs within two minutes to work over his room. The hotel was clean. This shift, at least.

Mac phoned reception again, told the girl not to worry about the bed. He secured the doors, grabbed a cold Bintang from the bar fridge, opened it and put it on the writing table where he watched it sweat. Then he stripped to his briefs, did fifty push-ups and four sets of fifteen ab crunches. He shadow boxed up on his toes for six minutes and rewarded himself with the beer.

He pulled the curtains and got into bed. Fatigue raced up on him and his brain swam: he thought of Diane, and what it would take. He thought of the Sydney Uni job and what he'd need to do to keep it on track. The Garvey briefing in Jakkers gnawed at him too. Judith Hannah was last seen – or not seen, depending on the quality of the intelligence – in Makassar, capital of south Sulawesi. With Garrison. Allegedly.

What annoyed Mac was how quickly Garrison had become the focus. Even Sawtell, the Green Beret, had assumed the mission was a hit on Garrison. Then there was Dave Urquhart. Urquhart, the political liaison guy, the fixer of ulterior motives between the executive arm of government and Australia's spies. Where there was Urquhart, there was politics. Which meant some poor operational bastard was going to get screwed.

One guess.

Sleep crept up on him and he got a glimpse of the time he'd been wandering around The Rocks in Sydney with Diane. They'd drunk too much at dinner and were snogging under a restaurant awning while they waited for a rain storm to pass. A couple had come past, the bloke in a suit and his woman following behind. They'd obviously been fighting because the suit was withholding his umbrella. Diane saw it and reacted immediately. Yelled out, 'Give her your brollie, you selfish wanker!'

The bloke stopped and the woman moved under the brollie. The woman had turned and mouthed thank you at Diane over her shoulder.

That's what Mac had fallen for. A real piece of work.

* * *

Mac woke. It was dark. His civvie Omega on the bedside table said it was 3.11. He dressed in a polo shirt and rugby shorts. Dragged the top sheet from the bed, stuffed it under his arm. Pulled on a black baseball cap and dark sunnies and made for reception.

There was one person behind the desk. A young Indon with a bum-fluff mo. He was sleeping.

Mac bird-whistled and the guy woke with a start.

'Sorry to bother you, champ. Forgot to get something from my security box.'

The desk guy slapped his pockets as he stood, eyed Mac's bare feet, cap and sunnies.

Mac winked, friendly: '*Maaate*. The lights in this place.'

Just another crazy Skippy loose in the tropics.

The desk guy buttoned up his organ-grinder monkey suit, did a quick ID check of Mac's passport and then led the way through a door behind the reception desk. They walked along a dimly lit corridor, down two flights of stairs and into the basement security box area where the desk guy unlocked a thick steel door. Fluorescent lights flickered to life overhead as they entered. It was about twenty metres long, five metres wide and lined floor to ceiling with heavy brushed-steel lock boxes. There was a footstand at the far end, sitting on the taupe lino, near a table with two chairs.

The hotel was financed with Singapore-Chinese money and one of the first things they must have designed was the safe deposit area.

Mac could feel the surveillance camera on the back of his neck. The bloke turned, questioning eyes. Mac held up his red plastic key ring with the number 92 on it. The desk guy moved down to 92, looking for a key on his chain. The boxes between 90 and 100 were painted black, the long-term hires that required both the client's key and the hotel's master.

They both put their keys into the medium-sized door and turned. A brushed-steel enclosed tray lay inside. It was the size of four shoe boxes.

The desk guy stared at it.

Mac stared at the desk guy. 'Thanks, champ – think I've got it now.'

The desk guy smiled. Fucked off.

Mac whipped the sheet over his head so it draped over his security box and down to his ankles. He pulled out the tray and opened the lid. Bundles of US, Australian, Malaysian and Indonesian currency winked back through a seal-lock plastic bag the size of a decent cushion. It was all used notes, perhaps US$40,000 worth in total.

Mac riffled the rupiah, peeled off about US$5000. Trousered it, then resealed the money bag and dug around under it. There was a pile of Amex and Visa cards in various names, held together with a rubber band. There were also passports, drivers' licences, a digital camera, a BlackBerry and a red Nokia that had seen better days. There were two handguns – a Heckler & Koch P9S with a black plastic stock grip, and an American-made Walther PPK .38 – both holstered in navy blue hip rigs. Mac had never used the Walther.

There were four empty clips and several boxes of Winchester .45s and .38s. He couldn't remember how much ammo each contained. He grabbed the Heckler, two clips and three boxes of .45s.

Mac slipped the sheet off his shoulders. Turned it into a swag and put his booty in it. Then he left, walking backwards.

CHAPTER 6

Showered and made up like a sales dickhead, Mac ate up large for breakfast: bacon, scrambled eggs, fried potatoes, toast, tea, orange juice and half a rockmelon. He was hunkered down in a corner of the Pantai's huge tropical-themed restaurant, so he'd get a look at the whole room and everyone in it. He was surrounded by Anglo expats and Malaysians trying to cash in on the boom economy of Sulawesi.

Shortly before eight am Mac was running through his day: he needed extra phones, he needed a car – and maybe a driver – and he needed to get on the Garrison/Hannah trail. The Service didn't have employees or assets in Sulawesi. But they had Minky Bonuya, a local contractor primarily run by the CIA and a hub of the best intelligence on Sulawesi. His long, vulpine face was a real standout in round-faced Indonesia, and Mac wasn't a great fan of the bloke. But Minky was allegedly the one with the Garrison drum.

As he left the restaurant, Mac walked past a tourist at a fruit stand. She smelled of the soap that Diane used. Crabtree and Something. It annoyed him at first but he fell into daydreaming about perhaps travelling with Diane, when he wasn't working, when he was a regular university lecturer. When . . .

He snapped out of it. Gave himself a quick tap on the head with the middle knuckle. Thirty-seven years old, and in love for the first time. He didn't know how people did it.

Minky's shoe shop was two blocks inland from the Makassar port area. Mac did a figure of eight around it, then did some overruns, double-backs and triangulated patterns, with his black wheelie case in tow. Just an overworked salesman looking for his clients. Only this salesman had a P9S handgun sitting slightly behind the front point of his right hip bone, hidden from sight by a safari suit jacket.

Mac wasn't big on guns, which was why he hadn't even practised with the Walther yet. Didn't read the magazines, didn't have an emotional attachment to them. He had grown to like the unfashionable Heckler for practical reasons. At four inches, its barrel was nice and short, and it was lighter than the big semi-autos like the Beretta and Glock. Sure, it only had seven shots in the clip, but that meant it used a single-stack mag rather than the jam-prone double stacks. It also made it lighter and thinner, perfect for a hip rig. Banger Jordan had hated the shoulder rigs for their record of accidental shootings. He used to say that if he heard about any of his candidates using shoulder holsters in their careers, he'd come over and personally kick their arses. 'The most likely victim of the shoulder holster,' he'd said, 'is the poor cunt standing behind you – and he's on *your* side.'

The street looked okay. It was mid tourist season which meant more people to scope but also easier to spot eyes: people who were not relaxing. Some of the cars parked at the kerb – Toyota Vientas and Honda Accords mostly – had men sitting in them, but it wasn't unlike an Australian shopping district, the missus shopping while blokes read the sports pages. One of the car-bound blokes even looked straight at him: hardly a professional's technique.

Mac pushed through the door of Minky's shop into air-con dimness. Minky looked up from behind a glass counter. Smiled like a fox, lips parting to reveal big rodent teeth. Short and middle-aged, his hair was pushed back like an Asian Nosferatu.

'Aha, Mr Mac – welcome,' said Minky, coming around the counter in his white dentist's coat. He shook Mac's hand.

'Minky. How's business?' said Mac. The smell of leather was good – a blast of childhood.

57

'Oooh, so good, Mr Mac. So good.'

This would go on for a while. It was the Indonesian way. Mac used the interlude to case the place: rows of shoes up and down the sides, glass counter at the end of the shop and a glass door into the back room where Mac knew Minky kept his safes and tricky comms gear, including a military satellite uplink–downlink.

The last time Mac was in Sulawesi, Minky had helped him rescue a mining concession that a large Australian company had paid good bribe money to secure. It was being undermined by a bit of Chinese skulduggery and the resolution saw the Aussie mining company having to pony up more money to get what it had already paid for. Mac took it as a victory but he was always convinced that Minky had taken a cut of the extra fee. Real meaning: Minky had secretly foiled a number of Service-preferred solutions, such as blackmail, in favour of the cheque. After that gig Mac had promised himself that he wouldn't return to this beautiful and brutal island. During the operation one of his Indon contacts had been hauled off to the cells at the Makassar POLRI compound and beaten virtually to death. Mac always suspected Minky of informing. He'd have done it to ensure he was the only local asset that the Americans and Australians would use. He'd have done it for money. That was Minky.

Now they talked shit.

'How *are* you, Mink?'

'No, how are *you*, Mr Mac?'

And it was going on for just a shade too long. Mac started to get that cold thing in his gut. That thing when you're fourteen years old and you cross the dance floor of the school formal to ask the girl to dance, and you get that block of ice in your solar plexus. About half a second before she says, 'No thanks.'

That feeling.

He looked Minky in the eye. Rather than feeling warm towards the bloke, he saw him now as quarry. Minky clocked Mac's eyes changing and stopped blathering. Gulped. Gear change into scared. Pale-eyed people were not universally well regarded in South-East Asia, mostly because pale eyes couldn't hide their emotions in the manner required by a face-saving society. Especially violent emotions.

There was a slight movement behind Minky. A tiny shift of

reflection in the half-open glass door. Mac whacked Minky in the Adam's apple with a knife hand, grabbed the stunned mullet by the hair, pulled him backwards into his stomach and held his face still by wrapping his hand around the little guy's mouth. Then he squeezed his thumb and forefinger together on each side of Minky's face, so he was making the sides of his mouth push inwards on his tongue.

Minky's eyes bulged, his small hands mincing at Mac's paw and his legs thrashing.

Mac kept the air filled with pleasant nothings as he suppressed any noise of resistance, making it sound as if they were still talking. Mink's mouth gulped against the palm of his hand as he advanced slowly on the door to the back office. Mac put his hand back, drew the Heckler.

Minky convulsed, French-kissed Mac's palm. The vibration of stifled scream microwaved Mac's hand and he pinched Minky's nostrils shut to stop him moaning. Minky spasmed and vomit cascaded through Mac's fingers. It smelled like curried fish. With coriander.

'Yeah,' said Mac over his shoulder, as they crept forward. 'So if we went with the sirloins it wouldn't be the same thing as if it were blue. I said that to Dave.'

At the door he stared into the reflection and got a good angle, recognising the goon standing around the corner. He looked solid and fit: expensive black slacks, white trop shirt with his hand poised under it. He was one of the sports page readers. He had been in a silver Accord.

Mac whipped around, wanting to secure the front door against any backup. But he couldn't risk it. He wanted the goon alive and talkative, so he dropped Minky's semi-conscious head, walked around the corner and snap-kicked the goon under his left patella. The bloke's mouth fell open but no sound came out. One hundred and six kilos driven through the front foot will do that. The knee hyperextended but the goon stayed on his feet. Mac put his weight onto his front left foot and threw a low–high hook combination off his left hand. The low shot to the right kidney broke the goon; the high shot to the jaw finished him.

Dropped. Like a cheating girlfriend.

Still struggling for breath, Mac looked through Minky's front door to the packed street outside. He flipped the closed sign, slid the bolt, pulled the venetians down and walked into the back room with the goon's Glock in his back pocket and the Heckler in his right hand. He tried to control his heart rate with deep breaths. His mind raced. Who was the goon? What was the larger picture?

Minky was struggling to breathe through coughing fits, purple in the face and vomiting. The goon lay on his left elbow, eyes rolling back in his head, face slackened by the broken jaw, leg useless. In shock.

Neither of them said a word. They knew what came next. Minky would squeal straightaway. He was a pro. He didn't know much and what he did know he would give up fast for a torture-free morning. The goon was well dressed, probably Javanese – a contractor sent to woop woop to deal with the Skippy troublemaker. If that was the case there'd be at least another person. Mac thought hard but couldn't recall another man in the silver Accord.

His heart rate normalising slightly, he moved to the back door, bolted it. There was no glass. He moved to his right, along the back wall that was covered with electronics, and found a window high up. He stepped on a chair, peeked through the window. His vision was thwarted. Couldn't see the door area but could see the dusty Accord fifteen metres away in the dirt car park area. He clocked the registration plate. A man was in the passenger's seat: Asian, but he didn't vibe local. Black polo shirt, Ray-Bans and something familiar about him.

Mac got off the chair. He probably had five minutes before the cavalry tried to burst in. He pieced it as good as he could: the Americans had sent him to Minky to catch another American, a CIA rogue who was still Agency. So who was working for whom? Minky had a couple of Javanese thugs ready for a reception party. Or did he have no choice? Only one of the thugs went in. They didn't look bumpkin enough for Sulawesi, they looked very Jakarta. The goon gasping on the floor wore flash slacks and even smelled of Old Spice. That made him either American- or Australian-trained, which pointed to ex-BIN or maybe Indonesian Army special forces, the Aussie-trained Kopassus. However it worked, Mac was feeling fear.

Mac moved to Minky first. He didn't need prompting. 'I sorry, Mr Mac. So sorry, please.'

Sorry? They always were.

'Who's this, Mink?' asked Mac, waving the Heckler at the goon.

Minky shook his head.

Mac shot him in the bladder. Knelt on his chest so he couldn't scream.

Minky's face went purple.

'Who's this, Mink?' Mac pointed the gun at the other side of the bladder, intimating a second shot. Minky convulsed, groaned deep and vomited on Mac's safari suit pants.

The goon started moving. Mac stood, looked down on him. The goon wouldn't meet his eye.

'This a Garrison job?'

The goon looked at him, surprised.

'Where's Garrison?'

Now the goon went back to his studied nonchalance. He tried to shake his head but the jaw situation made him wince.

'Where's the girl?' This time Mac raised the Heckler, pointed it at the goon.

Minky sobbed, puked again. Blood soaked into his dentist get-up.

Mac didn't want to leave without having at least one part of the puzzle. And he didn't know where he was supposed to be looking.

The goon looked back at the gun. Mac looked at the back door, expecting a charge-in at some point. The goon lashed out with his right leg, caught Mac on the inside of the right wrist. The Heckler tumbled, bounced and slid along the white lino floor.

Mistake one: Mac's eyes followed the gun.

Mistake two: the goon had his hand on the Glock in Mac's back pocket before the Heckler had stopped sliding.

Mistake three: the goon didn't fire immediately.

Mac swung an arc with his left hand, grabbed the goon's gun hand, twisted it slightly away from pointing at his stomach. Grabbed the gun-hand elbow with his right hand and snapped the goon's forearm across his knee. The goon was built in the arms but Mac's adrenaline and speed broke the forearm bones as if he was about to start a camp fire.

The goon screamed. The cavalry would be coming.

Mac pulled the Glock from the goon's limp hand and hit him in the temple. Hard. The goon sagged back to the lino, blood running out of his head.

Mac frisked him for a wallet. There was none. He scooped the Heckler, checked for load. An unnecessary yet robotic habit from the Royal Marines.

A kick sounded at the door.

Mac breathed fast and shallow.

Another kick. A man yelling in Bahasa.

He knelt beside Minky, looked at him hard. Saw the bloke's eyes, saw a deeper fear. The penny dropped. 'They got your wife, Mink?'

Minky shook his head. The shock was making his teeth chatter.

'Daughter?'

Minky nodded, tears starting.

'I'll get her, Mink, but you have to tell me where.'

Minky was on his way out. His eyeballs were rolling back.

A shot fired outside the door. No splinters. Minky's back door was steel.

Mac slapped Minky. A bladder shot usually gives you ten minutes, but Mac's slug might have bounced into the leg's main artery.

'In Makassar? Is that where she is, Minky?'

Another head shake.

'Is she with Garrison? Tell me, Mink.'

Minky vomited again. This time green and red. It dribbled rather than poured. A bloke about to cark it.

Minky looked up, said, 'Eighty.'

Mac slapped Minky as his head lolled. 'What's that, Mink – you say "eighty"?' He didn't get it.

Minky nodded almost imperceptibly, his face pale.

Then he was dead.

Collapsed like a rag.

More gunshots. The sound of lead pinging around in the door.

Mac stood, raced to the front door, then had another thought and went back to the Javanese goon. He pulled back the guy's trop shirt collar. No luck. Then unzipped the bloke's pants, pulled them down. 'If we don't tell, then it never happened, hey butch?'

He grabbed the waistband, pulled it round. Bingo! A pink piece of paper stapled to the tailor's label. Mac tore the dry-cleaner's ticket off the pants, grabbed his black wheelie bag.

He prepared for the worst as he exited. It didn't come. He walked straight into tourist crowds. Malaysian lawyers and dentists with their kids all kitted out in genuine Sulawesi tribal headdresses.

He flowed with them, adrenaline bursting like fireworks behind his eyes. His vision darted everywhere at once, breathing shallow and raspy. His brain was working so fast he could barely think of anything else except silver Honda, black polo shirt; silver Honda, black polo shirt. Silver. Black. Black. Silver . . .

He walked for five minutes like that before he took his hand entirely off his right hip. There didn't seem to be a tail. Not from the silver Accord, at least. The two Western-style Javanese hit men probably hadn't wanted to take their business into the street.

Mac had got lucky.

He lurched to a stand of hibiscus behind a bus stop shelter. Vomited. For all his reputation as a tough customer, he hated shooting, hated guns and loathed seeing someone die. But no amount of training or experience could stop a trapped and scared animal behaving like a trapped and scared animal. Mac hadn't shot Minky because he was tough; he'd shot him because he was scared and wanted to control the situation by making the other guy more scared than him. It was a mistake. He'd known that as soon as he pulled the trigger.

He walked and walked. He backtracked, overlapped and did the oldest trick in the game: turned on his heel suddenly and walked straight back from where he came. It looked natural if you pretended you'd forgotten something. He walked past the markets, down to the waterfront, a thriving fishing town for a thousand years and now concentrating on netting South-East Asia's holidaying middle classes. The local jihadists were trying to reverse that with the aid of their old friend, potassium chlorate.

Midday turned into two-thirty real fast.

He dipped into a series of dime stores of the type that blanket Asia: the ones that sell cigarettes, incense and cigarette lighters where the girl's bikini drops when you turn it upside down. They sell the local rags as well as *Tempo*, the *Straits Times* and the *Jakarta Post*. Mac bought plain Nokias and pre-paid cellular network cards for a Philippines

63

telco called EastCall. He ducked in, he ducked out. He bought phones from different shops and bought a packet of wet-wipes. He ate goreng at a street stand, sitting back in the shadows where Grandma wrapped spring rolls. He didn't let his eyes leave the street or his hand leave his right hip, and he cleaned Minky's vomit off his pants.

He did numbers: six shots left in the Heckler, but it would have to be dumped. He didn't want to go back to the Pantai for the Walther – too risky now. He should have taken the goon's Glock with him, but now he'd have to pick up a gun when he RV'd with Sawtell. Would they have a spare? How many more did Garrison have coming for him? And who or what was Minky talking about when he said 'Eighty'?

He walked some more, looking for a car hire place that wasn't a big American brand – the CIA data-tapped those franchises quick-smart. And the Americans were starting to look like being part of the problem rather than the solution. Minky was an Agency contractor and the hit squad was probably the same. But whether the ambush was American or Australian, Mac felt relieved that he'd changed the RV with Sawtell from Makassar to Ralla, up the coast. Mac hadn't been thinking about double-crossings when he'd done that at the last minute. He'd just wanted to keep a posse of highly conspicuous special forces soldiers out of town until he needed them. Now it might give him a day's head start on whoever was after him.

He asked around and headed inland to a place called Paradise Holiday Hire Cars. A couple of locals had said it was cheap and reliable. And they took cash.

He passed by the Golden Hotel on the waterfront and watched a bunch of Anglo and Asian junketeers milling around, waiting to get on a tour bus. They looked like IT consultants or telecom engineers. Local police lolly-gagged with their assault rifles. Mac slid in amongst the junketeers, smiling and making quippish non sequiturs to no one in particular.

Hoo-fucking-rah!

The junket-lovers were putting their day luggage into a pile to be loaded into the luxury coach. Mac wandered among them with his wheelie case. No one challenged him, probably because he was Anglo. One of the great weaknesses of the coalition of the willing's

War on Terror was its inherent ethnic bias. Something was wrong when a pale-eyed white man could wander through the world's largest Muslim country and receive less attention than a local.

Mac bent down, pulled his blue Service Nokia from his wheelie and put it in the side pocket of a carry-all. The name tag on the bag said Richard Taylor, accompanied by a Melbourne address. The ASIS listening post would track the junketeers for hours, maybe days, before it sounded all wrong.

Mac walked another three blocks, found his rental car place and hired a white Toyota Vienta. He paid in cash for ten days and coughed up for an insurance policy which was worth more as emergency bog paper in Sulawesi than as something that would save him from being sued.

Driving to the outskirts of Makassar, he pulled over into an elevated tourist lookout and tried to collect himself. Rummaging in his safari suit pocket Mac gasped a little at his right wrist as it caught on the fabric. The wrist was now swelling from the kick he'd taken from the goon. He fished out the pink dry-cleaner label. It had a serial number under the name SUNDA LAUNDRY – PALOPO. Palopo was a mid-sized coastal town a day's drive north. If those flash slacks had been recently pressed, then Mac was prepared to bet that Garrison – probably Judith Hannah and Minky's daughter too – were somewhere in the vicinity.

It was all he had to go on. With Minky dead, it would have to do.

Mac grabbed a set of spare socks from the wheelie bag, tied them together in a knot and pulled the lever to open the gas tank flap. He found a stick on the ground, about three feet long, and moved to the back of the Vienta. Pushing the socks into the gas tank with the stick, he held the other end and waited for a few seconds before pulling the petrol-soaked socks out. Unclipping the entire hip rig and Heckler from his belt he knelt and wiped down the gun until the whole thing was shiny with gasoline. He dumped it in a rest area bin and went back to the Toyota, grabbed the Winchester loads and the spare mag, wiped them down with the socks and then dumped them too, along with the socks.

Then he got on the road for Ralla, where he was meeting Sawtell the following morning.

He was exhausted. Adrenaline does that to you.

As he drove he thought back to what he had done with that Service phone. It was only the second time in his career that he'd deliberately slipped Canberra's internal bugging and tracking.

And that time he had also suspected the Service had a mole.

CHAPTER 7

Mac's need to win was not a recent development. At Nudgee College in Brisbane, they drafted him into the first XV as a fifteen-year-old. They put him at half-back and the theory was that if he couldn't handle the knocks they'd pull him out.

Near the end of that year, Nudgee played Churchie in the annual grudge match: Micks vs Prods. Mac's mum and dad and sister Virginia came down for the occasion. Mac could tell they were intimidated by the school's Renaissance architecture and pillared buildings as they took their seats in the bleachers.

The half-back from Churchie was their captain, a senior and full of lip. The guy wasn't tall but he was built like a brick one. He got in Mac's face, sledged him something terrible from the start and didn't exclude Virginia from his abuse. Mac did it the Nudgee way, with a stiff upper lip.

At half-time, Mac was in the middle of the field listening to the coach when he became aware of a red-faced, pale-eyed maniac on the sidelines calling his name. In front of the high-society set of Brisbane, Frank yelled in his broadest North Queensland accent: 'Do something about this wanker – he's a flamin' ponce.'

His father was right. If the match had been played in Rockie,

Mac's opposing half-back would have copped a slapping quick-smart. No more sledging.

Mac gave Frank the nod. His father walked back up to the bleachers where Mac's mother whacked him on the forearm, rolled her eyes. Virginia stared at Mac, winked.

At the second half's first scrum, Mac had the feed. The sledger got too close, trying to edge Mac off his mark. So Mac shifted his weight, lifted his right foot, drove his heel down on the bloke's foot, putting all his weight on that heel. Wind rushed from the sledger's lungs, the alloy studs creating agony.

The sledger screamed, stood back, eyes rolling in his head. Mac winked at him, blew a kiss. The sledger threw a haymaker, wide-eyed with rage. Mac rolled slightly and copped it above the left ear. Felt like a bowl of ice-cream. The sledger threw another that completely missed. The ref stepped in, sent the bloke off. He had to be escorted by his team-mates.

Nudgee won and Mac wore the taunts about having the Mad Dad for the rest of his schooling. Mac learned this about himself: he could play the Nudgee game, but he preferred Rockie rules. Which didn't mean he was right to kill Minky. In golf you didn't get to choose how your ball lay, and in the intelligence game you often had to work with what you had. Mac's job now, simply, was to get Judith Hannah and, hopefully, Minky's girl too.

There were no guarantees on that second one. Mac was now cut off from Canberra and pretty sure there was a mole in the organisation, either in Jakarta or Australia. Something had gone wrong in Makassar but it had gone wrong in a way that felt basically out of step. In his profession there was a structure to every type of assignment, and small but badly placed elements could make it all feel wrong. It was like hearing a pop tune on the radio thirty times and on the thirty-first time you hear it, you hear the live version and someone changes a few tiny notes. Your brain still hears the song, and you can adapt, but you know instinctively that a pattern has been broken. That's where Mac was focusing: you didn't get a last-minute tasking to go to Jakarta from the Asia-Pacific director, and then a late-night briefing from a combined ASIS–CIA team to go into Sulawesi, and then on the first and only contact you are given, the bad guys are waiting for you. It didn't happen like that. Someone had set it up.

It came down to a case of who: Tobin? Garvey? Urquhart? That Agency wanker with the He-Man handshake?

Mac drove all night. He wanted to beat the heat, avoid taking a rest, stay ahead of anyone chasing him.

The Vienta wheezed up the hills, dying every time Mac needed extra grunt to overtake the hundreds of overloaded freight trucks that populated Indonesian roads by night. The driver's seat had no cushioning left and most of the asphalt on the blacktop had washed away. Every turn of the tyres was a new jolt that threatened to break the suspension and Mac was constantly throwing the Vienta onto the shoulder of the road as oncoming trucks used the 'third lane' to overtake straight down the middle. A nightmare, but negotiating it kept him awake.

He chewed gum, drank bottled water, plotted scenarios, babbled to himself, sang Beatles songs. The air-conditioning was rooted so he stank up the car with BO as he sweltered in the safari suit pants and shirt. Mostly, he lived in the rear-vision mirror. There was a silver Accord out there somewhere and he knew they wouldn't stop looking.

By midnight his right wrist was puffing like a stonefish and ached something chronic. He was getting to the point where he wouldn't be able to hold a weapon, let alone be efficient with it, and although Mac didn't much like guns, he disliked even more being injured in his gun hand. Especially when he was in the backblocks of Sulawesi with a hit squad on his tail.

That assumed he could get another weapon. He felt vulnerable without the Heckler, but it was lying in a rest stop garbage bin for the most practical of reasons. White men sweeping into town and killing the locals meant the police were going to be coming at you. All that rubbish about South-East Asian cops not caring was bullshit. Mac knew Indonesian detectives who would do anything to bag a pale-eye, particularly on something legit. The last thing he needed was to be picked up for questioning and have a warm gun sitting in the back seat. It would mean the local lock-up for two weeks while some fruit salad-endowed chief tried to work out how rich an Australian textbook executive might be. The dream that there was some all-knowing super-spook from Canberra who could appear in a Sulawesi police cell, flash a badge and get someone like Mac cut loose never came true. People like Mac were what they called an 'undeclared' – they had no diplomatic status and if they were caught doing something illegal, their fate was that of the criminal.

Having wiped and dumped the Heckler, Mac felt the POLRI were going to have a tough time nailing him for the Minky murder. But he still had work to do with the Americans. In his experience, soldiers hated being pushed around on mad missions by intel types. And this was going to be a doozy: the main contact – a CIA contractor – was dead. There were Javanese thugs in pursuit and they didn't look like amateurs. And Mac hadn't even got the drum on Hannah.

It was a complete fuck-up. Worst of all, the dry-cleaner's ticket pointed towards Palopo. It signalled a shift into central and northern Sulawesi. Southern Sulawesi had a cosmopolitan city like Makassar, as big as Brisbane. The north had a whole galaxy of shit-holes and pirate haunts. It could even mean dealing with the chief pirate and strongman of the north, Cookie Banderjong.

Cookie could be highly problematic, and Mac was not looking forward to selling that proposition to Captain John Sawtell.

The sun was just hitting the horizon as Mac pulled into the Motel Davi, near the ocean side of Ralla. Kids stood by a stand of trees, flying kites in the early morning half-light. There were fish hooks on the tails of the kites and they were trying to hook fruit bats. Get Mum to cook it up for lunch.

The town was a fishing village with pretensions to being a tourist trap. But it wasn't making it. It had a few restaurants, a wharf and a Pertamina gas station. It also had a motel where the management was discreet, or as discreet as you'd ever get in the archipelago.

Mac parked the Vienta, walked the line of thirty rooms arranged in a horseshoe, dragging his wheelie case across red dirt. He was looking for a marker, like a playing card or restaurant menu sticking out from under a door. It would mark the RV.

He didn't have to worry. The door to room 17 opened quietly and John Sawtell beckoned him in.

'You look like shit,' said the American as Mac entered.

Sawtell was showered and shaved, dressed in Levis and a black T-shirt, black Hi-Tec Magnums on his feet. The right-hand bed had been slept in, but it was perfectly made. There was one Cordura bag. Packed. One set of toiletries in a perfect line on the bag.

Mac threw his bag on the unused bed. He wanted to lie on that thing for seven hundred hours but it wasn't going to happen.

'There's an alteration,' said Mac as he undid his stinking business shirt. He kicked his shoes off, dropped his trousers, picked up the threadbare white towel on his bed. Wrapping it around him he pulled his toilet bag from the wheelie.

'Like what?' said Sawtell, eyeballing him, hands on hips like he was hearing some lame excuse from a private.

Mac didn't want the military–intel thing to start. Not here, not when he could barely think straight from fatigue.

'Like we're going north. Girl's up north.'

Sawtell didn't move. 'That the mission?'

'Is now.'

A big pause gaped between them.

'Snitch told you that?' said Sawtell, referring to Minky.

'Something like that.'

'Something?'

'Near as.'

'The mission is south.'

'Mission is the girl, John.'

'Mission is don't die, McQueen.'

The whole thing happened in low tones. Mac knew that Sawtell put the safety of his guys above all else and that going north represented new risk. After the Abu Sabaya thing in Sibuco, Sawtell and Mac had sunk a few cold beers and they'd been frank about the tension between soldier and spook. The intel guy would get the senior rank, but the military bloke really ran the show. It was what special forces soldiers called a 'bullshit rank', when you seconded an Agency geek into a military mission and ranked him as a major so he could trump a captain like Sawtell.

71

Mac turned to the bed and pulled a handful of Nokias from the bag. 'We need those charged,' said Mac as he headed off to find the communal shower block.

Sawtell sighed, looked at the carpet and shook his head in resignation.

Mac took Sawtell and his three men to breakfast at a place on stilts over the river. Just along the bank from the restaurant there was a young male macaque monkey chained to a spike in the river bank.

They ordered omelettes and coffee. Mac asked for a fruit bowl and the owner's daughter brought out a basket of mangos and pineapples. He asked her if there was a laundry in the town and she shook her head, but took Mac's clothes bag anyway, held up two fingers, like 'peace'.

Mac liked the initiative, asked the girl her name. 'Arti,' she said.

The boys hoed in when the omelettes arrived. One thing Mac had noticed working with military blokes was that they were incredibly focused on food. Never knowing when they'd be left hungry for days, they ate like maniacs when the eating was good. Some of this fruit would no doubt be produced tomorrow as an informal rat pack.

Mac felt better for his shower and shave. He was comfortable in his blue ovies, which he preferred to the salesman get-up. The lads hadn't done too badly on the civvies front, wearing an assortment of chinos and polo shirts. The comms expert they called Limo – a large Latino bloke with a shaved head – wore a Metallica shirt which was a no-no in the intel world. You never wore anything that the human eye picked up subconsciously: no tattoos, no piercings, no hair colour, no jewellery and no message T-shirts. Too easy to remember. Mac made a note to get him something plainer.

Then there was Hard-on, a slow-talking black American with a boxer's body, who had gone for the preppy look of chinos and polo shirt. He would be the athlete of the crew, the guy who could climb any wall, make any jump, beat anyone in a fight. His sidekick was a paler and taller black American called Spikey. He couldn't keep his eye off the monkey on the river bank, and finally asked what the animal was doing.

'Local shit – don't worry,' said Mac, smiling.

The four Americans had that special forces thing about them;

not arrogant, but totally self-confident. People who liked to get a job done. Mac recognised Hard-on from the Sibuco thing four years ago. The others were new and he hoped they were as good as the Green Berets crew were that night.

Mac spelled out the mission: go to Palopo, snatch the girl, call in the helo from Watampone, do the Harold Holt.

'The Harold who?' said Hard-on.

Mac smiled. 'You know, like the ice hockey player?'

Hard-on winced with concentration, but Limo nodded slowly with a smile. Mac gave Limo a wink. Hard-on sifted the sands.

The monkey started snivelling. Then it was screaming. It was only thirty metres away and its eyes were pleading while it yanked at the chain around its neck. The air filled with the sounds of its terror.

Spikey shook his head, looked at Mac. 'You gotta tell me, man. What's with this ape?'

Arti poured water, smiling at Mac.

'Maybe that'll explain itself,' said Mac.

Spikey nodded at him slowly, not satisfied.

The monkey screamed again. Spikey shrugged, went back to his food.

Suddenly there was a cacophony of noises. Water splashed, something roared and a monkey screeched.

Mac looked over. A large crocodile had launched itself out of the river and had the monkey in its smiling mouth. Flipped it. Rolled it. Disappeared back into the river. Monkey's arm waving.

Spikey fell backwards out of his chair with fright. Fumbled for his Beretta. Which wasn't there. Eyes wide, panting breath.

Sawtell laughed at him.

Limo slapped his leg, pointing at Spikey. 'Look at chu, man. Like your girlfriend just told you she got the clap.'

Spikey's mouth hung open, his eyes glued to the river bank where there was nothing left but a spike and a chain. And a collar.

'That!' sputtered Spikey. 'What the fuck was that shit?'

Arti came back to the table. Smiled. 'Croc catchee monkey. No catchee family.'

The Americans' cover was bodyguarding the Australian forest products executive, Richard Davis. Mac had his cards ready to go:

RICHARD DAVIS

GOANNA FOREST PRODUCTS LTD.

It had a Brisbane address but the phone numbers all diverted to the Southern Scholastic office in Sydney. The bodyguard cover was totally natural in South-East Asia, as were the side arms. And there would be no reason for the hired goons to know anything about the business venture, which meant four less people requiring background and cover.

Mac and Sawtell had discussed the need to avoid telling the lads that there was a rogue CIA component in the picture and keep it basic damsel-in-distress stuff for now. Sawtell's aversion to Palopo and Sulawesi's north was pure professionalism. He was based out of the southern Philippines and knew all about Cookie Banderjong, the strongman who ran northern Sulawesi. A former BAKIN operative who had been educated at an exclusive Melbourne boarding school, Banderjong was a rich kid with family ties to Suharto who got to play spy-versus-spy in places like Paris and DC.

When the Suharto regime fell in '99, Cookie had gone back to the last real asset he could put his hands on: the family's old clove plantations and logging concessions in northern Sulawesi. He expanded his power, made millions from Japanese and Malaysian loggers, brought Western managers into the plantations, bought out small-time competitors and seeped backed into the political wheel-and-spoke structure. As it turned out, many Suharto cronies were rebirthed in the new Jakarta, and many of them were Cookie's former BAKIN colleagues.

Cookie had built a private army to protect the foreign logging companies. He organised the pirates and bandits on operating concessions and he dealt with the jihadists with brutality. He ran the north of Sulawesi like a medieval fiefdom – so much so that Westerners who had had any dealings with the man referred to northern Sulawesi as Cookie Country. And Mac and Sawtell's men were driving to the very edges of it.

Sawtell had told Mac: 'Any freaky stuff up there, and I'm pulling my boys out. Got it?' His tone had been uncompromising. Mac didn't take it personally; he didn't have a choice.

* * *

They hit the road before lunch. The Berets had picked up a blue Nissan Patrol from the base in Watampone. It was the big turbo diesel version. Comfortable as a car and would go anywhere. It had no special comms gear or plating. Mac had been clear about that. He wanted to move around like a party from a logging company, not in a 'civvie' Hummer with comms aerials sticking out of it like a game-fishing boat.

It was stinking hot outside, air-conned in the cabin. The boot was filled with guns. Limo drove like a soldier, slightly over the limit but controlled. At Mac's behest he'd changed into a plain black shirt. All the lads wore baseball caps Mac had bought from the Pertamina. It was beyond him why the American military retained those ridiculous hairstyles that set them apart wherever they went in the world. No way was he going to have kids racing out onto the streets of Palopo pointing at the Yanks like the 101st had just landed at the wharf.

Mac took the front passenger seat but there was a tension in the air. The lads mumbled, weren't relaxed. It built for ten minutes then Mac turned to the back seat, looked Spikey in the eye. 'Okay, play the fucking thing. But if I hear the word "nigger" or "ho", it's coming off. Right?'

The lads whooped. Spikey high-fived Hard-on. Limo put his hand back like he was carrying a fish platter. The lads gave him skin and a CD appeared from somewhere; gold-coloured, black texta on it.

'Enjoy it while you can, guys,' said Sawtell. 'Won't get played on my watch.'

Mac turned back to the windscreen and heard Hard-on say, 'That's my *Pizza* Man!' Mac laughed quietly. They were kids. Fucking kids!

Winding his seat back, he pulled his black Adidas cap down over his face to grab some Zs as the R&B ramped up.

CHAPTER 8

There was only one dry-cleaner in Palopo and it was the Sunda Laundry. They drove past it once and came back for another sweep. Mac saw cases of Bintang in a stack at the entrance of a roadhouse. They stopped, bought a case.

After finding a rundown Dutch Colonial guesthouse near the southern approaches to the small fishing town, they hunkered down for the evening and ordered in food.

Mac went through a long tale with the guesthouse owner about not sourcing the meal from a place that would make his friends sick. Though Mac had grown used to the food in South-East Asia, the Americans ate steaks from Texas and corn from Iowa, all flown into Camp Enduring Freedom in Zam. The last thing Mac needed was an extended case of the trots from these elite special forces. It didn't mean the owner would listen to a single word. Indonesians nodded and smiled at every request. Whether they did anything about it depended on if they could. Or wanted to.

Mac realised there were a few kids around the place. Kids were expensive and demanding in any part of the world, so he tipped the bloke large. Gave him the wink and a slap on the bicep. He seemed to get that Mac wanted some privacy from the bloke and his family.

The owner's teenage son delivered the food. Mac looked him in the eye. Couldn't see fear. Asked him his name.

Kid said, 'Bani.' Quite tall, good-looking, athletic and cocky in that globally fifteen-year-old way. He wore a white singlet and Mac clocked a crucifix through the fabric. Mac walked with Bani down to where the Patrol was parked. The boy was still at school, learning English and science, playing soccer. He wanted to stay in school but by the way he shrugged and looked around him Mac could tell that education wasn't part of his future.

Mac dragged the Bintangs out of the boot, hauled them up to the room. They ate and drank. The food tasted good, clean.

Forty-five minutes later, when they'd all kept it down, Mac knew for sure. Hunger satisfied, they sat around, dished out guns and loads from the Cordura bags. Sawtell let Mac have his own Beretta M9, but not before he made Mac spill on how and why he was without a gun.

Mac told the lads most of the truth but stopped short of the Minky details. He didn't want to admit that he'd panicked and shot the intel source – the only intel source.

Sawtell eyed him. Flexed through his wide neck. 'Just so you know – that piece ain't goin' nowhere near no garbage can. Reading me?'

'Crystal,' said Mac.

They fired up their mobiles and programmed each other's numbers into their address books.

At nine-thirty pm local, Mac slipped out into the night to have a butcher's. It had been a year since he was last in Palopo. For a small town with barely any profile, it was the crossroads for a lot of travel in Sulawesi. From Palopo you drove north towards the major port city of Manado, to the south was Makassar, to the immediate west was the remote highland areas with their weird architecture reminiscent of boat prows, and further west was the airport hub of Palu.

Palopo itself had changed. There was more neon, more people on the streets after dark and some real restaurants, not just the goreng and fish shops that populate rural Indonesia.

Mac moved towards the centre of town, keeping to the shadows. His cap was low, his ovies covering his body shape and the chunky Beretta handgun in its webbing rig.

Sunda Laundry was down a side street off the shabby main plaza area. Mac walked past it on the opposite side of the street and then came back right in front. It was a double-wide joint and through the glass doors Mac could see a few washing machines and tubs, some dryers too, and a large folding table. A small pilot light was on in a back room.

Mac did another circuit, sweat trickling down his back, and couldn't see any surveillance. Ducking into the laneway running adjacent to the back of Sunda Laundry, he pulled the Beretta out from under the ovies. He hated Berettas. They had been OK'd and rejected several times by the US military in the 1980s before going into service. They were prone to jamming, the trigger was too far from the grip and, especially annoying for Mac, they had double-stack fifteen-round magazines. That was fine for a soldier or cop, where simply showing a nice big gun was a bonus in itself, but no good for a spook. A handgun with fifteen rounds in the handle was like carrying a small shoe box around with you. Who the hell needed fifteen rounds?

Mac moved down the unlit alley, smooth and slow. He held the Beretta cup-and-saucer, his body pointing two o'clock. He heard his breath rasping and his Hi-Tecs scraping on greasy soil. He moved past garbage bins and mangy cats. It smelled like an open sewer.

He hesitated as he got to the back of the laundry, looking for that pilot light. Heart pumping, he got closer to the fence, moved along it and paused at the point where the laundry's backyard started.

He turned, out of habit, cased his six o'clock. Nothing, except mangy cats getting back on their piles of garbage.

He looked back at the laundry. The pilot light wasn't bright, but he could make out the yard. There was no car, certainly no silver Accord. He kept his eyes on the place, checked his G-Shock. Almost ten pm. Sweat ran freely down his back now.

After an hour, nothing.

He walked back to the guesthouse, crossed the streets a few times and backtracked. All quiet.

He hit the mattress at 11.25 and fell asleep wondering if he could call Sydney on his mobile, whether Diane would be sweet with that.

It was just before eight am when Mac got to the Patrol, showered, shaved and back in his salesman dickhead get-up. As he opened the front passenger door, Limo put the big 4x4 into drive. Mac held up his hand. 'Just a tick, mate.'

Bani came out the side door of the guesthouse and Mac signalled he get in the back seat. The kid was excited – his first interpreter work.

Sawtell shot Mac a look, then got out of the Patrol. Mac caught his eye and followed.

They moved away from the vehicle as Bani got in the back seat.

'What the fuck's this?' said Sawtell, far from friendly.

'We need someone to do the talking. Bani's keen.'

'Spikey's the languages guy – that's why I picked him,' said Sawtell. 'Shit! That's a kid! You want that on your conscience?'

John Sawtell had the kind of eyes that could hand out slaps. He had that way of getting up in a man's face and talking soft, just like Mac's father used to.

'Thought about Spikey,' said Mac. 'But you know, John, these guys are intimidating to the locals.'

Sawtell cocked an eyebrow. Disbelief.

'It's not racist – these are big, scary guys to the Indons.'

Sawtell gave him a *you're so full of shit* look. 'McQueen, he's a kid.'

Mac could smell the Ipana on Sawtell's breath.

'You're not going to drag a kid into this shit,' said Sawtell, lifting a finger.

'It'll be fine,' said Mac.

Sawtell shook his head. 'The look on your face when you arrived at Ralla? That wasn't fine, my man – that was fear.'

Mac looked back at the Patrol, where all eyes were on them. He looked back at Sawtell. 'John, if I take Spikey into that laundry, and it turns serious, chances are the dry-cleaning guy makes a call. It goes to shit. Spikey doesn't do what I do, John. He can't keep it light.'

Sawtell laughed. Big laugh. 'Light?! Oh, that's good. That's so intel-guy.'

'Back to that, are we?'

'Do we ever leave it?'

Sawtell was right. That part of things never stopped.

The American wasn't letting this go. 'First time I worked with you, in Sibuco – call *that* light? My boys talked about nothing but you for days.'

'Sure,' said Mac. 'But it was the pizza delivery part that we had to finesse. It took months – not everything's about kicking in doors and killing bad guys.'

Mac didn't believe that last bit himself. Sawtell didn't believe what he'd just heard.

They stared at each other. The audience looked on.

'I guess that's it, huh?' said Sawtell.

Mac deadpanned. Nodded.

The dry-cleaner episode went fast and well. Mac played the dumb-shit Anglo salesman looking for his local businessman contacts. He described Fancy Pants and Ray-Bans and through Bani he explained that he had lost the piece of paper that said where they were staying.

The dry-cleaner told Bani where to go. A hotel in the middle of town.

Bani made one last push, unbidden, asking the dry-cleaner something else. The dry-cleaner answered, giving Bani the name of Fancy Pants. Seems there'd been a delivery to the hotel.

Bani was beside himself with excitement when they got back to the Patrol. Mac gave him a pat on the back, Bani beamed. Then Mac stopped it dead, told the kid not to get in.

The boy almost cried. Mac pulled an envelope out of his safari jacket, told Bani he had to make a promise. 'If you take this, if you accept this gift, then this is the deal: I want you to go home, pack a bag and catch the midday bus to Makassar. Got it?'

Bani nodded, sniffled.

'I want you on that bus. There's a letter in there for Brother Tom at the Makassar Brothers' school. Got that? He's a friend of mine, I've called him this morning. He's expecting you. His pupils go to university, in Surabaya. You want to go to university, Bani?'

Bani looked up at Mac. Nodded, looked into the envelope. Saw a wad of greenbacks, looked confused.

'That's the deal, Bani. You did good work here today, but this is the deal, huh?' Mac shook the boy's hand. 'You beauty.'

Bani hugged him. Mac saw the crucifix again, through the gap in the boy's trop shirt. Sadness flooded him. '*Dominus vobiscum*,' he said, pointing at the cross.

Bani smiled. '*Et cum spiritu tuo.*'

They parked by the fishing wharves, two blocks away from the Grand Hotel. Mac told Sawtell the name of Fancy Pants, then he got out of the Patrol. Grabbing the wheelie bag from the rear luggage compartment, Mac said he'd see them in fifteen minutes.

The Grand Hotel was a seven-storey modern place, built for the thriving tourism industry. Mac moved along the drive-through area that led into the lobby. Palms rustled overhead as he doubled back and walked down the side road and into the car park in the back. He did a slow circuit among about fifty cars and minivans, looking for a silver Accord and anything else that might look out of place. There were no eyes, no silver Accord. He was nervous and the Beretta sitting in the small of his back gave him little comfort.

He came in the front entrance, amidst a crowd of Japanese businessmen in golf clothes, and had a good nosey-poke at the reception staff as he walked past into the dining and bar areas. They seemed to be the real thing, although most Indonesian hotels had at least one person reporting to POLRI, the military or the intel agencies, depending on which department was protecting the place.

There was no one untoward or out of place in the eateries. Mac had a very strong sense of those who were professional watchers, and those who were not. All he could see in the Grand Hotel were civilians.

There was a solid patch of wet down his back when Mac got back to the Patrol. Limo had kept the motor running and the air-con felt icy as Mac got back inside. They confabbed: Mac grabbed the Shell map, sketched the layout on the cardboard cover. Then he handed over the operation to Sawtell.

'I want the girl alive, okay?'

Sawtell barely heard him. He'd turned deadly serious, muttering, the crew all ears. They transformed from laidback boys to killers in a split second. A special forces hallmark.

Limo got the Patrol moving, they drove the two blocks and pulled into the car park behind the hotel. Not even nine in the morning and it was already thirty-eight degrees and dripping humid. Mac's stomach churned, his right wrist ached, the greasy omelette breakfast wanted to come up.

Limo backed the Patrol up to a hedge and the Berets walked around to the back, opened the doors and got into their weapons cache. Most of the chat was aimed at Hard-on, whose surname was Harding. He seemed to be the key guy. They focused down like Mac wasn't there.

Mac had done lots of snatches in his career; he was known for it. But he didn't want to go into these building situations with a military crew. They trained together, they did this as a job and one loose screw in the unit was going to get Mac shot. Or it would distract one of the military guys and risk him being shot too.

The lads tooled up and walked across the car park. Casual but menacing. They wore stadium jackets and field jackets concealing M4 carbines, a sort of shortened M16. Mac was sure there'd be some stun grenades in there too.

He sat in the driver's seat with the diesel running. When the Americans were all inside he slowly pulled away from the hedge and rolled towards the lobby area. The place was not busy. One tour bus sat away from the lobby entrance, the driver smoking, reading a newspaper.

Mac looked in, saw the desk guy being marched to the elevators with Sawtell and Spikey. Hard-on scarpered, probably for the stairwell. Limo stood like a rock in the middle of the lobby, big bulge under his stadium jacket.

Mac had insisted they dispense with field radios on this trip, hence the Nokias. If Garrison was out there with the girl, he was expecting military to come after him and he'd be prepped to pick up the field radio signals.

Mac parked out on the street in the pre-arranged RV. He thought about Minky's girl and how he was going to introduce that topic to Sawtell.

Four minutes later, Mac's Nokia trilled. It was Sawtell, displayed as JS.

'Yep?'

'We're here. Nothing,' said Sawtell, panting slightly. 'Manager says they checked out last night, in a hurry, no idea where they're headed.'

'Is he lying?'

'Shit, McQueen – that ain't my thing.'

Mac thought quickly. He could go in there and break the guy real fast, make him remember. But the whole thing was dragging on and there was no telling who was protecting the hotel. It was a big tourism concern, which meant someone was paying for the staff to turn up and not steal from the Westerners. The call might have been made already and Mac didn't want to be a sitting duck when the POLRI commander or Kopassus colonel turned up.

'Is there anything there? Anything they've left?'

The sounds of Sawtell snapping at Hard-on and Spikey echoed from the background. Sawtell came back on the air. 'A few things.'

'Get 'em,' said Mac, 'and ask the manager what they were driving.'

Sawtell came back, said, 'Silver Accord.'

'How many?' asked Mac.

There was a pause, then, 'Three. Anything else, McQueen?'

'Yeah,' said Mac. 'I want the phone logs from that room.'

'Got it. See you soon.'

The Berets got to the Patrol at a canter. They piled in, Mac pulled out quickly and drove north, out of town. No music now, adrenaline retreating. After twenty minutes they pulled into a bushy wayside area. Hard-on pulled out a bed sheet, put it on the ground and opened it.

First impressions: Mac could smell the Old Spice wafting off the sheet. He saw several empty steel bandage containers and a ripped-up chewing gum wrapper, shredded thin and purposefully, bits of loose foil everywhere. A surviving piece of green paper said BARTOOK SPECIAL MINT. There was a paperback book in Tagalog. Not much.

Sawtell had the phone logs. There were fifteen outbound calls, made in the last nine days. One number wasn't like the others.

Mac looked at it. Couldn't get the picture. He grabbed his Nokia, dialled a number in Jakarta, Telekom Indonesia.

No connection.

Mac swore. He'd forgotten the state of the Indonesian phone system. Telekom Indonesia installed cellular towers where the tourists were starting to come, but the locals had no coverage even a few clicks out of the towns.

They drove back towards Palopo. Mac used a pay phone on the outskirts. Called an old mate at TI, an engineer called Dougie Foster. They swapped greetings, then Mac said, 'Mate, I've got some numbers. Can you run them?'

'Shoot.'

Mac read the numbers. The lone wrong 'un was a Manila area code. A silent address. Mac asked for as much info as he could get and Dougie told him to hang on. After a few minutes he came back. 'Got a pen?'

Mac wrote it down. He had the telecom exchange that the number would have been connected to, and Dougie gave him an area: Intramuros, a suburb on Manila Bay that Mac knew well.

The other fourteen numbers were closer to home. Dougie said, 'You're in luck, Mac – there's only eight numbers on that series.'

Mac wrote it down. They were heading north again, for Tenteno.

CHAPTER 9

They made good time on the road to Tenteno. Limo drove the Patrol, Hard-on rode shotgun. Spikey was in the middle of the back seat, Mac and Sawtell either side. Mac's wrist was now bandaged and Limo had slipped him some anti-inflammatories. But he agreed with Mac – a chipped bone in there somewhere, and the only cure was going to be resting the thing, something that was not going to happen on this trip.

They'd be arriving in Tenteno after dark and Mac wanted to case the place, have a chat to whoever was around. He wasn't expecting miracles. This was Sulawesi, the world's eleventh largest island and basically unpopulated. Fishing villages dotted the coastline and highland tribes did their thing in the interior. It was all rainforest and mountains, and people trying to win forestry and mining concessions. If the trail went dead in Tenteno, Mac would give the intel guys in Jakarta a chance to come up with some piece of genius. That would set the hounds running. If the mole was in Jakarta, he or she would make a move. Which would give Mac a chance to pull a counter-ambush.

But the trail didn't go dead.

Mac and Spikey went into the general store on Tenteno's main road as soon as they'd driven around the small lakeside town. The store owner was helpful, but didn't know anything. Spikey kept it calm, doing small talk. Mac watched the owner clench and unclench his left fist. He only did it once but it betrayed nerves.

Mac strolled out of the store, motioned to Limo and the others to drive round the back. He walked down an alley between the store and another wooden building, and came out in a rear yard. There was a lean-to on his left. Boxes and drums of cooking oil were stacked to obscure what was in the structure. Mac walked around the makeshift wall, saw a tarp covering a large shape and whipped it off, revealing a silver Accord. Same rego as the one behind Minky's.

Coming in through the store's back entrance, Mac took the owner by surprise. The bloke's eyes widened as Mac said to Spikey, 'He stays there, he doesn't move, right?'

It was near to closing time anyway so Mac fastened the front door and pulled the blinds. 'Tell him this,' said Mac to Spikey, not taking his eyes off the owner. 'Tell him he's harbouring a vehicle known to have been used in the terror bombings around Tenteno.'

Spikey rattled it off and the owner gulped, shook his head, gabbled something back at Spikey.

'He says it couldn't be,' said Spikey.

'Tell him if I'm wrong I can get my friends at the POLRI or Kopassus to come up here and check it out for us. Might all be a huge mistake,' said Mac, winking at the store owner.

The owner shook his head, fear in his eyes.

Mac pressed for the breaking point. 'Tell this guy that it might even warrant a visit from the boys from the BIN. And tell him, Spikey, that those boys will get to the bottom of it real fast by getting his wife and kids into the cells and helping him to remember. Memory is a funny thing.'

When Spikey had translated, the owner went quiet, looked at the floor.

Breaking point.

Mac started again, Spikey interpreting. Yes, the store owner knew the blokes in the silver Accord. They had been going out on the remote road to Sabulu. They'd made the trip several times and yes, they'd headed out that morning.

Mac got Spikey to ask what kind of people were travelling. The owner said two Javanese and one pale person.

'Yankee?' said Mac.

The owner nodded, said something to Spikey: a tall American.

Could be Garrison, thought Mac.

The three men had been travelling in a white LandCruiser, said the store owner. Mac's attempts to get deeper information met with shrugs. Yes, there may have been more than three and yes, one may have been a woman. The bloke had been paid to mind his own business, and that's what he had done. Mac believed him. He sliced the telephone lead with Spikey's Ka-bar and moved outside.

It was dark but some light from the back of the shop spilled on to the Accord, a 2002 model. Mac tried the doors. Locked. After putting a rock through the driver's side, Mac flipped the hood, and unplugged the howling alarm. That brought Sawtell and the others to the party.

'This it?' asked Sawtell.

Mac nodded, reached for the door handle, pulled on it.

Sawtell's mouth flew open, wide-eyed, his hand reaching out. Limo covered his eyes. Hard-on turned away.

Spikey stared at him like he was an honest-to-God dumb-ass honky motherfucker.

'Shit, McQueen! Holy fucking shit!' said Spikey.

'Maybe to you that's a car, McQueen!' gasped Sawtell. 'But to us, that's a fucking bomb!'

Mac looked down at the open door, looked back. Limo was peeking from behind his hands. Sawtell looked at the sky. Spikey still stared.

'Sorry, boys,' said Mac.

Mac stood back, let Spikey check the vehicle for pressure plates, wires and anything tricky on the ignition column. Then Mac had his turn. He went into the boot, the glove box, the centre console, the spare wheel bay, the centre armrest of the back seat, the tool box, the ashtrays, the radio and the storage compartments. Not much. Chewing gum wrapper again, Bartook Special Mint. Someone liked to get close to the ladies without scaring them off. Someone liked to rip it open in really thin strips.

He asked for a flashlight and got under the car. Positioned himself right beneath the windscreen washer reservoir and shone his torch straight up through the transparent plastic. It was a classic place to hide stuff and some people still thought the old places were best. Nothing.

Then he started on the carpets and before he got far he found something under the driver's seat. He fished out a key and shone the flashlight in again to see if there was anything else. He quickly went over the rest of the car's interior.

Coming up empty-handed, he turned his attention back to the key. Hard-on asked what it was. The other soldiers groaned as one, as if to say, *What does it look like, lame?*

It had a diamond-shaped, black plastic key ring with the letters MPS stamped on it in silver. The key was big, German, expensive and made of forged alloys suggesting a serious lock. The number was 46. Someone had lost a key. He wondered if they would come back for it.

Mac trousered it.

He turned back to the owner of the place, who was looking unsettled about what Mac had done to the Accord.

'Don't worry, sport,' he said to the bloke. 'I bet it's overinsured.'

The owner didn't look convinced.

'Ask him about Sabulu,' Mac said to Spikey. 'I want to know what we're looking for.'

The road to Sabulu was even worse than the general store guy had warned. From Tenteno, the road rose up into the highlands in steep, muddy switchbacks. It had been a bad, tropical road to start with and the logging traffic after the afternoon monsoon showers had torn it apart.

Mac asked Limo to drive. He was good, which was a change. Most Yanks couldn't handle that sort of terrain. At one point the Patrol slid across the track and threatened to slide off into a thousand-foot ravine. Limo kept his foot on the gas, counter-intuitively, and the Patrol came right.

'Not from South-Central, are you?' said Mac.

Limo smiled. 'Costa Rica.'

It was drizzling and everyone remained quiet as the Patrol's turbo squealed and cried its way up one ridge after another. The dark of the tropical night pressed in. The only universe was the one that the headlights illuminated, occasionally flashing on macaques at the side of the track, which had obviously seen a similar vehicle across several hours before. Mac could see off-road tyre tracks in the mud.

They were looking for a 'depot', which the store owner said was about seventy miles into the interior. Depots were sometimes shacks, sometimes compounds. Loggers and miners lived in them and the natives – the Toraja – collected weekly or monthly deliveries from them. The store owner reckoned they should be on the lookout for a depot called 'thirteen'.

They pressed on, the Patrol rolling and sliding. They got higher, past the mist-line where it was clearer and colder. Limo hit the heat. They glugged water from bottles and ate the fruit that Mac had known the soldiers would stash. They got to the top of a switchback and Mac asked for a toilet stop.

The stars shone huge and plush in the blackness above. A monkey argued with a bird somewhere in the rainforest canopy. It crossed Mac's mind that the next time he came through here it might all be felled. Instead it would be sitting in a backyard in Perth or Melbourne as garden furniture. He started pissing and Sawtell came alongside.

'You know that dude with the store is as good as dead?' said Sawtell, not pissing but staring.

'Hopefully we get to the bad guys first, huh?' said Mac.

Mac shook off early. Didn't like where Sawtell was standing. If Mac was going to poleaxe someone, that's where he would stand. At a bloke's four o'clock while he had his hands full.

Sawtell must have sensed the vibe. He moved around in front. They both felt the cold. Plumes of mist came out of their mouths.

'My boys weren't happy about the Bani thing.'

'I wasn't over the moon myself. But it's a good school,' said Mac.

'That was nice. What does he say to his folks?'

Mac didn't want to go into all the details. He'd had a chat with Bani's dad that morning before they went down to the dry-cleaners. The dad had thanked Mac profusely for the opportunity. Education in

Sulawesi was not like it was in the United States. Wasn't a birthright, wasn't an entitlement. Parents with the smartest kids watched all that potential go to waste most of the time. But there was no point in telling that to Sawtell. He was a good man, but he was an American good man.

Mac changed the subject. 'Mate, I don't know what to expect up here. Can we tool up now?'

Sawtell gave him a disappointed look. He stepped back, tapped on the roof of the Patrol, and the boys spilled out.

It was almost daybreak when they finally hit Depot 13. They were high enough to watch the sun come up over the Pacific. An amazing sight. The primordial rainforest started up like a soundtrack. In the space of twenty minutes it was deafening.

The depot was signalled by a couple of lamp posts dug into the ground, thirty feet apart. A track ran between them with a sign with the number thirteen strung above. They killed the lights. Mac handed off to Sawtell, who ordered Hard-on and Spikey to run a point. Then Sawtell got out of the Patrol and took a stance behind the rear fender; Limo did the same thing behind the front hood. Mac sat in the back seat with the Beretta on his lap, yawning, dreaming of some nosebag.

They waited for the all-clear and Mac asked Sawtell if Enduring Freedom was a success yet.

'Ha!' Sawtell snorted.

'I take that as a no,' said Mac.

'Holy shit! Oh man!' Sawtell seemed genuinely amused. So did Limo, who smiled his way.

'It's the wrong mission, in the wrong part of the world, for the wrong reasons with the wrong tactics,' drawled Sawtell. 'Oh, and the wrong leadership – political and brass.'

'We got Sabaya, didn't we?' asked Mac.

Sawtell was out of view, behind the Patrol. He didn't answer.

Half an hour later, Hard-on flashed three times through the trees in the dawn gloom. Limo drove the Patrol through the gates, Sawtell walked behind on the verge of the track. They drove like that for five minutes and came out into a clearing. There were six or seven mid-sized wooden buildings that looked like they'd been built a decade ago and then abandoned. Hard-on put his finger to his lips and beckoned Mac and Limo out of the vehicle. They walked behind him, guns ready, heading between two of the buildings and coming into another clearing, a courtyard with three accommodation-style buildings around it. It was a barracks of sorts. The place looked deserted, except for the white LandCruiser that dominated the courtyard.

Sawtell looked at Hard-on, who said, 'All clear, sir, far as we can tell.'

Sawtell looked around. Pointed at the LandCruiser. Hard-on shook his head. 'Haven't checked it. Waiting for you, sir.'

Sawtell nodded. Hard-on went to work on debugging the Land-Cruiser. Spikey jogged back into the courtyard to give him a hand.

Sawtell was distracted. He looked off into the distance and looked around very, very slowly, his face completely impassive. Mac had seen career soldiers do this before, and it usually meant the shit was on the doorstep. They just knew something was up.

Mac realised they were standing in the middle of a natural ambush. Surrounded by buildings, surrounded by jungle.

Sawtell slowly put his finger in the air. 'Hear that?'

'Helo,' said Limo.

They looked at each other and tried to find the source. Mac couldn't hear a thing.

'Ain't military,' mumbled Limo. 'That Euro piece of shit?'

One of the first things special forces soldiers learned to do was identify aircraft and vehicles by their sound. Much of what they did they did in the dark, without flashlights or open comms. The tales of tired soldiers piling onto the enemy's helo or onto the bad guys' boat were as legion as they were apocryphal. But the lesson was the same: know your hardware.

Sawtell indicated its position with his finger. Then shook his head. 'Gone.'

'Probably a logging scout,' said Mac.

They ignored him.

Hard-on and Spikey cleared the LandCruiser of booby traps. Mac found a map in the glove box, and more Bartook Special Mint wrappers. Torn thin.

The map was in relief, of the highlands. It showed broken lines in red, which meant dirt roads. And it had another series of thin blue lines, which Mac assumed were horse tracks, or whatever they used up here.

It wasn't that much use. Mac threw it back in the LandCruiser, slammed the door, moved to the rear. Then he had another idea. In the Royal Marines there had been an absolute ban on touching any map with a pen or a pencil. Anything that could possibly mark it. You put a map in a plastic sleeve, you pointed at it, you used bearings and you used coordinates so that everyone knew what everyone else was talking about. But if you marked a map in the British military someone was going to get in your face and accuse you of defacing Her Majesty's personal property. It was a 'back to base' offence.

Mac went back to the front seat, unfolded the map and had a good look. If these guys did not have that basic training, they might have absent-mindedly drawn on the thing. Even just touched it. Which was the universal human instinct.

He found what he was looking for on one of the central panels. A definite depression with a blue ballpoint at the end of one of the blue lines. A slight blue squiggle a couple of centimetres away – someone trying to navigate with the thing on his lap.

He called Sawtell over, showed him. Sawtell picked up the map and, without hesitating, turned due north, pointed into thick jungle and said, 'That way, nine or ten clicks.'

They tooled up. Sawtell was serious about this one, just like Mac had seen him in the Sibuco take-down; a bit nervy and controlling it with glacial calm. The lads sensed it. They checked guns and cammed their faces without saying a thing. When the Old Man went like that, it was time to get serious.

The boys took US Army fatigues out of Cordura bags. The guns were M4s – short, black assault rifles favoured by the US Army Special Forces.

They pilfered the rat packs and the stashed fruit. Ate up large. Then they headed into the jungle, Hard-on walking point.

The heat came up fast. The noise of the forest was thunderous and screeching at the same time, crowding in on the senses, enveloping the party with humidity, bugs and noise. They tabbed for an hour.

The horse track they were on was a steep climb. It was agony. Mac made a mental note: more running to balance the gym and boxing fitness.

Sawtell was a conservative campaigner. Mac wanted to stride out, get some blood going. But Sawtell stopped, peered, backtracked and did all the special forces hand-signal stuff. He was the jungle version of how Mac moved around a city: with total paranoia.

They maintained silence and walked Mac in the middle of their set-up. The tension was heavy. Every time Mac looked at Sawtell, he saw more concern. Concern that the American would not share. John Sawtell may have been a bleeding-heart boy scout but he kept it tight when the shit was hovering. There was a maelstrom of worry and contingency-mongering going on in that square head, but Mac knew he wouldn't spook his boys. Not a squeak.

Five clicks into the hike, they took a rest in a clearing. Limo produced water bottles from his pack. Mac checked a moss-covered log for snakes and spiders, and lowered himself.

There was a crack, a soft warm feeling in his head.

Then it all went black.

CHAPTER 10

Mac came to with the kind of head pain he'd experienced once during a bout of malaria. A sensation so powerful that you hit your head against a wall to make it go away.

He could hear something. People's voices. Then something else, humming like a machine. He took his time opening his eyes, let his right eyelid go up slightly. The rush of light was like an explosion in his brain. He groaned. His mouth was dry, tongue stuck to the roof of his mouth. He could barely think straight. Was he drugged? Drunk?

More voices. He tried again to crack an eyelid but the light shut him down just as quick. Sparklers behind his eyes. The noise got louder and he felt hands under his armpits. Hands on his feet. Then he was going up, like when he was a kid and his dad picked him up off the sofa where he'd fallen asleep watching television.

The noise got louder. It thromped and whacked and whined. It was fucking with his mind.

Mac thought: a helo.

Then he blacked out.

The patch was wet. Very wet. Mac shifted his head slightly and felt it cold and damp on his cheek. He must have been dribbling something chronic.

He opened his eyes. No pain in the eyeballs but a ton of it behind his right ear. He was lying on his side. There was a white sheet on him. A white pillow, white mosquito net over him that smelled of pyrethrum. He was naked except for his red briefs. He rolled over so he was looking at the white ceiling, fan turning.

He breathed, wiggled his toes, flexed his fists. The right hand was still swollen and painful. But he was alive and in one piece – for the moment.

He wondered who it was. Garrison's thugs? The Chinese? He prayed it wasn't the boys from Beijing. When intel hacks got gossiping they inevitably came to the Chinese torture scenarios: the drugs, the hypno, the implants, the beatings, the surgery.

There were no restraints. Whoever it was, they didn't see him as a threat.

He sensed movement. A face looked down on him. Large, round, male.

Maori. Fuck!

'How's the head, chalks?'

The guy smiled. A big, confident smile. Mac didn't know what to say. 'Sonny?'

The big Maori laughed, a high-pitched chortling giggle. 'You remember me, eh Chalks?'

Mac was a stunned mullet. He was looking at a ghost from his past: Sonny Makatoa.

Mac carried something on his CV that he reckoned he shouldn't. He was a veteran of Desert Shield/Storm. Technically. Straight from the Royal Marines he'd rotated into Basra in '91. The first Iraq war was winding down, the wells were burning, Bush Senior was pulling the boys out and novices like Mac were being sent into a war zone to see how intelligence worked in the shit. It was the only way to get that experience. The only way for the spy masters to know if this was your thing.

It was Mac's thing.

He deployed with a couple of older Australians, one of whom was Rod Scott. They were doing lots of sweeps for hidden missile silos and bio-warfare factories. There were loads of snitches and turncoats coming out of the woodwork in those final days. Saddam military wanting US dollars. Saddam military wanting Australian visas. Saddam military planted by his intel people as doubles and provocateurs.

Mac worked the 'show-me' detail, as in, *So this is the Brucellosis weaponisation program you were telling us about? Show me!*

The Australian SAS was in demand elsewhere, so in one of the last factory-checks the spooks were doing for bio-warfare manufacture, the New Zealand SAS stepped in as the escort. It was scary work: mines in walls, snipers on the peaks, everything booby trapped. They were into the cave systems of southern Iraq where the turncoat colonels reckoned the bio-labs were.

That's where Mac had met Sonny Makatoa. Sonny was only six years older than Mac but already leading his own unit. Senior ranks deferred to him, lesser ranks were shit-scared. His boys loved him. He stood five-eleven and was built like a tree stump. It was hard to imagine who or what could intimidate him. Sonny was tough in the strangest way. Tough like he was born to be in a war zone. Careful and professional but not nervous. Almost as if he liked it.

He remembered Sonny because on his first day Mac had turned up with a different kind of hat to the rest of the spooks and soldiers. They all wore khaki boonies while somehow Mac had ended up with a blue one.

Sonny had thrown him a spare hat at breakfast. Told him to put it on. Mac had hesitated. Sonny eyeballed him. Mac put it on.

It wasn't till late morning when they were waiting – and for some reason, war is all about waiting – that Mac had got talking to one of the Kiwi SAS. Asked him about the hat.

'Corporal's saving your lily-white,' said the Kiwi. 'Snipers round here fix on anything out of the pattern. Assume it's a commanding officer, or someone important. He likes you.'

So Mac had remembered Sonny. And Sonny had remembered too, probably for other reasons.

Mac swung his feet to the floor. He was in a demountable and from the decor and size of the room, he assumed it was the sick bay. The room was air-conned but that wasn't helping with his head. He had a dizzy spell, thought he would chuck. Put his hand to his mouth.

'Hem – fucking get in here, now!'

It was the same old Sonny. Barking, yelling, expecting everyone around him to be on the ball. A large Maori man in a black T-shirt and olive fatigue shorts scooted into the sick bay. Barefoot, tucking in his shirt. Sonny nodded at the bloke and they got on either side of Mac and helped him up. The headache subsided slightly as they walked him out the door.

'Put on some weight, Chalks?' said Sonny. 'You were a skinny little runt when I knew ya.'

The sick bay opened into a communal area with loads of natural light. Mac winced and squinted. There was a kitchen down one side, bench tables and chairs in the middle, and an area with sofas and a La-Z-Boy in front of a big plasma-screen TV at the end of the room. Barcelona was playing Liverpool. Mac took one guess who got to sit in the La-Z-Boy.

They sat him on the sofa and he saw rainforest through a window. He nodded to the offer of tea and the big guy called Hem moved to the kitchen. Mac had him at one hundred and eighteen kilos, about six-two, all muscle and moving like a cat.

Sonny grabbed a chair, sat on it, leaned forward with forearms on his fatigues. His black T-shirt had a white crest on the left breast, the words TOKOROA RFC printed in white.

'That's Hemi,' Sonny pointed. 'Played reserve grade for Canterbury-Bankstown. Couldn't control the temper, though, eh?' Sonny chuckled, then whistled low, shook his head slowly. Sombre. 'Big, strong cunt that Hemi. Good soldier, great fighter. Tough as.'

Sonny looked back at Mac, smiling. 'Just can't let him drink, eh Chalks?'

The teapot came back, along with a glass of water. Mac sank the water in one, wincing at the pipe that bulged in his brain.

'So what's the set-up?' asked Mac, who was getting his bearings and starting to worry about where Sawtell and his boys were.

'Private work, mate. Contracting, protection, a bit of law and order. You know how it is.'

Mac had a fair idea how it was. In places like Sulawesi, the foreign miners, loggers and oil companies wanted to be able to work their concession without complication. Mercenaries like Sonny removed the complications. Accountants back at head office called it 'pacification'.

Hemi moved to Mac's nine o'clock and Sonny changed the pace. 'So what brings you up here, mate?'

'Girl,' said Mac. 'She went missing from the embassy. Just checking she's okay.'

'Little out of the way to go missing, eh?'

Mac was getting his instincts back. He was going to tread very, very carefully. Sonny had said he was mercing. But not for whom.

'Well, she might be up to no good,' said Mac. 'Might be nothing. They sent me out for a chat. No biggie.'

Mac reached for his tea. He realised Sonny hadn't offered him any clothes. He was still in his undies – no Beretta.

'Coming out for a chat with the cavalry, Chalks?'

Mac looked up and Sonny looked straight back. It was a steady gaze and it gave Mac the creeps.

'Those boys would be, what, Yank special forces?' asked Sonny. 'Probably came in from Zam, right? Or Guam?'

Mac looked away.

'What's she done?' said Sonny.

Funny, thought Mac; three days ago he had asked the same question in exactly the same tone. And now here he was in the middle of Sula-fucking-wesi and still none the wiser.

'Don't know.'

'Don't know?' Sonny raised his eyebrows.

'Don't know – on the lam with an American as best I can figure it.'

'American, huh?' Sonny looked quickly at Hemi, looked back. 'Tall cunt? This Yank?'

Mac nodded.

'About my age? Dark hair?' asked Sonny.

'That's the bloke,' said Mac.

'And?'

Mac's training and natural inclination told him to always with-hold names and histories. 'Need to know' was a well-worn cliché but it saved a lot of complications. Then again, Mac didn't have many options. He decided to horse-trade. 'Where're my boys?'

'They're safe. But one of them didn't make it.'

'Which one?' said Mac, gulping.

'Big cunt. I was about to tap you on the shoulder and he took a shot at me. Hem took care of it.'

Limo!

Mac felt a wave of sadness. An American who could drive jungle terrain and not carry on about it. Dead.

'Quick?' Mac asked. Mac could feel something welling in his chest. He fought it off, kept it tight.

'About five minutes,' said Sonny. 'Billy – my helo guy – did all that Catholic shit with him.'

'And the others? They okay?'

'Sure. Got 'em locked up though. Don't wanna turn your back on those special forces cunts, eh, Chalks?'

Mac nodded, dazed. Pointed to his head.

'Yeah, sorry, cuz.' Sonny chuckled. 'Got such a fright from your mate that I spun and collected you with the butt. Got you a beauty, eh?'

Mac nodded.

Mac had a choice: play the game with Sonny and see where it could lead; or clam-up and try to bluff his way out with threats of government involvement. He wanted to keep his momentum, get Hannah and get out. So Mac spilled on Garrison. Told Sonny just about everything. Left out the bit about killing Minky and Minky's daughter being somewhere with Garrison.

As it happened, Sonny and his lads had been keeping an eye on Garrison's people. They were in an area which had been a Japanese mica mine in the 1940s. There were a lot of old buildings and tunnels up there, disused. But Garrison's people were in a forestry concession, and that's what Sonny and his mercenaries protected.

Mac couldn't read how their chat was going to end. What Sonny might want. Then the former SASer dropped the bomb. Talking about his boss, Sonny used the word 'Cookie'.

Mac's face must have betrayed him.

'What's up, Chalks? Seen a ghost?'

'You working for Cookie Banderjong?'

'What's it to you?' snapped Sonny.

The possibilities started mounting up. With Canberra out of the picture and Mac suspecting a mole, he needed private infrastructure, he needed a guy who could make things happen. But Cookie had to have a reason to help him. Mac decided to give it a burl.

'Does Cookie like stability? Is that what keeps business good?'

'Maybe,' said Sonny.

The sealed track to the mansion led up the hillside from the military compound. They walked by the helipad, where a white and blue Eurocopter sat on its wheels. There was a hangar behind it and further down the track was a long garage with cammed LandCruisers, the kind with the double rear axles. Mac noticed one of them had a turret in the top with what looked like a US military gun rail. There was a fleet of motorbikes in there too, orange KTMs.

Mac was back in his ovies and Hi-Tecs but he still had no gun. He had his G-Shock but the time – 2.34 pm – didn't compute. It felt like early morning and he still felt like shit.

'So where are we, Sonny?'

'Foothills of Malino. Santigi's that way.' Sonny gestured south. 'Nice up here, stays cool in the summer.'

'Sabulu's a bit far south for Cookie, isn't it?' asked Mac.

Sonny gave him the up and down look. Like Mac was getting cheeky.

'He's been going south, some power vacuum thing. But you've heard all about that, right Mr Spook?'

Mac hadn't heard any such thing. The truth was that Indonesian politics were a mystery to all but a circle of about two hundred insiders. In a nation of two hundred and twenty million that was a pretty tight inner circle. Back in the days when Jakarta's heart was up for grabs and Sukarno thought that 'non-aligned' meant not having to deal with the Yanks, the CIA had an entire desk devoted to Indonology. The big foreign newspapers still sent in their brightest journalists, the governments rotated in their expert diplomats and the spies trained for a year to get a posting in Jakkers.

And none of them knew what the fuck was going on.

Sonny veered towards a demountable building on the roadside. It was cool inside. A very large Fijian soldier in a black T-shirt and olive fatigue shorts sat at a desk. He leapt up on seeing Sonny, webbing gun rig swinging around as he did.

'How they going, Mosie?' said Sonny.

Mac looked to his right, saw Sawtell, Hard-on and Spikey. They were sitting at a table eating lunch behind a steel-mesh cage. They looked over: swollen eyes, split lips. Hate in their eyes. Mac was going to have to work on this.

'Good – no problems,' the Fijian replied.

The guy called Mosie looked quickly at Mac.

'Moses, this is Mr McQueen. These are his boys.'

Mac took his hand. 'Looking after them, Moses?'

'Yes, Mr McQueen.'

Mac winked at him. 'Set, brother.'

Moses beamed. There were two types of fieldwork: thuggery and enlistment. You either treated your world as eternally hostile – like the Israelis and Russians – or you cosied up to people and enlisted them. Mac preferred the enlistment model.

Mac moved to the cage. ''Zit going, boys?'

'The fuck *you* think?!' said Sawtell.

'You'll be out soon, Moses has it covered,' said Mac, trying to keep it light.

He saw a rack of guns and Cordura bags hanging from the white-washed wall as he left.

Time to get it sorted.

Cookie Banderjong was nothing like Mac expected. He had a full head of hair, pushed up and back in a pompadour. A good-looking, round-faced Javanese. The legs outstretched on a huge teak desk revealed a pair of Billabong boardies. His legs were muscled, his chest pushed out against the white polo shirt – the one with the alligator on it. His intel days were over but he was still working out. As Sonny and Mac entered he was talking on the phone, wearing a headset plugged straight into his computer. He twirled the headset cable in the air as he yelled at someone in Indonesian. Then it changed to English. 'Dave, that prick's got something wrong with his brain. Deadset, you make me come down there and it'll get ugly. Tell him that . . . okay . . . yeah . . . sweet. Sweet as.'

What stumped Mac was the accent: pure Strine. So it was true, Cookie Banderjong did grow up in Melbourne. You could read all the files but you never really got a feel for a person until you heard them.

Cookie was still into somebody. 'Yeah, I know, mate. Like I said, either the company starts getting eight-hour shifts – *of actual work!* – out of these blokes or I'll come down with Mr Makatoa and we'll have a word in the shell-like.' He smiled at Mac and Sonny, held his hand up in apology.

Mac felt expensive Sumatran silk carpet through his socks. They'd been asked to remove their shoes at the tradies' entrance.

Cookie signed off: 'Yeah, yeah, mate. I know. It's not your fault. Time to sort it though, huh? Sweet, no worries, catchya.'

He squeezed a button on the cable, tore his headset off and chucked it on the desk. Walked around the desk and across the chocolate-coloured carpet in his bare feet. Cookie was about five-nine and athletic. He put out his hand, smiled big like a movie star. 'You must be Alan?'

''Zit going?' said Mac.

'Can't complain.'

They shook. Mac smiled back. Couldn't help himself.

'They call me Mac.'

'Mr Makatoa's told me a bit about you – sounds interesting.' Cookie pointed to the white leather sofas by the huge PanaVista window that looked out over the valley.

So Cookie was an enlister too. He used the correct pronunciation of Sonny's name. He said it Maka-*tor*, knowing how irritated Sonny would get hearing the Anglo version of Maka-to-er. In Maori, *toa* meant warrior, and people with that in their names felt it was there for good reason. Enlisters noticed the small things; Mac decided he'd better be cagey with this guy.

Cookie's office was a sprawling thing up on the second storey of the mansion. Around the walls were the mementos of his life in BAKIN, the Suharto-era Indonesian intelligence apparatus which had also had a secret police function. There was a picture of Cookie smiling with an elderly Richard Nixon, both of them in golf clothes. A black and white photo of a group of men looking serious, standing around a strategy table. It featured a younger short-back-and-sides Cookie with a man who might have been Alexander Haig.

Cookie called for tea and came over to the sofa, saw Mac checking the walls.

'So you're ASIS?'

Mac didn't respond. In any other company he'd have done the old *then I'd have to kill you.* But he wasn't going to say that to Cookie Banderjong. Not here. Not in front of Sonny.

'You'll like this one,' said Cookie, moving to a picture on the wall. He took it down and gave it to Mac. It showed two men of similar age talking to one another in what looked like a banquet hall. A Chinese banquet hall. Communist Party dog collars and Liberation Army fruit salad displays filled the background. The two men in the foreground were in suits and ties: Cookie animated, the other man sullen but intent. The unmistakable face of Vladimir Putin.

Mac smiled. 'Where and when?'

'Beijing, '93,' said Cookie. 'I went through our surveillance footage with the technical guys after the dinner – as you do – and there was this one. He was such a strange guy: very smart, very intense. He was nothing then, just one of those over-serious Commies with the Russian legation.'

'You guys got a camera into a Chinese state function?' Mac chortled. 'Are you fucking nuts?'

'Only when I drink.'

They shared a laugh. It was funny. But Cookie was also pulling rank, showing Mac that he was hardcore. The real thing – a bloke who could waltz into Beijing and pull counter-surveillance on the MSS, on their own patch.

Cookie warmed to the story. 'I saw Putin on the news a few years ago when he became president, and I'm like *Holy shit – I know that prick.* Went back to the old surveillance prints, pulled some strings and got that little beauty on my wall.'

Mac was being played. He handed back the picture and Cookie gave him the wink.

The tea came through with the housemaid and kids' screams echoed through the open door.

'Thanks, Rosie – and tell those kids if I have to come down there I'll take the damn PlayStation and chuck it in the bin. Okay?'

Cookie eased back into the sofa. The enlistment was over, his face slackened a bit. 'What have we got down there, Mac? And what's in it for me?'

Mac told Cookie as much as he could about Judith Hannah and Peter Garrison. Mentioned the ambush in Makassar, but not that he thought it was Canberra-connected.

Cookie squinted at Mac. 'This Garrison, is that the northern Pakistan Garrison? The police compound guy?'

Mac nodded. 'Drugs for guns for gold. A clever guy, good at playing everyone off.'

'That wasn't a terrorist attack, was it?' Cookie smiled but with no conviction.

'Nah. Garrison called in an air strike far as we could see.'

Cookie looked out on the valley. 'And Garrison's still Agency?'

'I was briefed three nights ago, and they were claiming him then,' said Mac.

Cookie looked at Sonny. 'Well this might be a nice coincidence, hey Sonny?'

Sonny had most of his mercs running cover and clearances for a Malaysian logging company in the Tokala peninsula. At the same time, Cookie seemed to want Garrison shaken down to see where the money trail led. Sonny needed a slightly larger crew for that gig and Cookie wanted Sonny to use the Americans to make up the numbers.

'Works for me,' said Cookie to Sonny. 'I want a chat with this Garrison prick, and these guys want the girl. Everyone's happy.'

Sonny didn't like it. 'Those Yanks aren't happy, boss. Might have their minds on payback, not on the mission.'

'Your call,' said Cookie.

Sonny and the boys had been monitoring the activity up at the old mine, but now that Cookie knew who it was on his turf, he wanted them out of there.

'I'll have a chat to the Yanks,' said Sonny, not convinced. 'See if they're up for it.'

Cookie looked at Sonny. Looked at Mac. 'So let's do it.'

CHAPTER 11

Sonny and Mac walked down from the house in the heat, the cicadas deafening. Sonny suddenly stopped and put a finger in Mac's face. 'Here's the deal, Chalks. We go and talk to the special forces boys, see if their hearts are in it. Right? But whatever happens, you're vouching for them. Got it? They're your problem.'

Sonny ended this sentence with a poke in the chest. Mac got the point: if Sawtell fucked up, Mac got whacked.

The lock-up was still cool when they let themselves in. Moses walked out of a door, zipping himself, his SIG handgun in its webbing rig on his chest.

Sonny didn't waste time. 'Hey, Mosie – let 'em out,' he said, pulling up the chair behind the desk and sitting down. Moses opened the cell door and positioned himself in front of the confiscated weapons.

Sawtell stalked out of the cage, looking like he could kill someone with his bare hands. Sonny put his hands up, palms facing Sawtell.

'Time to talk, eh boys?' When Sonny said 'boys' it sounded like he was saying 'boice'.

Sawtell and Sonny talked and talked. They talked about campaigns, about people they'd lost, bullets they'd taken, idiot superiors and the stresses of dealing with friendly fire in a combat zone. They even realised they'd both been in Somalia at the same time.

When Limo's death came up they talked about how much it hurt to tell a bloke's mum that her boy had bought it, but how important it was to make that call yourself, not let the bureaucracy do it for you.

Sawtell welled up. Sonny didn't blink. He said you knew you were in deep when your boys' welfare meant more to you than your own. 'That's not weak, John – that's being a professional. That's the way it has to be.'

Sawtell sniffled. Wanted to say something but his lip quivered and he stared at the ground. Mac didn't know where to look. He'd never been in the inner circle of the military when soldiers did this kind of debrief. He'd assumed they just got drunk.

'Tell you something else, John – that boy, the big fella – he was the only one who clocked me,' said Sonny, his voice respectful. 'Got a shot off too. Good talent, good lad that one.'

'His name was Alvarez, Christian Alvarez,' said Hard-on, tears running down his cheeks. 'We called him Limo 'cos he was built for comfort not speed.'

'Well he was the fastest of the lot in that clearing, eh boys?' said Sonny. 'Billy the fucking Kid. Scared the shit outta me – lost it so bad I almost took Chalkie's head off!'

They all chuckled at that one.

'And then what'd we do? One less intel fuckwit to get us in the shit.' There were wry smiles as Sonny continued. 'Us simple army boys wouldn't know how to fuck it up without Chalks here to help us, eh?'

The soldiers laughed and Sonny ruffled Mac's hair, pretended to try again when Mac leaned away.

Soldier psychiatry: make it all about the office guy, get the team bonding.

Sawtell wiped his cheek with the back of his hand. Turned to his lads. Hard-on and Spikey looked like jocks ready to get back in the game. Something passed between the three of them.

Sawtell looked back to Sonny, said, 'What's up?'

The Green Berets were assigned rooms and had their showers, then ate with Sonny's skeleton crew in the mess. They ate steaks, mashed spud and then Hemi brought over a plate of steaming corn cobs.

Sonny's eyes went wide as hands reached from everywhere. Corn was a favoured military food if you could get it. It made you feel full and had a slow-burn energy effect.

'Hey, McQueen. This reminds me of that time in the desert. Remember?' said Sonny. 'In the Yanks' mess? Tell 'em the story.'

Mac had hoped Sonny wouldn't want to relive that episode. He batted it away. 'Some other time, eh Sonny? Let's talk Garrison.'

'Easy,' said Sonny. 'You get the girl, Hemi grabs Garrison, then we pick up Limo on the way back. Sounds like a plan.' He pointed his cob at Mac. Sly smile. 'Shit, Chalkie's embarrassed. A blushing Australian. Who would have thought.'

Mac put his cob down, leaned back, looked at the ceiling. Yes, he was embarrassed.

'It was a long time ago, Sonny – I thought I was doing the right thing,' he said. He could feel a constellation of dark eyes in brown faces staring at him. He felt like an iridescent son of Saxony. He looked back at Sonny.

'I'm not a racist, okay?!'

There was a pause. Then they all laughed. Mac put his face in his hands, moaned slightly. He was still very tired, lump on his head the size of a lemon.

Hard-on grabbed Spikey by the arm, made a high-pitched nasal mimic. '*I'm not a racist, okay?*'

The hard men of the military shrieked like a bunch of girls. Hemi had to hold on to the kitchen bench, like he was having a seizure. Sonny cried with laughter. Moses, who was sitting beside Mac, patted him on the back. Smiled a very big Fijian smile.

Mac let them go. He watched a joke go down that he was excluded from. Forever.

He finally held up his hands. 'Okay, Sonny, I'll tell the fucking story.'

'See this corn?' He looked at Hard-on and then Sawtell as they caught their breath. 'They don't serve it like this in the ANZAC chow tents. If you're Aussie and Kiwi, they pour loose frozen corn kernels out of white plastic bags, boil it till you can't taste it and then expect people to eat it.'

'Yuk,' said Spikey. 'Why don't they just get the cobs in?'

'That's what Sonny here reckoned. It was the end of the first Gulf War, there were two days till the airlift, and this madman here,' Mac pointed at Sonny, 'had heard that the Yanks served fresh corn cobs. So he invited himself to eat in the US Army NCOs' mess.'

'This in Basra?' asked Sawtell.

'Yep.'

Hard-on whistled low.

'They put up with him for a few days – the Yanks were getting ready to pull out and they were feeding a lot of people. I think they were being polite.'

'Sounds like us,' said Sawtell.

'I was seconded with Army MI for a few days and I was sitting in the NCO mess one afternoon. I had a pass.'

The lads *oooed*.

'Anyway,' said Mac, 'in walks Sonny with a couple of his SAS lads. And the bloke – what's he called, the steward?'

'Yeah, the mess steward,' said Sawtell.

'He intercepts Sonny and tries to tell him that lunch is off. Sorry, but that's the rules.'

'No dice?' asked Sawtell. He laughed, shook his head like *hard case!*

'But Sonny has already seen the corn, sitting there in the bain-marie,' Mac continued. 'And the cook seems okay to have it eaten, so the steward shrugs it off. But on the way to the bain-marie Sonny goes past this Army bloke.'

'US Army?' asked Sawtell.

Mac nodded. 'They let you wear T-shirts in the American messes, and this bloke had a very short-sleeved T-shirt on, and he had these tattoos down his arms. He was a skinny, blond guy. You'd call him a peckerhead, or a, a pecker . . .' Mac searched for the word.

'Peckerwood,' said Spikey.

'That's it,' said Mac. 'Peckerwood – Southern accent, and on one of his arms he had a Confederate flag.'

Hard-on whistled low again, turned to look at Sonny. So did Sawtell. Sonny shrugged.

'So Sonny stops. But he doesn't worry about the bloke's flag, 'cos on the other arm he's got a Maori design.'

'Moko, Chalks,' said Sonny. 'Fucking moko. Get it right.'

'Sonny goes "Nice ink you got there, Chalkie – perhaps you'd like to fill me in on its history?" And the Peckerwood doesn't have a fucking clue who this guy is or what he just said.'

The table laughed, egging Mac on.

'So Sonny says, "The tat, Chalks. The fucking tat – that's my family you've got on your fucking arm." And this Peckerwood is getting frazzled. Tries to shoo Sonny away.'

Sawtell was loving this. 'Bad idea, huh?'

'Terrible fucking idea. Sonny does that Maori thing, looks him up and down like he can't believe that such stupidity and ugliness exist in the same body – it just can't be physically possible.'

Hard-on and Spikey high-fived.

'The steward is coming over, people are putting down their cutlery. It's a bad scene because most of the people in the mess are black and Hispanic. They're tuning in and they're in no hurry to poleaxe Sonny Makatoa.'

The Americans swapped glances.

'So Peckerwood tells the steward "It's okay" and says to Sonny, "Why the fuck would I have *your* family on *my* arm?" like he wouldn't sink so low. And Sonny points at the tattoo and says, "'Cos you're wearing a something-or-other moko."'

'Ngati Tuwharetoa,' said Sonny. 'The tribe is Ngati Tuwharetoa.'

Mac continued. 'The guy doesn't know what the hell is going on. And then Sonny says: "If you don't know whose family you're putting on your body, Chalks, then don't fucking put it on. Understand that, boy?"'

Sawtell laughed. '"Chalks" and "boy" in the same sentence – bet he never got that in Tupelo.'

'So Peckerwood leaps up,' said Mac, 'and Sonny just looks him up and down. Doesn't move. Just leans further in. Peckerwood is clenching his fists and Sonny is ready for him. They were about to get into it.'

'Yeah, so?' said Hard-on.

'So I stopped it,' said Mac, looking at Sonny. 'Got between them. I shielded the Peckerwood.'

Hard-on slid his hands over his stubbly head, exasperated. 'Oh, man. You *stopped* it? Why?!'

Sonny stared at Mac.

''Cos that's how I reacted,' said Mac.

The good humour deflated. Mac looked down at his plate, said, 'The guy was ignorant, had no idea what someone like Sonny could do to him.'

'I wasn't going to hurt him – just wanted to know about the tat,' said Sonny.

'You were going to take him apart.'

Sonny chuckled, then went serious. 'You got it wrong, Chalks. The motto of the story is this: you don't spend a week under a soldier's protection and then side against him in a slap-up.'

Mac looked at the lads, who nodded sagely.

'Not how it works, cuz.'

The helo swooped in to the landing zone a little after four pm. Sonny had wanted to go while there was still wind around in the tops and the noise of an aircraft wouldn't drift. They landed downwind from the area they were targeting as an extra precaution. The bloke called Billy de-powered and the thing came to a silent stop.

They piled out in an assortment of clothing: the Green Berets in their fatigues, Mac still in his overalls and black baseball cap, Sonny's boys – four of them in total – all wearing the olive and blacks they'd had in camp. The new addition was the field radio with throat mics. They were wired again and Mac could see the Americans were more comfortable with it.

Sonny pulled them in, spelled it out: no heroics, no rock stars. He wanted to turn the thing around real quick without anyone getting shot. If that meant Garrison's blokes just threw down their weapons, all for the better.

He wanted to pull the classic special forces trick: attack at about three am with maximum force and see if the enemy had the ticker for it.

Mac had one proviso on that: he'd rather take one guy – Sawtell or Hard-on – into the structure and try to snatch the girl. He'd want to do it while there was a diversion elsewhere.

Sonny gave him the okay. 'But pick your target well. Once the shit starts there's going to be fire everywhere. Once it starts I can't guarantee the girl.'

They started out and made good time across bad terrain. There was a moon and the lads were fit. This was a lightning raid and everything they needed they carried on their webbing. M16 A2s and M4 carbines sat across their chests. Hemi hauled a heavy calibre machine gun and Mac had a borrowed SIG 9 mm handgun, with a customised suppressor that he stashed in a webbing pocket. It wasn't as good as the Heckler but it was better than nothing.

Mac was still woozy and he struggled to keep up. He was also worried about his wrist. It was still puffed and he couldn't get his hand properly around the SIG's grip. But he kept that to himself.

Hemi walked point and Hard-on swept from the back. It was steep, and dark where the branches hung low; roots tripped them. But there was little noise from the party.

Sawtell hung back a bit and Mac slowed to walk with him. There was something on his mind, something he had to clear before any shooting started.

'John, can we talk?' he said in a rasping whisper.

Sawtell looked at him. Mac saw a cammed face and the whites of Sawtell's eyes.

'What is it?'

'Ah, the girl – Judith Hannah,' said Mac.

'Yeah?'

'There's another one, I think.'

'Another girl? With Garrison?'

'Yeah. Kidnapped.'

'Who?'

'Remember I told you about Minky?'

'The CIA guy?'

'Yeah. Well, he's dead.'

'Who?'

'One guess.'

They stopped, Sawtell looked away, put his hands on his hips. 'Fuck!'

'Yeah – not good.'

'You shot him?'

'I was ambushed. I got scared, carried away.'

'And this girl?'

111

'His daughter.'

'Minky's daughter?'

Mac nodded. The entire thing was a less than ideal situation and one that he had been hoping would go away. But here they were, about to storm a compound, and a young girl was in there somewhere. It didn't seem fair not to warn the soldiers.

'You thought maybe some of us might like to know this? Shit, McQueen, how old is she?'

'Dunno – eight or nine.'

Sawtell bit his bottom lip. He looked angry. Real angry.

Mac tried to dilute it. 'Look, I didn't want to tell you guys in Ralla 'cos I was embarrassed, and I was hoping I'd be able to get her when I snatched Hannah. And then we ran into Sonny and, well, you've seen what he's like with me.'

Sawtell nodded. 'Yeah, I saw that.'

'So, whaddya reckon?'

'You'd better tell Sonny is what I reckon, 'cos if you put a young girl's life on his conscience it might be you he comes after.'

'Reckon?'

'I don't think he'd wear that shit.' Sawtell almost spat it. 'And I don't have a problem with that either.'

They eyeballed one another. They were strong words: if the girl got hurt, Sawtell would stand back and let Sonny whack the culprit. Soldiers were a whole different breed.

Mac thought about his next words very carefully. 'It's just that I don't want to get Sonny distracted with the racial stuff just before we do this thing.'

'And why wouldn't he be distracted by that? You focus everything on the cute white girl and a little brown girl can go to hell?'

Mac swallowed hard. This wasn't going the way he wanted it.

'That it, McQueen? You know that if a bunch of black and brown men know there's a little brown girl up there, they might just give her equal priority?'

'Look, John –'

'So you get the black man to make peace with the angry brown man?'

'Umm . . .'

'Five minutes before go?'

Sawtell was looking at him like he was a different species. 'What is it with you intel guys?'

'John, it's not like –'

'Fuck you, McQueen.' He hissed it. 'I'll tell Sonny. We'll do what we have to do. But fuck you.'

Sawtell moved off, shaking his head.

Silence in Mac's head. Like a drum.

CHAPTER 12

Mac lay on the ridge, behind a log under a low-hanging canopy of branches. Hard-on lay beside him. Below them was a compound of eight oldish wooden buildings, like pre-war public schoolhouses. A generator drove a floodlight system that illuminated a courtyard. The place had been built with little evidence of permanence and the main buildings were arranged in no particular order or angle, except that they surrounded the courtyard.

Thirty metres up a scree and clay slope Mac could see why the compound had been built: there was a mine entry with a small railway coming out of it. During the Second World War the Japanese had exploited the mine for mica, the prime ingredient in silica gels.

They took turns with Hard-on's binos, looking for the main residence and a lock-up – difficult given that the buildings looked so similar to one another.

Mac had to think it through: he was either going to stealth into the right building, or he was going to stealth into the wrong building and start a shooting match.

There wasn't one girl, there were two. What if they weren't in the same area? Mac would bet they were. This was hardly a prison set-up and criminals were usually lazy when it came to managing incarceration.

His mate Jenny Toohey from the AFP once told him about a raid she'd led on a child sex-slave ring in Semarang. They stealthed in to find the boys and girls watching TV in their pyjamas while the kidnappers slept off an opium bender.

So Mac was going to take a calculated gamble. All he needed was a good odds-on pick on which building the girls were in. He didn't want to be wandering in and out of barracks at three in the morning, saying, 'Sorry, fellas, wrong building.'

According to Sonny's local intel, there were ten or twelve people in the camp. A dozen was doable.

The first part of the exercise was sacking the perimeter security. Sonny and Hemi had taken that job. There were two guards, as far as they could tell, and Mac wanted them both totally out of the picture before he wandered across that floodlit courtyard.

The radio system crackled. Hemi's voice: 'Blue team this is Red. Good to go. On your signal.'

The sentries were down. A good start.

The plan now was old and simple: Mac and Hard-on would break into their building and search as far as they could without starting the shit. If they couldn't go further, and needed a distraction or cover, they'd call in the Red team, who would come in with a lot more noise from the other side of the compound. The way these things worked, when they worked well, was highly effective. The louder distraction usually triggered the human instinct to protect; the enemy would hopefully race out of the place leaving the intruders and the abductees inside and unaccompanied.

Or, it could all go to shit. Like when the distraction didn't work, or you trod on a cat or someone was simply lying awake, helping himself to a bit of self-love in the dark. That's when it was close-range gunfire, which made even professionals rethink their career. It was scary, and someone usually died.

When Mac did these things, he liked to work with a military athlete, and with Hard-on he'd got lucky – a good operator with soft feet, a calm brain and a killer's body. Someone who kept their head still and their heart rate down.

He liked special forces blokes because they thrived under pressure. That was something the intel guy needed when he was trying to think things through. Like when you get to a cell and there's no one in there. Or there's someone in the cell, but they're hostile – don't want to go anywhere.

Hard-on and Mac mumbled to one another. They settled on the larger of the buildings as the most likely residential. It had a large three painted on it in black, faded but still visible. They could make out a clearly worn path through the clay courtyard to the steps which went up into the building. They couldn't see similar paths to the other buildings.

Sawtell agreed over the earpiece, told them he could see a cable from the generator room going into building three, but not going anywhere else.

The last thing they looked for was a security system. With two perimeter guards, Mac doubted it. Not out in the highlands of Sulawesi. But they did the grid-scans with the binos: started with the foreground, worked to and fro. Moved to the next grid, to and fro. They each did it once over, looking for small white plastic boxes mounted on the wall of a building or on a stick, hip-high to a man.

Nothing.

They checked each other. Mac had the SIG 9 mm. The silencer wasn't the best but it might give him a slight edge. SIGs had the fifteen-round mags which Mac hated. On a job like this, however, it was welcome.

Hard-on had his Beretta in his webbing and an M4 carbine lying in front of him. But he was going in with a Ka-bar as his primary weapon. Also in his webbing was a sealed plastic bag filled with a length of muslin soaked in the US military version of chloroform. If Garrison was inside, Mac had some questions for him and he didn't want the bloke dead. There was also the issue of female hysteria: a woman being woken in the early hours by one bloke in overalls and another in a black ski mask might not think she was being rescued.

Hard-on pulled black gloves over his fists. Clenched them. He pulled a black ski mask from inside his shirt, put it on.

Mac rubbed his right wrist against his face, hoping it would hold out. He could have sat back and let the soldiers do their thing, used his wrist as an excuse. But Judith Hannah was his responsibility, his mission.

He thought about Minky's girl and what Sawtell had said. He hadn't deprioritised her because she had brown skin; he'd done so to keep his mind focused on the mission. Still, it didn't look good. He admitted that. He just couldn't admit it to them.

His heartbeat rose in his throat. He took a couple of deep breaths, then held down an acrid sensation in the back of his mouth. Nerves rising, Mac pulled down his black cap, looked at Hard-on and nodded.

'Red team, this is Blue,' said Hard-on into the throat mic. 'Approaching.'

Mac's ears roared with nerves as he scooted along the south wall of building three. He was in shadows but still vulnerable. The moon was out and while that was good for his general vision it was also good for an enemy who might be watching.

He battled to control his breathing. Hard-on crouched in front of him. Before them was the expanse of the courtyard – about thirty metres across and flooded with artificial light. They'd spent the last fifteen minutes circling round behind building number three, now they were tucked in behind it, under the window line.

Hard-on took his time. Mac watched the soldier's back heaving through fatigues and webbing. You couldn't stop the nerves, but you could breathe with it. They waited. Listened for the slightest sound. Nothing. Except the sound of heartbeats roaring in Mac's ears.

Hard-on put his hand slightly above his shoulder. A get-ready signal. Then he picked up the M4, shouldered it and shifted his feet and hips into the marksman position.

Mac stood from his crouch, pulled the SIG out of its webbing, checked for load, checked for safety, slapped his breast pocket for the spare mag. He fished the suppressor from another webbing pocket, twisted it on, giving it a final hard screw at the end for good luck.

Then they heard it. Faintly at first, like it might have been a monkey. But they stopped, tensed. Waited. It came again. A yelp, some words. Indonesian, female, high-pitched. Yearning then trailing off.

Mac felt ice in his heart. They could barely look at one another. They'd just heard a young girl crying out in a nightmare. They had the right building. And one of the hostages was alive.

Hard-on looked at him through the holes in the ski mask. Mac didn't know how Sawtell had handled the bit about Minky's girl. But Hard-on seemed focused on the mission rather than angry with him.

Hard-on held up his right hand again, numbered down with gloved fingers: five, four, three, two, one. Then he thumbed-up. Mac moved around the Green Beret, trying to keep his eyes on the clay ground while also looking ahead. He kept to the short side of the building but the floodlighting increased. He felt like he was walking onto a stage. It got brighter and brighter until he was standing at the last corner before he'd have to turn right and go up the entrance stairs and into the front porch of the building. He squinted – a bug under a microscope.

He paused, stuck his head around. Looked. Nothing. Pulled back. Looked again. Realised he'd been holding his breath, and made himself breathe out.

To his left Hard-on was circling further into the courtyard, M4 to his eye line. He held a perfect shooting stance while also crabbing silently sideways – right leg over left – and keeping his sights trained on the building. He trained the weapon back and forth down the eight windows of the building. Anyone sticking their head up was going to get shot.

Mac swung around the corner, into the full blast of the floodies. He walked the twenty paces to the entrance steps, stayed close to the wall, under the window line. His footsteps roared like a rock concert. At the steps he stopped, lay on the dark red clay and pulled himself under the wooden steps like he was inspecting a car. Looked for weight and movement sensors, looked for grenades and trip wires.

Nothing.

He pulled himself out, his wrist aching and his head throbbing from Sonny's butting. He'd stopped breathing again. He wasn't feeling so good. Cold sweat soaked into his cap.

Hard-on moved in from the courtyard. No resistance. Still no movement from inside. Hard-on put a hand on Mac's shoulder, his eyes questioning. Mac gave thumbs-up.

Hard-on handed the M4 to Mac, and walked up the beam on the side of the stairs rather than the stairs themselves, landing like a cat on the porch. Mac covered the courtyard from beside the stairs. Took long sweeps with the assault weapon, looking for movement, sounds. He glanced over his shoulder a couple of times, saw Hard-on working his lock magic. When he looked back a third time, Hard-on had his gloved hand reached out. Mac handed over the M4 and pulled out his SIG. Then he joined Hard-on on the porch. The door was now slightly ajar and Hard-on took his standing marksman stance. Nodded at Mac.

Mac put his back against the wall, reached his left arm out and slowly, at arm's length, pushed the door open. It was silent for the first half of its arc. Then it made the slightest squeal which ended in a small croak. Hard-on stood like a statue, the door open before him. If anyone was waiting, or anyone just happened to be in that zone, Hard-on would nail them and the shit would start.

But there was no shooting. Hard-on looked briefly at Mac, held up his hand in a 'wait' signal. Lay on the floor, looked along it for thirty seconds, looking for tripwires and lasers. Mac thought back to the fear he'd evoked in those boys at the Honda Accord. Realised that to a special forces guy this whole mission might look like one big booby trap.

Hard-on stood and flicked his head. Mac came away from the wall, into the room. It was a kitchen. Mac held the SIG in cup-and-saucer, moved immediately to his right, around the side of the room. Pots and pans hung from hooks along the wall. Musty smell. Moonlight came through the window over the sinks. He moved around the right wall towards a portal without a door and took a position. He turned back and watched Hard-on check behind the door, look up at the ceilings and walls, crouch down to look under the large table in the middle of the area, even open a broom closet door.

They stood either side of the doorway. Hard-on took off his ski mask and stashed it in his back pocket, did a quick peek around the corner. Pulled back. Looked again, slower. Mac took his six o'clock.

Hard-on slipped the M4 strap over his neck so the thing was hanging horizontal across his chest. His eyes were fixed on something. He pulled his boot-blacked Ka-bar from the webbing, held it hammer-grip, blade up – less likely to cut one of your mates than if you held it hammer-grip, blade-down.

Hard-on turned to Mac, pointed to himself and held up one finger. He would go first. Pointed at Mac, held up two. Mac was backup.

Hard-on slid into the next room. It was darker, sheets over windows. Two camp beds, one on either side of the room. Walkway down the middle. On the left, an Indonesian man was asleep on his side, facing away from Mac and Hard-on. The other bloke was sleeping on his back, snoring, fatigues on, boots by the bed, M4 leaning against the wall.

Hard-on took two strides to the guy in his fatigues, clapped a gloved hand firmly over mouth and nose and slit his throat, all in one movement. He didn't hesitate, made two strides to the guy under the sheet, who made a humming sound – like he was waking up next to his girlfriend – and Hard-on did the same thing to him, except he entered the bloke's neck from the side, taking the carotid artery direct.

Total silence. No more snoring, no more breathing. The white sheet was now dark and shiny. The bloke hadn't moved from his sleeping position. The other bloke hadn't even opened his eyes.

Hard-on stood up too abruptly, the M4 clattering briefly on his webbing. They paused. Mac's wrist had almost seized up in the cup-and-saucer position. Nine-millimetre handguns actually had a decent amount of kick and with the suppressor hanging off the end, he was scared his wrist wouldn't be able to deal with it.

His breathing was plain embarrassing. Special forces blokes lived, slept, ate and trained together, and after a while their breathing got synchronised. So Mac knew Hard-on was probably spooked by the ragged, gasping sound coming from the intel guy. He could imagine the Green Beret having a beer with his boys after this was over, saying something like, 'That Pizza Man – he asthmatic or some shit?'

Hard-on put the Ka-bar in his webbing scabbard, brought his M4 up to his eye line again. Pointed. Now they were looking at another doorway, this one with an actual door in it.

Hard-on made a gesture with his hand to show he wanted a low–high team for entry. He wanted Mac covering left, he would cover right.

Mac crouched on one knee in front of the door knob. It was an away-swinging door. Hard-on was in standing marksman pose straight over the top of him. If there were people on the other side, they would look up and see the profile of one man. Less to aim at.

Mac went to turn the knob, an old brass number, nice and worn and quiet. His breathing was now coming so fast and shallow that it reminded him of what he was like after a fifteen-minute session with the jumprope at the gym.

He shook it off. Sweat fell onto his forearm. Took a deep breath. Exhaled. Pushed the door in, brought the SIG up to eye line. His heart thumped in his temples, throbbed at the lump on his head, roared in his ears.

The door opened into a long corridor with doors and rooms. This was not what Mac wanted. It was gloomy but he reckoned there were at least three rooms off the corridor. The only good part? Not all of them had doors.

Hard-on and Mac moved forward, Hard-on in the lead.

Same routine for the first door. Mac kneeling, Hard-on standing. Door swung open with a creak. They took it in. Moonlight came in the large sash window, a naked Asian man lay on the only bed. The bloke lifted his head, opened his mouth in surprise.

Mac rose, SIG ready, levelled the suppressor and was about to fire. Heard Hard-on say, 'No.' Then saw why.

There was a woman behind the bloke.

Naked, blonde, and out to it.

CHAPTER 13

Mac hesitated, then lowered the SIG so it was at hip-height and popped the Asian man in the forehead.

Blood sprayed on the girl, but he was pretty sure he'd missed her with the slug.

The sound of voices and feet hitting floorboards came from next door. Urgent commands.

Hard-on keyed the throat mic. 'Sonny, shit's started. Bring it. Bring it now.'

Almost immediately the staccato sound of short-burst machine gun fire came from further down the building. Glass smashed and someone screamed. Shots fired back, echoing inside the building.

Hard-on said, 'Get the girl.' Then he went to the doorframe, stood beside it and fired in short bursts down the hallway. The air filled with thumps and male fear.

Mac knelt on the bloody bed, pulled the dead guy off the girl. Two rounds came through the wall above him. He was full-on panting now, muttering to himself. The girl was Judith Hannah, he was sure. She was naked and from the breasts up she was covered in blood. There were bits of brain and bone in her hair.

She was tied to the bed head with cargo ties, both wrists, both ankles. He tried to get them loose. Reached for his own Ka-bar, fumbled, dropped the knife. He was not handling this well. Then he realised there was no response from Hannah.

'Judith – how are you?' He picked up the Ka-bar and slashed the ties on her wrists.

No response.

Panting, gulping and muttering like a madman, Mac checked for a pulse on her inside wrist. Pressed three fingers close to the bone. Got it in one. Drugged? Catatonic?

He gave her a soft slap on the left cheek. Her eyes didn't open. 'Judith – talk to me!'

The shooting went on around him. He slashed the ankle ties.

Hard-on popped shots like a robot and yelled, 'How we going, Pizza Man?'

'Almost there.'

'Where's the other girl?' shouted Hard-on before shooting again.

'She's not in here, mate,' he yelled over the gunfire.

He knew Hard-on would avoid firing in a downward trajectory until they knew where the younger girl was. Mac looked around in the gloom and realised he hadn't looked behind the door. He pulled it away from the wall and looking straight back at him were big dark eyes under a fringe; a cuddly blanket clutched into a naked chest. Total fear.

Minky's girl, alive.

Splinters of doorframe flew into the room.

Hard-on yelled, 'Fuck!' and staggered in, clutching at his right bicep. 'Fuck it!'

Minky's girl screamed.

Mac leapt up, took a crouch at the doorframe. Two men down the end of the corridor were laying down indiscriminate fire. It whistled around, sliced through the wooden walls, tore strips off the plaster ceiling. There were two sounds: loads firing and the building being torn apart. Mac pulled back in.

The radio crackled. 'Blue team, this is Red. Ten more tangos from another building. We're bogged down. Can you hang on?'

Hard-on winced, growled at his pain. Keyed the mic, said, 'Red

123

team this is Blue – we have both targets. Repeat both targets. We need cover. We need it now. Over.'

Radio contact ceased.

Hard-on took his hand away from his bicep. It was a mess. The shirt was torn and blood was seeping into it as Mac watched.

'It's a flesh wound,' said Hard-on. 'But a bad one.'

'Can you cover me if I get the girls?' asked Mac.

Hard-on nodded, reloaded, moved back to the splintered doorframe. The shooting had died down. They were probably waiting to see if it was safe to approach. Hard-on did a quick peek, then pulled back.

Mac went to the bed, dragged Hannah up to a sitting position. Kneeling on the floor he pushed her arms up, pulled them over his left shoulder and her body followed. He wrapped his left arm around the back of her knees and when he stood she hung limp down his back.

He turned for Minky's girl. She would have to run.

Hard-on counted his five then leapt into the corridor, laying down fire. Mac would have maybe ten seconds to make a dash for it with the girls, before the return fire came back twice as hard.

Smiling at Minky's girl, he put his hand out.

She shook her head.

Mac smiled harder, wiggled his hand, tried to grab her wrist. 'Come on. Let's go.' She pulled her hand away.

'Come on, darlin' – I'm here to help,' said Mac, clicking his fingers at her.

Hard-on looked back to Mac. 'On my five, Pizza Man.'

Mac made another attempt at Minky's girl and she pointed at her ankle. He looked closer: the girl was handcuffed to a pipe on the wall. The flesh around the steel cuff was worn and bleeding.

'Fuck!'

With Judith Hannah on his back, he knelt to the dead rapist on the floor. But the guy was naked. *Where would he keep his keys, Einstein? Up his arsehole?*

Mac was seriously losing it. Hard-on was losing ground and yelled into the room, 'Ready?!'

And then he smelled it.

124

Smoke!

The joint was on fire.

A bullet passed inches from his face, thwacking into the opposite wall. It was time to go. Mac returned to Minky's girl, pulled the SIG from the webbing holster, pointed it in close at the handcuff chain and pulled the trigger. Minky's girl screamed as his first shot missed. Mac got the suppressor's muzzle closer to the chain and tried again as the girl jerked around, scared of his gun. Her shrieks hurt his ears but this time the handcuff fell away. Mac put his hand out again and the girl took it.

They moved to the doorframe, which was now hanging by a few shreds of wood and plaster. Hard-on was ready to go, his right arm limp and dripping blood at his side. The M4 was in his left.

There was a lull in the gunfire. Mac gripped tighter on the girl's hand, but he could feel her pulling, scared witless. Hard-on flicked his head and Mac took the two girls into the corridor, but as he did more gunfire erupted. Hard-on fired back but in the confusion the girl pulled free as Mac ran in a crouch towards the exit. He looked back and saw the wall and door give way as the girl disappeared back into the room. She was buried in wood and plaster.

Hard-on and Mac looked at one another and Hard-on shook his head.

Mac fired back down the hallway with his SIG as Hard-on joined him, and they jogged out the way they'd come in.

The radio came back to life as they went down the entrance stairs and into the courtyard. A scene of carnage met them, fire billowing out of the far end of building three and bodies lying on the red clay. Spikey and Sawtell walked along the courtyard side of the building, aiming up at the spaces that five minutes earlier had been windows. Sporadic fire issued from the windows. The Americans returned with interest.

The fire was taking hold. More gunfire came out of the building. On the radio, it sounded like Sonny and Hemi were nailed down elsewhere. Mac wanted to drop Hannah and Hard-on in the bush and get back to rescuing Minky's daughter.

Hard-on was in a bad way as they headed for the RV, groaning every time his feet hit the ground. Judith Hannah bounced rhythmically against Mac's back. At least her legs were warm, which was a good sign.

Mac keyed the mic: 'Red team, this is Blue. We have one target. Repeat one target. Need help on the other. Over.'

No reply.

He tried again. 'Red team, Minky's girl is in building three, repeat building three, in one of the middle rooms. A wall has collapsed on her – can we get someone there?'

Hard-on, through his agony, shook his head. 'It's not going to happen, Pizza Man. This is one we'll just have to live with. Fuck it!'

They hit the cover of the jungle and made up the slope for the RV. Mac dumped the girl softly on the mossy forest floor. Hard-on almost collapsed in the leaves. He was in shock, losing blood and in a lot of pain.

Mac opened Billy's triage pack which had been left at the RV. He peeled back the flap to reveal morphine vials, bandages, needles, scalpels, hypodermic syringes, horsehair sutures and much more. He found a thick bandage then pulled a squirty bottle filled with pure grain spirit from the bag and tore open a packet of five sterile pads. Ripping away Hard-on's sleeve, he had a closer look. The bullet had passed on the inside of the bicep and out the other side. It had probably nicked an artery and chipped the bone.

'What's it like?' asked Hard-on in a small voice.

'A fucking mess,' said Mac, already working on the wound.

Hard-on's body spasmed at the pain of it, but he was a good soldier. Tears ran down his cheeks, he gasped, moaned and swore through gritted teeth as Mac cleaned the gaping thing out with spirit and the pads. Finally Mac squirted spirit on the last pad, placed it on the wound and strapped the bandage around the bicep.

By now Hard-on was full into shock: pale lips, chattering teeth and eyes rolling back. Mac kept him talking, asked if he wanted a shot and Hard-on shook his head.

'Just say no.'

They both chuckled, but Mac couldn't do anything more for now.

He got on the radio. 'Billy, I got a man down. At the RV. Repeat, man down.'

'Got that, Blue team. There soon, over.'

Mac turned to Judith Hannah. Not much change. He still had no clothes for her so he took off his webbing, dropped his ovies and put them on her.

Fishing in the medic pack he came out with a cap of smelling salts. Tried them under her nose. She reacted slightly but was still in some kind of coma.

He grabbed Hard-on's M4. Checked for load, checked for safety and then barrelled down the hill in his briefs and Hi-Tecs.

The fight was still going and the building was now completely enveloped in flame. Mac felt sadness about Minky's girl. He gulped it back and moved to the end of the building where the shooting was still happening. Sawtell leaned out of another building, called him in. Mac raced around, ducked in a side entrance and joined Sawtell, Sonny and Billy in the room. Across a small field, a posse of thugs fired intermittently from building five. Sonny, Sawtell and Billy fired back.

'Well that went to shit in a handcart real quick,' said Sawtell as Mac joined them.

'Cunts were waiting for us,' said Sonny. 'Had a whole backup team in number five.'

They looked Mac up and down, taking in his briefs. Didn't say anything.

Through the window they watched Hemi, behind a long-abandoned bulldozer, enthusiastically hammering away with a belt-fed .50 cal machine gun. Every time he loosed a burst, whole sections of building five fell away, as if someone were poking pieces out of a jigsaw puzzle from the inside.

'I'll give him ten more seconds,' said Sonny, 'then we roll, eh?'

Mac nodded. 'Hannah's okay. Local girl didn't make it.'

Sonny nodded.

'I tried,' said Mac.

'I know,' said Sonny.

Sawtell asked, 'How's Hard-on?'

'Not good. Needs a doctor.'

Sawtell looked at the blood on Mac's hands, then looked away, sad.

127

'You use the morphine?' asked Billy, getting ready to go.

'No,' said Mac. 'Didn't know how.'

'Good,' said Billy, and he left.

'Where's Moses? Where's Spikey?' asked Mac.

A pause.

'Didn't make it – got caught in there.' Sonny gestured at the inferno, shook his head. 'Fuck that for a game of cards. I'd rather be shot.'

Sawtell nodded.

The evacuation went smoothly. Hemi carried Hard-on, Billy took Hannah. Sonny took point duty, Sawtell ran the sweep.

They got to the helo as fast as you could carrying two people. They put Hard-on in a stretcher. Wrapped Hannah in a blanket and harnessed her into the back seat of the Euro. Her head lolled and Mac jammed a folded blanket under her left ear. He found a pair of orange ovies in the tool bay, put them on.

Billy got on the flight deck, made ready to fire her up. The whole crew was deflated, exhausted, sad, drained by the adrenaline come-down.

Sawtell suddenly pulled back from talking to a zonked-out Hard-on. There was a commotion outside and voices raised, slides clicking and the sound of a rifle being manhandled.

Mac grabbed the SIG from between his feet, poked his head out of the helo. Beneath him Sonny had his arms around Moses and Spikey. They all looked down, smiling and crying at the little girl lying in Mosie's arms.

Spikey's left hand was held to his ear, blood was crusted down his neck. He was saying to Sonny, 'Damned if Mosie don't just pick up that wall like it was litter.'

They got back to the compound at sun-up. Sonny and Sawtell went drinking in the mess, played Stevie Wonder, Rolling Stones and Grand Funk Railroad. Played it loud, talked loud, tried to sing along – a couple of boys with some pipes to clear.

Everyone else hit the hay.

Mac lay awake, remembering one night his father had got home late. Mac had been ten years old at the time. It was hot, the middle of summer in Rockie, and Mac had got up after midnight to get a glass of water. Frank was sitting in the darkness of the kitchen, sipping Johnnie Walker and sucking back Pall Mall Plains, an ashtray filled with white butts in front of him. The dark red pack was going end over end on the formica table between Frank's fingers. Mac got his water, and as he was going back to his bed Frank said, 'You've gotta promise me, mate. Never mix alcohol and firearms – got it?'

Mac had nodded, freaked at his father's slurred and bloodshot state.

In the morning the *Bulletin*'s front page was dominated by the story of a local girl killed while asleep in her bed. Her father had shot her. He was a wife-basher and a violent drunk who'd regularly threatened his wife with a Smith & Wesson .38. On this night, he tried to scare his wife and shot at a wall beside her. The slug went through the wall and hit his nine-year-old in the head.

Mac remembered his mother telling Frank that he should have locked that bullying prick up years ago.

Frank didn't tell her to shut up. Just wore it.

Mac thought about it.

Then he breathed again. It felt like the first time in days.

CHAPTER 14

Mac woke later in the morning in the air-conned men's quarters. He dressed in his blue ovies, which had already been washed, dried, folded and left on a tallboy in his room. On the ovies was the black diamond key ring with the MPS logo and the big German key. He looked at it again. Put it in his breast pocket and moved down to the mess.

After he'd finished eating, Hemi came over with a mug of coffee. 'Some shit last night, huh?'

Mac nodded. He'd never been shot at that much for that long. He was still a little jangled and deafened by the experience.

'Yeah, wouldn't want to go to a party up there,' said Mac. 'If that's what they're like on a week night, imagine them on a Saturday when they're really on the piss.'

Hemi laughed. 'Like some of the pubs back home, eh?'

'Where's that?'

'Fucking Gisborne. Heard of it?'

Mac shook his head.

'Fucking hard case.' Hemi shook his head.

Mac asked him about the girls.

'They're doing all right,' said Hemi. 'The little one is fine but the Aussie girl's still asleep. Don't know what they were feeding her.'

Mac's job had been to snatch Judith Hannah, but not interrogate her. That had been made plain by Garvey back in Jakkers. They'd given him nothing to go on, no reason to talk with her. Even in his initial briefing with Sawtell back in Jakarta, the whole emphasis had been on Garrison, not Hannah.

But Mac didn't give a shit now about what he was supposed to do. Minky was dead, Limo was dead, Hard-on had half his arm shot off, Hannah was in some kind of coma – probably drug-induced – and there was a little girl, now without a dad, who might or might not have been subject to unwanted sexual attention.

So Mac didn't give a rats about what Jakarta wanted.

He poured another cup of tea from the silver pot. 'Hem, tell me, who was doing the shooting last night?'

Hemi shrugged. 'Dunno, really. Looked like locals, I suppose. Organised though. Trained, I reckon. All kitted-up. No sarungs – that what you mean?'

Mac nodded. 'Well, yeah. Any Anglos in there?'

Hemi did the theatrical frown. Shook his head. 'Mate, it was dark, eh? All I know is they knew what they were doing – didn't run, kept fighting. Not a bad outfit really.'

Mac thanked him and got up to go. Then turned and asked if there were any special handshakes he needed to know in order to get in and see Cookie. Hemi said he'd handle it. He went to a wall-mounted phone, spoke briefly. Put his finger on the hook, let it go, called someone else. Came back.

'Mosie will meet you at the gate.'

Mac breathed the steamy equatorial air as he wound his way up the drive to the mansion. He had this place as Dutch-built. It was elevated and Sonny was right, it had been built precisely in the right rise of the valley to get both the breeze from the west off the Macassar Strait and the southerly that came up from the Sunda Sea and Flores. The rainforest came right to the edge of the driveway. Amazingly coloured hornbills strained the breaking point of branches as they gnawed at the fruit. There were also piping crows and cicadabirds, and the racket they made, along with all the insects, made the air vibrate.

By the time he got to the gate, the back of his ovies were wet with sweat. The black iron-work gate was at least two storeys high and wide enough for three trucks to pass through abreast. Those Dutch must have been a paranoid bunch. A bored-looking local made no attempt to leave the glassed-in guardhouse. Probably orders from Sonny. Moses appeared on the other side of the gate, said something to the guard, and the small walkway gate next to the guardhouse swung open silently. Mac walked through and the two men greeted each other with a thumb-grip handshake.

'Set, brother. Nice work last night,' said Mac.

Moses grinned big. 'Set, brother. Set.'

Moses wore olive fatigue shorts, Hi-Tec Magnums and a black polo shirt. He'd dumped the webbing and the SIG and now had on a hip rig with a large handgun in it.

Behind Moses three children were playing on a groomed and irrigated lawn. It extended all the way to the swimming pool area and the four-storey white mansion.

He recognised one of the kids as Minky's girl. She ran with the other kids, laughing. She wore a new white linen dress. She and another girl about her age teased a younger boy with a ball. Piggy-in-the-middle stuff, and the boy was about to lose it.

Moses turned and snapped something. The girls gave him a cheeky look. Minky's girl held the ball out to the boy, and when he went to grab it, she pulled it back. The girls ran up the lawn, shrieking with delight.

The boy lost it.

Moses rolled his eyes and they walked across the lawn. He put a friendly hand on the crying boy's shoulder and the boy leaned into the Fijian, walked alongside muttering something, probably about girls.

In the wealthy Indonesian families, they had a word for people like Moses that translated loosely as 'house boy'. Moses' job was to ensure that the family was safe from bandits, kidnappers, slavers, thieves and assassins. He was a hell of a thing to look at: about six-four, one hundred and twenty-five kilos and all muscle. According to Hemi, Moses was part of the same clan that included General Sitiveni Rabuka, the military strongman of Fiji. Mac remembered a bunch of journalists once asking Rabuka about his boxing and football prowess, and the general had laughingly remarked that he was the small one of the tribe.

Moses kind of explained that.

When Mac asked about Hannah, Moses led him behind the mansion to a modern annexe that at first glance looked like a guest wing. But when they walked into the air-con comfort, Mac realised it was a small hospital the size of a large vet clinic.

They got to a door. Moses knocked, opened it and Mac saw a nurse – a young local woman – wiping Judith Hannah's forehead with a wet towel, talking low and sweet to the girl. Hannah had a drip in her arm and her eyes were still shut. Pale, sickly.

'Billy don't want her talking,' said Moses. 'She gotta rest, brother.'

Mac looked at Mosie, thought about arguing. Thought again. Mac had a good idea what was wrong with Judith Hannah. A fast and clumsy way to get people talking was to hit them up with overdoses of scopolamine, which was a truth serum of sorts. Trouble was, it was derived from the Datura family of plants which also had hallucinogenic properties. It was a dangerous way to mess with someone's biochemistry. When you'd got the story you wanted, you administered a 'hot shot' of scopolamine and morphine which induced amnesia in the short term. Secret police used it more than spooks.

They headed for the house, running into Hard-on and Billy, who were on the way out. Hard-on's arm was now totally strapped and in a sling.

Mac gave a wink. "Zit going, boys?'

They went through the tradies' entrance into the mansion and both men kicked off their boots. Mrs Cookie demanded it and Sonny had warned Mac that 'the missus of the house is a real piece of work'.

Mac had grown up in a house where the missus was a piece of work and he knew the secret was to do it her way.

Moses took them through. Cookie stood from the desk, asked how the girl was going. Moses said, 'Real good, Mr B. She a happy one, that one.'

'All that screaming?'

'That lil' Santo, Mr B. Girls gang up. Two on one, not fair.'

Cookie put his hand up, like *Yeah, yeah*.

Moses was dismissed. He gave Mac the wink as he shut the door behind him.

Mac and Cookie sat on the white leather sofas. A housemaid came in with green tea and left. Cookie lit a smoke and they did small talk about Australia and big boarding schools. Cookie had been schooled at Xavier College in Melbourne, where he'd acquired the accent and the ockerisms. 'The culture of that place was "fit in or fuck off", so I went local.'

They talked about Australian politics, the problems with Melbourne Football Club and Aussie–Indon relations. Cookie was well read, smart.

'You did the right thing, telling Sonny about Lastri,' said Cookie, changing tack.

'Who?'

'Minky's girl. Her name's Lastri.'

Mac looked away. He hadn't figured he'd have to do this conversation again.

'Look, Mr B . . .'

'Cookie. Call me Cookie.'

Mac paused. He wasn't going to rush in with the racism disclaimer again. 'Um, it's been quite a few days, you know . . .'

Cookie leaned forward, poured the tea. 'You don't have to explain. The important thing is you told Sonny and that American before they went in. That's the part that counts. That's why Sonny let it go. Can you imagine if Mosie was running around with this girl he pulled out of the fire, and you're going, "Oh, yeah – her"? You think Sonny would let that go?'

Mac had always backed his ability in the blueing stakes, but Sonny and Sawtell deciding to teach him a lesson at the same time? That wouldn't work well for Mac.

Cookie chuckled. 'Don't be so hard on yourself, Mac. Thing is . . .' Cookie exhaled, looked at his smoke. 'Her mother's dead too. Made some calls this morning. Makassar cops all over it.'

'Shit, sorry.'

Cookie waved him away again. 'Problem's gone. You'll be allowed to leave Sulawesi, then the investigation will start again. For now, guess we have a new girl in the family.'

In Indonesia, families took in orphans. It was informal; it was the culture.

Cookie fixed him with a look. 'This business is hard enough on

134

you already without beating yourself up. You know, I once did things the other way round from you. I mean, I *really* fucked it up.'

Cookie moved forward on the sofa, flicked his smoke at the ashtray. 'We'd lost this computer programmer guy from our air defence program. There was all this evidence left around that he'd gone on holiday, but we tracked him down in a house at Kuta. The fucking Koreans had him. It was a tough one. We didn't want him dead – we needed to debrief him – but we didn't want him explaining launch algorithms and all that shit to the Koreans.'

Mac nodded.

'So it was like your one last night. We flew in the Kopassus boys, and they pulled an early am raid. Went great, everyone happy. Except the eleven-year-old daughter of our scientist who got shot in the leg.'

'What was she doing there?'

Cookie shrugged. 'Koreans had snatched the bloke's two girls as well. So there I am in the debrief and this intel idiot from Jakarta has turned up with the *full* file!'

Mac looked at him. 'You're kidding me.'

'Deadset.'

'Where'd they find that genius?'

'Dunno where they scraped him up from, but he's working presidential liaison now – briefs SBY on intel matters.'

They both laughed. There had never been any military commander of any rank who'd ever been given the full file on anything from intel. Soldiers were considered to be the 'operational' end of the gig; spooks saw themselves as the brains.

'So there I am sinking further under the table. I'm not kidding. I've got this Kopassus colonel, this damned gorilla, right beside me and he's reading my comms logs.'

Mac made the *eek* face. The comms logs were all the minutes made from phone calls and recorded meetings. They'd include all of the internal BAKIN briefings that Cookie had been giving his own controller, all the requests for Kopassus involvement and the reasons. They'd include the full rundown of who was in the house.

'So this Kopassus gorilla is looking at dates and times and my comments and who else is present – he's never seen anything like it.

He's got eyes like goggles, and he's looking at me and saying, "So you knew those girls were in there when you called us in? You knew they were in there when you briefed *me*?"'

Mac could hardly believe what he was hearing.

'What could I say? It was all there. Anyway, about an hour later I'm getting out of my rental car at the airport and I'm snatched, right out of the fucking Denpasar airport car park. Off to the police barracks. I'm bashed by these Kopassus goons, and down comes Colonel Gorilla for a word in the shell-like.'

Mac couldn't help himself, he was laughing.

'Gorilla gets in my face, says, "I don't care who you are or who you know, no one does that to my boys."'

Cookie pulled up the hair over his left ear. Mac saw only half an ear, ending in a ragged horizontal line. 'So then he takes a souvenir – cuts off the top of my ear, holds it in front of my face and says, "Be happy the girl didn't die. You pull shit like that again, and I'll take your heart."

'Then he walks off . . . with my *fucking ear*!'

They laughed, slapped their legs. Then they both sat back, realising it wasn't that funny.

'So the lesson was that soldiers are damned superstitious. You ask a lot, and they'll deliver. But they don't do kids. They won't cop that,' said Cookie.

Mac hesitated, then asked Cookie outright. 'Can someone fly me down to Sabulu? I need another look.'

'Let's go,' said Cookie, getting up.

They flew in over the site of the battle. The place was still smoking. Mac could smell the charred wood and the burned rainforest from a hundred metres up. Not a great advertisement for Cookie's protection service.

They walked down from the landing site, into the courtyard, armed with M16s. Billy walked point, Mac swept. Cookie was in the middle, dressed in olive ovies of the aviation jumpsuit style, sleeves rolled up to just under the elbows.

They strolled through the smoking wreck of building three, which was burned to the ground. Some of the foundations were still sticking up out of the ground.

Buzzards erupted into the humid air as they came upon bodies and charred boots. Mac smelled burned hair and toasted flesh. Cookie kicked a corpse onto its back, crouched down. Looked up at Mac, said, 'Look at that – Filipino, or Polynesian. Not local, anyway.'

Mac looked at where Cookie was pointing. The dead man's body had been burned down the back, but he'd fallen on his arm and the flesh was intact. There was a tattoo on the bloke's forearm, a scimitar and stars, done with the long curves of the Polynesian tats.

'Moro shit,' said Cookie.

They walked up to building five, where Garrison's extra boys had appeared from. It was still intact. They entered in a staggered formation, weapons at eye line. Billy went into the main room first, checked for wires and sensor pads, then waved the others through.

The walls boasted holes the size of large pancakes. The impact of the .50 cal gun had taken whole sections of the wooden walls off their studs. It smelled of old cordite and there were brass shells scattered on the floor amidst the rubble. Mac looked it over, still not really sure what he was looking for.

They cased all the buildings. In one of them, there was evidence of people having slept there. It had much better security and the beds were proper mattress jobs. There were two of them and they had their own rooms. The showers had been done right and Mac noticed that the power cable from the generator room ran underground, not over it. In the rooms, there were trapdoors in the floor. Someone had been worried about security and escape.

In the vestibule was a room with camp stretchers. The place was set up so intruders would have to go through the guards. Under one of the beds Mac found a torn strip of foil. It smelled of Bartook Special Mint.

Mac went back into the VIP rooms, had a quick look down the trapdoor of the one in the right. Nothing.

Looked down the left room's trapdoor.

A face looked back at him.

Mac leapt back, yelped. The trapdoor dropped and bounced on its wrong side. Mac tried to get his M16 around as fast he could. Flustered, jerky, he pointed it at the hole in the floor.

'Shit!'

He struggled to control his breathing as Billy and Cookie came through, guns ready.

Mac put a hand out. 'Watch it – someone's in there.' He nodded at the trap hole, breathing fast.

'Who?' asked Cookie.

'A kid. Looks like a kid.'

He swallowed hard, the adrenaline bursting through him from the fright. Cookie spoke to Billy without looking at him. 'Cover the escape will you, mate?'

Billy scooted out while Cookie and Mac trained their guns on the hole. Cookie started talking. Low, smooth, cooing. Mac couldn't make out all of what he was saying but it sounded good. He talked and talked, then sang something.

Mac was getting sweaty palms on the M16 – Sulawesi in summer was so hot. There was movement around the trap hole. First one hand and then another came out. Two slender hands up in the air – international sign of surrender. A mop of black hair came up. It was a boy, maybe seventeen, eighteen. He turned to Cookie, pleaded for his life. Mac didn't need a degree in Bahasa to get that.

Cookie snapped something at him and the boy stood totally still. He asked the boy something. The boy answered. Cookie cocked the M16, aimed up. The boy pleaded. Without taking his eyes off the boy, Cookie yelled, 'Billy, get under the building – see if this kid's standing on anything.'

Mac looked sideways. Cookie said, 'Could be standing on a mine or a grenade. That's what these pricks do, make a kid stand on a mine and then piss off. The kid has to wait till the cavalry arrives. Boom. We all go up.'

Billy's voice came back. 'He looks okay, Mr B.'

Cookie motioned the boy to come out. He stood, skinny and scared.

The boy's name was Setiawan, but friends called him Seti. He'd come along with his cousin because there was work up at the mine. He didn't know it would involve working with thugs. He'd been given a gun but when the shooting started he'd become scared and hid in the remotest building. This one.

Cookie was good. He kept the guy going, offered him cigarettes, then got Billy to get some water for the guy. Classic enlistment technique – the hard stuff could always come later.

Seti had no names. Yes, there were two white men – one of them a tall Yankee. And there was a broader Aussie. There was another man too. Asian, maybe southern Philippines, maybe Polynesian even.

After half an hour of the smiling act, Cookie turned to Mac. 'I reckon he's spilled. But I'll shake him down if you want.'

Mac looked at the kid, winked. The kid smiled big. Mac wished he had some rupiah to sling around. But it wouldn't have helped.

'Ask him about the Aussie.'

Cookie asked him and turned to Mac. 'Didn't see him – only heard. He only came up here once.'

'Ask him if there was a place called "Eighty" mentioned. Or maybe a person?'

Cookie asked and the kid became animated. Yes, the Asian dude was called Eighty. Mac asked through Cookie and got the answers. Eighty was about five-nine, good-looking, clean shaven, happy, well dressed in black T-shirts and Aussie board shorts. Had some business in the mine.

Then, said Seti, the other guys had said there was a white girl in the camp. They wanted to have their turn but Seti was brought up right, didn't want any of that.

Mac looked at the kid. Boy averted his eyes. Fucking liar.

Mac turned to Cookie. 'Does he have any idea what Eighty is, what it means?'

The kid shook his head.

'That's it,' said Mac. 'I'm done. That's good stuff.'

Cookie gave him a suspicious look.

'He's going to be helpful, Mr B. Honest.'

Mac shouldn't have said that last bit. Cookie laughed. 'I wasn't going to whack him. *Honest!*'

The buzzards rose like angels as the helo came down. The clearing where Limo had bought it was the size of a tennis court – just large enough for the Euro to land. Billy didn't like it but Cookie wanted it.

So they landed.

Limo's eyes and tongue were gone and the buzzards had started on his rear end, but Mac reckoned Sawtell and his boys would be happy to have something pretty much intact to ship back to Limo's mum.

Mac must have been getting better – he was sad watching this kid's face disappear into darkness as Billy zipped the navy blue body bag, but he wasn't as emotional as he'd been the last day or so. He was tight again, and it felt good.

Billy and Mac lifted Limo into the Euro, strapped him to the cargo cleats behind the last row of seats.

Billy moved to the cockpit. Mac looked out and saw Cookie sitting on the same log where he'd been butted a day earlier. Cookie beckoned him and offered him one of his smokes as he sat. Mac declined. Cookie took a swig of water, offered it. Mac took the bottle and finished it. Sulawesi was a steam room.

Mac had been waiting for this chat. The chances of Cookie Banderjong being this helpful and this involved without wanting something in return were between nothing and zilch.

Cookie looked down at his legs, flicked a piece of ash off the ovies. 'You run a database on Garrison lately?'

Mac hadn't, only read the file that Garvey gave him that night in Jakkers. Big oversight.

'Let's work it backwards,' said Cookie. 'Garrison's trade is drugs for guns for gold, right?'

Mac nodded. Cookie sucked on his smoke.

'He's good at it – making someone a shitload of money. He's doing his thing in northern Pakistan, right? He goes too far, bombs the police compound, and rather than being kicked out or dragged back to DC, he's suddenly in northern Burma.' Cookie turned his palms to the sky. 'And 'cos it's Burma, we're straight back into drugs, guns and gold.'

Mac kept nodding. One part of his mind wanted to get to Cookie's insights, while the other was on high alert for where Cookie felt Mac fitted.

Cookie continued, a man used to having the floor. 'So who benefits?'

Mac thought it was a trick question. It was obvious to anyone who had worked this area for any length of time. 'The Chinese.'

'Right – they've got the weapons, they want the gold. Burmese have the drugs, they want the Silkworms and radar arrays. All the good shit.'

Mac nodded. 'All they need is the middle guy who can turn drugs into weapons and gold.'

'Garrison,' said Cookie.

'Too right.'

Cookie paused, flicked the butt of his smoke into the forest, brushed ash from the leg of his ovies. 'So Garrison snatches your girl. Why?'

Mac's professional life rarely worked with this level of discussion. He had to keep his paramilitary missions secret from his colleagues, most of whom had no idea he was an S-2 operative. It didn't make him feel elite – it isolated him, put him in a position of being unable to swap information and talk things through with workmates. In a world of cellular information, Mac was usually in a cell of two or three people. So he was warming to the openness of Cookie's conversation.

'Dunno. An affair that went wrong?' Mac guessed.

Cookie shook his head. 'Garrisons don't think with the little head. Ever.'

Mac tried again. 'She was on to something – Garrison wanted that info.'

'I think that's more like it,' said Cookie, and changed tack again. 'Judith Hannah was a regular visitor to Sulawesi, did you know that?'

Mac didn't.

'Know her expertise?'

'China,' sighed Mac, the pieces slowly tumbling into place.

'Know what she was doing in Sulawesi?' Cookie was taunting, smiling. He didn't wait for Mac to shake his head. 'Counter-surveillance.'

Mac turned. 'Of what?'

'The Chinese maritime security team.'

Cookie laughed at the look on Mac's face, then said, 'Your girl is one of the world's experts on how the Chinese military intend to secure their shipping lanes for the next twenty years.'

Cookie smiled like the cat who got the cream, put his hand on the back of Mac's neck. Massaged it. 'Cut off from Canberra, mate?'

'Maybe,' rasped Mac.

Cookie laughed. Then paused. 'Let's work on this together, huh?'

Mac let a long slow breath out. It hissed between his lips. He looked back at Cookie, looked down at Cookie's extended hand, looked into Cookie's eyes. Cookie had guessed, correctly, that Mac wanted to know the truth behind the Judith Hannah rescue, and that the truth would bring Mac back to Sulawesi. Cookie was saying *We can all help each other, or I can make life unbearable for you in Sulawesi.* Mac didn't really have a choice.

Cookie winked.

Mac shook his hand and looked away.

CHAPTER 15

Sawtell's boys and Mac flew direct from Cookie's compound to Hasanuddin military base in Makassar in an unmarked Black Hawk. There they refuelled and ate, and then helo'd into Halim Air Base on the outskirts of Jakarta just after seven pm.

Mac was rooted. His back didn't agree with the Black Hawk seating systems, which basically entailed a canvas hammock that folded down from the rear and centre bulwarks. Judith Hannah slept lengthwise in a medic's litter, still zonked out. Hard-on and Mac sat with Sawtell and Spikey in the load space. Limo was strapped to the outside of the aircraft.

The Black Hawk was the loudest and most uncomfortable way to travel in the US military. When it had come into sight at Cookie's compound, Hard-on had groaned. 'Fuck that – just once you'd think they could send a Chinook out, huh? Would it kill them?'

Mac said his farewells under the tarmac floodlights, in the stinking heat. He clapped hands with the men, thumb-grip style. Sawtell was last. His eyes were rheumy and Mac could smell the booze on him.

'Well mate,' the American joked, trying to ape the Strine accent. 'Mission completed. We got the girl.'

'Nah, mate. We got both girls.'

Sawtell looked at the tarmac, shook his head, kicked at something that wasn't there. Embarrassed. 'Sorry 'bout all that. It got a bit loose out there, huh?'

Mac watched another American crew in black ovies pull Limo's body bag from the Black Hawk's external cargo rack and carry it off to a Dodge Voyager with no side windows.

'Sorry 'bout Limo. I liked the guy,' said Mac.

Sawtell nodded. 'He was good people.' Then he looked up with a slight smile. 'By the way, the boys have a new name for you.'

'Well I guess old Sonny had to be good for something,' said Mac, smiling.

Sawtell laughed. They shook.

The Americans stowed their Cordura bags and walked towards an unmarked Hino minibus where a couple of CIA guys waited. The way the US Army worked, Sawtell was going to be piloting a laptop for the next two days.

Mac's own debrief was leaning against a white Holden Commodore, which had turned orange under the glare of the floodies.

Garvey.

Beside the Commodore was a white Mercedes-Benz ambulance, a local behind the wheel. Three Anglo men – two of them from the Service, the other the chief medical officer of the Australian diplomatic mission – hurried into the Black Hawk as the rotors came to a standstill. The driver got out slower, walked round the back, grabbed a gurney. By the time the most self-important Anglo realised he needed a gurney, the local ambo was right behind him. The others raced to get Judith Hannah onto the gurney, but the ambo had to stop them because they were messing it up. Within five seconds the ambo was running the show.

Mac snorted. He turned back and Garvs was beside him. His tanned bald head glistening in the lights. The big tanned forearms stuck out from his hips like wings.

'Buy you a drink?' asked Garvey.

'Buy me ten and I'll let you get into my pants.'

Garvs pointed at Mac's strapped wrist. 'Got a girlfriend for that?'

Mac deadpanned him. 'I'm ambidextrous.'

* * *

Mac showered, shaved and got dressed in chinos and a short-sleeved business shirt before heading for the Lagerhaus with Garvey for a feed. Around them Anglos were getting pissed and yelling at the big screens. Mac saw a highlights package that featured Victoria smashing New South Wales in the cricket. Someone yelled out, 'You fucking bee-utey!'

Garvs, through a mouthful of tuna, yelled back, 'Yeah, yeah – put it away, ya fucking poof.'

When they drank together, it was always the same. Garvs was the loud one who started the fights. Mac made the peace.

The cricket fan stopped, wandered over, big stein of Becks in his hand.

Mac caught the bloke's eye, winked. ''Zit going, champ?'

He was Mac's size but dark haired with dark features and a cop haircut. About six foot, big in the shoulders and arms, thick in the legs.

'Not bad, not bad,' the bloke was sizing up Garvs, steaming. He had a group of four blokes behind him looking on. One called, 'Leave it, Keith, fuck's sake.'

Garvs looked Keith up and down. Snorted.

Mac came in fast. 'That was some shit you guys pulled in KL, huh, champ?'

Keith tore his eyes off Garvs to look at Mac.

'Don't know how you keep doing it.' Mac shook his head pensively. 'Resources they give you guys, yet you come up with something like that. Make the FBI look like a bunch of amateurs.'

Keith eyeballed him, looked into his stein, looked up. Mac saw unhappy drinking. He knew from Jenny Toohey that the federal cops posted in South-East Asia were overworked, stressed out and disillusioned about how much of a dent they were making in the slaving and drugs rackets. They were lonely, tired and constantly in danger of being assassinated. All for $71,000 a year plus allowance. So this bloke probably thought he deserved to have a few quiet ones with other cops and customs people without a countryman calling him a pony's hoof.

'You know,' continued Mac, 'you go through all that shit to break one bunch of slavers, and you think you're not getting anywhere, right? Well you've probably made thirty or forty parents real happy, huh? Gotta take the positives, mate.'

Keith was looking in his stein again. Slumped.

'So don't worry 'bout this prick . . .' Mac pointed his steak knife at Garvs. 'He'll get slapped, don't you worry 'bout that.'

Keith laughed. 'Thanks for that.'

Mac gave him the wink as he went back to his mates, then turned back to Garvs, who was making a face like *Who's the fucking boy scout?*

Mac swigged his beer, pointed at Garvs with the knife. 'You behave yourself.'

Mac had never figured out how it worked, the whole organisational thing. Garvs and Mac had started in the Service about the same time, trained together, always been deployed in similar areas and with similar goals. But right from the get-go Garvs had been pegged as management, while Mac was always going to be the operations guy. Garvs had an office and a team. Mac had assignments – Mac *was* the team.

He'd been so busy, for so long, that he had barely noticed the transformation in their friendship. One moment he and Garvs were bullshitting their heads off to get to the Malaysian F1 Grand Prix for a weekend on the piss courtesy of a Tommi Suharto company. Next thing, Garvs is sitting there shovelling him manure about Judith Hannah, shrugging too hard, giving the old *gee-whiz* look while knowing full well that Mac looked straight through all that shit for a living.

'Mate, let's make this the last one, huh?' said Garvs abruptly.

He must have clocked Mac's surprise. It wasn't even ten o'clock and Anton Garvey was piking. Garvs was not the kind of man to run screaming from a cold beer.

'Not like you, Garvs. Doctor's orders?'

Garvs called the bierfrau over. 'Nah, mate, but I've got you on the morning flight into Sydney. You know how early you have to leave.'

The Qantas morning flight out of Jakarta departed at 4.10 am and went through Singers before heading south. The drive to Soekarno-Hatta took an hour, and on a bad morning, clearing security could take an hour. Mac had drawn the crow.

'Not trying to get rid of me, are you, mate?'

Garvs' face told Mac that's exactly what was happening. 'Nah, Macca. If that was the case you'd have been on the night flight.'

The beers arrived. 'I have to talk to Hannah. You know that, don't you?' said Mac.

'Don't worry – we've got it from here,' said Garvey.

Mac remembered when 'we' used to have him in it.

Garvey had changed. Or had Mac? He remembered one of the first times they'd got on the turps together, in KL. It was one of those embassy functions where they pull out the big TV screen, fire up the barbie and turn on the booze for the Bledisloe Cup – Kiwis and Aussies on the razz. And locals looking on amazed that two nationalities could stand there giving each other a total shellacking and be laughing about it. Garvs and Mac had bonded on the schools thing since they'd both gone to a St Joseph's school: Garvs in Sydney, Mac in Brisbane. Mac had decided to have some fun with the bloke, said, 'Shit, if you're a real Mick then what happened to the Mac at the front of your name? Not one of them closet Prods, are ya, mate?'

Garvs had come back fast as you like, said, 'Mate, if we dropped the Mac off your name we might be getting closer to the truth, huh?'

That was pretty much how their friendship had continued. Always taking the piss. No one ever getting the last word.

Now, Mac's skin was crawling. He pushed again. 'So who's *we*, mate? This a Tobin thing? Urquhart?'

Garvey snorted through his nostrils. Shook his head as if to say, *This is all too tedious.* 'Oh, by the way, Macca. We found your Nokia. Bus driver. We got it pouched in from Makassar.'

Garvey pulled the blue phone out of his breast pocket, like he'd just remembered it was there. Threw it on the table.

Mac smiled. 'Damned things – got a mind of their own, huh, Garvs?'

Garvey stared at him too long. 'Mate, the listening post is for your own safety, you know that. You take things so personally.'

Mac could have made an allegation about the Minky ambush, could have pushed the conversation into there being a mole, or at the very least someone on the Garrison payroll. Could have got on his high horse and asked how that was contributing to his safety.

But he didn't. His friendship with Garvs had run out of gas, right there, right in front of him, after knowing the bloke for almost fifteen years. Garvs wasn't going to let him talk to Hannah, wasn't going to let him stay in Jakkers for a second longer than he had to. For the first time in his career Mac was not really being debriefed. He was being dismissed.

Mac thought back to the warning Banger Jordan had given them about office guys being the most dangerous of all. He realised that it wasn't the fact that Garvs had become an office guy that had thrown him. What got his defensive instincts going was that Anton Garvey wanted a bigger office.

CHAPTER 16

Garvs left before finishing the last beer, the farewells were hollow. Looking around the Lagerhaus, Mac thought about old times, thought about mates, thought about another drink. A hand waved from the bar. Keith, pointing down at the taps. Mac gave thumbs-up, thought, *What the hell: last time in Jakkers with a false passport, I may as well go out with a king-size hangover. A real Barry Crocker.*

He grabbed the Nokia, fired it up as Keith approached with two steins in one hand. Mac pegged him as similar to himself: a small-town bloke who hadn't been quite good enough to play footy for a living, so he'd had to find something useful to do with himself.

Keith plonked down, slid the Becks over. Put out a hand: 'Keith Cavanaugh.'

They shook, keeping it soft.

'Richard Davis.'

They chatted, Keith had some stuff to get off his chest: like how do you stop the sex-slavers with all these Aussies and Yanks arriving with their hard currency and willing to pay a thousand dollars to rape a child? How was a mere cop from Victoria supposed to tear down the police, military and politicians who were either behind the trade or protecting it?

Keith kept shaking his head, not in a good way. Some of the stuff he'd been exposed to was well beyond how they did it in the Mallee. He had a fiancée, but working up here was putting him off having kids.

Keith wanted to talk about 'this thing' that had gone pear-shaped. Mac knew about the Lombok incident, even though Keith only alluded to it. In August a combined AFP–FBI–POLRI transnational sexual servitude taskforce had finally cornered a gang of child slavers in an old factory. The Aussie and American cops had only got that far because of the amount of information they'd kept from their POLRI colleagues.

In the last hours before the planned raid, the slavers were tipped off. When the Aussies and Yanks got there, the place was already ablaze, destroyed, the 'evidence' with it. The evidence in this case was an estimated eighty-three children, both genders, ages ranging from four to twelve.

Mac only knew how distressing it had been for the cops because his friend Jenny Toohey had described finding a dumpster behind the factory. It was filled with soft toys.

Women cops had an ability to turn that sort of thing into a stronger resolve to catch the bastards. Men found it much harder for some reason; hit the piss, got depressed, didn't see out their rotation. Jenny had been up here for years. She was one tough girl.

'Take it easy, champ,' Mac said as Keith shook and left to get back to his boys. He'd bet Keith already had an application in for stress leave. This just wasn't his go.

Mac leaned back, had another look at the Nokia. Three messages: the first two from Garvs – office shit.

The last had been left little more than an hour ago.

Diane!

His heart raced as he listened, flustered. Diane was in Jakarta, staying with her dad at the British compound. Had some big client to schmooze. Mac smiled, he could have listened to that voice for hours.

Then came the clincher. 'Richard, I didn't hear back from you about my, er, message. Did you get it? I'll be back on Thursday – can we talk then? We could go for a drink, right darling?'

Relief poured through Mac and he laughed at the ceiling – he adored the way she called him 'darling'.

Mac tried to sober up. Diane thought he was in Sydney. He'd surprise her, but not now. He had no idea who was sitting at what listening posts.

He ordered a coffee, asked for Saba. The bar manager came over, went to a phone, came back, pointed at a small CCTV camera up near where the Glenfiddich and Grey Goose lived. Mac looked at it for four seconds. Looked away.

Sipping on the coffee, Mac waited. Saba's bodyguard came to the entry of the toilet corridor wearing a white trop shirt that didn't hide the gun bulge as well as his last ensemble. He looked around slowly, glanced briefly at Mac, flicked his head very slightly.

Mac moved to the corridor and down to the security door. Took the pat-down and scraping behind the ears. They walked into the office, out through the door that Sawtell had walked through five days earlier.

The room they entered looked like a store for booze and snacks. It was cool, musty. Behind piles of cartons the bodyguard opened a security door using a key from a retractable key chain and hit the fluorescent lights. There were a dozen black strongboxes bolted to the wall, each one the size of a mid-range TV set. The bodyguard made straight for the one marked 9, pulled out his key chain again, rattled through some keys and opened the box. Then he walked outside, standing where he could see Mac. He snarled slightly, reminding Mac of the small detail: this guy's uglier brother was a professional cage fighter in Manila.

Mac slid out the drawer on its rails, lifted the lid which was hinged at the rear of the drawer. In the box was a typical assortment of passports, drivers' licences, credit cards and guns. There was also a clear plastic seal-lock bag filled with cash. He grabbed the pile of Singapore dollars, and gave it a quick fan. He reckoned maybe three thousand. Trousered it. He grabbed a third of his rupiah, stashed that too.

The passports, drivers' licences and credit cards were strapped into single units, held together lengthwise with rubber bands. He picked up one. The rubber band held a small stack of cards in the name of Brandon Collier, Vice president, Sales, Orion Forestry Consulting (Aust.). There was a passport, a NSW driver's licence and a Visa card.

Mac had always worked under two main identities in this part of the world, but this was not one of them. He'd never used Collier as a name and the Service didn't know it existed. Most people in his business had some sort of fail-safe identity and credit card. Some had their 'pensions' stashed in credit card accounts under these names, which ran out of banks in the Cook Islands or Fiji.

Mac didn't have a 'pension'. What he had was a valid incorporation of Orion Forestry Consulting in Singapore, with a DBS business Visa card in the name of Collier and Orion. The bank account was legit, so was the company. An old associate of his – Benny Haskell – had done the incorporation. Benny was one of the accountants who worked on the original incarnation of AUSTRAC, the Australian federal government's money-tracking neural-net. Now he had a thriving banking-domicile practice, with an Australian solicitor, in Singapore. Benny had spruiked the taxation benefits of incorporating in Singers but Mac had just wanted the banking secrecy laws. Besides, when his days with the Service were done, forestry consulting might be his fallback gig. There was certainly enough work to go around if things didn't work out as a university lecturer.

He trousered the whole bundle, went to another bundle and pulled out a laminated ID card. It was an Australian Customs Service ID in the name of Richard Davis, allowing him access to bond stores and restricted parts of airports and container ports.

Picking a black toilet bag out of the bin, he motioned with his hand to the bodyguard. The guy swaggered over.

'The Heckler, thanks, champ. Plus a clip,' said Mac.

The bodyguard pulled out the Heckler & Koch P9S in the black nylon hip rig. Picked up one clip.

'Can you load it?' asked Mac.

The bodyguard sneered, handed Mac the clip. Mac loaded it himself from the box of Winchester .45s in the bin. In Saba's bar only one person ever touched a firearm, and that was Saba's bodyguard. Mac wouldn't get his Heckler until he was standing in the back alley.

Mac stood on the back steps, unzipped the black toilet bag. The bodyguard put the Heckler in it, looked left and right, stood back and shut the door.

Mac walked the blocks to the Aussie compound. He had a mild sense of being followed but it felt like light surveillance. Felt like Garvey doing something for Mac's own safety.

A knock sounded at the door at 2.15 am. Mac was showered, shaved and had only a mid-sized hangover. It was Garvey's lackey, a bloke called Matt. They piled into a red Commodore, hit the airport freeway.

Matt was about thirty, tall, Anglo, educated. He was confident without being full of himself – a good lad to put on Mac's case. Mac wondered if he had someone on the plane with him, or another tail waiting at Singers. Wondered if Garvs was just testing Matt, to see if he had the ticker.

They parked in the consular annexe of Soekarno-Hatta, went through the consular security clearance and into the consular ticketing for Qantas. The girl behind the counter was a pretty local and Mac hammed it up with a back injury, trying to get an upgrade to Singers. The federal government had an eight-hour policy for travelling business class: you flew under that and you flew in the back, unless you were SES. Jakarta–Singers was way under eight hours.

The girl didn't smile, didn't react. But she gave him the upgrade.

'Wish they did that for me,' said Matt.

They walked into the main concourse. It was 3.20 am but the place was packed. Lines for the Qantas flights stretched out of view. Kids moaned, dragged on their mums' arms. Other kids snored on top of bags on the trolleys. They passed a group of Aussies with a state hockey team emblem across their cabin luggage. Mac slipped the wink to one of the blokes. ''Zit going, champ?'

Mac walked towards the huge security clearance section that transitioned passengers from the public concourse into immigration and the airline lounges. It stretched the width of the building and looked like a tollgate for humans. POLRI stalked back and forth with the low-hanging peaks on their caps. German shepherds, beagles, metal detector wands. Colt M4 carbines hanging across their chests. Mac made a note of the M4. The Indon government's anti-terrorism unit, Delta 88, had been equipped by the US government with flash new toys such as the M4 assault rifle and Mac was glad to see they were actually being deployed rather than sold on by a general with a Ferrari habit.

Mac turned to Matt, shook his hand. 'Thanks, champ. Let you get back to sleep now, huh?'

Matt smiled. They both knew Matt was going straight back to a listening post where he'd give regular updates to Garvs.

Mac had replaced his wheelie bag with a small black Puma backpack that had been lying in his room. Inside was the Service Nokia and the toilet bag, minus the Heckler. That was in the mail with his ovies and Hi-Tecs, posted from the Australian diplomatic compound by the night manager, Conzo. Conzo was an Indon who Mac had helped out a few times with money after his betting sprees at the Pulo Mas track in North Jakarta had gone awry.

So when Mac gave Conzo a package at midnight and asked him to mail it to Mac's PO box in Jakarta, Conzo was straight on it. He parcelled it and addressed it, put a franking stamp on it and put it in the mail bag, all the while telling Mac about his latest losing streak at Pulo Mas.

The 38s were too big so Mac asked the shop girl to bring him the bone-coloured chinos in the 36. The girl swung the pants over the change room door. The 36s fitted. He left them on, along with his new navy blue polo shirt, before heading into the Ralph Lauren shop barefoot. Sitting on a fitting seat he asked the girl to bring over a pair of dark brown boat shoes – size 10. Asked for a couple of pairs of socks and got a brown leather belt.

It all fitted, it was all good. Mac asked the girl if she could also hook a pair of dark blue 38 chinos and an XL white cotton Oxford shirt from the racks.

She was quick. He put his backpack in front of him on the counter to shield the transaction, put his blue chinos and white shirt in the pack. His old clothes went into a shop bag. He sauntered out into the giant mall that Soekarno-Hatta had become and walked straight up to his tail, an Aussie Vietnamese girl in a red Nike T-shirt, blue jeans and runners who was pretending to read the *Economist*.

Mac sat down beside her. She was mid-twenties, just learning her stuff. 'Don't tell me – too smart for the federal cops, too good-looking for the diplomats, huh?' he said.

She looked up from the magazine, said, 'I'm sorry?'

'The spying thing? Thought about the cops, thought about foreign service, but settled on this. Can make a real difference, right?'

The girl feigned confusion. She was good at it. 'Umm, sorry – think you got the wrong person.'

She had a nice voice. Low register, good long vowels. Smart but sensitive.

'Your mum doesn't get it, right? You can't tell her what you do, but you can't get engaged to that lawyer she's lined you up with. Holy shit! Not the lawyer.'

Mac was going for the mum connection. When he'd first seen her he'd noticed a slight pronation of the left ankle. In gait psychogenics the Israelis would say she had an ongoing dispute with her mother. Mac guessed it was to do with having some bullshit corporate cover yet a total lack of interest in suits.

The girl turned to him slightly, said, 'Like I told you, mister, you got the wrong person.'

Mac was almost there. 'By the way, the worst thing you can do in this business if you're a girl? Sleep with a colleague. Doesn't matter how profound it was, the blokes will call you a slut.'

Mac let it hang. He waited. Waited. The girl looked into the distance, she turned back. 'Like I said . . .'

She trailed off. Looked away.

Mac shook his head. 'Even if he said he loved you.'

He watched her eyes refocusing.

'Wasn't Matt was it?'

She kept looking away.

'Okay,' said Mac. 'Gimme the mic. I'll have a chat to the bloke.'

He pretended to be going for the ear device that Mac was guessing was hidden by her hair. The girl pulled back, put her hand to her ear.

Bingo!

'Don't worry,' said Mac. 'I'll tell him what's what.'

The girl was on her feet. 'Like I said, sir, I think you have the wrong girl.'

She picked up a blue backpack and walked away. He watched her walk across the mall area, down past the Gucci and Vuitton stores, along the cafes and up to the toilets. She looked into shop window reflections to check on him, then she disappeared into the ladies.

Mac had one minute before she finished her conversation with Matt, was yelled at for losing eyes, and then came back out.

Mac turned, unzipped his backpack and took out the Nokia, while heading across to a Swiss watch emporium where the hockey players were ogling the price tags. He had a look at something that cost $5200, looked closer, dropped his clothes bag, bent to pick it up and deposited his Nokia in a mesh water bottle holder that sat on the side of one of the hockey boys' bags.

Had another look at the $5200 watch – was happy he had a G-Shock habit.

Scooting over to a garbage bin, he dumped his old clothes out of the plastic shopping bag, put his backpack in the bag, then sat back down where he'd been with the girl.

The conversation he'd had with Garvs the night before was too pat. His one-time friend had made a point of giving the Nokia back to him, which Mac took to be a decoy gesture – it meant Garvs was going to microdot Mac's clothes. Microdots were the size of a very small bindi and they stuck to clothes just as easily. You couldn't guarantee you'd get conversations off one but they were a great location device. The good thing about them was you could place them on a person by touching them on the sleeve or patting them on the back.

Now Garvs was going to be tracking Mac to the local dump.

The girl came back into sight. Mac's flight was called. He stood, walked past her, winked. Smiled. Stopped.

'The worst thing about spooks?'

The girl said, 'What?'

'All twenty-second wonders, mate. Are they coming? Are they going? Who can tell?'

He thought he saw a smirk, made a wiggling sign with his little finger as he moved off.

The girl laughed, looked away.

Good-looking bird, thought Mac. Shame about the circumstances.

* * *

He reached immigration at Changi at about five-thirty am. He'd made a point of changing his ticket from a transit to a stopover from the public phone at the Lagerhaus. Matt would have checked – would have known. He moved through the arrivals lounge looking for the tail and found it easily: early thirties Chinese-Aussie, white short-sleeved business shirt, black slacks, paper under his arm, pretending to talk into a mobile phone. The bloke wasn't too bad.

Mac moved straight to the gents, the shop bag now in his backpack. Getting into the last booth, he pulled the shop bag and the toilet bag out of his pack, put them on the toilet seat. Then he stripped off his shirt and stashed it in the pack, unzipped the toilet bag and pulled out its contents: passport, driver's licence, credit card, business cards, Customs ID. Pulled out more: three unmarked screw-top jars, a travel pack of Wet Ones, a pair of owl-eye spectacles, a rolled-up dark neck tie, a black plastic hair comb and what looked like a red plastic compass box of the type a student would have for geometry class.

He went to work rubbing the contents of the small jar around on his hands, smoothing it through his hair; forward, back and both sides. Next, he combed his hair, giving it a left parting. Opening the compass box he pulled out a dark, hairy mo and a tube of theatre make-up glue. Squeezing the glue onto the back of the mo, he rubbed it with the tip of his index finger and then pressed the mo down across his top lip.

He put on the specs, changed into the size 38 trousers, used the Wet Ones to wipe around his neck and hands, which were covered in black residue.

He put on the too-large shirt, buttoned up and put on the tie. The spare clothes and Richard Davis ID went into the backpack. The jars and containers went into the toilet bag, apart from one of the unopened jars. The toilet bag went into the backpack. The backpack went into the shop bag. He took his shoes off, put a coin in each, face down. Put the shoes on again, picked up the shop bag and moved into the washroom area. There was one last thing. Pulling a dark contact lens from the jar, he put it in first go. He hated the sensation. Did the other. He was lucky: his pale eyes and blond hair were such beacons in South-East Asia that changing them to dark rendered him almost invisible. He hoped.

He hadn't been more than seventy seconds in the booth. Someone moved quickly to take his place.

He examined himself critically in the mirror, hoping he had at least two more minutes before the tail wandered in. This was the moment of truth: he pretty much matched the photo on his driver's licence and passport. He was now Brandon Collier – a dark-haired, spectacled bloke whose baggy clothes were hiding a pudgy body. The coins would alter his gait slightly, and gait was a more powerful identifier to the human brain than just about anything else.

He went out the door, the coins in his shoes making him walk upright and jerky. The Collier character, Mac decided, was confident about his nerdiness. So he put a superior smirk on his face and walked down the concourse with his 38 pants giving him an elephant arse. He didn't look, just walked like a man with all the time in the world.

Mac found the Singapore Airlines ticketing right beside the transit desk. People were yelling and carrying on. Mac got in line behind a Dutchman lecturing his wife. The Dutchman then took his turn lecturing the Singapore girl. He shrugged a lot about what kind of a country this was, had some long story he wanted to tell, with spittle flying off his lips in that guttural way the Dutchies speak. His wife nodded a lot.

The SIA girl gave customer service a good name. She smiled and nodded and sent them on their way without them getting what they wanted.

Mac stepped up, put down his passport. 'Some morning you're having, huh?'

She smiled. Tired, late thirties, smart. Once pretty, she was now just sexy. Her shift would have started at midnight and she'd be getting all the crazies, the ones who hadn't slept, or who had flown in from the West and had no idea what was happening to their circadians.

'Bloody Austrians,' said Mac. 'How rude can you get?'

'They were Dutch,' said the girl.

'Germans, Dutch. All look the same to me, mate,' said Mac, winking.

She smiled as if she really shouldn't.

'You're not the girl, are you? You know, with the parasol and the geese?' asked Mac.

She looked confused, then suddenly got it. Smiled big, looked at her screen too intently, looked back. 'No – I'm not *her*.'

Mac asked for a one-way to Surabaya.

She asked, 'Economy?'

Mac nodded.

She shook her head. 'Economy's sold out on the 7.35 flight. I can get you on the evening flight in economy.'

Mac shook his head. 'How much is first class?' he asked, fanning out his Singapore dollars on the counter.

She looked back at the screen, chewed her bottom lip. Said, 'I think we can do this.'

Mac flew first class on an upgrade. The food was great, the leg room was even better, the brand new Airbus was out-fucking-standing. He grabbed a cold orange juice, reclined and had a think about what the hell he was doing. Five days ago he'd had a soul-weary feeling about this profession – just wanted it to be over, get into uni life. He could have walked away that morning, jumped the south-bound flight for Sydney, sunk a few cheeky ones, then stretched out in business class and slept all the way into Kingsford Smith. The Service apartment was valid until the end of January so he could have spent some time working out how a mortgage was going to happen. Could have booked into the Coogee Bay Hotel for a couple of nights, lain on the beach, knocked back cold beers, inspected the insides of the eyelids. Could have spent Christmas with his mum and dad at their retirement home in Airlie; taken up some pressies for his nieces, spoiled them rotten, annoying Virginia big-time.

But Mac wasn't going home. He was heading back into a potentially ugly situation, partially blind on info and with no Commonwealth backup. A regular boy scout running into a snake pit.

He laughed out loud at the absurdity of it. At some point every bloke turns into his father.

Mac remembered the summer of his last year at UQ. Virginia had just started uni. She came home with a bloke called Miles who she'd been seeing. Mac had seen Miles too. He wore John Lennon glasses and got around in bare feet, beret and a rat's tail of hair down his back. He had a 'Meat is Murder' T-shirt and a Mao lapel badge on his WWII great coat. Mac had first seen Miles with a megaphone in his face on the vice-chancellor's steps at the St Lucia campus, banging on about Palestine or Guatemala and saying things like 'fascist' and 'pigs'.

Then Virginia turned up with the bloke, who sat there at Sunday lunch telling Frank how it was with human rights and the corrupt pigs and the brutality against protestors. Frank didn't say a word. Finally, Miles challenged him, said, 'Okay – so why are you a cop?'

Frank looked around, put down his fork, said, 'Because it needs to get done. 'Cos most people can't.'

If Mac was honest about why he ended up in public service when he could have done a lot of other things, it had a lot to do with what Frank had told Miles.

But it hadn't helped Frank much. The last time Mac had been in Airlie, the federal election was on and Mac was amazed that his father had become a silent voter – a good man trying to disappear beneath the radar while the criminals who would harass him roamed free.

Frank had looked at Mac a bit sheepish after he told Mac. 'Things sure changed, didn't they, mate?' said Frank.

They sure did.

And people like Mac just kept stepping up for it.

They touched down at Juanda airport mid morning. Mac hired a Honda Civic from Avis with the Orion Visa card. If anything was going to come up strange on a neural-net system, it was going to be a car rented on a Visa card that had been issued five years before and never been used. But someone would have to be looking for that. They'd have to realise that the only way for Mac to slip off everyone's radar would be that he'd assumed a new identity. And when they couldn't find any flags on the IDs they knew of, they'd have to backtrack and go looking for new ones. That's what Mac would do, but a lot wouldn't. And he hoped that the people who were now following him were as hopeless as he used to think they were.

He pulled out of the enormous Juanda rental car parking lot, hit the air-con as the heat started to grip and took the direct feeder on to the Trans-Java Highway.

Then he headed west, for Jakarta.

CHAPTER 17

Mac hit the first toll road, to Mojokerto, paid in cash, keeping off the databases. There were toll roads all the way west to Jakarta and he could have used the e-tag on the rental car to speed straight through and be billed when he took the Civic back. But if Matt found a one-off credit card usage, he could cross check it with the toll road databases and the rego of the rental car. He'd have the time and everything.

He stuck to the speed limit while trucks flashed past him. No excuses for the POLRI to pull him over. A white Commodore followed him for a while so he pulled over, let them pass, got right in behind them. The Commodore took an off-ramp fourteen minutes later.

He pulled into a shopping area, bought water, fruit, cotton buds and nail polish remover. Sat in the car park, removed his mo. He did it slow. If you looked after those things you could get three uses out of them – maybe four if you weren't getting into fights.

He found a local band on the AM radio dial playing covers of Billy Joel, Phil Collins and Olivia Newton-John. Hard to tell if they were in Bahasa or bad English. He'd re-strapped his wrist but the worst seemed to be over. The swelling was on its way down and the lump behind his ear was much better. He felt okay and kept his spirits up by slugging water from a large bottle on the seat beside him. And tried to sort himself out.

Garvs had said, 'It's over.' It was far from that for Mac. He'd been through this before, in East Timor. The politicians and Service lunchers had wanted him out, but Mac had gone back in. That had been a clearer scenario and he'd been vindicated, made the office guys look good. This wasn't clear, and Mac was confused about his next move. He didn't know what Garrison was up to, didn't know what his connection might be to someone in the Service. He needed to know more about Eighty and where he fitted. He also had no backup in the embassy, since there'd be a general low-level alert out for him.

Mac's main role at the Service was in trade, banking and finance. It wasn't what they'd sent him to the Royal Marines for all those years before but it's what he'd spent most of his time doing. That's where Mac overlapped with Judith Hannah. She was tailing the Chinese intelligence blokes who were working on a maritime security system to protect Chinese trade. Indonesia was the key to it, given it had the world's worst piracy problem in the world's most valuable shipping lanes: the Malacca Strait and the South China Sea.

Mac and others – including many people in the US State Department – knew that the Chinese approach to maritime security was ultimately the establishment of a Chinese naval base in Singapore. They'd been hinting at it, enlisting cocktail drinkers to it and generally seeding the idea for most of the 1990s. It was a simple piece of arithmetic: if your booming economy relied on making lots of stuff really cheaply, then you had to be able to transport lots of stuff really cheaply. Every time there was another act of piracy in the South China Sea, another maritime terrorist warning in the Malacca Strait, or another blue-water heist in the Java Sea, you added more slices of a per cent to the costs of your goods. Once those slices rose too high, either your profit margins eroded or your buyers in Italy, Bahrain, Malaysia or Australia had an excuse to buy elsewhere.

And the Chinese economy was not able to handle an erosion of margin.

China had annoyed the region and the Americans by trying to establish a PLA navy base in the Spratlys in the 1990s, as an attempt to patrol the South China Sea. But the People's Republic really needed to have its ships on the Malacca Strait. It couldn't get a base in either

162

Indonesia or Malaysia and the Chinese had threatened to go to Burma, which would mean pumping billions into the Burmese junta's military. It could even end up in an independent Aceh.

But it really had to be Singapore – ethnically Chinese, the unofficial banker to Chinese Communist Party cronies, and the controlling maritime presence in the Malacca Strait.

What had infuriated the PLA generals was the successful lobbying in the 1990s for the US Navy to build a military pier at Singapore's Changi Naval Base. On completion in 2001 the pier was large enough to birth a Nimitz-class supercarrier, making it essentially the US Navy's hub in the western Pacific. Far from dousing the naval base aspirations of the Chinese, it merely intensified their efforts. Even during Mac's time in South-East Asia, Singapore had turned into a lobbying bazaar where every official, professional, business person or public servant now had strongly held views on Chinese naval involvement in Singapore. The Chinese-Singaporeans were either pro- or anti-PRC; they either took their messages from the CIA or the MSS – China's Ministry of State Security. You could go to cocktail parties or symposia where the room was divided in two.

But when Mac knocked this around with what Cookie had told him, he came up with nothing. What did a CIA rogue like Garrison and his Asian friend called Eighty have to do with Chinese maritime security issues?

It didn't make sense.

Mac filled up at the Pertamina roadhouse just out of Bandung, dashed into the gents and pulled out the dark contacts. He bought a coffee and a roti and grabbed a white plastic table by the window. The coffee was crap – there was no excuse given the island they were on. Nibbling on the roti, he flipped through a transportation trade mag that had been left on a neighbouring seat.

Mac read the editorial: about the importance of foreign investment in vital infrastructure. The boring stuff. The kind of issues that Mac did for a living. He was even driving on the result of some of his work: the Trans-Java Highway. It was going to be completed over the next decade and would cost billions more than the government had. The missing link was foreign investment and the problem was a thing called sovereign risk – the risk to bankers that the government would renege on loans, resume assets or fix components of the market so investors couldn't make an economic return on the asset. The way around the sovereign risk issue hinged to a certain extent on internal regulations and anti-corruption measures; but it also rested on the banks being able to own not only the asset, but the land it sat on. That was a big cultural problem in a place like Indonesia, where the ability to control territory or shipping lanes was the source of all power.

Mac and a Malaysian spook worked on it for years and finally found the gap – one of the big Golkar powerbrokers was a firm opponent of ceding land titles to foreign financiers. A Suharto-era, old-school oligarch, he was TNI-aligned and steadfast in his opposition. He was also homosexual. Least, that's what Mac took from the video footage and recordings he had of the bloke. Mac and his counterpart had a word in the shell-like with a couple of lads from BIN – the president-controlled intelligence service, which luckily had its own rivalry with the military-controlled intel group called BAIS. They sat back, waited for the announcement. Later, it was the Malaysian and Aussie bankers who announced they were taking first lick at the low-hanging fruit that was Java toll roads.

He flipped on, a typical Indonesian journal in that it was written in both Bahasa and English. He was about to chuck it aside when something caught his eye, and he flipped back. There was a half-page display advertisement in black and white. Mostly in English, the banner read SURABAYA PORT STORAGE, followed by the acronym SPS. The artwork showed a group of gabled dock warehouses and a cartoon man in overalls holding a key. They were short- and medium-term freight transit facilities, self-service and non-bonded.

Down the side of the ad was a list of Surabaya Port Storage's other sites. Mac felt his pulse lifting. Looking around the room out of habit, he ran his finger down the list and found it two from the bottom: Makassar Port Storage (MPS).

Mac got into character, convinced himself that the number on the MPS key was 46 and fed some change into the roadhouse TI phone. Rang the direct number on the magazine ad. It answered in three. Mac said, 'G'day, that Gerry?'

There was a confused sound at the other end, whispering,

someone who didn't have English handing over to someone who did. A new male voice, slightly younger, came on the line. Said, 'Hello?', like he was asking a question.

'Yeah, sport, Collier here. Brandon Collier from Orion.'

'Hello, Mr Brandon.'

'Mate, having one of those days – had a bunch of stuff in number forty-six. But I've just got the consignment and it's all linen, mate. Those useless bastards got me the wrong goods.'

Silence.

'So I'm trying to work out what's been left in forty-six, if what I've got is the frigging linen consignment. With me, sport?'

'I not know, Mr Brandon.'

'Can't you just have a look for me, champ? I don't want to send someone all the way to Makassar just to look in the damned shed. With me, sport?'

'Can't look, Mr Brandon. No rule.'

Mac wanted to keep the bloke talking in the hope he'd just go and have a peek, see what was in the joint. But there was something else there – fear. They probably had his family or had threatened to do something similar to what they did with Minky if any Anglos or POLRI turned up for a butcher's. Mac decided not to push it. He'd just have to look for himself.

Mac made it into Jakkers in one go, without getting lost. The outer and inner freeway rings of Jakarta were notoriously confusing, especially where they interchanged. Even the locals who drove them every day found them a nightmare. The worst was a three-level interchange which saw extra flyovers being added every ten years to alleviate the confusion that had been created previously with the one below. A total Barry Crocker.

It was early evening when he drove through the leafy affluence of south Jakarta. The Australian Embassy was on one of the grandest boulevards, called Rasuna Said. Mac skirted it, then made for a commercial area. He pulled into the off-street car park of a large private mail centre. It was fluorescently lit inside. Walking in, Mac made for the service counter. A middle-aged Javanese face stared back blankly.

'Georgie, it's me, Richard.'

Georgie's face sprang to life. Big smile. 'Mr Richard – I did not know it was you.'

'Like the hair, mate?' he said, pulling the black hair off his face and smiling.

Mac found that joking about sudden changes of appearance was better than trying to fool people with it – especially people you knew, and wanted to use.

'Mate, I left my key at home,' said Mac, slapping at his pockets. 'How're the kids by the way?'

'Teenagers! Mate! Forget it!'

Georgie waved his hand dismissively and walked behind the bank of mail boxes. He kept talking. 'I say to my son yesterday, "How come you turn fifteen and you suddenly the genius? You're having the lend."'

Mac loved it when Indons went all Strine on him. That was Indon–Aussie diplomacy, right there.

Mac was laughing when Georgie got back in front of him. 'Mate – he knows it all. Just ask him!'

'It true,' said Georgie with the Javanese wide-eyes. 'It true!'

Georgie put down some letters, and the package Mac had parcelled up the night before. Consular mail sure beat the public version. Georgie put it all in a white plastic shopping bag with the mail centre's logo on it.

There was a stack of TI phone cards on a rack behind Georgie. Mac asked for a 10,000 rupiah version, paid in cash and left.

He opened the package in the Civic. Everything was there. He put the Heckler in the centre console and unfolded the blue ovies, praying he hadn't chucked the key in some fit of efficiency. Shaking the ovies, out came the cheapo pre-paid phone he'd bought in Makassar and the black diamond MPS key ring followed it.

He was about to start the Civic, but saw a TI phone booth beside the mail centre and decided to save the pre-paid phone for the more important calls.

Secretaries put him through to PAs, and finally Diane came on the line, 'Richard! How are you, darling?'

Mac could have been a pool of melted heart, right there on the pavement. He choked a little. 'Yeah, no worries.'

She chuckled, she pouted. She was making up with him and Mac was dissolving into his shoes. Total squirrel-grip.

He apologised for doing a runner in the restaurant and Diane apologised for dumping him by voicemail. They had a laugh. Diane said they should apologise a bit more personally over a few chardies. Mac said how was tonight? Diane didn't hear him right. So Mac lied that he was in Utara – the north of the city. Diane was speechless for a few seconds.

'You okay?' he asked.

'Something caught in my throat,' she said, then gathered herself. 'So where are you staying?'

'Well, I was going to check into the Sultan. I've just got into town.'

'Why not stay down here?'

'Where – at the embassy?' asked Mac.

'Sure. I'm in one of the cottages.'

'Okay,' said Mac. 'What's the secret handshake?'

Diane gave him the drum. Said she'd have his name at the gate.

'See you at nine, darling.'

Mac signed off, breathed out. There was at least one game that he was playing in.

He pushed in the TI card and dialled again. Jenny Toohey came on the line. 'Can we talk?' he asked.

She said sure, she was going to be home at seven.

He was about to make another call, but hesitated. The last few days had seen him surviving more attempts on his life than he was happy with. He wondered about tempting fate. Wondered who really gave a shit about Garrison and his snatch on Judith Hannah. Maybe Garvs was right. Perhaps he should walk away and leave the whole wash-up to the politicians.

He looked into the middle distance. Tapped himself on the head with the blue plastic receiver. Tried to make himself see it the cynical way. Tried for once in his life to think like an office guy. But he couldn't make it come. He looked up at the sky, said, '*Faaarrrk!*'

Then he called Lion Air, and booked the morning flight to Makassar.

CHAPTER 18

Mac drove north, dropped the Civic at Avis's downtown depot and took out the plastic mail centre bag with the ovies. He put the hip rig on, letting his white shirt out a little to cover the weapon. Putting the cheapo phone in his pocket he grabbed a cab to the finance district. Got out. Walked both sides of the street. Looked for eyes, swapped taxis and made for the trendy port area of Jakarta.

Jenny had lived on and off in the Aussie residential compound. But a couple of years ago she'd moved to a private residence. It kept her from having to reject advances from workmates but also increased her risk of dying from misadventure.

Mac had the taxi drop him three blocks from Jenny's address. He walked one side of the street, then the other, counter-surveilling, looking for eyes. Satisfied, he walked up a frangipani-lined path to a modern block of apartments in a five-storey building.

He smelled cayenne pepper and coriander – dinner time in Jakkers. Walking up the stairs to the second level, he rang the bell. The door opened slightly and Jenny Toohey's pretty face peeked out. She smiled, opened the door, looked over both his shoulders. Mac stepped in, hugged her. She hugged him back, but with one arm – the other held a Glock 9 mm pointed at the floor. They kicked at the door at the same time. It slammed.

Jenny stood back, flashed a smile. She was looking good – tall, athletic, fresh-faced, dark hair back in a ponytail. She filled out a pair of Levis and a T-shirt like God had poured her in. Mac would have done the business if he didn't have his mind on another woman.

'Ooh, aah – the hair. Decided being brunette makes you sexier *and* smarter, huh?' she said, squeezing his bicep playfully.

''Zit going?' asked Mac.

'Not bad for an old girl.'

'Thirty-five's not old,' he smiled. 'It's fucking *ancient*.'

She laughed in mock rage. 'Need a beer? I got some cold ones.'

'Sure, Jen.'

'So,' she pointed at his crook right wrist. 'You got a girlfriend for that?'

Mac slapped her arse with his good hand. What was it with Australian humour and the subject of self-service?

They walked into the kitchen–breakfast area. It was clean, nice, but not a home.

She cracked two VBs, handed one over. They clinked bottles. Drank.

'Aah,' said Mac, looking at the stubbie like he was appraising a fine wine. 'Nothing quite like the taste of Mexican bat piss.'

Jenny rolled her eyes. 'Queenslanders! The day you lot can explain the appeal of rum, then you can slag off our beer.'

'Simple, mate,' said Mac. 'Makes everyone look the goods, and we need all the help we can get.'

Mac had a strange bond with Jen. They'd met six years before at a Boxing Day embassy barbecue in Manila. The Ashes was on the telly and a bunch of Aussie, Kiwi and Pommie diplomats, law enforcement and intel types were sitting around in the residential compound getting completely shit-faced on Aussie booze.

Mac was introduced to Jenny via a Pommie bloke who was trying to crack on to her. Jenny was the going-somewhere golden girl of the Australian Federal Police. She was all ironed-out and buttoned-down. Beautiful, and a former university basketball star.

But an ice queen.

The Pom spoke down to him, with a plum stuffed somewhere. He wore a tie on Boxing Day – a wanker.

Mac and Jenny had done the polite Aussie thing, smiled and nodded, tried to make the best of it. Then the Pom told the Aussies how 'privileged one felt to be part of the world's oldest diplomatic legation'. Mac had told the nonplussed Pom, 'Mate, you'd wanna get your hand off it at some point, wouldn't you?'

Jenny had ejected her mouthful of chardonnay through her nostrils. It took her five minutes to compose herself.

The ice queen had a sense of humour.

Soon after they became on-and-off lovers – drank a bit, laughed a lot and joined forces on their loneliness. They liked each other's company.

She cried after sex.

Jenny had gone into the Feds straight out of uni. After doing the usual ambitious-girl rotations she'd ended up working narcotics details out of Darwin, Perth and Brisbane. She was going places. Groomed for management and the SES structure of the Australian Public Service. A place where you flew business class, stayed at the Marriott and no one told you in advance what your expenses claim was going to be.

Jenny was twenty-six when her life changed. During an ongoing investigation into a Vietnamese heroin importation ring the call had come through once again from Australian Customs in Vietnam. A husband, wife and kids were on the same route out of Saigon into Brisbane via Singers. All over again. The personnel changed regularly, but they were always a family unit and the intelligence placed them with the same drug gang.

Jenny was in the Feds' tail car, riding passenger and working the radio. She told the lead car where to go and let the backup car know where they might have to cut in. It was late January, the stinking Brisbane heat making a mockery of the Falcon's air-con. Everyone was over it. They'd been tailing this mob and others from the same syndicate for almost two years and the heroin was still hitting the streets. The one bust they'd pulled seven months before was a roadside swoop in Logan City as the suspects had driven south to their Southport unit. It yielded nothing, except the gang complained about the racist treatment given that the mother had a young baby with her at the time.

The complaint stuck. Official reprimand. The whole suits versus cops bit.

On the day her world changed, Jenny's mind was elsewhere. Six days earlier she'd had a termination at the behest of her fiancé – an ambitious lawyer who wanted 'a life'. She'd wanted the baby.

Jenny was still bleeding and eating Nurofens, pale as death, as she tailed the Vietnamese family south-bound out of Brisbane. Suddenly, she'd had a flash. It went like this: 'The baby!' It was like she was sleepwalking.

She turned to her superior, a guy called Steve Hornby who, in spite of his clumsy attempts at charm, was a good operator with the kind of arrest and conviction record that cops love.

'Steve – the baby. The fucking baby!' Jenny screeched.

Hornby had recoiled. 'What?'

'Steve listen to me – pull them over. Do it!'

'Fuck that for a game of soldiers,' Hornby had replied, his left eyelid twitching, nervous about the vibe and uncomfortable with angry women.

Jenny reached forward for the lights and siren switch.

'Don't you fucking do that, Toohey. That's an order.'

Jenny had never used her looks with her male colleagues – she didn't want the reputation. But she leaned over, pushed her breasts onto his arm, slid her hand up Steve Hornby's thigh.

'Steve, it's the baby. Trust me.'

She sounded crazy and far away, even to her own ears.

Steve broke a forehead sweat, his eyelid going crazy. 'There goes my super.'

Jenny hit the lights and they swooped on the Vietnamese.

Which was how Jenny Toohey came to be standing on the side of the M1 at Rochedale in the early afternoon heat, holding the cadaver of a baby that was stuffed with the highest-grade Laotian heroin. Jenny's mouth open, but no scream, looking down on the baby's dead eyes staring out of heavy make-up.

Packets of brown heroin fell out of the baby's hollowed-out back as Jenny unwound the swaddling.

Steve Hornby on his knees vomiting in the grass, begging for mercy. *Please God, no!*

Feds from the lead car chased the 'mother' and 'father' down the nature strip, the mother's right sandal flying off as she veered towards a wire fence.

Panicked, out-of-breath yells came over the radio system.

Jenny Toohey made no sound, heard only the roar of emptiness in her ears.

She took stress leave and dumped the fiancé. She ducked counselling, didn't cry. She retrained, redeployed as AFP intelligence liaison in an area that hooked from Saigon to Jakarta and up to Manila. Mac happened to know she was very good at what she did, which was busting the slave rackets – what they called transnational sexual servitude.

Mac suspected she was in love with him, but she didn't say it. She let him come and go. Mostly he went. She didn't ask him about Southern Scholastic, she didn't seem to need the details of what he did. In Mac's experience, this was an almost super-human effort for a female cop.

In return, he ignored the salt-crust she left on his chest when he slept over.

She had only one stipulation: 'I don't cry, understand?'

Mac said, 'Good as gold.'

They sat on her dark green canvas sofa, her giving him the look. Like she knew something was up.

'Jen, it's over – I'm out.'

'What? The ASIS thing?'

'Book company, yeah,' he said, winking.

They smiled at each other.

'When?' asked Jenny.

'My official last day is January thirty.'

Jen narrowed her eyes, thoughtful.

'But there's one last thing I have to do,' said Mac. 'And they don't want me doing it.'

Jen shifted forward on the sofa, looked at him with big dark eyes and said, 'I know.'

Mac cocked an eye.

'That bloke – what's his name? – Matthew, sidled up to me today. Asked me if I was in contact with you. Said something addressed for you had turned up in his pigeon hole, you know, and it was the kind of thing he had to give to you *personally*.' She was being facetious, had that same cop disrespect for casual deception that his father had.

They laughed. Sometimes spooks made it way too complicated.

'And you told him?'

'I said, "Matthew, wherever McQueen is hiding I'm sure it's not down the front of my blouse."'

Mac laughed. Jenny could do that to him. Take all the stress and chuck it out the window.

'Holy shit! You're a piece of work, you are.'

'Me?! It's that bloke who's the boob-talker – ask any of the girls.'

Mac ran the options. Either she was part of the program and was carrying a wire, or she had dismissed Matt cold. The third option was that Matt had heard some talk round the traps and had Jenny's apartment under surveillance. Mac would have done it.

'Any tails?'

She shook her head.

Mac trusted Jen. She was highly tail-sensitive. A foreign female cop, living alone in Jakarta, spending her life tracking the kind of crime gangs that would steal children and sell them to paedophile brothels. If Jenny said there was no tail, there was no tail.

A pause opened up. She stared at him, stared at the beer, gave him the hard eye. 'Okay, Mr Macca – you can ask away, but if I say no, then it's no. That fair?'

Mac nodded. He couldn't ask more than that.

He started with the Sulawesi adventure and the Hannah snatch, ending with the Jakarta return and the instruction to get on a plane to Sydney. Only, he kept it vague. If she was a journalist, she wouldn't have been able to write a story on what he told her. No names to follow through on.

She stared at him.

'Something's a bit dodgy about the whole thing,' he said, flustered. They had never really spoken like this. 'I'm – I want to cover-off. I have to . . . I'm looking for maritime activity around Sulawesi in the last week. Not necessarily terrorism,' he shrugged. 'Could be something else. Something out of the ordinary.'

Jenny made a face. That was nothing she had heard of.

'No chatter?'

Chatter was what people in the intelligence community picked up in their rounds but perhaps wasn't the stuff of reports and memos. It was the daily gossip gleaned from being around people, making small talk.

Jen shook her head. 'I've heard that Chinese naval base thing – you know, in Singapore? I've heard that a couple of times in the last ten days or so. It's getting talked up again. But you know how the Chinese are.'

Mac knew how the Chinese were. But he'd been out of South-East Asia for long enough that he wasn't hearing this stuff. If Mac was Garvey, he'd want him the hell out of it too, before he started connecting back into his networks. He'd want him in Sydney, cut off, thinking about his new life.

'No piracy or terrorist alerts in the Java Sea?'

Jen shook her head.

'Malacca? Macassar Strait?'

Jen stared blankly.

'What about Maluku?'

He was grasping. If anyone would know, or had access to the knowledge, it was Jenny Toohey. Her role was to coordinate intelligence from organisations as diverse as POLRI and FBI to the Jakarta Container Port and TNI, the Indonesian armed forces. And her main briefs – narcotics, people smuggling and sex-slavers – were all connected with shipping. She was also one of the few people Mac had ever heard of who had good relations with both BIN and BAIS. Even in the Indonesian bureaucracy and government, you were aligned with one or the other intelligence organisation. You were either the President's people or you were TNI's people.

Mac slumped back, sipped the beer, thought about what he had. Not much. Tomorrow he'd find out what was in the MPS warehouse in Makassar, hopefully. Right now he was flailing. He was also tired. Rooted.

The phone rang. Jen got up, took the call, and by the sound of it the caller was in southern Thailand. Mac could hear the voice: high-pitched, male, hysterical. Jen talked him down, stayed calm. She was a

174

natural leader. Mac had no doubt she'd make it to the upper echelons of the AFP. Maybe take a right turn and end up in PMC.

Suddenly something clicked.

The phone logs!

The phone logs Sawtell had brought out of the hotel in Palopo. Mac had read them, got on the blower to his contact in TI and most of the numbers had pointed to Tenteno. But one had been in the Philippines, in an area of Metro Manila called Intramuros: trendy, expensive, latte-sipping, intellectual. Most important, it was coastal – right on Manila Bay, with views of the container terminals if you were in the right building.

Jen said something gentle to the bloke on the other end, hung up, paused, big sigh. Made a quick call to someone else. This time her tone was less conciliatory. She was remonstrating.

She rang off, walked to the fridge, grabbed two more VBs. 'Thai water police.' She shook her head. 'A bloody worry.'

When she sat down again Mac said, 'What about the Philippines? Manila? Anything out of there?'

Jen looked at the ceiling. 'There was something I read today in a circular. Didn't look like my go.'

'What was it?'

'Heist. Container. Whole shipment lost, unaccounted for.'

'Any ideas?'

'Containers go missing all the time. They're not supposed to. Not after the Yanks went and spent all that money on the tracking protocols. But stuff goes missing. They're ports, and people work at ports.'

Mac looked at her. 'So why was it circularised?'

Jenny shrugged.

'I mean, what was in it? Where was it going?'

Jen stood, walked to the phone.

Mac piped up, 'Umm, not a good idea.'

She clocked his embarrassed tone, did a double take. 'Fuck, Mac. You people are too much! I'm a fucking federal *cop*! A *senior* federal cop!'

Mac looked away. It'd be good to be civvie again – weird, but good.

Jenny walked to the kitchen area, shaking her head. Pulled a Nokia out of a charger, made to turn it on. 'I'm one of the good guys – remember that part?'

Mac looked over, scratched the back of his head. 'Uh, yeah . . . You got a personal one?'

Jenny shook her head, rolled her eyes like *Are you people for real?*

'I'm serious,' said Mac. 'You got a non-Commonwealth phone?'

Now Jen had her hand on her hip, giving him the evils. Giving him the ice queen. Slight tooth-grinding motion in the mouth, she slowly shook her head.

Mac pulled out the cheapo pre-paid. 'This should do.'

Jen stayed where she was. Mac had to get off the sofa, walk to her, pick up her hand and put the phone in it. Close the hand around it. She didn't take her eyes off his face. Not hate – another thing, like his sister Virginia used to give him. Like the time he had to deal with the bloke who'd been grabbing her on the dance floor of a footy club bash, lifting her dress up and that sort of carry-on. Had asked the bloke to stop it which turned into Mac having to give the bloke a little something to go on with. Didn't help that the drunken groper was Ginny's boyfriend.

Mac and Jen stared at each other for thirty seconds. Mac needed this. Jenny didn't.

'Please,' he said.

Jen looked down at the phone, mumbled something, shook her head and dialled AFP, Manila.

Mac had once vowed he wasn't going to foul his own nest. That whatever he was asked to do, it wouldn't involve mixing his personal life with his professional. The Service encouraged people to observe those limits. It was why you didn't tell friends and family where you worked. When he started out Mac had imagined that the issue would be more to do with something that Frank was investigating that Mac would be asked to whitewash. But it had come down to another cop in his life: Jen. He'd just stepped over his line and he felt sick about it.

Jen came back to the sofa, sat down and put a white pad on her lap. 'My guy says it was an unmarked ro-ro container ship, shipping for San Francisco.'

'Ro what?'

Jen shrugged, used to the lingo. 'You know – roll-on/roll-off.'

'Unmarked? You mean no name?'

'That's it.'

'Believe that?'

'Just telling you what he said.'

Mac thought about it: unmarked or non-commercial ships were usually military, government.

'Go on,' he said.

'Not much else. When the alarm went out the whole place was swarming with US Army. A section's been shut down. Media blackout. Local cops on the outer. There was a bunch of blokes with bio-hazards on – not *that* unusual.'

'Serious?'

'Yeah, but there are spills all the time at container terminals and you never quite know what's leaking. They send them out in the suits and breathers just to be sure.'

'US Army is normal?'

'No, it's not.'

'Does your guy know what's in it?'

'Nah – it's hush-hush.'

'Hushed up?'

'Well . . .'

'Come on, Jen.'

She looked at him like she might be going too far.

'Okay. Gary was in Bangkok a couple of years ago, at a maritime security symposium – one of those events that the British put on. Turns out one of the guys who gave a paper at the symposium is running the show at the Manila thing.'

'Know who he is?'

'Gary couldn't be sure, but he was ninety per cent certain the guy was DIA.' Jenny shrugged. Threw the pad aside.

The evening was over. Mac made a promise to himself; that he would make it up to Jen. She'd recovered from her annoyance, but Mac knew there were other things she wanted to discuss, possibly even the future and commitment. It might have been. Before Diane.

'By the way, Jen,' he said, stepping to the front door, 'you don't think I'm racist, do you?'

Jenny thought about that, and said, 'No. No I don't.'

They stared at one another, Jen imploring him with her beautiful dark eyes. Mac knew what she wanted. She wanted him to unload, talk about stuff like fear and regret. But he couldn't. He felt blocked up, like he had a piece of concrete in his throat. As her eyes softened, his were getting harder – she reached out, he defended. He wanted to tell her he had another bird but he didn't know how to say it.

So he said, 'Thanks, mate,' and did the Harold.

Jen shifted her weight. Both hands in the back pockets of her Levis. He saw her staring at the ceiling as he slipped out. A proud girl.

I don't cry, understand?

Mac took the third cab that stopped. He trusted too-easy cabs like he trusted fish and chips in Alice Springs. He went north to the retail district in downtown.

The DIA connection was odd. The Defense Intelligence Agency was a super-group connecting all the military intelligence outfits of the Pentagon into one collection and counterintelligence bureau. It was extremely powerful and operated in a far less publicly accountable way than the CIA. Globally connected, it had at its heart one of the most powerful networks of any intel organisation, with 1.4 million defence personnel who could become agents, co-optees and sources at any time. It could use more than seven hundred bases and facilities in forty countries. What was a DIA guy doing shutting down a section of Manila's container terminal? What was in the missing container?

It spelled 'United States military' and Mac knew only one person under that heading who he could call right now: John Sawtell.

Mac got on the cheapo phone, called DC and got a listing for Camp Enduring Freedom in Zam. He mumbled the number to himself as he dialled, wondering if one of these days his knack for short-term recall of numbers and names was going to evaporate. You only got it with practice.

The switch came on the line. Mac asked for Captain John Sawtell – US Army Special Forces. After Mac didn't settle for 'not available', the bloke said Sawtell was in the mess. The bloke asked for a contact number and Mac said he'd try back soon.

They got to downtown in twenty-one minutes. It was eight-thirty pm and still somehow the rush hour. Mac got out of the cab with the mail centre bag, walked fast through a large shopping mall and came out the other side, on a whole new block. There was a big cab rank out the front of the mall – lots of Vientas lined up waiting for shoppers, lots of drivers in white trop shirts, black chinos and plastic sandals, leaning on hoods, smoking, talking on mobiles, shooting the shit.

Mac walked the line, the bag under his arm. He was looking for someone in his mid thirties, someone with overheads and middle-class aspirations. Someone with kids.

Someone with shoes.

He focused on one guy, about five-eight, oval face, sensitive expression and a full head of black hair. He was groomed, no sandals and there was a dark blazer hanging against the inside right door. The guy had pride and his cab looked clean.

Mac stopped, gave the bloke a wink. "Zit going, champ?'

The driver was all smiles.

Mac sat up front, had a natter with him. His name was Rami, which in Indonesia could have been his first name, a contraction of his surname, a family nickname from childhood or a name given to him by his local religious teacher when he came of age. You never quite knew in Indonesia. The bloke could have gone his entire life being known simply as Rami and that would not have been considered strange or unhelpful in the archipelago.

Rami was trying to finish an IT qualification at a local technology college, but he had to drive a cab to find the money and that meant studying part-time. Which slowed the whole middle-class dream to a crawl. Rami shrugged. What could you do? Couldn't ask your wife to work when she had two kids.

'Maybe we can help each other out,' said Mac.

Rami dropped Mac in an area four blocks south of the British Embassy residential compound. Mac got out, looked around, walked to the rear of the Vienta. Rami joined him. He opened the boot. Mac put his plastic bag with the ovies, MPS key and Heckler in the trunk, jamming it behind the back seat so it didn't slide around.

Rami shut the boot lid. Mac put a hundred-dollar greenback in the breast pocket of Rami's white trop shirt, held two more US hundred-dollar notes up in front of the cabbie's disbelieving face.

'Here's the deal, champ. Six o'clock, on this corner, tomorrow morning. You get the rest of the money. Sound fair?' Mac winked.

'And no one touch the bag,' said Rami, underlining it with a stern Javanese shake of the head.

Mac had no choice but to trust him. He didn't feel entirely safe without the Heckler but he was close to making something happen with Diane and he wasn't about to blow it by trying to smuggle a handgun into the British Embassy compound.

He walked the remaining blocks, crossed the street, stopped and looked in window reflections. Stalked the few cars allowed to park around the embassies, looking for eyes. Around this area of south Jakarta your average punter couldn't just park and have a nosey-poke. Anyone on the streets would be diplomatic, intelligence, cops.

He doubled back and presented himself at one of the glass-cage gatehouses that had sprung up all over South-East Asia in the past five years.

'Richard Davis. For Diane Ellison. Thanks, champion.'

CHAPTER 19

Mac waited by the gatehouse in early evening heat. The sky was orange-red – a tropical barn-burner of a sunset. Behind the bullet-proof glass a big Anglo was looking over the shoulder of the local guard, checking out Mac's passport. The big bloke looked up at Mac's face, looked back, leaned further over the guard's shoulder, flipped at the passport and looked up again.

Mac winked. 'Look better with the goldilocks, huh?'

The mo was in the container, the contacts were in the jar but his hair was still black.

The big Anglo was expressionless.

Mac had him as former HM Customs, intel section – big, beefy, red-faced sort of bloke who clocked faces like he was a biometrics computer. It had been a long day and the last thing Mac needed was some customs robot getting in his face about where he'd been and what he'd been up to. Just some old chat, maybe throwing in one of their trick asides about swimming at a Darwin beach or the famous train journey from Madras to Chennai. Mac had had his hairy moments in many airports with blokes just like old Beefy here, and he didn't have the ticker for it after the kind of forty-eight hours he'd just been through.

Beefy smiled, said, 'No luggage, Mr Davis. Not intending on staying?'

'That depends on her ladyship, champ. She might get lucky.'

Beefy snorted, smiled, slipped the passport back under the glass. Mac gave him the wink and giddy-up. Beefy stepped away from the bullet-proof screen, shaking his head slightly, keyed the radio handpiece on his left shoulder, mouthed something. Came back, flipped his head to the right. The pedestrian gate slid straight back into the gatehouse. Mac said, 'Thanks, lads,' and walked into the residential compound of the British Embassy. Just another Aussie sales dickhead with a thing for tall blondes.

He didn't have to wait long, only about ninety seconds before a sapphire-blue Jag came around a corner between a stand of topiary. Mac went to get in the front, by habit, then realised Diane was in the back. He slid onto leather, into air-con, smiling at the figment of his marriage fantasies.

''Zit going? All right?'

'Ooh, the hair, Richard! I love it!' she said.

Mac felt the car surging forward as he was pulled down into a kiss. He felt Diane's breath blowing out of her nostrils like plumes of desire and he got his arms around her waist. She shifted her mouth to his jaw and then his left ear, which tickled.

'God it's good to see you again,' she whispered, then kissed him on the mouth, slipped her right hand down to his bicep, sinking her talons into it.

Mac finally came up for air. They were driving what he reckoned was north. He pushed his hair back, thinking, *Do I have enough Brut on? Is she going to get black dye all over her hands? Is it kinky if another bloke's sitting two feet away?*

Mac sat back, took her in. She was smiling, pale eyes sparkling in a strong, oval face. Intelligent and not cowed. She filled out her sky-blue linen dress, which came to just above the knee. Black shoes with a single strap, cute little gold watch on tanned skin. Mac was used to birds in Levis and runners, boardies and tank tops. Diane was a whole other level.

'Where we going?' he asked.

'Sunda Kelapa – that fish place we got trashed at once.' Diane said it with an air of smiling collusion, as if her world was made of two people and Mac was one of them.

Sunda Kelapa was the original fishing village Jakarta had been built around. It was still used for fishing and was probably the only part of Jakkers where you'd see a man in a sarung who wasn't hamming for a tourist photo. It was old-school Jakarta and after dark there was a chance of being mugged. Mac let it go. He wanted one night of non-paranoia. He'd leave the worrying to the driver, who seemed to know what he was doing.

He was back with Diane, as if Sydney hadn't happened. He was giddy, intoxicated with it all, in love.

They ate up large: curried crab, salty fish, prawns in the banana skins, buckets of goreng. The whole Javanese bit. Being back in Jakkers seemed to have a calming influence on both of them. In Sydney, Diane's personality had brought out a chip on Mac's shoulder, a nagging sense that he may not be good enough for a diplomat's daughter. The morning that had started with the interview at the University of Sydney, and included being tailed, and ended with that awkward lunch, was really just the climax of a lot of worries that Mac had been feeling in Sydney. The fear of not being able – or allowed – to make the shift to civvie life. Or the deep-seated suspicion that perhaps some people just weren't equipped to have wives, mortgages and financial planners. There was also the loss of control, the ebbing away of his carefully crafted internal walls and walls within walls. He knew it was happening and he blamed Diane for how weak it made him feel.

Maybe it was just the age-old worry, that he'd ask the girl to marry him, and she'd laugh, say something like, *You? Why would I marry you?!*

All of it had come together that morning, and he'd taken it out on Diane, right at a point where she wanted to talk about where she fitted in his future – which, now he was relaxing over a meal in Jakarta, seemed to be the most acceptable thing a woman might want to do when she'd been going out with a bloke for six months.

One of the things Mac had always liked about Diane was that – chips on shoulders aside – she didn't make him feel like a pig. She ate as much as he did, also spoke with food in her mouth and laughed about how gross that was. She was one of those women who jam their fork into a piece of food and feed it to their bloke.

The inferiority bit was all in his head.

They were actually a right pair: sinking cold Singhas, taking the piss out of uptight Germans at exhibitions and laughing about their short-lived break-up.

'I'm sorry about the whole voicemail thing, darling,' she said, grabbing his forearm. 'What a cliché! I can hardly believe I did that!'

Mac apologised for avoiding a chat about what they might do in the future. And for doing the Harold Holt.

'The what?' she asked, laughing.

'You know – the Aussie prime minister, the Chinese sub, the MSS?'

'Tell me more.' She widened her eyes.

'Then I'd have to kill ya.'

Mac didn't know why he'd said that. It was an intel in-joke; you only really said it to someone in the community, someone who already knew. He was exhausted. Maybe he just wanted to come clean with her? Maybe that was part of his anxiety the last time they'd met?

Mac changed the subject. 'Remember that wine we got here last time? Time for a comeback?'

Diane made a face that said, Bad idea.

Mac remembered how they'd sunk a couple of bottles of the Balinese white muscat a few months ago. They'd got so drunk that Diane had tried to go for a swim in the harbour and had got down to her bra and undies before Mac and her driver could bundle her back into the car. The muscat gave Mac a hangover that would kill a wild brown dog, and Diane had an IT trade show to attend the next morning which she could only endure through a pair of very dark sunnies.

So they ordered the wine.

Carl, the driver, who had been standing against the wharf railing since they arrived, approached the table as Mac gave back the wine list. Carl looked at the owner, pointed at the table. The owner nodded, came back with the bottle, showed Carl the seal. Carl nodded, stepped back to his railing and let the owner cork the bottle and pour.

Mac gave Carl the wink. 'Thanks, champ. Anything we can get ya? You eaten?'

Carl shook his head, his hands hovering over a black pouch-bag slung around his waist that was actually a disguised holster. 'No thanks, Mr Davis. I'm right.'

The British used ex-soldiers and ex-cops for their diplomatic protection details. The main risk in Jakarta, for people like Diane, wasn't terrorism. It was snatches. And Carl had the body, the presence and the handgun that made Asian kidnappers pause. He was about five-eleven, one hundred kilos and filled out his jeans and polo shirt like he was made of arms and legs and nothing else. His presence said, *I don't hesitate and I don't miss.*

Mac relaxed with it, and drank.

They fell into Diane's cottage a little after midnight. Carl had already entered and done his recce, gun drawn. Diane held Mac against the vestibule wall in a deep kiss. She tasted of Balinese muscat. Smelled of shampoo and sea air.

Carl walked past them, stood at the door, cleared his throat and looked at Diane. She rolled her eyes. Mac came forward instead, shut the door and turned the key to deadlock. Asked through the door, 'Only one, mate?'

Carl said, 'Corner bolts, if you would, sir.'

Mac slid the big stainless steel bolt at the bottom of the door into its hole in the floor, pushed the top one up into its steel slot above the doorjamb.

'Thanks, sir,' said Carl.

'Goodnight, mate. Thanks for everything.'

Mac pulled Diane onto his chest, so their faces almost touched. They were both naked, sated. Looking at her, he wrestled with the idea of coming clean. But it felt wrong. Like going into a forbidden zone. He hadn't even had that discussion with his parents or sister.

He wasn't sure how he was ever going to unhitch himself from the lies, starting with his name. Diane had been forthcoming about her past: the dropping out from Cambridge, the attempt at being a kept woman in London in her early twenties, the Kuwaiti fiancé and her unanticipated drift into the world of IT and high-level sales – something she was good at and well rewarded for.

Mac couldn't tell her that kind of story about himself. Where would he start? With ASIS? The Royal Marines, Desert Storm, East Timor, the Bali bombing? Abu Sabaya? There were whole chunks of his life that not even Garvs knew the full story about.

He decided to try a smaller bit of candour.

'You know, that day at the restaurant in Chinatown? In Sydney?'

Diane nodded.

'I had a ring in my pocket. I was going to ... umm ... you know ...'

Diane smiled at him. 'Do I?'

'I was going to ask you to ... aaah, be my fiancée.'

'Marry you?'

'Aaah, yep.'

She raised her head, smiled. 'Really?'

'Yeah, but I couldn't. It's why I did a runner.'

'Why?' Diane pushed his hair back, looked from one of his eyes to the other.

Mac almost said, *'Cos I've been bullshitting. Lying to you.*

But he didn't, pulled himself back.

'I was too scared.'

'You silly thing,' said Diane, her eyes reflecting disappointment.

Mac lay awake while Diane snored softly. She'd taken it well. Said she was still in love with him. Said she wanted to think about the marriage bit.

He was in love but confused. He found himself wondering about privilege and pecking orders and the level of personal security you got when you were born into the right world.

He lay there thinking that it would work out just perfect if Jenny was assigned a Carl. Someone to guard the perimeter and let her relax at a restaurant: no more asking for the table furthest from the front window, no more demanding the seat that faced the door. Whenever he'd gone to a restaurant or movie with Jenny, she'd worn a holster-bag just like Carl's. It sat on her lap like a security blanket.

He'd never mentioned it to Jen. Never told her that if she got rid of the disguised holster, she might get herself a bloke.

CHAPTER 20

Rami was early. So was Mac. They greeted each other on the arranged corner. Mac stood at the back of the cab, looked around for eyes while Rami popped the trunk from the driver's seat. Mac leaned in, opened the mail centre bag and checked the five strands of cotton he'd left across the velcro strap of his holster. The cotton was intact. No one had been in there.

Mac walked to the driver's seat, gave Rami one of the hundred-dollar notes and said, 'Gimme two minutes, champ.'

He leaned into the trunk and opened the toilet bag, got the moustache on in twenty seconds, took longer with the contacts, but still fast for a bloke with no mirror. Trousering the passport and key, he tied the neck-rag and then pulled out the black backpack and pushed everything into it.

There was a sudden racket, like mortar shells dropping on their tails and firing. *Clunk! Whoosh! Clunk! Whoosh!*

It scared the shit out of Mac, who hit his head on the boot lid as he swivelled to find it was just the sprinklers going on at exactly six am, all the way up and down Embassy Row. He was labouring under a hangover that felt like a croc was trying to death roll his brain. The airport was going to be a hoot.

They made good time to Soekarno-Hatta. The air-con worked,

which put a few more miles in Mac's white shirt and chinos. He'd definitely have to buy more clothes in Makassar.

He made small talk with Rami, who was excited about the money. His missus was excited too. Mac asked him to promise to use it for college. He had lived in South-East Asia long enough to know that when the missus of the house was a piece of work, it often meant household wealth was being siphoned to her parents or sibs. A weak husband was not a good thing to be in this part of the world.

Rami promised, laughed as he saw Mac's worried expression, and said, 'My wife is my friend too, yes? But it always good to do what she says.'

'When she says it, right?' said Mac.

Rami laughed, genuinely amused. 'You married too?'

'Nah, champ – but I'm aware of the general situation.'

Mac stood outside Terminal 1, Rami's cab waiting in the honking traffic of the set-down area. Mac's pack was in the back seat and Rami was waiting for the last hundred-dollar greenback – waiting for Mac to take a quick recce and come out with the all-clear. The airport police and POLRI were at the other end of the apron and Mac reckoned it would be at least three minutes before Rami got a face full of German shepherd.

Mac still wore the specs, too-big clothes, his hair dark to match his black moustache. The coins were under his heels, the Heckler in his pack. The fear of God was in his head, helped on by his hangover.

The Heckler was a calculated risk. Domestic flights out of Soekarno-Hatta were checked by security, but they would be selective in their searches, and Mac was hoping no one would make him for a hijack risk.

Mac held up one finger to Rami, then walked slowly to the air-powered sliding doors of T1. Paused in front of the heavily tinted glass, looked at himself, controlled his shallow breathing, walked into the terminal.

The place was almost packed – long lines at check-in, cafes, ATMs. Not bad for 6.50 am. Soekarno-Hatta had been stealing market share from KL, Singers and Honkers for several years and was now a Top Thirty airport by passenger movements. It suited Mac – he liked busy.

He liked Top Thirty because they were the airports the drug mules targeted, which meant the cops would be looking elsewhere. From Mac's perspective, he wanted the men and women behind the two-way glass in the observation rooms to be looking for the real bad guys. It was another reason Mac flew Lion when he travelled inside Indonesia. The major Indonesian airlines – Garuda and Merpati Nusantara – were housed in T2, the international terminal of Soekarno-Hatta. And it was T2 where all the ghost-corridors and two-way glass and surveillance equipment had been laid out like a customs man's wet dream. That was good for Beefy, but not for Mac.

Mac kept to the wall, staying relaxed in that nerdy way he'd developed for Brandon Collier. He walked down the side of the check-in hall where all the seats were arranged, heard families arguing about why a child couldn't have Coca-Cola, watched businessmen reading the *Jakarta Post*, saw teenagers fiddling with iPods, annoyed to be up so early with parents who so obviously sucked.

Mac kept his eye on the Lion Air suite of check-ins. It looked clear. No eyes, no magazines being read upside down. He walked further, to the end of the T1-A section and as he was about to turn, saw something.

Totally froze.

Held his breath.

Hangover throbbed.

Walking south from T1-B, straight towards him, past the Air Batavia and Kartika Air check-in suites, was a person he recognised. Shapely, tall, very good-looking. Female. Vietnamese-Australian.

Mac was hungover enough to actually say 'Fuck' as he turned as smoothly as he could.

A disaffected teenager looked up, a bit spooked that an oldie was more disaffected than her. He took off back to the Lion Air suite and around the corner. Back into the set-down area. He did it smooth but he was burning inside. The ASIS bird was there, which meant Matt was there.

He stood on the set-down apron, saw the sun coming up, felt the heat and humidity starting to move into the air. Airport police were walking the lines of cars and cabs, telling drivers to move on: beagles for drug mules, German shepherds for those with a reading disability.

Mac stared at Rami's cab, coming to grips with something he'd just seen in the terminal. Something other than the ASIS bird. As he'd walked to the doors, he'd looked over to his right, where an Aussie surf clothes emporium beckoned shoppers with massive posters of young Anglos enjoying their unfettered lives in southern California and Surfers Paradise.

Dominating the main window was a huge poster of Kelly Slater, the famous Californian surfer. The surf company had named their latest range after him. They called it 'SL8TR'.

Mac's thought process had gone like this: that's a clever marketing ploy in South-East Asia because of the acronyms and contractions the locals use with one another's names. They contracted long multi-word names into one short one, such as Hispran, the Indon-Islamic leader from the 1970s whose full name was Haji Ismail Pranoto. Or they used acronyms, such as with Indonesian President Susilo Bambang Yudhoyono, known as SBY.

Once they had their contractions or acronyms, they filed them down so they became a word in their own right. If you were an outsider, you could pick up the word but never know what it really meant.

Mac stared over Rami's cab, out over the sprawling megalopolis of Jakkers, where the brown haze was starting to rise. Acid rose in his throat. When Minky had told him the name of the person who had snatched his daughter, he had said 'Eighty', but Minky didn't mean eighty, like the number. He was using an acronym: AT, the teenage nickname for an aspiring actor from the southern Philippines, whose name had been Aldam Tilao – before he'd changed it to Abu Sabaya.

Abu Sabaya: pirate, bandit, terrorist and the most dangerous man in South-East Asia. Supposed to be dead.

Peter Garrison and Abu Sabaya. Two psychos. Two very, very smart psychos. Now acting together? In league with someone in the CIA? Being helped by someone in ASIS? Or both?

It scared Mac. He had to get to Makassar, start putting this thing together.

He looked to his right, saw POLRI approaching, a shepherd straining on its leash.

Rami was in front of him. Right there in front of his face. Mac came to. Shook it off.

'You okay?' asked Rami.

Mac nodded, knowing there'd be little colour in his face, that his pupils were probably dilated. He turned to the POLRI guy, smiled, tapped his G-Shock. 'My fault, officer – moving on now.'

Rami turned, saw the POLRI guy and the shepherd and ran to his cab. Mac followed, leaned into the back seat, picked up the black pack.

'Here you go, champ,' said Mac, handing over the last hundred-dollar greenback. Rami smiled, took the money, turned to his right, wound down the window to talk with the POLRI guy. Mac noticed Rami averting his eyes, not actually looking at the cop. A car parked outside a public building was no big deal in Australia. In Indonesia it meant plenty, and Rami obviously didn't want to be mistaken for someone with an ammonium nitrate experiment going on in the back seat.

Rami put the cab into drive, and Mac said, 'Mate, I just realised I need a blazer for my meeting in Makassar. You take Singapore dollars?' He nodded at the blazer hanging on the rear passenger's handle.

'Um, yeah. How much?'

Mac showed a wad. Said, 'There's five hundred there. For the college fund.'

Rami smiled. 'Sure.'

Walking into T1 in his too-small dark blazer, Mac heard an announcement that included the words 'Ujung Pandang, Makassar'. He guessed the flight would be boarding in five minutes, closed in twenty.

He found the biggest group of travellers and mingled through them, up into T1-B and T1-C. His stomach churned with fear but it helped him focus. He hopped from group to group, finding camouflage, then he saw what he was looking for: Matt, walking away towards the end of the T1 hall. Mac watched him stop, talk to the breasts of a pretty Kartika stewardess.

Boob-talker.

He looked back, got on his tippy toes, saw the ASIS bird back at T1-A. Mac realised what Matt had done: he was simply covering the two departure gates that led into the departure lounges. He was waiting for Mac – knew he was heading for Makassar, knew it wouldn't be on the major airlines.

Someone knew.

Mac would have to go through them, and if they'd been doing their job they would have looked through the surveillance tapes from Changi and realised what Mac now looked like.

Mac couldn't get through.

And he couldn't not go to Makassar.

He had about two minutes to make a decision. He hadn't even checked in.

He saw a local bloke in a sports jacket and cream chinos. Black shoes, strong build, wide in the stomach and hips. Five-ten, about Mac's age. Radio on his belt. A cop.

Mac drilled further into the large group, pushed his hand into his pack and came out with the Heckler and the hip rig. He wouldn't have time to set the whole thing up, thread it through all the belt loops, so he stripped the belt component out of the holster and put the holster and Heckler under his belt, just in front of his right hip bone. He took the specs off, trousered them. Then he edged up to the cop, keeping his back to the ASIS bird. Pulling out the Customs ID in his right hand, he folded it back slightly to obscure the picture page.

Then he leaned into the cop, kept his voice down. 'Federal Agent Collier, AFP.'

He showed the bent-back ID, flashing the photo and badging, but looking around – furtive, serious – as he put the ID into his inside blazer pocket. The cop looked Mac up and down, looked into him. Mac faked it out, leaned into the bloke's ear. 'This is embarrassing, but my radio's rooted. One of those useless American jobs.'

The cop warmed to that. All cops have problems with radios. All cops think it's the fault of some office guy who's trying to save money. Mac did a cop-like hands on hips, let the bloke see the Heckler, put his hand out. 'Name's Brandon – with the JOC.'

'Samo.'

They shook and Mac watched the wheels whirr, watched Samo realise that he was talking with someone from the Jakarta Operations Centre. Mac had Samo's attention: this wasn't about catching mules or credit card fraudsters. JOC oversaw the counter-terrorism joint effort between Indonesia and Australia.

'Some pen-pusher's still lying in bed, getting his beauty sleep, huh?' snarled Mac. 'And here's us out here at sparrow's, and they give us radios that don't work!'

Samo shook his head, looked away disgusted. Mac wondered how long a graveyard roster lasted for Jakarta cops. A month? Two months? Working through the early hours hurt no matter what country you lived in.

'They got a million people a week going through this airport, and I have a team of ten! *Ten*! I don't believe. I don't believe!'

Enlisted.

Samo was just getting going. 'You say that to senior person, but they not know. Why they care?'

He did the big Javanese shrug, a gesture that made the Gallic shrug look like a mere tic.

'My people are all over the shop,' said Mac. 'Can I get some backup on my detail?'

'Sure,' said Samo.

Matt and the ASIS bird walked towards one another from opposite ends of T1. Matt was wearing a pair of dark chinos and a pale blue polo shirt. No gun – ASIS officers weren't allowed them unless they were S-2. The bird was in her Levis and an Aussie surfer T-shirt.

Mac was waiting for them. As they got within twenty metres of one another, Mac broke out of the group he was camouflaged in and walked straight up to Matt. Into his face. Pretended to be surprised and scared. He turned, ran.

Matt hadn't been sent out to physically restrain Mac. He'd been sent to do words in shell-likes and escort him to a Sydney-bound flight. But he reacted like anyone would. He gave chase. Mac pretended to run for three strides and saw the ASIS bird start to react towards him. Mac suddenly stopped and turned. Matt was caught unawares, couldn't stop his momentum. Mac grabbed him by the front of the polo shirt and the forearm, pulled the young bloke down on him. They went to the white lino. Matt struggled, but he was on top of Mac and couldn't get off.

Mac smiled in the youngster's face. Said, 'Steady there, fella. Steady!'
To Samo it would look like Matt was attacking.

'Fuck you, McQueen. Fuck you!' said Matt as he grimaced with the effort of the struggle.

Mac made sure he couldn't move. The ASIS bird made it to the two men and didn't know what to do, so Mac grabbed her ankle with his free hand. Made it look like she was stomping him as she struggled for balance.

'Help!' yelled Mac, and Samo's team moved in.

The first one to hit was a female called Suzi. She had a ten-inch snout and a set of teeth like a wolf. She had something personal against Matt's rib cage, thought Mac. The boob-talking thing must have done the rounds.

CHAPTER 21

Mac sat at the front of the 737, which he didn't like. But he did his breathing exercises and attempted to relax, analyse everything, see if there was something about his life he hadn't completely screwed up in the past five days. The Soekarno-Hatta madness had worked out but in the excitement he didn't have enough rupiah to buy the ticket so he'd paid with the DBS Visa card.

The Service and the CIA and anyone else who had been taking an interest in Mac over the last few days would now have a known alias and an electronic funds trail. Which meant he was probably travelling into a welcoming committee in Makassar without a weapon – he'd dumped the Heckler rig in a concourse bin at Soekarno-Hatta after the kerfuffle made the security bulls move in.

Sometime during the next twenty-four hours he'd be going back to the Pantai. An option with its own problems.

Mac munched on fresh fruit, drank bad coffee. Thought about where Sabaya might fit.

Mac had started with the Service at the end of the Cold War, and in those days the emphasis had been on trade, finance, technology and political influence. It was clever, intricate espionage, and it was what Mac was really trained for: infiltration, surveillance, covert ops, snatches, provocations, bribes and blackmail. Mac's mentors were Cold Warriors – people like Rod Scott – and their craft was the subtle stuff. Finding key influencers in South-East Asia and turning them, finding the bad guys and making them doubles, manipulating the media as much as possible – pretty simple when you could 'leak' the inside story to journalists at the Jakarta Marriott, see it turn up in print the next day.

The Service would find where the illegal technology transfers were taking place, and why a rival nation might want a certain microprocessor or titanium self-sealing O-ring. In those days, discovering why the Chinese or Koreans were trying to influence a certain Indonesian political or bureaucratic figure was almost as informative as if you had one of your people inside their organisation.

The main mission was to secure South-East Asia against Chinese political, military and economic hegemony.

That was during the 1990s. The Chinese economy was in double-digit growth and their MSS people were stealing as much mid-level technology as they could from the US, Germany, Japan, the UK and France. The Chinese became brazen but they were stealing 'secrets' that were well behind the cutting edge – sometimes three or four years out of date. Mac remembered the time a group of Chinese posing as scientists had followed a photographic and imaging trade show around the South-East Asian circuit, stealing as much as they could. The scientists were going down to the Agfa booth, pretending to be looking at something and dipping their ties in an improved fixing solution. The Service lost interest in technology transfers when Mac and others realised that the technology companies were employing Indonesian and Malaysian go-betweens to fence illegal technology transfers. The companies were making money from the Chinese by selling them old rope. It took the fun out of it.

Mac had two main identities during this era: textbooks executive and forestry consultant. Textbooks allowed you cover for just about any trade show or discussion with a government official. And forestry gave you access to the interior of countries like Indonesia, Thailand and Philippines while creating an excuse to be around ports, rail yards and trucking depots. In the embassy, he was Alan McQueen, second assistant trade attaché. He was plain old Macca with a face that blended in the crowd.

But when September 11 happened, ASIS hit a snag. The Prime Minister's office needed a ton of intel and analysis, and they needed it yesterday. They needed counter-terrorism intelligence, what was known as CT. Australia was camped on the doorstep of the world's largest Muslim nation, which meant some fast re-aligning of regional interaction. It meant knowing what the hell was going on. And the people with the CT answers weren't the spy agencies of ASIS or ASIO or the military intel operations. The organisation with both the intelligence and operations reach into Muslim South-East Asia was the Australian Federal Police. Which is why Mac had found himself hunting Abu Sabaya. The Service needed to win back some influence and favour in Canberra by proving it could partake in America's 'War on Terror'. And the Service dreamed up an adventure.

Mac was in the middle of a dangerous infiltration of a Chinese front company called Mindanao Forest Products when he was called into a meeting at the embassy in Manila one afternoon. Sitting in the embassy intel section meeting room when Mac walked in was Tony Davidson, director of the Asia-Pacific region. A large grey-haired bloke with jowls who had once opened the bowling for Western Australia, Davidson was the spook who controlled the spooks across India, China and South-East Asia – Australia's most important region. The ASIS station chief for the Philippines, Joe Imbruglia, leapt up to greet Mac, who was dusty, sweaty. Imbruglia had one of those smiles Mac's mother used to give him when friends popped over unannounced. It said, 'Please be nice?'

Mac had liked Tony Davidson immediately. He had a soft hand-shake, oozed power and confidence, and he was one of the few intel chiefs left in the Western world who actually had some operational experience. Davidson had ignored his lackeys, leaned his large forearms on his thighs, and spoke like it was just Mac in the room. 'Tell me about Sabaya,' he said.

Mindanao Forest Products had started as a name on Mac's to-do list. It was a known front company for the Chinese government's attempt to control its offshore primary produce sources, timber being one of them. At some stage Mac was going to find a way to infiltrate some of these organisations, maybe see how far Filipino officials were implicated. Mindanao Forest Products wasn't special in his list. But before he could infiltrate the company, Mac took a phone call which led straight to Abu Sabaya's people.

In one of those weird twists of the intel world, Mac had got a call for Thomas Winton, Goanna Forestry Consulting. It was a Service front company. You gave out the card, you played the part but you never expected to be taken seriously as a professional. Now, a representative of Mindanao Forest Products had asked to meet him. Someone wanted his forestry expertise. He would get to invoice and everything.

The fronts for Mindanao Forest Products met Mac at the Peninsula Hotel in Manila. Mac had taken Kleinwitz, the accountant. The fronts had a problem. They had a forestry concession for Mindanao – the Muslim-dominated island of southern Philippines – but they couldn't log the place.

Mac was confused. 'Why not?' he asked.

'Because they stole our machinery.'

'They', as it turned out, were Abu Sabaya's crew: Abu Sayyaf. The Chinese had got their wires crossed, had thought that some casual baksheesh in Manila would carry weight in the boonies of Mindanao.

It didn't.

Sabaya was an economic force. He was known to the world as a terrorist who ordered bombings, kidnappings and beheadings as a way of securing Mindanao as a Muslim state separate from Manila. But Sabaya also operated a traditional protection service – he was a person who did for foreign loggers and miners in Mindanao what Cookie Banderjong did for those people in Sulawesi. You didn't pay the man, you didn't get protected.

'So why don't you pay him?' Mac had asked.

The head guy had shrugged. 'Don't know where these people are.'

Abu Sabaya was no dummy. The shareholders and CEO of the forestry company were no names he'd ever heard of. His bankers and accountants ran the databases, did the numbers. Couldn't get to the bottom of who ran Mindanao Forest Products. So Sabaya stole all the logging and hauling equipment shipped in for use in the Malaybalay region. Then he sat on US$10 million worth of plant and machinery and waited for the Chinese to come to him.

'That's what the Chinese wanted me to do,' Mac told Davidson. 'Find Sabaya, broker an agreement, get the machinery back and get the logging started.'

Davidson looked at him. 'How you doing?'

'Logging's started. First invoice was paid,' said Mac, then winked.

Davidson laughed, pulled back and looked at a very nervous Imbruglia. 'An intelligence officer out there making money – the accountants are going to love that, eh Joe?'

Imbruglia was sweating, nervous, not a man who understood how field people preferred to interact. All he knew was that one of the most powerful men in Australian intelligence was in his meeting room, having a laugh with his most independent-minded officer. An office guy's nightmare.

Davidson's face slackened. He turned to an offsider who handed him a piece of paper. Davidson looked at the paper, handed it to Mac.

Mac, on high alert, looked at it, whistled low.

'Had a meeting last night with some people from the American side,' said Davidson, leaning back and sliding down in the Aussie hardwood chair. 'They're going in hard in Mindanao – already in build-up mode.'

Mac nodded. He'd seen the circulars about Zamboanga City and the old school site being prepped by US Army engineers. Now he was looking at a plain piece of foolscap with a few simple lines of typeface printed on it. It mentioned a thing called Operation Enduring Freedom and listed a bunch of names as South-East Asia's most wanted terrorists.

Abu Sabaya was Number One, ahead of Khadaffy Janjalani, Azahari Husin, Noordin Mohammed Top, Radulan Sahiron, Abu Sulaiman and Hamsiraji Sali. The remaining names included two CIA agents and a plant from Pakistani intelligence.

Davidson said, 'I saw that name at the top, and it rang a bell. Asked around and someone told me you were on top of this bloke.'

'I wouldn't say on top. I met him once. But I deal with his people,' said Mac.

'Yeah, Alan, but there's no intel bloke I've heard of who would know how to get to this guy. I mean, other than you. Right?'

Mac had looked from Davidson's smiling face to his Service lackeys, and to Imbruglia. What Davidson was saying was, *There's no AFP or CIA person infiltrated to the extent you are.* Davidson saw a chance to win back relevance in the Prime Minister's office. And Mac was getting the tap on the shoulder.

He was used to these conversations. He'd had them in the East Timor thing, in the Kosovo shit, even the Samrazi snatch where at the last minute he'd been fitted up with the missile-homing devices. It was always the same. Mac was never asked directly to do what they wanted him to do. Davidson had flown up from Canberra on short notice to get Mac to kill Abu Sabaya, but he wasn't going to ask him. Not in a taped and logged ASIS meeting room. They never did.

Davidson smiled, leaned forward again, said, 'It's actually quite fortuitous, wouldn't you say?'

Mac said nothing.

Davidson got quieter. 'I mean, given your background and everything.'

Mac became an expert on Abu Sabaya, studying his file, following his MO, doing endless face-to-faces with Mindanao villagers, small business people and cops. He enlisted where he could.

The overall impression of Sabaya? Too smart to catch, too tough to kill. Aldam Tilao wasn't purely a terrorist, he was more a businessman who had seen the level of money flooding in from Saudi, Syria and Iran in the early 1990s and made a commercial decision. Sure, he was a Moro – which was what southern Philippine Muslims were called. But his business was stealing stuff, the same business that entire families and villages around the South China Sea had been doing for a thousand years. Piracy, banditry, kidnap, protection. He'd simply switched to jihadist rhetoric and put his hand out for some of that Middle Eastern cash.

The cash had flowed, and with it his gang and their equipment levels had flourished. At one point, the CIA had the gang at two hundred strong. Which, if you wanted to get technical, was a private army. He gave them a name too: Abu Sayyaf. And with the name came a political goal to make Mindanao a separate Moro state, much to the annoyance of the two existing Marxist-based Moro separatist organisations.

Everything about Sabaya was clever and ambitious. He didn't just kidnap Westerners and ransom them. He rode boatloads of his soldiers into coastal resorts on huge speedboats and took off with twenty tourists at a time. In one year – between mid 2001 and 2002 – Sabaya's crew abducted more than one hundred foreigners, beheading several. He taunted the Americans, and the Filipino commandos who were working with them. It was classic stuff, such as offering to buy the Philippine soldiers' brand-new American-provided M16 A3s and M4 carbines, or making an offer for the Stinger shoulder-launched surface-to-air missile systems. Offer these poor soldiers so much money that they couldn't say no. So when John Sawtell's boys – or the US Rangers or SEALs – had to storm Abu Sayyaf fortresses like Basilan Island, they were facing the latest American ordnance coming straight back at them.

Abu Sabaya went to ground as soon as the Americans arrived in Zam. He moved around in his trademark black T-shirt, jeans, sunnies and black backpack. He was generous and charming. The poor folk of Mindanao loved him. But the main thing going for him was the incredible support of the womenfolk. On Abu Sabaya's patch, there was no sex slavery, no sex tourism, no freak shows with mothers and their kids. Mac had once seen a bloke crawling around a village in the boonies behind Cotabato, with no hands and no feet. He'd asked what was up and a local told him that the crawler had tried to set up a child sex freak show for Australian paedophiles. Abu Sabaya had used his own *keris* – a short, South-East Asian sword.

He loved money and he loved pizza.

Mac's digging finally nailed down Abu Subaya's favourite pizza joint in Sibuco and he found that Sabaya would have his pizza delivered when he was in the area.

Mac had co-opted a worker in the pizzeria, Davey, and given him a couple of the tiny microdot locators just starting to be introduced by the Americans for shipping. Mac had some false starts – hot pizza grease wasn't great for the microdots. Davey also tried to run away. He was scared of what would happen to him if a microdot was found or someone saw him trying to insert it into the cardboard box.

Mac had found Davey and talked him round – even though the bloke had every right to be scared.

When the deal finally went down, the Americans had flown Mac into Zam, dropped him on the quay with Sawtell's boys and the Philippine Navy commandos, the SWAGs. It was a lynching party: no cops, no flexi cuffs, no spare boat to transport prisoners, no evidence bags. No one brought a notebook. The only camera was the Coolpix in Mac's breast pocket.

They closed on Sabaya's pump-boat at speed. A pump-boat is a daggy wooden, high-sided harbour vessel. They're old, slow, running on tiny diesels that give them a top speed of ten knots, if they're running downwind. Mac had watched Sawtell stand in impatience as Arroy made the request for the pump-boat to shut down power and prepare to be boarded.

But the way it happened was this: the Philippine Navy commandos hit the spotties, yelling obscenities, and the gunfight started immediately. The Americans had lost a guy they called Jacko to an Abu Sayyaf bomb a couple of months earlier, and they weren't going to screw around that night. The Philippine commandos had lost their own people.

Having worked with many special forces outfits over the years, Mac knew they always engaged in gunfights with their assault rifles set to 'three-shot' mode. But that night, Mac didn't hear the tap-dancing of three-shot. He heard a roar of lead and felt the air shake with full-auto. The Green Berets and the SWAGs put so much lead into the pump-boat that it listed to port, dipping its gunwale into the diesel-slick waters. Mac remembered the heat and the metallic smell of human plasma, diesel and tropical salt water biting into the back of his throat.

Mac had to ask Sawtell to stop the firing. Arroy overheard the request on the headset, shut it down himself. Then the whoops started up.

Mac grabbed the CIA guy they called Pencil Neck and tried to get him onto the pump-boat. 'Come on, champ, time to go to work,' he'd urged, but Pencil Neck couldn't move. He was vomiting, crying. A bit of human scalp had stuck to the sleeve of his pressed battle fatigues. Mac flicked it off, ruffled the guy's hair. But Pencil Neck was frozen to the seat.

Mac, Sawtell and a couple of Yank troopers went instead, slipping on the blood-covered decks of the listing pump-boat. They turned over bodies, Mac insisting that a semi-submerged corpse be brought to the surface.

Mac photographed faces, some of them torn off by gunfire. One had lost an arm. He found it near the prow, fake gold Rolex glinting under the SWAGs' spotties. They found a black backpack floating, black sunnies inside.

He remembered getting increasingly agitated. Mac had two corpses on the foredeck of the pump-boat, but neither of them was Abu Sabaya. They searched the area for an hour. Mac asked the SWAGs commander, Mig Arroy, to get a frogman down there. He sent down two with their marine spotlights. Sawtell wanted to know what they were looking for.

'I told you – a body,' said Mac.

'We got 'em, ain't we?'

'How many were we shooting at?' asked Mac.

Sawtell called Arroy to his boat where they confabbed. Pencil Neck joined them.

Mac said, 'I've got two bodies.'

'There were five on the pump-boat,' said Sawtell.

'I saw four,' countered Arroy.

'There's a couple of bodies down there,' said Sawtell. 'They're just not floaters. One of them's Sabaya.'

'You know this?' asked Mac.

Sawtell nodded, unsure.

Arroy said, 'There's no way we're going to retrieve all the bodies out here. No way.'

One of Sawtell's guys leaned out of the pump-boat's wheelhouse, waved a blood-splattered pizza box. 'Mmm – Hawaiian Surprise. My favourite.'

Pencil Neck vomited again.

Mac leaned back in his seat as the 737 dipped slightly and headed into Makassar. He churned over the Abu Sabaya story. It had been the turning point of his career in more ways than one. He'd done more positive work in East Timor, but the Abu Sabaya thing had got him a name among the Americans and British as well as the Filipinos and

Indons. It had given him an aura he hadn't wanted, a reputation he'd never asked for. He hadn't killed a major terrorist – he'd stood there and watched a bunch of soldiers cut a bunch of bandits to ribbons. He wasn't ashamed, but he wasn't proud. To Mac's mind, if you wanted to wage war on terror you had to stand for something a bit better. It didn't mean that Catholicism should win out, or that Islam should lose. His mother used to say that being Catholic didn't mean you were always right – just that you'd always try to do the right thing.

The official US–Philippines statement said Sabaya had been killed in a gunfight along with two others, and that four people had been captured. Actually, no one had been captured. It hadn't been that kind of mission. It was the kind of rubbish intel people leaked into the media to make other terrorists nervous, to flush out traitorous types who might be ready to squeal before the supposed prisoners started to sing.

Mac was debriefed but not asked for a report. It wasn't going to be logged, at least not as an assassination. Davidson phoned, congratulated him on the whole thing, laughing at the pizza delivery aspect. Then he'd asked Mac for an informal report.

Mac's report was written on a piece of white printer paper, with a blue ballpoint. It had been pouched to Canberra. It was short. It said, *We killed two Abu Sayyaf people. Abu Sabaya was not among them. He planted a black backpack containing a pair of sunglasses – he wanted me to find it. His death is a hoax.*

As the Lion Air flight descended, Mac wondered back to his paranoia about there being a mole in the Service. He mulled, making connections and wondering who else in the Service had seen that note.

CHAPTER 22

The passengers from the Lion Air flight moved from the heat of the tarmac into the cool of the Hasanuddin terminal. Mac stayed mid pack, looking for eyes.

He passed through the terminal and out into the heat again. It was a minute past eight am and just another day in the Sulawesi steam bath. The cabs were lined up, about twenty of them. People milled, still no eyes.

Mac took the third cab. He gave an address in the south of the city. Taking the seat directly behind the driver, Mac dug the cheapo cellular phone out of his pocket, hit redial and patched through to Camp Enduring Freedom in Zam. Asked for Captain John Sawtell. Sorry, said the bloke, he's in the mess.

Military types never seemed to stop eating.

He sat back, thought about his day. He needed to know what was in the stolen container out of Manila, he needed to know what was in the MPS warehouse. Were they linked? He needed a gun. And he needed to know who was following him right at that minute.

In the driver's rear-vision mirror Mac saw a red Subaru Liberty, staying back two cars. He had asked the driver to go south into the city rather than use the main westward route. The red Liberty was following.

They drove with traffic along a two-way stretch of secondary road, dodging trucks and buses. The old Dutch-built bollards of the bridge loomed and they slowed. Mac turned and watched the Liberty, three cars back now, edging out, looking for a way to get closer.

They made it off the bridge and took a right at the next traffic lights and drove north, the Liberty now only two cars away. They pulled up to an intersection which turned right into the major road into Makassar. It was rush hour in Makassar – eight-thirty and it was jammed up, everyone sounding their horns, trying to get onto that bridge.

Mac paid the bloke with rupiah, tipped big. 'Thanks, champ. One more thing you can do for me.'

They got so they were almost at the front of the queue to get onto the main artery into Makassar. The lights changed to amber. They went red. Mac said 'Now.'

They flew into the intersection, the driver veering to his left slightly to get in behind the last right-turning car. They made it as the main north–south traffic started grinding through the intersection again. The red Liberty had pulled out too, into the wrong lane of the feeder road, but couldn't get out into the intersection. The north–south traffic started moving. Mac's cab moved with it. He looked back, saw the driver of the Liberty with his arm across the back seat, having to reverse. The driver stopped, looked over at Mac's cab. He was Ray-Bans – the thug in the silver Accord behind Minky's. Mac knew that face from another time, too – but where?

There was another guy in the front seat with him. Turquoise shirt, Javanese.

The cab moved onto the bridge that would take them into Makassar and Mac asked the cabbie to get into the left lane heading north. Mac looked back and saw that the Liberty had thrown itself into traffic to the sounds of even more horns. It was now eight cars back.

The line slowed again and stopped. Mac took a deep breath, controlled the fear, and slipped out the rear left door. He jogged along the bridge in a crouch as close beside the left of the stationary cars as he could. He was betting Ray-Bans had his car right on the centre line trying to see where the cab was. He wouldn't trust his sidekick. He'd be giving himself the eyes.

The bridge was three hundred metres long and Mac kept a solid pace. The only way Ray-Bans and his mate could catch him would be to get out and run, or hope the rush-hour traffic abated. If that happened, Mac would slip back into the cab.

The traffic stayed snarled and Mac made it onto ground again with what he reckoned was a forty-car lead on the Liberty.

The intersection on the other side of the bridge was snarled too. So Mac ran straight across it, to the amazement of the locals who peered at him like he might be an escaped lunatic. In late November and early December, south Sulawesi had average temperatures not too different to Sydney. What was different was the humidity, and Mac could barely get air into his lungs. He got to the other side of the intersection, stopped, hands on hips, gasping, looking to the sky like he was searching for more air.

He heard a voice. Looked down. A cabbie was leaning through from his seat, smiling. 'Hey boss. Where we going?'

Mac got into the cab. 'Sedona, thanks, champ. Fast as you like.'

Mac wasn't a fan of the Sedona. It was great for tourists and business people, but for someone always thinking about how to leave the place without being snatched or killed, it wasn't so great. It was a high-rise hotel, for a start, meaning limited escape opportunities. And it fronted a major boulevard, which made it a lot easier for people to put surveillance teams in the area without being picked.

Mac was looking out over the sea and the historic Fort Rotterdam from his fourth-floor room at the Sedona for one reason: the Sedona didn't always check or photocopy passports. So for now, he was Gary Penfold.

Mac turned to the paper bag on the room's letter-writing table, emptying its contents: hair dye, nail polish remover, cotton buds and a bunch of recharge cards for the mobile. He picked up the Schwarzkopf 10N blonder – the most powerful you could get – and had a read of the instructions. Then he set to work on the mo: took his time stripping it with the nail polish remover. Next, he shook out the hair dye pack, mixed the two liquids in the bowl, got into the shower, wet his hair down, and then got out. Stood there in the bathroom painting the 10N onto his dark brown hair with the black brush, latex gloves on both hands. Dark brown, of the type he'd dyed himself with two days earlier, was about the darkest you could use and still reverse it with a chemist product. Anything darker and the only thing he could have used would be a peroxide. If he did that, he'd end up walking around Makassar with his hair all frizzy and screwed up, looking like a punk surfer.

He sat in a chair at the window, a shower cap on his head and a towel round his waist, watching the *pinisi* sailing boats coming and going from the old harbour between the new commercial ports. The *pinisi* boats were ancient working craft that still hauled sandalwood and cloves from the river systems and coastal towns down to Makassar. The G-Shock sat on the table counting down twenty minutes. The phone was plugged in and charging. Mac picked it up and hit redial. He got through to the switch bloke, who recognised Mac's voice. Bloke did a hissy sigh, so Mac wound him up, said, 'Hi darling – I'm home.'

Another big sigh. A click and a clunk. Mac thought he might have to have a word in the shell-like, but then suddenly it was a voice he recognised. 'Hello. Hello!'

'G'day, champ. 'Zit going?' said Mac.

Sawtell laughed. 'I knew it was you. We had Taylor running around worried about some psycho with an Aussie accent.'

'I've been called worse.'

'I bet you have.'

They had a bit of a chat. Mac wanted to follow through on Limo, wondering if he could contribute to the pension that traditionally accompanies a dead soldier. Sawtell said the envelope had already been sealed and went with Limo's effects to his mum. But thanks anyway for the thought.

Then Mac tried to ease Sawtell into things. 'That's some shit you guys have got up in Manila, huh, John?'

'Manila? Yeah, we're on stand-by. SEALs are already up there.'

'Pretty big, huh?'

'It sounds it. Dunno what they have.'

'It's chemical or bio, isn't it?'

Sawtell laughed. 'You playing me, my man?'

Mac laughed too. He couldn't play John Sawtell, as much as he'd like to.

'Where are you, anyway?'

'Lombok,' said Mac.

'How's Judith?'

'She's good. But still wasn't talking when we got into Jakarta.'

'How's she now? She remember anything?'

'Mate, it got taken out of my hands. Delivery boy. You know that movie.'

'Sure do, my man. Sure do.'

'Anyway, mate – I'll let you go. Be careful up there though, eh? They've shut down the whole port. Got DIA running the show, what I hear.'

'Not for long.'

Mac said 'No?', trying to keep the curiosity out of his voice.

'DIA are just securing the place,' said Sawtell. 'Doing the media and government control, what I hear. They're waiting for the Twentieth to come in from Guam.'

Mac tried to remember. The Twentieth? What the fuck was the Twentieth?

'Yeah,' he said. 'The comms guys?'

Sawtell sniggered. 'No, man. CBRNE. The big leagues. All that wacko scientist shit.'

Mac said, 'Fuck!' Couldn't help himself.

'That too. I'm on need-to-know – can't tell my boys. You know how the guys get when they know they goin' to be round that shit.'

Mac did know. CBRNE stood for Chemical, Biological, Radiological, Nuclear and enhanced Explosive. It was the skunk-works end of warfare and your average soldier would pull any sickie, come up with any kind of excuse, to stay away from anything that had CBRNE attached to it. Which was why people like Sawtell were given orders to stand-by on a need-to-know.

Mac's heart was racing. CBRNE! He was getting a really bad feeling about the whole thing. The worst of it was who they were flying in – the Navy SEALs and Green Berets, hardly experts in chemical spills. You didn't pull in special forces to man road blocks and write press releases.

A trickle of Schwarzkopf 10N ran down his temple. 'John – what have they lost up there?'

'Don't know,' said Sawtell. 'But Poppa Bear wants it back.'

Mac stepped out onto the waterfront drive of Somba Opu in front of the Sedona. Palms waved in the breeze that came off the Strait. Makassar was one of the oldest ports on the planet. From a time when all trade was maritime, Makassar sat on the crossroads of the most heavily used shipping lanes: north through the Macassar Strait to the Philippines; south across the Java Sea to Lombok, Surabaya, Madura and Bali; west down the Java Sea to Singapore, Jakarta and Penang; east through the Banda to the Pacific. It was still strategic. Mac wondered where Hannah's expertise had fitted with Garrison and Sabaya. Wondered what the MPS warehouse had in it.

Everything was coming back to maritime.

He was back in his well-fitting khaki chinos and dark blue polo shirt. He looked at his reflection in the hotel's tinted windows and saw thin blond hair, short and pushed back from his face. He looked all right for someone who was exhausted, cut loose and scared to death.

He turned south, walked casually, some inoffensive Anglo waiting for his bird-watching tour bus to arrive.

If it was Mac doing the tail he'd only be looking at four or five hotels, and the Sedona would be one of them. The Pantai Gapura would be another. So Mac wanted Ray-Bans to show himself. The oldest trick in the military book also applied to being tailed. If you're smaller with less firepower, don't meet your larger adversary on the ground of his choosing. Be moving, be erratic, be nimble. Mac knew his adversary was not going to do what he had to do in the street. He didn't want to languish in a Sulawesi lock-up any more than Mac did. So Ray-Bans would set an ambush, do it the easy way.

And Mac would try to make the bloke show himself.

Mac ducked into a side street. One of the old Dutch lanes built in the 1700s. It was narrow, filled with tourists and local traders. It smelled of cloves, of incense and dirt. He found a fish shop, sat back in the shadows and watched American tourists around him.

The owner approached and Mac pointed at the cook in his bolt-hole, saying, 'I'll have what he's having.'

The woman bowed, smiled and yelled something at the bloke in the tiny open-sided kitchen. The bloke looked at Mac. Mac gave thumbs-up. The bloke smiled. Nodded.

Turning his eyes back to the street, he saw what he was looking for. A bloke in a bright turquoise trop shirt with a bulge under the right hip made two passes, looking sideways into the restaurant. The passenger from the red Liberty was late twenties, about five-eight and ninety kilos with a strong upper body but maybe not athletic. Mac thought he detected flat feet. He had a cop haircut and flat cheekbones.

The meal came quick. Swordfish chunks stir-fried in a coriander and chilli sauce, goreng and an assortment of vegies. He asked the woman for a cold Bintang and hooked into the sword.

The cook brought the Bintang out himself.

'Thanks, champ. This is some great tucker,' said Mac.

The cook was chuffed. He smiled and tried to get through the language barrier. 'Merry Carn?' he asked.

Mac shook his head. 'Nah, champ. Skippy.' Mac did his bush-roo impersonation, paws up under his chin.

The bloke laughed out loud, put his hand on Mac's shoulder before making his way back to the woks and gas rings. Javanese social inter-action had two speeds: serious appraisal verging on suspicion, and outright joyous laughter. Laughter got you closer to the gods, so if you could get a laugh out of a Javanese, they owed you.

Mac finished the meal and dawdled with his beer, turning it round and sipping at it. Something nagged at him – some chatter he'd picked up a couple of years ago when he was posted in Manila. His barber, Ramon, had been a National Police intelligence officer during the Marcos era. Ramon cut hair for all the Customs guys, cops and the Port Authority bulls. He was like a clearing house for all the good chatter, all the stuff you couldn't get from an embassy cocktail party or a keyhole satellite feed.

Which was why Mac had got his hair cut there.

He tried to get his memory working. Ramon had once told him about a discovery at Clark, the old US Air Force base about twenty minutes' drive north of Manila. Apparently, in their haste to decommission the joint in 1992, an entire cache of hush-hush matériel had been left behind by the Yanks. There were huge underground systems at Clark. You could drive all day around the base and never see daylight. Someone forgot about an underground storage garage, and ten years later the Philippines government had demanded that the Department of Defense come back and pick it up.

Mac had remembered the last part of the conversation because Ramon had said, 'It's going out to Johnston – all being handled by the spooks now.'

Mac had remembered the Johnston bit only because he was dating a Canadian girl called Bethany Johnstone at the time. She was Canadian Customs intel – gorgeous, but a little on the bossy side. Mac had chuckled at the thought of a bunch of hush-hush hazardous matériel being shipped to Beth.

He'd never taken it further. Conspiracies weren't his thing and in truth the Filipinos loved nothing more than tales of forgotten caches of precious stuff. The story of Yamashita's gold was a classic example. During the Pacific War, the Japanese military under General Yamashita had looted gold reserves from wherever they invaded throughout South-East Asia, and they had hidden the vast caches in secret caves around the Philippines and northern Indonesia. Filipinos had grown up on stories of where the Yamashita Gold might be hidden.

The reference to spooks at Clark linked it for Mac. He wondered if the US cache at Clark was the same stuff that had now gone missing in Manila Bay. He wanted to get on the phone to Jakarta and just ask Jen to look it up. He wanted to have a serious conversation with Garvs – cut through the bullshit. But it wasn't going to work that way. He wasn't going to get Jen in the shit and he wasn't going to give Garvs a chance to order him home.

He wolfed the beer, flattened some rupiah and stood to go.

Suddenly he had a flash: when he'd brokered the logging deal with Sabaya's business negotiators, one of the entourage had been a tallish Eurasian-looking Filipino with a huge chromed handgun. He'd never said a word, just sat in the background and stared.

Mindanao '02 – the guy was Ray-Bans.

CHAPTER 23

Mac let himself out the back of the shop and walked to the end of the rear alley. He paused, poked his head out. Looked left and right down the cross street and couldn't see a red Liberty or men sitting in cars.

He walked west with the other pedestrians, the streets buzzing with large tourist buses and Malaysians and Americans in tour groups.

There was no sign of Mr Turquoise. Mac assumed he was around the corner, waiting in the street the restaurant fronted on to. He slowed as he approached the corner where an old man sold newspapers and magazines. A monkey sat on the guy's cart, chain attached to his collar. He walked wider, stopped, put his hand in his pocket, pointed at a *Straits Times*, came out with rupiah. The guy flipped the newspaper into four, held it out and cupped the same hand for some brass. Mac hit him with some dough, leaned over and around and clocked the street. Mr Turquoise had moved on from the restaurant. Mac took his change, tossed one of the 500 rupiah coins to the monkey, who caught it and put it in his little canvas pouch, gave Mac a wink.

Mac looked round the corner again and saw Mr Turquoise staring into a shop window. There was no sign of Ray-Bans.

Mac walked out from the corner, exposing his position to Mr Turquoise, who was forty metres away. Turquoise stood up, turned around slow, clocked the street. Clocked Mac. Did a double take. Mac pretended to see him for the first time too and, feigning surprise, turned and moved away. He kept going back down the cross street, though not as fast as he could.

Turquoise followed Mac around the corner with his hand under his trop shirt; Mac kept moving away, down the cross street. Turquoise hesitated, probably warned to be careful. Then he came after Mac.

Game on.

Mac knew that flat-footed guys tired quickly, especially in the legs. That's why regular army never took them. A flat-foot who tried to join the Royal Marines, the paras or a diggers' infantry outfit would be carried out on a stretcher. Everything was speed marches, every day was a route. There were no stragglers, no excuses.

Mac assumed that if Ray-Bans wasn't with Turquoise, he'd be covering the Pantai. So Mac was luring Turquoise north, away from his support, diluting the numerical advantage. If things turned out Mac's way, he'd even up the firepower equation.

Mac got to a pedestrian crossing and waited. Turquoise closed as the light went green – he was already puffing and Mac moved off again, through the strollers, keeping a distance of about fifty metres, keeping it straight. He wanted the tail at his six o'clock, giving the guy confidence. They crossed another street. Mac paused at the light, turned and had a look; Turquoise was purple in the face, shirt getting wet. Mac wondered if he smoked. They came to a street behind the Sedona. Mac stopped, looked around as if he was confused. He wanted Turquoise to think he had the upper hand. Wanted him overeager to end it.

Mac turned left into a cross street and slowed. They weaved between other pedestrians, Turquoise closing, wheezing, and Mac pretending to be scared and tired. He let Turquoise get within fifteen metres and then ducked into one of the alleys, stopped, dropped the newspaper, ran straight back the way he'd come. As he flew out of the alley, Turquoise looked up in surprise, his right hand under the shirt, on his right hip.

Mac slapped his left hand down on Turquoise's gun wrist, at the same time throwing a heavy open-hand strike into the guy's throat.

Right up high near the jawbone. He straightened his arm, drove up through his right leg and threw his right hip behind it. Turquoise's feet left the pavement and he went down on his back, winded, his eyes wide with fear and surprise. Mac pulled the bloke's gun hand away from the holster with a Korean wrist-lock, belted the guy in the temple with a right-hand punch. Turquoise went slack.

Mac's wrist pulsed white-hot with the impact. Agony.

He looked around. A couple of people had watched, but now quickly turned away. Mac shook his hand but it made his wrist hurt even more. He dragged Turquoise behind a pile of garbage in the stinking alley and pulled the handgun out of the holster – a Browning. He stuffed it in his belt in the small of his back. He checked the guy's two breast pockets in the trop shirt: nothing. Had a feel in his pants, came out with a laundry slip from the Golden Hotel. What was it with Javanese men and their goddamned pants? He looked closer and saw Turquoise's room number on the docket. It was 414 – level four, harbour-facing.

There was something else: a scrap of paper with a series of numbers written on it in ballpoint. He trousered the scrap, checked the other pocket and laughed as he came up with a red plastic rectangle with the gold stamp of 414 on it.

He put the key and the laundry docket back, then input the eleven-digit number into his phone. A bank account? He put the scrap back too.

Turquoise mumbled something, came to, looked at Mac, and panicked. Mac slapped him with the Browning. Turquoise slumped again. Picking up the *Straits Times*, Mac opened it and spread it over him. Just another drunk sleeping it off. Then he took off.

Mac's instinct was to go straight to the Golden, enlist his way into Turquoise's room and have a good old nosey-poke. Messing around in other folks' lives was what Mac had been trained for. But he wasn't going to do it. He remembered Ray-Bans' presence and general demeanour from the Mindanao Forest Products infiltration, and he hadn't seemed stupid. In fact, as Mac ran it through his memory, it could well have been Ray-Bans who'd engineered the doubling of Tony Kleinwitz. So Mac wasn't going to go stumbling into a hotel room which could be an ambush. The hotel key in the pocket? If Ray-Bans was smart enough to double Kleinwitz right under Mac's nose, he was smart enough to plant that key knowing that Turquoise might not be up to the job.

Mac walked north, his wrist aching, sore as. He moaned softly to himself as he tried to get his wrist comfortable. It just got worse. He'd have to attend to it.

Ducking into a convenience shop, he bought arnica ointment and crepe. Continuing on, he came back to the rear of the Sedona, checking for eyes and cars. He walked in the rear loading bay, passing waiters having a smoke and laundry girls flirting with the guys having a smoke. Pushing through saloon doors into the lobby, he checked for eyes before going through to the bar, asking for a bucket of ice to be brought poolside.

Then Mac raced up the fire stairs, made two passes of his room door, and paused outside it: the DO NOT DISTURB was still in place and the soap-scum he'd laid across the underside of the doorknob was still set in one glob, right where he'd put it. He bent down, sniffed the door knob – no solvent smell. You could remove soap scum with solvent and then put your own scum back on. But the solvent smell would linger.

He entered the room, nervous as hell, dumped everything into the black backpack, then swung around and left.

Mac sat by the Sedona pool, in the shadows of the palms and poured the contents of the ice bucket into the plastic mail centre bag from the pack. Screwing the top of the bag closed, he laid it on his wrist.

Gasped. *Sore as*!

Mac leaned back, trying to let the stress go, trying to breathe out the pain.

After twenty minutes he rubbed as much of the arnica in as he could without yelling aloud and bandaged the wrist as tight as possible. Stars flashed in his eyes, darkness closing in from his peripheral vision. He was almost in tears as he pulled the last of the bandage around behind his thumb, held it there with his teeth and fastened it with the bandage claws.

Agony!

* * *

Mac's blue Commodore rolled up to the big security gates of the Port of Makassar. He'd hired a private car and a driver called Sami to give him a better image.

Mac got out, walked to the glass security cage, showed the MPS key. The Port Authority guy looked him up and down, put his hand out. Mac turned over the Richard Davis passport. *Please don't scan it; please don't scan it.*

The bloke could have run it through his database, the same as Indonesian Customs. But instead he wrote the passport number and Commodore rego onto his log sheet, gave the passport back and flipped his head slightly. By the time Mac got back to the Commodore, the boom gate was up.

They drove onto Hatta Quay, one of the huge container aprons on either side of the traditional *pinisi* wharves. Sami said he knew where the non-bond stores were and they drove north to a set of buildings.

Mac left Sami at the security gate for MPS and strode across a concrete courtyard until he stood in front of a shed with the number 46 painted in huge gold letters on a black industrial roller door. It was the same as a whole group of the same doors fronting four large buildings. The warehouses were subdivisions.

There was a single pedestrian door in the main one, and Mac put the key into the welded padlock and turned it. The door swung inwards. Mac pulled out the Browning behind him, turned back and went into the warehouse.

It was about thirty metres long and twenty metres wide, with natural light coming down from glass panels in the gabled ceiling. Mac guessed it was eight, maybe ten years old.

Empty.

He walked around the edges, the Browning in his left hand. He felt stupid. Confused. He'd gambled everything to get back to Makassar and here he was strolling round in circles in an empty warehouse. Nothing but the sound of scuffs on a concrete floor.

He put the Browning back in his belt, breathing deep, and rubbed his temples and eyes. He was *so* tired; fatigued like he used to get in the Marines. Rooted.

He went through the options. He could go back to the gatehouse, try to either enlist or terrify the locals, find out what the fuck was going on. But he didn't see that as productive. He already knew they were scared of someone and he had a good idea who. He'd have to hurt someone and he'd only end up with intel along the lines of, *Some guys turned up in a truck, they paid in cash, they unloaded the stuff, then they picked the stuff up, then they fucked off.* And if he didn't kill them, he'd be caught by the cops or the Port Authority bulls and charged with terrorist activities or economic sabotage. They'd think of something.

His biggest problem wasn't Ray-Bans or Garrison or Sabaya or the Service, but allowing too many hours to go past without telling Cookie that he was back in Makassar.

He locked the door as he left, then went for a walk to get some air. Finding a path across the concrete apron and the rail tracks, he walked to the water's edge. It was an area where standard loose cargo was stevedored – cargo that wasn't in containers. A lot of Indonesia's trade saw feeder ships bringing goods from secondary regional ports to the larger ports, where freight forwarders and merchants would aggregate the stuff into containers for on-shipping. That's what MPS was for. To his left were the huge cranes of the Hatta container terminal. To his right was a breakwater made of large concrete blocks. Two boys stood on the blocks, casting lines.

The sight of the boys put a smile on his face. They reminded him of growing up in Rockie.

He wandered over. The boys were nine, maybe ten. Skinny, cocky, big smiles. No fish.

Mac asked how they were doing. Their English wasn't great, but fishing is the same in any language. They shrugged. Mac noticed one of them had a Brazil soccer shirt. He pointed, said, 'Ronaldo, Ronaldinho.' Said it sagely.

The boy burst into a smile, forgot about his fishing line and jabbered something at his mate, who was getting shitty. Brazil pointed at his friend and said, 'Enger Land.' He made a face.

Mac said, 'Beckham? Rooney?'

That triggered off an excited exchange between the two boys. Mac was amazed at the global reach of soccer. The passion was just as strong in Makassar as in Rio or Liverpool. Mac asked when Indonesia was going to a World Cup final and Brazil shook his head slowly. 'No good. No good.'

Mac turned to go. Saw the MPS warehouses had a gantry along the roof line. Realised those glass panels in the roof were hinged. He'd been ten once and he'd poked around where he shouldn't. With half a hunch he turned to Brazil and asked if he had the courage to climb the building. Mac pointed. 'Too high?'

The boys arced up, ten-year-old egos worn on their sleeves. Mac tried to get them going. They smiled secretly at one another. Mac pulled out some rupiah. 'How much is one of those World Cup footballs – you know: the Adidas ones. Silver, aren't they?'

Brazil looked at the rupiah with eyes that said, *The whole lot should cover it.*

Mac folded it, handed it over. 'We go all time. All time,' Brazil said, swinging his hand outward, like it was no big deal.

'Yesterday?' asked Mac.

Brazil shrugged. 'Sure.'

'Must see interesting things?'

Brazil shrugged, said, 'Sure.'

Mac looked over at MPS. Noticed a yellow tractor unit parked beside the back of warehouse 46. He pointed at the tractor. 'Interesting things in that one?'

'Sure.'

'Like what?'

The boys got coy, looked at each other like, *You tell. No, you tell.*

Mac smiled. 'You climbed in?'

'Sure.'

'See?'

'Sure.'

Mac put his hands on his hips and did the disbelief-at-their-bravery tone. 'Get some?'

'Sure.'

'No!'

Brazil nodded frantically. 'Sure. Had lots. Much.'

Mac went for goal. 'Show me.'

Brazil led them across the concrete boulders of the breakwater, England smiling at Mac. *You'll see how cool we are.*

They got to a point where the huge boulders didn't meet along their flat planes, revealing a gap that made a sort of cave. Well, cave enough for a ten-year-old boy. Brazil went into his cubby-house, England smiled at Mac. *You'll see!*

Brazil came out with his haul.

The blood drained from Mac's face and he gestured urgently for Brazil to put the fucking thing down. Slow!

Brazil's eyes went wide with fear and he lowered it, staring at Mac. Scared. Mac called the boys to him. They were shitting themselves. Mac could have done with the rubber undies himself. His heart jumped as they reached him. In a few years' time they'd be finding human teeth on the moon, he thought.

Sitting on the concrete boulder in the early afternoon was a yellow plastic box with a built-in handle. It looked like a tradesman's drill case, with a bit more grunt. CL-20: the planet's most powerful and unstable non-nuclear explosive. Enough to vaporise the three of them.

CHAPTER 24

Mac walked the boys back up to the MPS sheds, still panicking. There were two ultra-high-yield explosives Mac was aware of: CL-20 and Octanitrocubane. Both of them had about twice the expansion rate of Semtex and C4, which in turn had about three times the power of TNT.

He tried to remember back to one of his specialist rotations with the Americans. They'd been shown CL-20 and Octanitrocubane and the difference between them had been explained. One of the super-explosives was highly stable and could be burned without exploding. They used it to detonate thermonuclear warheads. The other was lighter and odourless but was highly unstable. Mac was stuffed if he could remember which one was which, but the skull-and-crossbones on the CL-20 box was enough for him.

As they walked up to the guardhouse, he kept the conversation going. Difficult when a couple of young boys think they're in trouble. He wanted to know who they'd seen around the warehouse.

Brazil managed to describe a tall Anglo man with dark hair. 'Merry Carn.'

Garrison.

England perfectly described Abu Sabaya: the teeth, the hair, the general aura. Abu Sabaya, here, in Makassar!

Mac tried to stay calm. He didn't want to spook the boys into silence. They were almost at the guardhouse. He stopped, asked Brazil, who had better English: 'When were these people here? One day?' He held up one finger. Then two. Then three.

Brazil thought about it, rolled his eyes like he was looking for the word.

'Morning!' He was proud of getting it out.

'Morning? Which morning?'

'Today morning, today,' said Brazil.

Mac just stared, horrified, both boys recoiling from his look.

He looked Brazil in the eye, pointed both index fingers at the ground. 'This morning? Today morning?'

Brazil nodded furiously, scared.

'Two men?' Mac held up the two fingers again.

Brazil nodded. Held up one finger and said, 'Lay.'

Mac shook his head.

Brazil used both hands to make the international sign of the female figure.

'Lady?' Mac asked.

Brazil nodded.

Mac asked what she looked like but Brazil looked confused.

'Mama? Mak?' asked Mac.

Brazil and England laughed at each other. Giggled.

So she didn't look like anyone's mother.

Brazil did his hourglass signal.

So there were three of them. He wondered where the bird fitted in. With Judith Hannah safely back in Jakkers, he wondered who it could be. Maybe just a gangster's moll. Some girls would put up with anything to get some excitement in their lives.

Mac thanked the boys. Pulled out some dough, but he was all out of rupiah. He showed them each a twenty-dollar greenback. They grabbed for the dough. Mac pulled it back. Twenty dollars US in Makassar was like having a thousand dollars in Sydney.

'You promise – give to Mak, right? To Ma,' said Mac.

The boys rolled their eyes, looked at each other. So Mac pulled the money back, pretended to put it back where it came from. They chorused that yes, the money would be going to their mothers.

After doling it out, Mac shook their hands and then shooed them away. He wanted them off the docks as quickly as possible.

Mac got to the guardhouse, got in the Commodore and asked for the Pantai Gapura.

Mac waited until they'd driven away from the port area before he fished out the mobile phone and made a call. From his recollection, sensitive explosives could be triggered by something that disturbed the atmosphere. Cellular systems ran on microwaves which did plenty of atmospheric disturbing.

He patched through to Cookie's compound in the foothills of Mount Malino. A local took the call, patching him on, probably to Cookie's sat phone. Cookie came on the line. Clear, but with noise in the background. A helo or a logging site.

'Yeah?'

'Mr B – it's Mac. Alan McQueen.' He still didn't have the ticker to call him Cookie.

'Ah, Mr Mac. How's it going?'

'Yeah, good mate,' he lied, his wrist throbbing and his eyelids heavy with exhaustion.

'So you're in town?' asked Cookie.

'Um, yeah, arrived yesterday, Makassar. Been busy.' Mac tried to work out how much of a lie he could tell. He was cut off from the Service, chasing a CIA bloke and the former number one terrorist in South-East Asia. Or were they chasing him? He needed the reach that Cookie could bring.

Cookie laughed, loud, like a pirate. 'Just checking, Mr Mac. Knew you wouldn't lie to me.'

Mac expelled a lungful of air. He needed someone on his side, couldn't do this by himself.

'Mr B, I need to talk.'

'Don't we all.'

'Remember that hocus-pocus a couple of years ago? The story about the cache of hazardous matériel found in a secret bunker at Clark? You remember that bullshit?'

There was a pause, then Cookie said, 'Was that bullshit?'

'Wasn't it?' asked Mac.

'It might not have been,' said Cookie.

Which in the intel world was code for *We were infiltrated – we had eyes*.

Mac wanted him to spill, but couldn't sound too eager. 'Oh well, I guess a bit of Agent Orange never hurt anyone, huh?'

Cookie scoffed. Too smart. He'd written the book on that ploy.

'Mate, while I'm digging into my memory, tell me what's going on with this Garrison prick,' said Cookie.

'For a start, it's not just Garrison anymore. I think I have enough to say he's now operating with Abu Sabaya. They're a team.'

Mac winced, held his breath. Waited for the laughter or the scoffing.

'That could make sense,' said Cookie.

'It could?'

'Sure. I never thought the guy was dead. They never found the body, never even ID'd him on the boat. I mean, did *you* see him that night?'

Mac didn't respond – Cookie already knew the answer.

Cookie seemed to be thinking something through. 'You know, if Sabaya's part of this, then it's big, right?'

'That's my guess,' said Mac.

'So where are they?'

'They were here this morning. In Makassar. Don't know where they are now.'

'In Makassar?!'

'Hatta container terminal. They cleaned out a warehouse and took off.'

'Which way?' asked Cookie.

'Umm, sorry?'

'Which way did he go? Garrison?'

Mac was lost. 'You mean, which road?'

'No, I mean he's standing on a dock. How did he leave? Land, sea or air?'

Mac felt like a dickhead. He'd become so exhausted, was following so many pieces of the puzzle, that he'd missed the obvious issue.

'I – I don't know,' he said, wondering if he could double back, ask those boys how Garrison and Sabaya had left the dock.

The Commodore stopped at lights. There was a thud, and a thunk, and Mac was suddenly looking down the barrel of a Glock 9 mm. He looked up into Samoan eyes. Steady Samoan eyes.

From the other side of the car, a door slammed and the phone was ripped out of Mac's hand. Mac turned away from the Glock to a big, big smile from a big, big man. The bloke hit the disconnect button on the phone, tossed it over his shoulder. It landed on the back dash.

'G'day, Macca,' the big man said with forced friendliness.

''Zit going, Boo?' said Mac, his smile icy.

Mac had inadvertently given Boo his nickname, and Boo had hated him for it ever since. It was during a Christmas party at the Jakarta embassy compound a few years back. Those who weren't going home fired up the barbie, cranked up the AC/DC and Helen Reddy and hooked into the piss, big time. Christmas in Aussie embassies meant the spooks, the law enforcement, the diplomats and the trade people all mushing in together. Drinking, dancing, pashing.

And it all stayed on the field.

It also meant socialising with a section of Australian Protective Service known as the I-team. The I-team removed Commonwealth people abroad who'd developed drug habits or were going to paedophile brothels. That sort of thing. Their leader was a hulking ex-navy Military Policeman called Barry Bray.

Barry had annoyed some of the women at the Jakarta embassy because of his forced removal of a young woman who'd got hooked on the then-new drug that Japanese teenagers were calling ice. The woman had had the full psychotic episodes and, because the situation wasn't entirely medical, Bray was called in.

The thing that got the women going was Barry's use of a straitjacket before he put her on a Qantas flight. It was the first time Mac had really noticed Jenny Toohey. The womenfolk had been going off like a bunch of hens but it was Jen who stepped up to Barry, told him to cut it out and let her and another female AFP officer do the escort. She'd stood there in front of Barry, poking him in the chest, giving him the old what's what. Barry brushed her aside. Jen complained to the Ambassador, complained to the Jakarta AFP station chief. She was a piece of work, all right.

Not long after, the I-team was back in Jakarta for Christmas and wanting to party like nothing had happened. The ladies were bristling but were standing off. Barry was a large, arrogant man with a reputation for violence.

Mac had got a bit boozed, noticed that Barry had the dirtiest teeth he'd ever seen. He'd said to the Customs bird he was cracking on to, 'He looks like Fu Manchu with a mouthful of bamboo.'

The Customs girl loved that, and the next day Jenny Toohey was calling Barry 'Bamboo'. Saying it with a wink and a giddy-up. The girls soon shortened it to Boo. Female revenge, served with laughter.

Boo stuck. Barry tracked it back. Never forgave Mac.

Now Mac, Boo and his sidekick, Marlon, sat in a suite at the Pantai Gapura, waiting for the evening flight out of Hasanuddin to Soekarno-Hatta. Boo had rightly surmised that the crowded concourse of a major airport might be a better place for Mac to stage a getaway than facing off in a hotel room. So they were waiting.

Boo turned his chair around, sat down like he wanted to have sex with it. Marlon stayed on his feet. He was heavy-set in the chest and arms, about five-eleven, one hundred and ten kilos and carried a handgun in a shoulder rig under a blue blazer.

'So, Macca, what's been up, mate?' asked Bray.

'Oh, you know,' said Mac. 'Just enjoying the weather. Sulawesi's beautiful this time of year.'

'Temperate climate. That's what it is . . .'

Mac chuckled. He could do this all day – a former Navy MP would get the shits before he did. But he didn't want to sit there all day. He had a call to make to Sawtell and a call to Cookie to finish. He was either going to talk his way out, or fight his way out. His wrist was begging him to do it with charm.

'You know something, Boo?'

Bray raised an eyebrow.

'It wouldn't hurt you guys to just get me my phone, let me cover-off, huh?'

'Oh really?' Bray smiled over at Marlon.

'There's things happening around here that you could be helping with, rather than screwing up,' said Mac.

'Shit, *really*? You hear that Marlon?' Bray sniggered. 'There's things happening round here, mate! Chrissakes, Macca. Sounds like *The X-Files* comes to Makassar!'

Marlon laughed and Mac winked at him. He liked that the bloke had a shoulder rig. They were about three times slower than drawing from the hip and they had the added problem of leaving the right arm straddled across the chest. That was a bonus for Mac and potential disaster for Marlon.

Boo was another story. He was getting on in years – maybe forty-seven, forty-eight – but he kept his Glock in a standard hip rig and at six-three he was still a handful on the blueing side of things. Mac had played footy with him in the ANZAC Day Aussie versus Kiwi rugby games in Jakkers. They were supposed to be special sporting events on the embassy calendar but Boo always managed to turn them into something much more. He had no problems scrapping with blokes half his age. He liked it.

Mac looked back. Dropped the funny stuff. 'Boo, I need to make a phone call to US Army Special Forces in Zam. It's urgent.'

Boo scoffed.

'I'll tell you the number. You call,' Mac pushed.

Boo stood, walked around the table, sat on it so he was looking down on Mac. He wore grimy off-white chinos, grey plastic shoes with a zip up either side and a lemon polo shirt with the penguin on it.

'Urgent, huh?' said Bray. 'Only urgent thing I've heard about lately is Alan McQueen, on a plane, into Canberra for a little word in the shell-like.'

Mac breathed out. 'Mate, just get me the phone. You can sit here, listen to me. What's the problem?'

Boo and Marlon both laughed. Then Boo pointed at Mac's wrist and said, 'Got a boyfriend for that?'

Mac laughed and pointed at Boo's mossy fangs. 'Got some Steradent for that?'

Boo iced over while Marlon pissed himself.

Mac opened his hands. 'I mean, you do floss, right?'

Marlon put his hand to his mouth, trying to stop the laughter.

Boo's big forearms flexed. It wasn't going to be fun getting a slap from Boo, but it might be worth it in the medium term.

Mac edged forward on his chair, getting his weight onto his right thigh. Tensed. 'You know, Boo – it's probably one of those tropical things, like, um, moss river fever.'

Marlon spluttered. Boo's eyes flashed and he threw a right-hand punch. Mac slipped under it and let loose the perfect right-hand uppercut, collecting Boo on the tip of the chin and snapping his head back. Boo fell back onto the table like Mac had just felled a tree.

Mac's wrist screamed for respite but he turned for Marlon, taking two paces to get to him. He watched Marlon reach across his body and under his left armpit for the shoulder rig. Mac planted his left foot as he watched Marlon prepare to draw, then lashed out with a right-foot snap-kick aimed at Marlon's right elbow, right on the point that would either break the elbow or dislocate the shoulder. His snap kick connected, one hundred and six kilos of accelerating mass behind it. The elbow snapped back against Marlon's chest, busting the joint, his right shoulder popping out in an anterior dislocation. Marlon's eyes went wide with fear as he cannoned backwards into the hotel room wall, air sucking straight out of him with the pain and shock. He was unconscious before he hit the floor, his arm mangled and twisted into a shape it shouldn't have been in.

Mac reached into Marlon's shoulder rig, pulled out the Glock and stood. Boo was mumbling, trying to raise his head, his hand fumbling around for the Glock on his hip. Mac stepped over, brought his Glock down hard on Boo's right wrist, breaking something. Boo screamed and pulled his hand to his chest. '*Faaarrrkkk!*'

Mac left Boo's gun. No time. Sweeping the room, he saw a phone, couldn't remember the numbers. He raced to Boo's black briefcase, riffled through it and found his cheapo mobile phone. Shoving the Glock into the belt of his chinos, he pulled his shirt over it, put the phone in his pocket and made for the door. Bursting through it, he came face to face with another Glock 9 mm, behind it a person he knew as Sami. The driver of the blue Commodore.

'Fuck!' said Mac. 'You too?'

Sami shrugged. 'It's a living.'

Mac put his hands up, shook his head. Behind him Marlon was moaning, Boo was gasping.

'Mate, I need to make a call,' said Mac, going for his pocket.

Sami started to say something.

Then his head shifted sideways so fast his hair stayed put for a split second. It looked like a Buster Keaton gag. In place of his face was a large fist and forearm.

Male.

Maori.

A bloke in a set of grey ovies stepped in front of Mac and brought his right foot down hard on Sami's gun wrist. Sami shrieked, moaned then passed out. The Maori turned back to Mac, raised his chin and widened his eyes.

'G'day, Chalks.'

CHAPTER 25

Boo and Sami sat on the wicker-sided sofa, right forearms cradled in left hands, ashen-faced, tons of pain, no fight left. Marlon lay on the floor, in la-la land.

When Billy arrived with his medic's backpack he set it down on the table, looked around and said, 'Shit, guys, didn't leave much of them.'

Billy unzipped the medic pack, went to Marlon who'd been vomiting, passing in and out of consciousness. Didn't matter how big and tough you were, a dislocated shoulder was more trauma than the human body could handle. Billy gave Marlon a green stick of laughing gas, told him to breathe deep on it. Then he got him upright and tried to get his jacket off. Marlon screamed and passed out again.

Sonny spoke in a low voice with Hemi at the table, which had a pile of Glocks sitting on it, then he picked up his sat phone, hit a speed-dial and wandered out to the terrace. Hemi got up to help Billy.

Mac put his hand in his pocket, grabbed his mobile.

Boo looked up and said, 'Gotcha phone, eh Macca? Hope it was worth it.'

Mac looked at him, thought about the situation. If he ever got out of this there'd be a lot of explaining to do to a lot of office guys. 'What can I say, Boo? I told you I just wanted the phone. It was urgent.'

Boo shook his head. 'What is it with spooks? Think you're above the law?'

'What is it with I-team and straitjackets?' said Mac, though his heart wasn't in it. Wished he hadn't said that.

'Mate, ever seen what a girl looks like on ice? Scary, mate. That jacket was for her protection,' said Boo.

Mac scoffed.

Boo shook his head. 'And don't give me that shit, neither. I didn't ask her to take that junk.'

Mac weighed the phone, watching Hemi get the blazer off Marlon, dribble coming out of the Samoan's pale lips, his head lolling. Mac looked back at Boo and his broken wing.

Mac breathed out, said, 'Sorry 'bout the arm, Boo.'

Boo laughed. Big, bamboo-toothed laugh. 'Missus won't be happy, I can tell you.' He let his mouth fall open in a big leer. 'Might have to play nursie to poor old Barry. Know what I mean?'

Mac shut the bathroom door, sat on the toilet lid and fired up the phone with his left hand. His right was so far gone he couldn't even make a fist with it. He scrolled down 'dialled calls' and hit the one starting with 63.

The switchboard bloke came on and Mac asked for Captain John Sawtell. Mr Switchboard said, 'No can do,' like he was relishing it. When Mac asked why not, the bloke said, 'He's operational.'

Mac thought back to their last conversation. Sawtell had said he was on stand-by to go into Manila. Now the CBNRE boys needed more special forces? It must have turned weird.

'Can you patch me through?' asked Mac. 'It's urgent.'

'Sorry, sir. Can't do that from a civilian line.'

Mac knew the rules and why they existed. If you had the right gear and a bit of luck you could pinpoint a military handset from a civilian-originated call. Not something most people would think about, but a handy tool for terrorists and spies.

'Can I get a message to him?' Mac pushed.

'I can try, sir, but no guarantees.'

Mac gave him a mobile number and the Indonesian country code.

He didn't want to do it that way, but since the I-team had found him he figured there wasn't much cover left to blow.

'Tell him I've got something down here that the Twentieth are going to be very interested in, okay?'

Sonny wanted to move out. He gestured at Mac. 'Let's go, Chalks – got something you might want to see.'

Sonny, Hemi and Billy stowed real quick and made for the door. In their grey ovies they looked like the Beagle Boys.

Mac lingered, wanting to ask more questions. Sonny stood at the door with a Glock behind his back and flicked his head at Mac. Impatient.

Mac held his hand up and, turning back to Boo, asked, 'Mate, how did you track me to Makassar?'

Boo shrugged. 'Didn't.'

Mac looked at Sonny, and Boo got the picture quick-smart.

'You know, Macca, let the mountain come to Mohammad,' said Boo.

'What the fuck's he talking about?' Sonny demanded.

Mac said nothing.

'We didn't have to chase you, mate,' said Boo. 'Just sit back and wait for you to come to Garrison.'

Sonny let the door spring shut, came straight over, got in Boo's face, fist clenched. 'Garrison?! What the fuck you know about Garrison, huh Chalks?'

Mac put his hand out to pull Sonny back, said, 'Boo, why were you tailing Garrison?'

Boo shrugged. He was into territory that was now confusing him too. 'We came in from Tokyo couple of nights ago. Jakarta put us on you; briefed us on Garrison.'

Mac still didn't get it. 'Yeah?'

'The theory was since you were associated with Garrison, if we could find him then you'd be around the shop somewhere.'

Mac was incredulous. '*What?* I'm not associated with Garrison. They sent me out here to kill him five days ago! Jesus Christ!'

Boo shrugged. Sorry.

Mac pulled his temper back a notch. 'Who briefed you, Boo? Garvey? Urquhart?'

'Nah. Internal, APS.'

'Who?'

'Steinhardt and that sheila with the bloke's haircut.'

'No one from the Service?'

Boo shook his head. 'They met us as at the airport, wanted us into Makassar quick-smart.'

Mac breathed out. He'd been set up. Getting briefed at the airport or a bar was how it worked when someone didn't want the order taped and logged. It was like a briefing that had never happened, a 'tasking' that never existed. He'd bet the Australian Protective Service had no record of Boo's assignment and no paper trail linking it to ASIS. All that would remain was a verbal connection between Mac and Garrison. It was as good as saying that Alan McQueen was rogue.

Mac rubbed his temples with his left hand. He had to think, had to think.

Sonny stepped in, menacing, gave Boo that look, said, 'Where's Garrison? Where is he right now?'

Boo shrugged.

Sonny prepped a straight right and Mac leapt in.

'Mate, give me a chance,' said Boo, holding his good hand in front of his face. 'Last I saw of Garrison, he was getting on a speed-boat down at Hatta.'

'When?' said Sonny.

'This morning, 'bout ten to eight.'

'Yeah?' said Sonny, his nostrils flaring.

Mac saw fear in Boo's eyes. 'Listen, Boo, you and I – we've been set up against each other. Right? Me and Sonny, we've been chasing Garrison. We're not with him, right? Had a gunfight with his boys three nights ago,' said Mac.

Boo nodded.

'So Sonny isn't going to kill you, right?' said Mac, turning to Sonny for assurance.

Sonny said, 'Not if someone tells me what the fuck's goin' on,' said Sonny.

'Okay, we watched them load up the speedboat – about a forty footer – with six large gear bags. An Asian bloke seemed to be running the show. There was a girl . . .'

Mac was getting impatient. 'What happened then?'

'They got in the boat, three of them, and took off west.'

'Out to sea?'

'Like there was no tomorrow.'

Mac could feel Sonny getting restless. Cookie didn't pay him to try hard, he paid him for results. The way it sounded, Garrison – the walking payday for Cookie – had just sailed off into nowhere. Mac thought about the missing piece of it all. 'Boo, what puts Garrison together with me? Where did that come from?' he said.

'He's been porking your missus – didn't you know?'

Mac's jaw dropped.

'She was the one on the boat,' continued Boo. 'I was coming to that. On the boat with Garrison. Tall, blonde. Big sheila.'

CHAPTER 26

Mac had only been gulled by a female once in his career and that was early days, in China. Part of his early training with ASIS had seen him infiltrating the Chinese Cultural Exchange Program, which was still a big tool for the People's Republic into the 1990s.

The cultural exchanges and scholarships had become a joke. The Commies would announce that some academic, teacher, political researcher or journalist from a Western country had won one of their friendship junkets and then bring them over to China for a couple of weeks of official wining and dining. They would tour them around the countryside, get them drinking at all opportunities, and wear them down with isolation, fatigue and flattery. Then they'd lure them into compromising situations and record the whole thing, and when those people were settled back in Melbourne or San Francisco or Auckland, contact them and have a quiet word. The Chinese liked it best when their leftie was closet gay, liked children or had a money problem, gambling debts or a secret heroin habit. Strangely, a sense of being underappreciated was often the best lever for creating an agent.

The cultural exchange program was an old Soviet trick that had already been overdone by the KGB in the 1960s and 1970s, producing a stream of Marxists in culturally influential positions. But the MSS was still having fun with it when Mac joined up.

In the first couple of years in an intelligence organisation, the brass would let the recruits have a shot at different things, to see where their aptitude lay, and also detect weaknesses. When Mac asked if he could infiltrate the MSS exchange programs, his regional director said, 'Go for your life.'

He posed as a freelance journalist, writing socially important articles for the *Courier-Mail* and the *Age* under the name of Andrew Stevens. He picked on subjects that the Commies loved: wealth distribution being appalling in the West; the education system not working for those with no money; women living in Melbourne's suburb of Broadmeadows having fewer rights than females living in northern Pakistan; Australians and Americans were richer, but Cubans and Vietnamese were happier. All the classics.

Mac was amazed how easy the stories were to write. Academics spouted forth to him, statistics could be pulled out and twisted to mean what he wanted and social workers would say anything to get in print. He even won an award from a Sydney 'peace institute' that had been set up as a KGB front in the 1960s and had somehow become self-perpetuating after the Soviet Union imploded.

One day the letter from the People's Republic of China arrived, containing the kind of flattery and enlisting techniques that Mac knew well. It even quoted lines of his stories back at him. Mac got into character with a shabby suit and a bad haircut, developing a dreamy yet self-righteous manner that he remembered from the socialists at UQ. The Chinese interviewers saw a bloke who started every second sentence with, 'I feel it's so important that . . .' and appended anti-capitalist remarks with 'not that I'm really an average Australian'. The panel were impressed, looking at each other and nodding at each other as if to say, *He'll do*.

In hindsight, the MSS probably knew who he really worked for before he landed. And wouldn't you know it, Mac was bedridden with gastro four days into the junket and was assigned a woman to keep him company while the main junket pack moved on into the interior to look at hydro dams and tyre factories. So Mac lived in Beijing's Palace Hotel for a week with a woman whose first name contained a jumble of xs and vowels, but who was known in intel circles as Daisy Dau.

Daisy's basic approach was to have lots of sex, drink lots of wine and flatter a man or woman into incriminating confessions. The Palace was part-owned by the General Staff of the People's Liberation Army, and it was wired like a recording studio.

When Mac got back to Canberra and debriefed, the older guys got a laugh out of that for a while. Every young Westerner got pounced on by Daisy Dau. She was beautiful, smart and sexy and renowned for comparing her male companions to Kevin Costner. *Ooo, you such strong man, you so handsome, like Krevin Cottner.*

Those had been early days. The Service wasn't trying to trip him up. He was allowed to call it a learning experience. He didn't know much and wasn't a great pillow-talker anyway. He joked with the guys that the MSS listening post had a stack of tapes of an Aussie bloke growling energetically for about thirty seconds, followed by hours of snoring.

This Diane thing was in a totally different league. It had completely blind-sided him. Through her he had glimpsed a new life, a new way to be in the world. It wasn't just her sexiness. She was the kind of woman you could have a laugh with and be serious with inside the space of five minutes. She had an appetite and loved a drink, she was shallow *and* deep. When Mac was a teenager he used to flip through Virginia's magazines, the ones with the sealed sections. He remembered the fresh-faced girls with their clean lines, tans and their flashy, confident smiles. He'd thought girls like that didn't actually exist in his world, and even if they did, a boofhead from Rockie wasn't allowed to meet them. Diane was one of those girls, and he hadn't had to change a thing about himself.

She was the only woman in Mac's adult life who had got him up for a dance. Even though she'd regretted it.

He'd wanted to go civvie for her.

He'd bought her a ring.

And she was screwing a rogue CIA agent.

Looking back now, there'd been lots of small clues, of course. There were the subtle deflections from Mac meeting Diane's father which, in retrospect, shouldn't have been a big deal. There were smaller things he could have picked. The fact she thought the 'A' in ADSL referred to 'advanced'. Or the time he'd made a joke about

IUDs – the contraceptives – and Diane, a bit drunk, continued what she thought was the joke, but punchlined with something about using Nokia phones for detonation. Mac had been confused until it clicked: she must have thought he'd said 'IEDs'. There were only three types of people who really spoke in terms of IEDs: cops, military and spooks. Certainly, you'd have to be one of those to reflexively translate IUD to IED. You must have it in your head, on your brain, recently been at a symposium or rotated through one of the Israelis' excellent specialist courses. The ones where they make you dress like a terrorist, show you your raw materials and then get you to make your own Improvised Explosive Device, just like they would in Syria or Malaysia.

The thing that Mac should never have overlooked with Diane was the occasion when he knew she was at a big IT trade show down at the Jakarta Convention Centre. He'd found her at the Atlas Network Security stand and surprised her. Atlas was in the same area as the stand for a computer security organisation called ASIS. Mac had looked across, seen the ASIS – ADVANCING SECURITY WORLDWIDE signage and quipped that the name certainly had a ring to it. Diane had touched her nose, eyes darting to the left and back again. Now why would a Pommie IT maven have even a clue what Mac had been smiling about, let alone react to it like that?

It was amazing how much information a bit of love could gloss over. But it sat there in your subconscious, waiting for the moment when you were ready. And suddenly there was the information, clear as day. A warning light you'd never miss if the agent was a hairy fella with bad breath.

It reeked of the old squirrel-grip. That and Chanel No. 5.

Sonny leaned around from his position in the front passenger seat of the LandCruiser. 'Any big ideas, Chalks?'

Mac shook his head, 'I'm waiting for a call from Zam. I don't know what's going on.'

'That doesn't help me, does it?' said Sonny.

Mac shrugged, overcome with exhaustion, suffering excruciating pain in his wrist and still in shock at the news about Diane. He was rooted.

'Let me say that another way,' said Sonny, getting annoyed. 'It doesn't help us much, right?'

'I'll talk to Cookie if you want, say it's my fault,' said Mac, looking out the window at the passing scenery.

They were on their way to Hasanuddin Air Base, the military facility that fringed the commercial airport outside of Makassar. They'd opted for the scenic route to the Eurocopter because of certain cargo in the luggage compartment – a bound and gagged bloke Mac knew as Ray-Bans.

Sonny ignored Mac's offer. 'You get something out of that cunt back there and no one will have to take the blame for anything. I mean, you're the spook, right Chalks?'

This was the time that the military guy looked at the intel guy and said, *Okay smartarse, do your thing.*

But Mac had no answers. He wasn't a torturer, didn't get off on that kind of interaction. Hemi and Sonny had already beaten their captive to a bleeding pulp and it was amazing the bloke was still alive, let alone conscious. Mac had no insights into what the guy might know or not know. Garrison was Agency and Sabaya's techniques were notoriously cellular, so they'd both be secretive. And Diane was starting to look like a very smart operator who would not be giving much away to the hired help. If Ray-Bans said he didn't know what was going on then Mac was inclined to give him a fifty per cent assumption of honesty. He didn't think the bloke knew anything. He was a Sabaya henchman, hired to get Mac out of the way.

'The answer is in the Macassar Strait. Garrison and Sabaya are out there, you can bet on it,' said Mac.

'I don't want to bet on anything, McQueen. Understand?' Sonny fired back.

Mac could see why Cookie used him.

Sonny and his team were being called back by Cookie for a mining situation – something that required a little more pressure than the local cops could exert. They'd want to know that they'd taken care of their excess baggage problems before they left.

Mac had got Boo and his boys spared on the basis that they weren't so unlike Sonny and his boys. Mac had had to work on that, emphasising that dead APS blokes would bring POLRI's Criminal

239

Investigation detectives in from Jakkers. But he didn't know about the bloke in the luggage compartment.

They drove past the turn-off to a popular family swimming hole where the waterfall emptied straight into a big pool. Mac's mind worked overtime, struggling to work out what Garrison and Sabaya were doing, what the missing container in Manila contained and why Garrison had Diane working as a double agent months before this thing had gone down. He had to stay clear on that without the feeling of betrayal muddying everything.

His immediate goal was to create a scenario where the guy in the back didn't have to die.

Mac leaned forward, whispered in Sonny's ear, 'I reckon I can get something out of this bloke if we're alone. You guys go on, leave him with me. Whaddya reckon?'

'I don't care if you want to fuck him, make him your missus. All I want is something I can take to Mr B. Got that?'

Mac nodded.

Sonny's sat phone trilled and he took the call before passing it back to Mac.

'Hello,' Mac rasped.

Cookie Banderjong wanted Mac to stay in touch. Reckoned there was still life in the Garrison–Sabaya thing. Said, 'Don't be a stranger, mate. Remember your friends.'

Cookie was really saying, *The trail's dead for now but if you come back to this island, you're dealing with me.*

Mac's head spun and he struggled to breathe properly.

As Cookie was signing off Mac had a sudden thought. 'Mr B, if the US military is shipping something to Johnston, what are they doing?' he said.

Cookie chuckled. 'They're burying their mistakes, mate.'

Mac said nothing; he was beyond riddles.

'Johnston Atoll is a US Army base about two hundred miles south of Hawaii. It's a huge incinerator plant out there in the Pacific. Hush-hush, run by DIA,' said Cookie.

'What do they burn?' asked Mac.

'All their CBNRE stuff – diseases that don't work, explosives that don't meet stability specs, dogs with two heads. All that scientist shit.'

Mac was totally awake again, his heart thumping.

Behind him, someone groaned. A long, animal-like exhalation of pain.

'Mr B, the secret cache at Clark – what was it?' demanded Mac.

'Oh that. About four thousand tons of VX gas,' said Cookie. 'Nerve agent. Nasty shit.'

CHAPTER 27

Mac tore the grey duct tape off Ray-Bans' mouth, sliced the white flexi cuffs from his wrists, and watched him slump to the carpeted floor of the HiAce van. It was late afternoon, the temperature was low thirties, and dust seemed to float on the heat. Wafts of kerosene and scorched rubber came from the helos and military air-lifters around Hasanuddin Air Base and the F-111s from the Indonesian Air Force's Eastern Command screamed as they took off.

The HiAce sat beside Cookie's LandCruiser in a private hangar that looked over the whole spread of Hasanuddin Air Base and the airport. A security bloke strolled with a German shepherd about eighty metres away near the huge sliding doors.

Mac put a bottle of water in front of Ray-Bans. Watched the guy squirm and wriggle to get comfortable. Blood was smeared down his dark red polo shirt and across the thighs of his cream chinos, and his right eye was puffed, dark purple and about to get a nice yellow yolk in the middle. Struggling onto his right elbow, he pushed himself up against the wall of the HiAce with his boat shoes. He put his hand out for the water, revealing a heavily muscled arm. Couldn't reach it, so Mac opened the top and gave it to him.

Mac stayed at arm's length. The guy was an athlete and Mac was in no shape to go close-range with him.

Ray-Bans drank, convulsed slightly, then wiped his mouth and spat. A tooth bounced on the black nylon carpet.

'This when I die?' he asked, in a London accent.

'That depends on both of us,' said Mac.

Mac had developed paranoid ideas about Ray-Bans for the last couple of days. It wasn't just that the bloke was put together and looked like he knew what he was doing. It wasn't just that from Minky's place and all the way up Sulawesi and into the highlands the two had been playing cat and mouse. It wasn't even that Mac had finally clicked and realised that the bloke was part of the Sabaya retinue during the Mindanao Forest Products infiltration. The big thing Mac had been overlooking, and which hadn't occurred to him during this totally out-of-control mission, was that Ray-Bans might be a lot more like him than he was comfortable with. He had the same aura Mac drew around himself in the field: the unknown quantity, the person who could be from anywhere, doing anything. About the only people who noticed the kind of blandness Mac affected were other spooks.

'Smoke?' asked Mac.

Ray-Bans nodded.

'Bad luck, I don't,' said Mac.

They both laughed, Ray-Bans through a busted-up mouth. He stopped himself quick.

'What's your name?' asked Mac.

'Call me Paul. Yours?'

'Then I'd have to kill ya,' said Mac.

Paul snorted, looked out the HiAce window, still casing his surrounds. He was a good-looking man up close, even with the facial he'd got from Hemi. He could have starred in *General Hospital*, sort of an Asian Rick Springfield.

'You knew during the Mindanao Forest thing that I wasn't a forestry consultant,' said Mac.

Paul looked at the floor. 'Didn't know what the fuck you were, tell the truth. You were a pretty good deal-maker for an impostor.'

'You liked that?'

Paul looked at him with one eye, nodded. 'Chinese liked it too.'

'And Sabaya?'

Paul grinned, looked away. 'Embarrassed him, getting a pale-eye to broker something between a Filipino and the Chinese. Didn't really live up to some of his ethnic ideas . . .'

'But you let it go.'

Paul shrugged, slugged at the water, winced slightly.

'You NICA, one of Garcia's boys?' asked Mac, referring to Philippines intel.

Paul shrugged.

Mac waved the Browning. 'I'm the one with the gun. In the movies, that's good for me, bad for you.'

Paul smiled, looked Mac in the eye. 'I'm not NICA.'

'Agency?'

Paul shook his head.

The van was getting stuffy and Mac got up, pulled the sliding side window back. Let some air in, sat down.

'Paul, there's something worth knowing. I'm really tired, really stressed. I'm even a bit emotional,' he said, looking down at the Browning on his lap. 'I'm not going to sit here all day asking questions like I'm on a date with a difficult bird. I'm sure you'd like to get on your bike too, huh?'

Paul nodded, said, 'Mate, I'm Old School.'

Mac looked at him. Old School was intel-speak for MI6 – the oldest intelligence organisation in the Western world and the one that most others were in some way modelled on. ASIS, the CIA, Mossad and the Canadian SIS had all turned to MI6 for guidance during their set-up phase.

'SAS, paras?' asked Mac.

'You're quick.'

'The looks and the accent . . .'

Paul shrugged. 'Mexican father, Filipina mother. Grew up in Manila, high school in London. Usual shit.'

'Spanish, Tagalog, good Yankee accent?'

'That's the one.'

'Useful guy.'

'The expendable ones usually are.'

'Tell me about Garrison,' asked Mac.

'The American?'

Mac nodded.

'Don't know much. He's apparently Agency but a bit unorthodox. Likes money.'

'Weren't briefed on Garrison?'

'Basic file. I know he was in Burma doing stuff with the junta and the Chinese. But my entry point was Sabaya. He'd been off the map since you finished him.'

'Wasn't me.'

'That's not what they say.'

'What do they say?' said Mac.

'Then I'd have to kill you.'

They looked at each other for two seconds.

'Sabaya came back on the map again in '05,' said Paul. 'He'd been lying low down in Sulu for a couple of years. Been into Burma, somehow hooked up with Garrison. But Garrison was never my end. Sabaya was my end.'

'Where does the girl, Judith Hannah, fit in?'

'We met them at the airport ten days ago,' said Paul, pointing out the window. 'Garrison was shooting her up with something, so I hear. He wanted something from her.'

'What were they using?'

'Don't know – scopolamine, I guess. That's the Agency thing, isn't it? But I wasn't around. I was chasing you round the manor, remember that?'

'What did they want from her?'

'Don't know. I never got to Sabaya's inner circle. He thought I was a mercenary, hired muscle.'

Mac suspected the guy was stonewalling, but he pushed on. 'What about the other girl?'

'I tried to stop that, believe me. I'm Army, mate – got a policy about kids.'

'No, not Minky's girl. Adult, blonde, English. Calls herself Diane.'

Paul shrugged. 'Who's she with?'

'Garrison, as far as I know.'

Paul made a face. 'Just 'cos she sounds English, mate, doesn't mean she works for the English. Know what I mean?'

'It's important.'

'Sorry, mate. Don't know about an English girl.'

Mac thought about it. 'So what are these blokes up to?'

'You can't ask that in the Sabaya camp,' said Paul. 'They'll drop you for that.'

'What's in that old mine?'

'Nothing. Fucking beats me.'

'Nothing?'

'I had a quick look a week ago – empty. They've laid track in there, but there's nothing in it.'

Mac was exhausted, close to passing out. He stood to a crouch, pulled the sliding side door back, got out backwards and gestured for Paul to follow.

They walked to the hangar door. Mac reached into his chino pockets, came out with about four hundred US dollars. Handed it over.

Paul took it, turned to go, said, 'I owe ya.'

'No worries, champ.'

Paul looked down at Mac's wrist and nodded. 'Got a girlfriend for that?'

'Go on,' said Mac, gesturing with the Browning. 'Fuck off.'

Definitely paras.

Mac headed through the military checkpoint of Hasanuddin in the HiAce and drove into the hinterlands behind the airport thinking back to his conversation with Cookie. Cookie had called VX nasty shit. But it was way beyond nasty. A substance that attacked the central nervous system, VX was something the most depraved scientists had concocted and yet even the most psycho generals and politicians could never find an excuse to deploy. Death started with a runny nose and a headache. Before you knew it, your bladder and bowels were doing their own thing. Then your lungs wouldn't work. If you inhaled it, you died in about fifteen minutes. If it landed on your skin in very small doses, you'd die in four to ten hours. If you ingested it by way of drinking or eating, you might have two or three days up your sleeve.

The scientists had a measurement called a Threshold Limit Value for how much an average adult man could be in contact with the agent for an eight-hour day in a forty-hour week. The TLV of VX nerve agent was 0.00001 milligrams per cubic metre of water, an infinitesimal amount – essentially a bit of vapour in the air. It was odourless and colourless.

VX had been developed to do one thing: wipe out entire urban populations while leaving the buildings and other infrastructure in place.

The big weakness of VX was the way it had to be used. If Mac remembered correctly, the optimum usage of VX entailed it being turned into trillions of microbe-sized droplets so it was suspended in the air which then had to drift with air currents over the unlucky populations. To make VX as deadly as it could be, you needed it to be sprayed like fertiliser. The technical term for this state was an aerosol. Aerosol was easy to say, difficult to achieve. Perhaps not so hard with a container of VX wrapped in CL-20.

He found a lay-by and parked by a river under the trees, out of the heat of the afternoon. Then he got in the back of the van, laid his head on his backpack and felt himself going under.

Mac awoke with a start, panicked by the ring-tone of his Nokia. It was dark and hot, he was drenched in sweat and his right arm was useless from pins and needles. An eerie yellowish light illuminated the HiAce. He fumbled, got the glowing phone, croaked, 'Yep.'

'McQueen. Sawtell. You called.'

Mac tried to clear his head. *What's the time? Where am I?*

'Ah, yeah John. 'Zit going?' said Mac, trying to push his hair back with his bad hand. He couldn't make a comb.

'Good, my man. Uh, you okay?'

Mac could have cried. It seemed like forever since anyone had asked him that. 'Mate, I'm all over the shop. I need . . . I mean . . . Look, where are you?'

'Come on, McQueen.'

'Okay, if there's a guy from the Twentieth nearby, tell him this. Tell him Abu Sabaya is on a ship with a container of VX and twenty cases of CL-20.'

'Sabaya? *Alive?!*' said Sawtell.

'What I said,' replied Mac.

'Well, how? When? Um, I . . .' Sawtell paused.

'Do this for me, champ, and I won't bother you again. Swear to God,' said Mac, his head clearing.

Mac heard Sawtell exhale. Probably tired too. Mac looked at his G-Shock: 1.07 am. There was background noise behind Sawtell. Mac bet he was in a situation room with the Twentieth, DIA, the SEALs and Green Berets, and nowhere to deploy.

'Shit, McQueen. *Sabaya?!*' said Sawtell, still reeling from the revelation.

'He's with Garrison,' said Mac. 'They left Makassar this morning with a bunch of cases of CL-20. I reckon they'll RV with a container ship carrying some lost goods from the US Army.'

Sawtell's breath hissed over his teeth. 'Gimme a second, okay?'

Mac heard a raised voice. A big pause. Some murmured questions. Bigger pause, then a Southerner's voice came on the line: 'Hatfield. Twentieth support command. Who's this?'

'Call me Mac.'

'Don't jerk me around, son, I said *who is this?*'

'Ask Sawtell.' Mac wasn't going to get into a game of proving who he was. He'd let Sawtell vouch for him.

Hatfield turned away from the receiver and Mac could tell from the bloke's tone that Sawtell was giving a decent rendition of who Mac was. Just as well Sawtell had no idea what the Commonwealth of Australia thought about Alan McQueen at that minute.

Mac heard Hatfield say, 'This is it, last chance, Captain. You quite sure?'

Pause. Mac could envisage a bunch of special forces jocks, CBNRE propeller heads and a team of poker-faced DIA spooks all looking at Captain John Sawtell, thinking: *There goes the oak leaves.*

Hatfield came back on the line. 'Okay, tell me, Mr McQueen. What have we got?'

Mac told him about Abu Sabaya being alive. 'You remember the Sabaya slaying in '02?'

'Yes, saw the news,' said Hatfield.

'Captain Sawtell was there.'

'You?'

'That's not important,' said Mac. 'Thing is, sir, I developed a lot of the HumInt on Sabaya. I met him once, brokered deals with him.'

'Yes?'

'He always had a much bigger commercial operation than he did a terrorist one. Terrorism was his calling card, but everything he did, he did for money.'

'Ransoms, wasn't it?'

'Sure, and protection rackets for the miners, oil companies, what have you. But his biggest moneymaker was piracy, though not piracy of the bluewater kind. What he did was much smarter. He infiltrated the stevedores and freight forwarders and had some Philippine Customs people on his side too. He'd switch containers before they even got on a ship.'

'Shit!'

'Yeah. So there'd be a container of DVD players shipping out of MICT for Long Beach –'

'I'm sorry?'

'MICT, sir. Manila International Container Terminal.'

'Go on.'

'So the container would ship, and it would be a legitimate box with the right weights and scans. But it would be filled with logs or old TV sets. The freight forwarders and importers wouldn't know they'd been robbed until the containers were opened in Anaheim. Sabaya wouldn't even touch the containers. They'd be on another boat, shipping for Singapore or Brisbane, the consignment sold already.'

'Smart guy.'

'Very smart. His best trick is the microdot tracking. I bet you can't get a signal, right?'

'Damned right.'

'Sabaya worked out early how to nullify that whole microdot thing. I think he did it by degaussing the containers with a cheap electromagnet. That make sense?'

Mac heard a sigh of annoyance. 'Yes, Mr McQueen. That makes sense.'

'If it's any consolation, sir, MICT is one of the most secure dock facilities in the world. Can't take anything in or out without it being weighed, photographed, scanned and logged.'

'I know. That's why it was cleared to ship our stuff.'

'Sir, Sabaya's the best. He knows he can't get the containers through the security gates so he finds what he wants on the docks and on-ships them instead.'

Hatfield was enlisted. Mac could feel it. He'd flown in from Guam to find a lost load of VX and finally someone was telling him something he didn't know. The Twentieth support command had enormous powers in the United States and beyond. Hatfield could shut down ports, impound 747s, close down entire trucking hubs if he had reasonable grounds. But right now he had nothing. Mac wanted Hatfield to need him on one of those Army helos.

'So where's my container?' said Hatfield.

Bingo! thought Mac. 'My guess is it was on a ship in the Macassar Strait this morning. It was met by Sabaya and Garrison.'

Mac sensed eyes, looked up: saw a face peering in the van window. He freaked, grabbed the Browning, loosed three rounds. The glass imploded and the noise woke the forest. Mac rose, Browning in a cup-and-saucer, his wrist aching from making a grip. He opened the side door and switched off the interior light. It was pitch-black outside and, changing the Browning to his left hand, he dropped to the ground. He walked a few paces away from the van, ears rushing, heart palpitating and unable to see a thing. Then he tripped on something. Looking down he saw it and let his gun arm drop. It was a macaque, minus a head and right arm.

'Sorry, champ. Not your night.'

He'd always liked the macaque for its intelligence and soulfulness and the way it could wink. It saddened him to know that the animal was the preferred test-bed for the type of people who had created VX nerve agent. Didn't seem right: bunch of psychos in lab coats standing around, seeing how fast one of the magnificent animals lost bowel control. His sister Virginia had always teased him about liking animals more than people. Didn't seem so strange to Mac.

He wandered back to the van, sat down and heard the phone going haywire. Grabbed it, said, 'Yep?'

'That you, McQueen?'

'Yes, sir.'

'Holy shit, son, you okay?'

Mac tried to say something, but it wouldn't come. 'Umm, yeah,' he said eventually.

'Talk to me, son,' said Hatfield.

'Yeah. Fuck. Just killed a monkey.' There was something in the air choking him up. *Fucking pollen.*

Hatfield talked him back into the game, talking about long nights, tough missions and the need to focus to overcome disappointment.

'Gotcha. I'm good. Yep, good to go,' said Mac.

Hatfield had more questions. 'Captain Sawtell said something about CL-20?'

'They have about twenty cases of the stuff,' said Mac.

'Twenty *cases!*'

'Yep.'

'That's a lot of ordnance for something that was supposed to be experimental.'

'That's Sabaya for you. He's a piece of work.'

'Any ideas?'

Mac thought about it. Didn't want to throw up a false alarm. 'If I had to bet on it, I'd say they were heading south, across the Java Sea. For Surabaya, maybe Fremantle.'

'You know what that much CL-20 would do to a container load of VX?' said Hatfield, almost whispering.

'Aerosol effect?'

'Damned right, son. Damned right.'

CHAPTER 28

Mac made good time to the Pantai, then drove up and down the road on the main entrance, looking for cars and eyes. There was a white Commodore with two men in it. Australian by the look of it.

He parked at the front doors on the far side of the drop-off area, positioning the HiAce side on to give him some cover when he got out. Leaving the motor running, he went in through the front lobby, hoping it would look like a trade delivery. He slapped down his Richard Davis passport at the front desk. The girl behind the desk was reading *Vanity Fair*. She got up in a hurry, smoothed her skirt.

Mac winked. 'About that story on me – don't believe a word of it.'

The girl rolled her eyes and Mac showed his deposit box key. 'Like to make this fast. Got a plane to catch.'

They made their way down into the security basement and Mac walked up to the box behind the desk girl. They opened it and Mac simply piled everything from the box into his backpack, zipped it up, shut the deposit box and left the basement.

He got to the van and pulled out into the street, keeping an eye on the white Commodore in his mirror. It pulled out, followed.

Mac had choices: lose them or confront them.

He sped up, slowed down, waiting to see if they'd make a move. It was two am in Makassar and the two cars had the roads largely to themselves. He sped up and slowed down, ran a red light and made the tail come with him. There was a line of taxis outside the Kios Semarang, an upstairs nightclub haunt of the expat community. Across the road from it was a narrow Dutch-built alley.

He drove around the block again and, finding the other end of the alley, pulled in beside it so the HiAce blocked it lengthwise. He leapt from the van and took off down the alley. The Commodore pulled up behind him and he could hear a door open and a bloke say 'Fuck it' in an Aussie accent as he realised he couldn't get by the van to get into the alley. The door shut again and Mac heard the V6 scream off round the block.

Mac stopped and sprinted straight back to the HiAce, leapt in and swung around, making a dogleg exit from Makassar with as many illogical turns as he could. He drove conservatively, not wanting POLRI asking questions about the monkey window. On the outskirts of the city it was dark with no street lighting. Mac swung onto the road to Hasanuddin and floored it.

He had a flight to catch.

Mac waited under the trees over the road from the floodlit security gate at Hasanuddin Air Base. He'd left the joint hours ago with no worries because Cookie had arranged it. But he wasn't game to stand there at two-thirty am and tell some MP and his dog that he should be allowed back in. He didn't want to test his luck in the early hours.

He was back in his blue overalls, the Walther .38 in a hip rig beneath the ovies. He wore his black Adidas cap. Everything else he might need was in the pack.

Lying down, he looked at the stars. Conserving his energy, he tried to map out exactly what he was doing. Boo and his boys had obviously escaped from the Pantai, where Mac had left them in their flexi cuffs. The spook who called himself Paul and claimed to be MI6 seemed to have slipped out without anyone noticing and the four hundred dollars would get him from Hasanuddin to Manila. Maybe.

Where Mac went from here was a bit of a guess. He was as surprised as Hatfield when he came up with his Surabaya scenario.

He hadn't been planning to say it. Didn't want to sound like a nutter, but that's what it had sounded like: a container ship carrying what amounted to a VX bomb would sail into a major South-East Asian port and detonate.

The impact would be incredible. If you could get the right winds behind you, and get the VX to erupt far enough into the atmosphere, the body count could be huge. Mac had said Surabaya because he was thinking about a ship sailing south-bound from Manila down the Macassar Strait. Where was the biggest city? Across the Java Sea in Surabaya, where the city of three million people was totally built around the ports and most of the citizens lived in densely populated shanty towns. Surabaya was also built at sea level – low enough to have flooding problems. A nerve gas vapour would have no problems descending to where lungs were inhaling.

Mac had no idea what Hatfield and his CBNRE team were going to do. They had the weight of the White House and Pentagon behind them. But how would you search every ship? And if the ship was already in port, wouldn't an interdiction by the US Army just get the bomb detonated?

The Madura Strait that passed by Surabaya was a busy shipping lane – one of the world's busiest for oil supertankers. And Surabaya's port was as busy as Jakarta's. The shipping world measured container movements by the shortest containers – the twenty-footers – even though many of the containers were thirty and forty feet. So all movements were listed as TEUs, or Twenty-foot Equivalent Units. Surabaya's major port, Tanjung Perak, had a throughput of about seven thousand TEUs every day. The three hundred ships that went through Surabaya each month had a pre-paid schedule for berthing and loading/offloading. The commercial disincentive for the port master to shut down the port and allow the docked vessels and those standing off to be searched was substantial. If the request came from a Yankee and the substance they were searching for was odourless and colourless, Mac couldn't see how that was going to work. Indonesia's path to full economic development would be predicated on its maritime importance and it could not afford to be seen as a dangerous or money-losing shipping destination. A container ship had to carry a stowage plan showing exactly which container was in which bay, row and pier. They were all numbered, sure, but when you had a ship with eight thousand containers on board you'd be looking at three or four days to search it. And what if the ship with the VX wasn't going to Surabaya? What if it was bound for Lombok or Denpasar? That was turning into a shitload of containers to be searched – and when? Tonight? Dawn? All at once?

His other concern was that last sighting in Makassar. Just because Sabaya, Garrison and Diane were seen speeding westward from the dock, it didn't mean they intended to board the ship with the VX on it. They could have been planning something totally different. Sabaya's chosen MO had always been to travel separately from any heisted cargo. The VX could be going in the opposite direction, up to Shanghai or Yokohama, or across the Pacific to Oakland or Long Beach. Garrison might have spotted a tail, decided to put everyone off the track.

That's what Mac would do.

Intelligence people didn't work on 'cases' like cops. Spooks built a picture, synthesised information, had an area of specialty. The only reason Mac's specialty had any currency with the US Army's Twentieth was that his covert work had a regular overlap with Special Forces.

He couldn't afford to screw this up. He needed some shuteye to deal with it properly. Lying down and using all the meditation tricks he'd been taught in the Royal Marines – as well as being chosen for their ability to deal with extreme pressure they'd been shown a trick or two – he slipped into a restless sleep.

Mac awoke to his phone vibrating in his breast pocket.

'McQueen, Hatfield. Twentieth. How you doing, son?'

Mac croaked something out. He still felt rooted. Could have slept for another day.

'We'll touch down in about five. Refuel. I'll send someone over to the main gate. Still up for this?'

'Sure am, sir.'

There were a few mis-cues between the men. Mac made to start a sentence a couple of times and then stopped.

'Everything okay, son?'

'I was just wondering what Jakarta had to say, sir. About me, I mean.'

'I have a request in for a secondment of Alan McQueen, aiding the United States Army in a crucial CT operation,' said Hatfield.

'Yep?'

'Well I had to go through the proper channels, Mr McQueen. Through CINCPAC. Which means I haven't heard back yet.'

'Gotta love those office guys.'

'Pride of the Pentagon,' Hatfield chuckled. 'By the way, McQueen, I don't have to lecture you on Army SOPs, do I? Helos, comms, appropriate behaviour – that sort of thing?'

'Right as rain, sir.'

Six minutes later an Indonesian Air Force MP came out of the bullet-proof glass cage and signalled with a flashlight into the trees, calling, 'Queen, queen!'

Mac presented himself for the search and the wand. Another MP stood back with the German shepherd. Mac declared the Walther. The bloke put his hand out and Mac handed it over.

They were halfway across the sprawling area of Hasanuddin in a black LandCruiser Prado when Mac had a sudden pang about Diane. He'd been dumped before. He'd been told off, passed over and left behind for better things. But he'd never felt such a cold touch. He wondered if she'd known who he was. Odds on. Wondered if she fully knew the reputations of Garrison and Sabaya. His mind circled the past. *How far back? That trade fair in Jakarta in May? Was she a plant? Had she just seen me as a target of opportunity? All that bullshit he'd told her about what he did for a living? Was she part of the 'Paul' set-up?*

There was another feeling, even stronger than his embarrassment. Diane and Garrison had made a fool of him, but his real instincts were protective. He prayed to God he hadn't left them a trail to Jenny.

The US Army contingent milled in front of an unmarked hangar at the northern edges of Hasanuddin, the whole place lit up like a Vegas showroom. There was refuelling going on and the air was thick with fumes, humidity and dust. Mac clocked two Chinook CH-57D tandem-rotor helos, four Black Hawks and lots of US military types with their bad haircuts and drab T-shirts.

The MP stopped the Prado, walked Mac over to a group of soldiers and asked for Hatfield. One of the soldiers peeled off, escorting them to the second Chinook. The soldier walked up the fold-down stairs, stuck his head in. Came back down. They waited. A middle-aged man in tropical battle dress uniform stuck his head out, full head of white hair. 'McQueen?'

'That's me, sir.'

Hatfield came down the stairs, shook Mac's hand with a soft grip. 'Pleased to meet you, son. Sorry about all this fuss.'

Mac liked him immediately. In a huge military outfit like the US Army, there was a lot of discretion about how much plumage the brass could wear. Hatfield wore BDUs of the same pattern and cut as his men. His only identifier was the word HATFIELD on standard tape over the right breast pocket. His aide sidled up while Mac was being introduced to Hatfield's offsiders. Mac noticed that he and the retinue called him 'General'. Mac liked that too – they could have said 'sir'.

Mac sensed an outfit where there weren't too many office guys round the shop. He might just fit in. It was unusual for US Army generals to fly around in Chinooks. Earning that rank gave you the right to sit in leather armchairs in DC and go to five-star lunches in Manila. Mac only knew of two other generals who flew around the world in helos, commanding directly some of the brightest people in any military organisation. They did so because of the decisions that had to be made on the ground in real time. They weren't the kind of judgements that could be phoned in and they couldn't be made by a less experienced or qualified person.

The MP handed Mac's Walther back to him. The seven-shot .38 felt like a pea-shooter among the special forces gear.

'Thanks, champ,' said Mac.

He looked across the US Annex apron, saw Sawtell and his boys stowing extra bags from the back of a Toyota pick-up truck, saw what looked like Navy SEALs in black Nomex doing the same thing at their Black Hawks. The Army Special Forces boys were eyeing off the SEALs, Spikey sneering at one in his biker bandana. The Green Berets might be the hard men of the special forces world, but the SEALs were certainly the rock stars.

Hatfield motioned the team, including Mac, into his Chinook. Four of them filed in and Hatfield waited at the top of the fold-down steps. He shepherd-whistled at Sawtell, waved him inside.

The Chinook was large. Shorter than a 737 but wider. There was a situation room near the front, just behind the cockpit stairs. It consisted of a round map table bolted to the floor and five padded swivel stools also bolted down. There was a bank of three computer terminals along the side of the aircraft. One of them was a black SGI screen, the hardware behind the Powerscreen systems that allowed the Americans to take satellite imagery and computer-model them into 3-D, moving images.

Further aft of the situation room, there were eight airline-styled seats with what looked like pillows and blankets on them. Mac felt his eyelids drooping just looking at them.

Two men looked over the table at him, one in Army BDUs with no name tape, the other in grey ovies. Hatfield introduced them as DIA and referred to Mac as Australian intelligence. 'This is Alan. The guy who put that pizza box thing together with Abu Sabaya. Remember that?'

The DIA spooks showed no enthusiasm as they shook hands with Mac. The senior one, in the ovies, called himself Don. He got straight to the point.

'You know where the shipment is?'

Mac shook his head. 'Do you?'

'It's serious, Mr McQueen,' said Don.

'Sure, so why'd you lose it?'

Don narrowed his eyes at Mac, who looked back, unblinking. The bloke had got all cute with knowing his last name. It was a no-no in the intel world, unless you were desperately trying to prove something.

'For what it's worth,' said Mac, 'Sabaya's like a black belt in this stuff. He wrote the manual on it. He'd have had one person, maybe two, in the security annexe – what's it called?'

'Hazardous Cargo Control area.'

'That's the one, HCC. I'd say the VX will be in the same container your Technical Escort guys loaded it into. It'll just have new, non-military markings and it may have been painted.'

'I don't follow how Sabaya could defeat the microdot tracking,' said Don. 'What's this about degaussing?'

Mac wasn't much of a scientist, but he could give the basics.

'Well, every steel structure has an electromagnetic current running through it, and it runs in one direction which creates what they call a signature.'

'Like a ship?' asked Don.

'Yeah. And you can change the current and therefore the signature by introducing electromagnets and strategic copper coils. Navies do it to defeat signals intelligence on their ships and subs.'

'So . . . ?'

'So the container pirates in this part of the world use degaussing on containers, and if they get it right it defeats the microdots. You can't track them.'

Don and Hatfield glared at one another.

'So the agent is still in the same box?' asked Hatfield.

'That's the Sabaya MO, sir. There's about twenty million containers in circulation around the globe with an annual theft rate of four per cent. This is happening all the time.'

Don couldn't grasp it. 'Why wouldn't they take the material out of the container and put it somewhere else?'

'Because Sabaya isn't a terrorist in the traditional sense,' said Mac. 'He's not on a suicide mission, he wants to make money. So he makes it easy for himself and pulls a sort of three-card trick. You know those guys on the corner?'

'Yep, sure do,' smiled Don.

'That's what Sabaya does. The container doesn't get opened. Who'd want to try and open a container full of nerve agent?'

The group nodded.

'The container just gets put somewhere else. It's just another container box, going onto a ship, coming off a ship, being stacked. It's just that they think it's something else.'

'So where does it go?'

'It goes on to a different ship at Manila, but with a new RFID tag on it. A legit RFID tag. A tag that the stevedores can tick off as belonging on the ship they are loading.'

The RFID tags sealed most containers going between major ports. They identified the container and included an electronic manifest which could be checked by scanning. They were 'sealed' onto the container doors so an RFID tag meant that the shipping company and freight forwarders certified what was inside. The US Department of Defense sealed all its containers with proprietary RFIDs. Mac knew you couldn't ship a container through MICT without such a tag.

'The DoD container with the new tag is shipped to another port where it comes off as a legitimate container and can be moved to a warehouse somewhere. You let the shipping system work for you. That's how most heists now work across South-East Asia.'

'That easy? Can't be that easy,' said Don, sceptical.

Mac gave them the example of a car with a tollway e-tag on the windscreen. The tag is registered to the car. But if someone took the e-tag off that car and put it on another, the electronic scanners would record that the original car had gone through the toll gates. It was the same with RFID tags on containers.

'There is a catch,' said Mac.

'What's that?' asked Hatfield.

'Catch is, General, that I need two things to do this properly. I need someone on the inside, down at MICT, to do the actual switcheroo. It should take five, ten minutes. Second, I need to have another RFID tag to seal that box. And it will have to match with what the Customs guys at Surabaya are expecting. This only works if I have a mimic of what the next port is expecting. So I need to find a real container with a real RFID tag going to a real location. And then steal it.'

'Actually,' said Don, 'we've been using smart boxes on those shipments. We'd get a tip-off if they were being tampered with.'

Mac nibbled on his bottom lip. Looked at Sawtell as if to say sorry. The smart boxes were an American attempt to stop container heists and terrorist infiltrations via container. They combined RFID tags and seals, GPS location beacons, and anti-tamper sensors, all built into a single anti-tamper box bolted to the container. They were the new wave in maritime security.

But they had a simple weakness.

'I'm here without prejudice, right?' said Mac to Hatfield.

'My personal guarantee.'

Don turned his hands up, looking to the other Yanks for help. His look said, *Who is this guy?*

'Well, smart boxes are driven by a boxful of C-size batteries,' said Mac.

260

'Are they?' said Hatfield.

'Um, yeah, and it doesn't take much to shut down a bunch of C-size batteries. Decent magnet will do it.'

Hatfield looked at Don, aghast. 'That could be why we've lost Box 138 off the screens, hey fellas?'

Sawtell gave Mac a look. Mac shrugged. Yanks might as well know this stuff.

CHAPTER 29

The group tore south out of the Macassar Strait and into the stretch of ocean separating Java from Borneo. If you were ever going to be accosted on the high seas by smiling looters with sarungs and AK-47s, the scimitar-shaped body of water where the Macassar Strait turned west into the Java Sea was where it was most likely to happen.

The CH-47D Chinooks flew line astern; the four Black Hawks flying abreast in a stagger, creating an arrow-head effect. The sea was only fifty feet below the Chinook Mac was in, pitch-black except for the intermittent flash of red aviation lights. The Chinook thromped, its turbine exhausts whining. Mac sat around the situation table with Don and Hatfield, having briefed them on the CL-20. They were still amazed that so much of the stuff was in one place, astonished it was being hauled around in gear bags in a speedboat.

'I'd love to know where all that CL-20 came from,' said Don as if Mac might have the answer, just like he knew how to kill battery power in the smart boxes. Mac wasn't going to hurt Don's image even more by admitting that most of his shipping knowledge came from a female Aussie cop.

Behind them, the guy called Brown was working on screens and liaising with Manila over his headset. Brown's subordinate had a big real-time screen with a bunch of white cigars on it. The major shipping companies had GPS locators on them and each of the white cigars had a small legend beside it which identified the vessel with a series of letters and numbers.

Mac had suggested they work back, get Manila International to find the orphan container left somewhere on the docks, the one with no RFID tag. Maybe also stripped of markings, maybe not. Then see what ship it was supposed to be on. It wouldn't be able to leave the MICT apron because the security gate would impound a container that was supposed to have an RFID tag, but didn't.

It was going to be a long search. MICT turned over about four thousand containers each day. The unions and management were on performance markers for their pay and, given that Manila had already had their hassles with the Americans, they were probably not going to drop everything and go looking for one untagged container in a seventy-five-hectare storage area. Not when it was the Americans' own fault. Mac reckoned if Sabaya's team had done their job, it would take a week to find that container, which was an unmarked red forty-footer. Just about the most common sight you'd see on a dock or container ship.

The guys on Hatfield's Chinook worked forwards too. Hatfield and Don had the sailing schedules of eight ships that had left Manila in the last eighteen hours, south-bound through the Sulu Sea to Surabaya or Lombok. There was a list of the vessels sitting in front of Hatfield. Mac was still betting it would be Surabaya. Lombok was busy but it still largely serviced 'feeder' container ships which also carried loose freight. Surabaya was more likely to service a large container ship from MICT.

Hatfield worked the main phone on the situation table. He was not in good shape. People from DC to Honolulu to Manila and Jakarta had questions. And Hatfield ate crow, said things like, 'We're working on it, sir. I have no idea, sir, but we're getting there, sir.'

From the odd cold stare Hatfield gave him, Don must have been silently churning with fear. Though the Twentieth's Technical Escort people had arranged the transportation of the VX to Johnston Atoll, Mac suspected the command responsibility had been DIA's. Another one of those soldier versus spook things. Intelligence people were not supposed to make mistakes. Ever.

Brown kept turning back from his heated conversations with MICT and Surabaya, cursing to himself, getting ratty. 'I can't *believe* this.'

While intra-Asian trade was the busiest in the world, they hadn't developed an advance-manifest system of the type used by the West. In the US, Canada and Australia each ship had to forward its electronic manifest – collected from all the RFID tags – to the destination port authority twenty-four hours before berthing. But in most of the Asian ports, the only way the port authority knew what was coming in was through the freight forwarders and shipping companies.

Mac knew from Jenny Toohey that finding the containers criminals didn't want you to find was uniquely frustrating, especially when, like Jen, you were looking for container loads of women and children. She could spend two or three days without sleep, going out of her mind, while port security, customs and operations managers at the terminals shrugged, said things like, 'Show me the box, I'll get someone to open it.' Jen always took that personally. It was probably why she was so good at it.

Hatfield was waiting for a confirmation from CINCPAC in Manila that he was going to get cooperation from the Indonesian Navy. These were Indonesian waters and its navy was overworked and under-resourced for a military force expected to cover seventeen thousand islands. Back in the late 1990s, when Western powers wanted Indonesia to get tough on Malacca pirates, their navy had only twenty operable vessels.

Hatfield was starting to get cranky, acutely aware that time was ticking away. The atmosphere at the Chinook's situation table was becoming smelly with fear and stress. The cigars on the screen were getting closer to the landmass of eastern Java. Mac couldn't add anything more.

Hatfield looked at his G-Shock. Pushed his hand through his white hair. The Chinook they were on had a direct patch to the most powerful comms and signals-intelligence apparatus ever developed. The Americans had keyhole satellites that could take images of a ten-inch object from one hundred and fifty miles aloft. If it was cloudy or dark, they'd use their Onyx satellites, which could only distinguish objects of ten feet and over. They could point a directional mic from space and listen to conversations, pick up keystrokes on a keyboard or hear a number being dialled on a mobile phone. The United States had the computing capacity to simultaneously intercept thousands of emails and mobile phone calls and have those communications translated and logged in real time.

All of this infrastructure was buzzing and whirring in the background. Brown and his sidekick brought up screens, ran numbers, yelled at Manila, yelled at Surabaya, yelled at CINCPAC and pleaded with the propeller heads at the satellite imaging agency called NIMA.

But nothing. A cagey terrorist from Mindanao and his CIA mate had managed to have a US Army shipment of the second-most toxic substance known to science simply disappear off the screens.

Hatfield breathed out. Looked away from the table. Composed himself, then asked Don for options.

'Pick the most likely ship on our list,' said Don. 'The one with the closest time-correlation to the VX going missing, and board her.' He cleared his throat. 'General.'

Hatfield looked at Mac, who said, 'I agree. We have to stop one of these ships and have a look. Otherwise we're going to have to shut down the whole shipping lane and I don't know if the Indons will buy that. If we get into that discussion we could spend more time arguing than searching.'

After a silence, Hatfield breathed out, said, 'Okay, let's hear it.'

Mac grabbed the list of south-bound container ships from MICT. Put it in front of Don. 'We can strike out *Golden Ram* and *Star of Bengal* because one's stopping in Cebu and the other is in Makassar as we speak, right? We know Sabaya and Garrison were motoring out into the Strait around eight o'clock yesterday morning, so we're looking for a ship that left MICT around ten pm the night before.'

'Which is a rough overlap with the time we realised the material was missing,' said Don.

'Right.'

Don ran his pen through a group of names: the ones on the top, too early. The ones on the bottom, too late.

Of the eight vessels, two were left: the RSL *Puget Sound* and the *Hokkaido Spirit*. Mac ticked two names, turned the list, slid it over to Hatfield.

Mac and Don held their breaths.

'Which one, boys? And make it quick,' snapped Hatfield.

Mac looked at Don, who wasn't game to say it.

Mac turned back. 'Both, General.'

Hatfield chuckled, almost laughed, until he realised Mac was serious. It was four in the morning and he was looking for a container of VX somewhere on the Java Sea. He had the most powerful military machine at his fingertips. And no one knew what the fuck was going on.

He shook his head, eyes looking tired, mumbled, 'Fuck me sideways.'

Then he picked up the phone with a grunt, hit a speed dial. 'Admiral? Hatfield. Twentieth. We have a target.'

Mac watched the boys from the Twentieth suit-up in their OSHA Level-A bio-hazard uniform, the only suit you could wear around nerve gas spills and what they called 'unknowns'.

The soldiers on the Chinook were all sergeants and above. Working with CBNRE was a delicate and exact business and you couldn't have some young dickhead wandering around deciding he knew best, especially when you were going to try to board a vessel at sea.

Mac watched the preparations. As machines were pulled out from the cargo area behind the airline seats, he recognised the percussion disrupter, an angular device that used shotgun blanks to stun detonation devices out of commission. He thought he saw a portable X-ray machine too.

Gantries were swung into place as Hatfield briefed a captain who was getting into his Level-A. Unlike the general-issue JSLIST suits that the world had seen on television during Operation Iraqi Freedom, the Level-A didn't have a canister that cleaned air from the outside. Level-As had their own forty-five-minute supply.

Brown yelled over his shoulder, 'General. CINCPAC on two.'

Hatfield picked up the receiver, hit a button. 'Hatfield. Twentieth . . . Got that, Admiral . . . Good to go, sir.'

The general put down the phone. 'Brown! Sawtell takes *Hokkaido* and Myers takes *Puget Sound*. Tell 'em stand-by for ten minutes and counting.'

Hatfield raised his G-Shock, squeezed two buttons and pushed another five or six times. Others around him did the same. He picked up the phone again, hit a button, waited. 'General Hatfield, Twentieth Support Command, United States Army. I'm –'

He was interrupted. He waited, tapping a pen on the situation table, sweat marks under his armpits. He nodded, dragged a hand across his brow. Scratched it. The rest of them looked on. Big tension.

Hatfield blinked long, said, 'Thank you, Commander. Appreciate your cooperation. Hope we can meet some time under better circumstances.'

'Gentlemen, The *Hokkaido Spirit* and *Puget Sound* have been ordered by the Indonesian Navy to shut down power and stand-by to be searched. They're giving us an hour. Let's go,' said Hatfield, clapping his hands.

The soldiers leapt to it. Through the gap behind the airliner seats, the guys in their Level-A kit were having what looked like white, plastic car-vacuum cleaners slung over their shoulders. Mac knew they weren't vacuum cleaners. He'd spent enough time on the docks with customs guys to know he was looking at explosives detectors. Mac thought he'd make a small point to Hatfield.

'General, I thought the point of CL-20 was that it's very hard to detect. Could be impossible through a steel container wall.'

Hatfield had the phone to his ear again and was distracted. 'Didn't I tell you, son?'

Don could sense something awry and he cleared his throat too loud.

Hatfield ploughed on. 'We'll be detecting the VX shipment.'

Looking away, he mumbled 'Thank you' into the phone.

Don was now a little pained, trying to physically get between Mac and Hatfield.

'But, General, VX is odourless. We can't detect it,' said Mac.

'I know,' said Hatfield with a smile as he looked back from the handset. 'But the bomb casements they're in have a nice big signature, believe me.'

CHAPTER 30

Hokkaido Spirit was a ten-year-old container ship with a capacity of four thousand containers. A mid-sized carrier working a line from Yokohama to Kaohsiung, to Manila, Surabaya and Fremantle, and then back again, once a week.

Sawtell's Black Hawk hovered over the starboard side of the ship while men in bio-hazard suits roped to the decks.

In the Chinook, the soldiers finished zipping Mac into a white OSHA Level-A, velcroed the collars and the ankle-ties and handed him a hard hat. Underneath he wore long woollen underwear, chemical-resistant overalls and a supplied-air NIOSH respirator with a full-face glass breathing mask. He felt totally uncomfortable and tried again to get Hatfield to see it his way.

'Know what, General, I could be more use up here in the helo. More of an advisory role,' he said.

Hatfield laughed. 'You're in good hands, son. Captain Alden here will walk you through it. Just no sudden movements, okay?'

The loadmaster threw back the large sliding doors on the side of the Chinook, and Alden and Mac stepped up.

Mac came down the winch lift onto the fo'c'sle deck, the Chinook's downwash so strong that the men could barely stand up under the pressure.

Brine smashed into the bow of the ship five storeys below, and the ship slopped around, swayed side to side. Sawtell's boys met him, unhitched him, told Alden to come on down. They were wired but the din of the Chinook's tandem rotors was so loud that communication was done with hand signals.

Alden landed and the Chinook moved away. They joined the five Special Forces troopers and Mac saw Sawtell smiling behind his mask.

'Let's go to work,' said Alden into the radio system.

Mac's breath rasped and wheezed into the respirator. The entire Level-A suit added ten degrees of temperature and about fifteen kilos of weight. The boots alone – chemical-resistant, steel-toe jobs – must have weighed as much as a medium-sized dog.

Alden asked Mac to join him to question the skipper, and then ordered Sawtell's boys to fan out.

'Mate, if they're on this ship, then at least some of the crew is on their side. See what I mean? This is Abu Sabaya we're talking about. Major league terrorist,' said Mac.

'Any ideas?' asked the captain.

Mac suggested the Green Berets and Mac go to the bridge, search the quarters and communal areas for people and make their move on any VX nerve agent from there. 'If the captain's not kosher, we'll know pretty quick.'

He recommended that Alden get moving on the detection systems with his guys. Hatfield had been ahead of Mac on that one. Had already determined that since you couldn't remotely detect for VX agent, they'd have to test for high explosive.

Fucking great!

Mac had assumed the VX was in forty-gallon drums or sealed canisters. But they had to store the stuff in warheads bolted to the front of one-hundred-pound bombs. The whole thing clicked into place: the secrecy when the stuff was discovered at Clark, the involvement of DIA, Don's shit-scared paranoia, the sight of an experienced army general gulping down the stress.

Sabaya had picked well. Those VX devices had been designed in the 1960s to spread the VX nerve agent as far as possible and the CL-20 was going to give that a boost. The scenario had got even uglier.

He forced himself to stay calm and focused. The captain had his blokes with their explosive detectors. Problem was you had to be virtually on top of the stuff to get a signal. Through the high-tensile steel of a shipping container, it could be pushing shit uphill. And looking up at the mountain of containers rising fifty feet in the air like a multicoloured Mayan temple, it seemed ridiculous.

The party split. Four went with Sawtell and Mac down the starboard inspection gantry. The captain and two guys from the Twentieth went down the port side.

They got to the deckhouse. It was the high-rise of the container ship that had the engine room at its base, the accommodation quarters and communal areas in the middle levels, and the bridge and comms rooms at the top.

A Japanese man called Tokada met them. He wore a white shirt with merchant marine pips on the shoulder. He greeted Sawtell in good English and then took a look at the rest of the suited-up crew. Got green around the gills, wide-eyed, like *Holy shit!*

His look of fright, complete lack of comprehension, told Mac this guy wasn't part of anything.

Mac and Sawtell got into the elevator with Tokada; all that could fit. As the lift got going, Mac reached his breaking point, whipped off the hood and respirator mask and took a deep breath. Everything around him was white: white lino, white formica walls, white ceiling.

'What are you looking for?' asked Tokada.

'We'll tell you if we find it,' said Mac.

Sawtell took off his head gear too, said to Tokada, 'This is Mac. Don't worry about his manners. He's Australian.'

Mac sat in the bridge and Captain Nagai helped him operate the computerised stowage system. You could run down the containers on board by any number of searches: port of offload, port of loading, twenty-foot containers, thirty-foot containers, and reefers that kept goods cool.

Mac was looking at the stowage map that allowed you to click on a position of a container on deck and bring up the details. He called Brown on the radio but there were still no clues out of Manila International.

Sawtell was searching the quarters and the engine bay and kitchen/ living areas. Mac doubted they'd find Garrison or Sabaya, or Diane. Sabaya's MO never put him with the stolen containers or the actual crime. Hokkaido Spirit might be carrying a VX bomb without knowing it. In that case there'd still be one or two crew who were in on it.

Mac clicked on the container locations and the files came up with port of loading, manifest, port of destination. Most of the containers originated in Kaohsiung and Yokohama and the main port of destination was Fremantle. Nothing obvious was coming up. Mac stuck to the outside piers of the container stack. If Sabaya was going to do this, he'd try to do a good job and he'd want access to his little bomb factory. The layout of a container ship made it very hard to open up a container at sea. The lashing systems that held the stowage in place were one-inch steel bars that ran across the small ends of the containers, preventing doors being opened. The stacks themselves were so closed up that you could barely get a person between them. Mac asked the captain for a heads-up on which containers could be opened. Nagai called over the XO and they conferred. If these people were friends with Sabaya or being threatened by him, they were incredibly relaxed about it. Mac was sure they were wasting their time.

They showed him the containers that were stowed in such a way that they could be opened at sea: when you looked at a stack of containers so all you could see were the doors, the ones you could open were at ten o'clock and two o'clock. Sabaya would have picked those spots.

Exhausted, Mac's brain buzzed, his eyesight was not doing well under the greenish tinge of the ship lighting.

He keyed the radio mic. 'Captain Sawtell, you there?'

'Sawtell, copy that.'

'Mate, I'm going out to help Alden. There's nothing I can do here.'

'Mac, can you support us down here first? We've got crew secured in the mess. Over.'

'Haven't told them what we're looking for, have you?'

'No.'

'Good.'

* * *

271

Mac took Nagai down with him. Wanted a bloke with authority and good English. Wanted to look at these blokes' eyes, see the reactions.

They were lined up, those who'd been sleeping in their underwear, others in pale blue ovies, the default uniform on commercial shipping. Mac looked for the odd man, the stare, the aversion, the wide eyes of the guilty guy, the slits of the liar. He looked for hands too deep in pockets, feet splayed all wrong, hips cocked with the wrong kind of tension.

But Mac saw only fear. Not all Japanese were sophisticated urbanites, as Westerners were led to believe. What Mac was looking at was a bunch of rural hicks who were just clever enough to know that men in bio-hazards didn't land on your ship in the middle of the Java Sea unless something was very wrong.

All the Green Berets had stripped back their hoods and respirators, their glass masks hanging under their chins.

Mac saw Spikey, and turned to Nagai, said, 'Captain, could you tell them something for me?'

When Nagai had finished translating, the crew was in an uproar. Tears, pictures of children being waved at Nagai. Mac had no Japanese but the general feeling was: *Get me the fuck off this floating freak show!*

Mac looked for the guilty one. He wasn't there. The Green Berets held their line, guns shouldered, the crew begging with them. The words weren't understood, but the eyes pleaded – one working man to another – to take them off this death ship.

Mac had laid it on pretty thick, describing what nerve agent did, how it killed you and how irreversible it was once it was out of its bottle.

Sawtell's men looked at Mac. Sweat dripped off top lips.

Mac looked at Nagai, said, 'Thanks, Captain. We're going to search the decks. Crew seems okay.'

'Did we have to do it like that?' asked Sawtell as they got to the elevator.

Mac nodded his head. 'Only way to do it, mate. If any one of the blokes was in on it, they'd be giving up their own mothers by now. No seaman will go along with that caper once they know what they're sailing on.'

* * *

Mac looked up at the main stack of container boxes. It was like a small building at sea. The ship wallowed and Mac had to distribute his weight not to fall. He saw what Nagai and Tokada had told him: three containers at two o'clock were not closed off by lashing or bracing. He and the others had been on the *Hokkaido Spirit* for thirty-five minutes. The respirator would be out of air soon.

There were huge steel ladders stowed lengthwise beside the gantry that ran bow–stern down each side of the container mountain. They were the lashing ladders. Stevedores used suspended cages to do the lashing in port but at sea the crews used the ladders for emergency work. Mac pointed, rasped through his mouthpiece to Alden. 'Let's get a bloke up there.'

It took three of the Twentieth's science guys to pick up the ladder and set it where it had to go. Mac and Alden held the feet of the thing which had large neoprene pads on the bottom. They couldn't quite get the angle they wanted. It stood almost upright and felt incredibly unsafe.

The soldier made good time for a bloke in a bio-hazard. He was rasping too by the time he got to the top. If it felt unstable at the feet, the top of the ladder must have been swinging like a metronome. Mac didn't like it, said to Alden, 'Poor bastard must have wondered why he didn't bring his life vest rather than the *China Syndrome* costume.'

The bloke up the ladder heard that and chuckled. Alden was about to pull him down when something came in on his radio.

Alden looked out at Mac through the Level-A hood and the glass mask. Held up his hand for quiet.

'Manila International found the orphan box. Should have been on the *Golden Serpent*.'

Mac's heart jumped a little. 'Where to?'

'Singapore,' said Alden.

CHAPTER 31

The Chinook could cruise at a little under two hundred miles per hour – pretty quick for a lumbering freight donkey, but still about ten mph faster than the smaller Black Hawk. Neither of the aircraft had much more than two hundred miles range in the tank. So the first thing Hatfield ordered when they were back over the sides was a fuel stop at Surabaya Naval Base.

Mac was soaked with sweat, tasting rubber deep in his lungs. He stood in line to get de-suited as everyone took turns helping the other guy out of the suits. The other blokes kept on their first layer of protections, the coveralls. This was just the beginning of their day.

The situation room was going crazy. The brass in Manila and Honolulu screamed over the air phone to get the hell into Singapore. Yesterday.

The screens showed the *Golden Serpent* alongside a landmass. When Mac asked Don where the ship was, he slumped his face down on his hands. 'Port of Singapore. Keppel Terminal.'

Hatfield had his BDU jacket off, going ape into his phone. 'I don't give a shit, you hear me?! I have one hundred and eighty bombs containing nerve agent sitting in a container on that ship!'

Mac saw a new map on the situation table. It was of the south side of Singapore Island. A steel marker – like a stainless-steel chess

274

piece – sat on an area called Keppel Terminal. It was just a few blocks from Cantonment Road. Straight up the hill were the big residential suburbs of Queenstown and Newton. Behind it were the skyscrapers, the hotels, banks and shipping companies. Keppel was on the doorstep of Singapore city.

Hatfield wasn't getting through to someone. He was trying to explain that the Twentieth was ninety minutes away at least and the Singapore government had to go to what he called Em-Con – Emergency Contingency. His folder said Singapore had one. The bloke on the other end had no idea what Hatfield was on about.

The air phone crackled with breathless, panicked American voices followed by laidback Singaporean accents saying, 'Yeah. Right. Uh-huh. Yeah.'

Brown worked his panels like a piano player. He was kicking something upstairs, but while CINCPAC in Manila had become involved on a joint military level, nothing seemed to be happening.

'I need to speak with the security chief,' Hatfield blared into his phone. 'Okay, okay, the vice-president of security, whatever. I – I know what time of the goddamn morning it is, thank you very much. What? Hatfield! General Louis Hatfield, United States Army!'

The atmosphere in the situation room was pandemonium. The Twentieth was a classified operation, reports on their operations didn't go before house committees, they weren't picked apart on CNN. Their only mission was to respond to any CBNRE emergency at any time, anywhere in the world. Their budget wasn't limitless but it was in the same deep-pocket league as Delta Force and the geo-spatial guys. Now they had American VX nerve agent wrapped in American CL-20 and a rogue American spook running it.

And the whole freak show had sailed into the Port of Singapore, the world's busiest port.

Mac felt the revs coming up and the massive surge of turbine exhaust and shrieking of horsepower as the Chinook lifted away from Surabaya Naval Base.

Hatfield barely noticed. He was a dynamo.

Mac thought about how Sabaya and Garrison had probably lured the tail and, once out of sight of land, got an airlift to the other side of Borneo, RV'ing with Golden Serpent, and leaving the tail nothing but assumptions.

275

Mac might have picked it if he hadn't been so tired. But even then, you had to start with the obvious. You never wanted to get lost in the double-reverse psychology department. That was for theorists and second-guessers, people who wanted a bigger office. Sabaya and Garrison had probably had a couple of insiders on board *Golden Serpent* and no doubt one of the captain's kids was hidden away somewhere. He wondered what they wanted.

What they wanted!

The missing piece.

'Mate, what do they want?' he asked Don between phone calls.

Don stared at him. 'Who?'

'Garrison and Sabaya. Has anyone talked to them?'

Don shrugged.

'Has MPA spoken with the skipper?'

Now Hatfield was listening too. 'MPA?' he asked.

'Yeah. Maritime and Port Authority,' said Mac. 'Their harbour-control people. The Port Master and operations manager will be there.'

Hatfield leaned down on the phone cradle, hit a speed dial, got back to the person he'd been speaking with. Took a deep breath, said, 'MPA operations. Port Master, please.'

The situation room stopped and looked at Hatfield, who sat down, said, 'That the Port Master? General Hatfield, US Army . . .'

Hatfield nodded, pulled over the piece of paper. 'There's a message for me, huh? Now why am I not surprised about that?'

The group was about fifty-five minutes out of Singapore when the ends came together. Mac was not needed. He got out of their way, took a seat, reclined it and tried to get some sleep. Let the boys from the Twentieth and DIA do what they were paid for.

A mix of MPA emergency response, Singapore Police and Singapore Armed Forces tumbled out of the speaker phone. There was a government guy in there too, somewhere, and the panic was now coming from the Singapore side. The biggest worry seemed to be how to deal with the threat and not close down the port. Port of Singapore's four huge terminals turned over just under half a million containers every week. It was the busiest port in the world and the island republic's raison d'être. No one – especially not a screaming American – shut down the Port of Singapore.

Hatfield put on a pair of half-glasses, looked down at his notes and said, 'Gentlemen, this is the message from the bridge of *Golden Serpent*: "Don't approach the vessel. Don't fly over the vessel. Don't contact the vessel. We will be in contact soon with our demands."'

The Singaporean politicians and generals went up as one and Hatfield winced away from the speaker phone. Silenced them again.

'The message has been directed to me personally. General Hatfield, Twentieth Support Command. Which means they know what we do, they expected our response and they know there'll be a special forces aspect to how we proceed.'

A person who Mac thought was the Minister of Defence piped up, 'Why are they talking to the American army? Why not us?'

'Don't know, sir, I suspect it's a control thing,' said Hatfield. 'But if you think it's a good idea to step in, then by all means. I'm just reading you the message. Our principal mission is the return of the stolen material and the protection of human life.'

The Singaporeans kept yelping. Hatfield repeated the message, said that was all he had. That the message had come through MPA. He was trying to keep the Singaporeans focused on what they could actually do: evacuation plans, general preparedness, emergency services stand-by, logistics, comms. And the big issues: how to inform the shipping community without creating mayhem, and how to evacuate the residents without causing a stampede across the causeways into Malaysia – a stampede that the Malaysians might want to slow.

The general wanted to know the Singaporean Em-Con. The answers weren't clear; it sounded like a bunch of office guys blamestorming: 'No, I told you. Remember?' 'No, but then I sent you that memo. You got that, didn't you?'

The army guys and the police had a jurisdictional overlap. The Port Master had the legislative oversight and the MPA emergency and fire service seemed to wield executive power over the lot of them when it came to hazardous and chemical emergencies.

There were other things the Singaporeans could be doing, such as stocking up on water and taping their doors and windows if they couldn't make a run for it, said the general.

Hatfield defaulted back to the basics. 'Gentlemen. This is what we know: the people who left this message have almost two hundred bombs that contain VX nerve agent. We also believe they are in possession of an experimental explosive material called CL-20. It's about three times more powerful than C4, and we believe they have in the neighbourhood of twenty cases of it.'

'What could it do?' asked the Singaporean Police voice on the other end.

'Well, you remember Bali?' asked Hatfield.

'Sure do.'

'Those were homemade potassium chlorate bombs. When detonated, the air around them expanded at about three thousand five hundred feet per second. CL-20 makes the air expand at about forty-five thousand feet per second. It's more than twelve times as powerful.'

'So what would twenty cases of this stuff do?' asked someone.

'I've only seen it detonated one brick at a time. Experimental stuff. And that was enough to flatten a small building. And I mean *flatten*,' said Hatfield.

Voices rose on the other end of the phone.

'Each case contains five bricks,' said Hatfield. 'So you get the idea.'

The voices started shrilling over one another before one voice dominated. Mac thought he heard him introduce himself as Colonel.

'General, I'm more interested in what's in the container. Last time I saw any literature on VX, I calculated that two of those American bombs would be enough to finish Singapore. How many did you say you had?'

'Well, Colonel, *we* don't have them. But if none of the shipment has been touched or removed, there's one hundred and eighty.'

The roar went up again.

Hatfield was stressed but calm. 'Gentlemen, we'll be landing inside of fifty minutes. May I suggest the Em-Con be in place and a military or police command be operating when we arrive?' he said.

Hatfield had just, in the kindest tone, suggested they get their shit together.

Mac awoke from his doze. Don and Hatfield stood in front of him; the general's BDU shirt was back on.

'We're detouring for Halim. Drop you off. Been good meeting you, Mr McQueen,' said Hatfield, putting out his hand.

'Halim?' said Mac.

'Yeah,' smiled Don. 'This just in.'

Don threw a printout onto Mac's lap. It was an order from the CINCPAC offices in Manila, and included was the cc'd request from the military attaché at the Australian Embassy in Jakarta to render *all Australian personnel* at earliest convenience.

Mac smiled. The system worked. At some point it always did. Frank used to tell him that.

Don was enjoying himself. 'Time to get back to the reservation, huh, tough guy?'

Mac looked at him. The word 'reservation' was meaningful in American intelligence circles. The suggestion was that Mac was rogue.

Mac winked at the bloke. Don wasn't going to bed for another three days. Mac knew what that was like. Decided to let it all go.

'Thanks, General. Thanks, Don. It's been fun. Hope you resolve this whole mess,' said Mac.

When the two Americans had left him alone, Mac eased back in the seat. It was over. He'd taken his shot, got Judith Hannah back to the clubhouse. He'd put the loose ends together in what might become one of South-East Asia's defining moments. He'd saved a British spook's life. He'd killed a man, by mistake. Killed another for good reason. Been put in hock to Cookie B.

Had his heart broken.

The Chinook peeled away from the group. He looked to his right through the window, saw the other helos keep tramping for Singers and had a brief flap of fear and hope for Sawtell and his boys. He'd found Captain Sawtell a bit robotic and terse in the early days. But they'd forged a friendship of sorts. They'd been on the same side in two gunfights now, and in the world Sawtell inhabited, men didn't get much closer than that.

Mac closed his eyes.

CHAPTER 32

Mac had grabbed some sleep and was now watching CNN. The main story of the hour was the International Maritime Organisation security committee annual conference in Singapore. The theme was Maritime Security: Asia fixing an Asian problem. He waited for the news flashes and the ticker along the base of the screen but there was nothing on *Golden Serpent*. It was just before eight am and he guessed the incident at Keppel Terminal might still be under wraps.

He sat in an office at Halim Air Base, on the outskirts of Jakarta. The white, square two-storey building was an international cooperation zone used by foreign spooks, diplomats and military types as a forward staging area for all sorts of comings and goings. Australian law could be applied in the zone, so someone like Mac could be arrested by the AFP just as if it were happening in St Kilda. He was resigned to that.

Through the open venetians, the sun was coming up. An APS bloke called Nigel was next door, in a secretarial area, trying to talk surreptitiously into the phone. It was the third call he'd made and Mac could guess what was being said at the other end as he listened to Nigel.

'Well, yeah. I mean, he's here.'

Silence.

'Davis.'

Silence.

'No, he's okay. Friendly.'

Silence.

'Okay, okay. Don't worry, he's not moving around.'

Silence.

'No one else is here.'

Silence.

'Just the cuffs.'

Silence.

'Okay, I got that. But he's not going anywhere, I mean –'

Silence.

'Only got one set. Actually, there's more in the car . . .'

Silence.

'Okay, okay. I'll stay with him.'

Mac chuckled. The APS guy was big and built. He was straight-forward too, probably recruited from a detectives' room in Brisbane or Perth. Mac had already seen three chances to incapacitate him, get the cuff keys from the leather pouch on his belt, take his Glock and get on the run again. He could even have switched into the bloke's blue ovies, taken his cap and his Commodore, driven out the security gates like he did this for a living.

But it wasn't going to happen. Mac's wrist was playing up and he'd asked Nigel to secure him at the ankles.

Nigel came into the office, put a mug of tea on the fake wood-grain desk beside Mac, keeping his distance, his hand unconsciously dropping to the Glock on his right hip.

'Cheers, mate,' said Mac.

'No worries.'

Mac checked out the mug he'd scored. 'Couldn't have got something even more appropriate, could ya?'

He turned the mug to Nigel. It said *All Men Are Bastards*.

Nigel laughed. 'Sorry, mate. Secretaries!'

The CNN story churned on. They had a reporter called Stan in front of what looked like the convention centre at Raffles City. Stan seemed excited . . . *still no confirmation, Betty, but insiders at this IMO security conference are telling us to expect a surprise guest speaker this morning. The military are already moving people back and it looks like we're going to have half the downtown area shut down for this.*

And I can inform our viewers that the worst-kept secret around here is that we'll be hearing from the Chinese Army's Xiong Ming . . .

The anchor, Betty, cut over, *And who is Xiong Ming?*

. . . Betty, he's the PLA's Supreme Marshal and as such he controls the PLA General Staff. The PLA General Staff is enormously powerful – it's military, of course, but it's also political, economic and social. The PLA General Staff has an influence over all Chinese government policy and –

So what's he doing in Singapore for this conference? asked Betty.

Betty, we can only guess at what Xiong Ming is going to say. But the first point is that Xiong is not known for public appearances, and it's rumoured that he's never left mainland China in a declared manner. Secondly, we know Xiong has been the loudest voice in the East Asian area for a concerted military approach to maritime security in the South China Sea and Malacca Strait. Xiong was one of the architects behind the push for the Chinese naval base on the Spratlys and he's considered more of a hawk in maritime matters than even the Americans. So – because this is an IMO security conference – insiders are expecting him to spell out the Chinese vision for secure trade in the future. Singapore is buzzing with the rumour that Xiong is going to publicly – for the first time – advocate an official Chinese naval presence in Singapore. If that's what he does, it's worth noting that he's also the senior voice in Beijing for a 'Greater China' policy. Betty . . .

The shot was on the anchor again, who thanked the reporter and segued into a story about a new tollway.

Mac liked hearing Stan in the mornings. The Aussie accent and everything. But the story itself worried him. Xiong was an immensely powerful figure in Beijing and his Greater China outlook even scared a lot of the political hard-heads of the Communist Party. Xiong speaking at an IMO conference in Singapore was symbolic and Mac hoped the speech wasn't about naval bases. He didn't think the Singaporean police were going to like the story either. If Xiong was flying in and it was already being broadcast as a rumour, the police would go to controlled airspace, a total hassle for any law enforcement or civil aviation type. They'd be doing that while also trying to deal with *Golden Serpent* down at Keppel.

Mac could just sense some of the outbursts and recriminations being flung around down at MPA operations centre right now. Hatfield saying, *Where's your Em-Con? Who's in charge?* The Singaporeans saying, *How do you lose one hundred and eighty bombs loaded with VX nerve agent?*

'Politicians are all the same, aren't they?' said Nigel, snorting. 'Doesn't matter what language they speak, they're always talking about what they're not talking about. Know what I mean?'

Mac smiled. Knew what he meant.

It was 8.20 am when Garvey turned up, Nigel walking him through to where Mac was. Mac put down the new IBM mug he'd been given.

'Garvs. 'Zit going, champ?'

Garvey put his hands on his hips. No shake. Looked around the office, nodding his head. Looked at Mac.

'What? No broken wrists? A bullet wound, perhaps? Not losing your edge are ya, mate?'

Mac smiled. No heart in it.

'Saw Marlon last night. Down at MMC,' said Garvs.

MMC was the Jakarta hospital used by Americans and Australians.

'How was he?' asked Mac.

'Oh, I dunno, worried about the shoulder reconstruction. Worried that his kids might be worrying about their dad. That sort of thing.'

As Garvey moved to sit on the desk, Mac noticed a Glock on his hip, under his shirt.

'Didn't know you were S-2, Garvs.'

Garvey shrugged. The two men stared at one another as if fifteen years of friendship had never happened.

'Still looking for a flight. May be this evening, get you into Darwin,' said Garvs.

Mac nodded.

'Mate, just go along with the process, huh? Let's see if we can salvage something.'

Mac looked at him, unsmiling. Garvs was the sort of person who'd hear phony Americanese like *process* and *salvage* and tell someone to get their hand off it. Times had sure changed.

'We going to debrief?' asked Mac.

'Haven't been asked to. But if you want to talk . . .'

Which strongly suggested that Garvs was wired.

Mac changed tack. 'What's Xiong doing in Singers?'

'Maritime security. That's the conference, isn't it?'

'Why would Xiong come in to talk about that? Bunch of pirates, terrorists messing with the Chinese economy? It's a pretty old story.'

'Could be that naval base shit again,' said Garvs, sniffing and looking away.

Mac's ears pricked up. Skin crawled. A sixth sense, when someone has verbally slipped and is using nonchalance to recover. Where had *naval base* come from?

He looked at Garvs, but the big guy was looking out the venetians. Trying to change angles.

'So where you been, old man?' said Garvs, too casually.

'Just looking into things,' said Mac.

Garvs crossed his arms over his chest. 'Things, huh? Where?'

Either Garvs was foxing or the Twentieth's reputation for maintaining a fully classified operation was holding true.

'Round the archipelago. You know how it is.'

'How it is was that you were on a plane back to Sydney, last time we spoke,' said Garvs, forced smile.

'Yeah,' said Mac, like he was a teenager weighing which rock concert he would get tickets for. 'But there were loose ends. Things didn't add up.'

'What's this? *Hawaii* 5-0?' said Garvs.

'In your dreams I guess that makes me Dano.'

The two stared at each other, the years compressing.

The front doors suddenly opened and an Aussie girl in her twenties and two British girls came through, laughing about what someone did to 'Bridge Over Troubled Water' at the karaoke last night. Realising Mac and Garvs were there they blushed, shut their mouths, walked through to the admin area.

Garvs got up, shut the door behind them. 'See, Macca, I can't work out why you went back to Sulawesi.'

Mac shrugged. 'Told you, things didn't add up.'

'What things?' Garvs was making swirls with his finger on the desk.

Mac fixed him with a look. 'I realised Garrison had to be working with one of our guys. I decided to find out who.'

Mac thought he saw an eye tremor, wondered if Garvs was dissembling.

If he was, Garvs rescued it quick with a laugh. 'Don't tell me, Macca – a mole, right?'

Mac didn't let the stare go, even though Garvs was laughing at him. 'Mole sounds very Cold War, doesn't it, Garvs?' he said. 'Let's say there's another kind of black operator who's no mole, not a double and maybe isn't even behaving illegally?'

'Okay.'

'Might be a good man, asked to do something. Something he's not completely comfortable about, but which gets him into the Big Boys' Club.'

'Really?'

'Yeah. Might not know the whole picture. Only be told the outcome or only told about the benefits.'

Garvs shot his eyebrows up too quick. 'How would someone work that?'

'It's an old move. If blackmail and threats don't work, try some reverse flattery.'

'Really?'

Mac was taking Garvs into areas he hadn't been into. Truth was, Garvs wasn't very good at the things Mac excelled at. Thought he'd give a glimpse of himself in operational mode.

He altered his voice, got into character. Did what he'd done a thousand times, all over Asia. 'You know, "Garvs, it so amazes me that you're still only an IO after so many years. You're so smart. So much smarter than these smarmy pricks who are getting paid twice as much as you and deciding your future. Don't know who the halfwit is who's been passing you over, but you know, I see you as director material. Fair dinkum, Anton, you're the type of person we need for these new taskings. No one else knows what the fuck's going on. But hey! Here's an idea! I'm having lunch with the DG next week in Tokyo, it'd be great to know I had your permission to put your name forward . . . "'

Garvs was embarrassed. Had broken the stare. Put his hand up. 'Okay, okay.'

Mac pushed on. 'How it works, mate. Only, as an afterthought, I'd say something like, "You know, Anton, we've been having this little problem. Been working on it with the American side. Hush-hush, classified, of course, but thought you'd like to sit in, lend us a hand while we get you in front of the DG, huh?" '

Mac didn't know if he'd hurt Garvs. Or if he'd struck something else. The big guy exhaled, looked through the venetians at the heat shimmers now coming off the concrete of Halim. He shoved a hand in his pocket, brought something out, popped it in his mouth. It was chewing gum.

The front doors flew inward and a bloke Mac knew entered the building, bandage across his nose, black eye – one of those ones with an egg yolk in it. A black cap on his head, he was dressed in grey ovies. He had a man and a woman in his wake as he stormed along the entry corridor.

The party went down the hallway and the MI6 guy called Paul suddenly reappeared. He'd reversed up, didn't miss anything. Paused at the door, smiled at Mac and entered the room.

'You're up early. You shit the bed?'

Mac laughed. 'Nah, that was your missus. You can have her back now.'

Paul came forward, shook Mac's left hand. Mac did introductions with Garvs.

Paul turned back, kept the musical Pommie accent going. 'You could be the man we're looking for, McQueen.'

Mac looked at Paul, looked at Garvs. 'Yeah?'

'Got a small thing in Singers this morning. Need a bloke who's all over it.'

'Short-staffed?' asked Mac.

'All at a conference. They pulled me out of MMC.'

Mac thought about the IMO security bash at Raffles City and realised that that's where the Service would always have deployed him. Natural fit: his turf, his specialty. The penny dropped. They wanted him out of Singers too.

Garvs cleared his throat. He seemed nervous around Paul.

'Mate, you didn't see the ankle bracelet. Makes him look like a tart, if you ask me,' said Garvs to Paul.

Paul looked down. 'He's right, McQueen. It's tarty. Lose it and let's get going.'

Garvs stood, looked at Paul, chewing furiously. 'He's in custody, mate. Understand?'

'Sure,' said Paul. 'But we'll be needing him.' He walked to the door. Turned back to Garvs. 'Have him ready in two, thanks mate.'

Garvs shook his head, like this Pommie was going to get a word in the shell-like. Paul put up his hand. Yelled 'Anthea' over his shoulder. Garvs and Paul eyed off for eight seconds. Something colder than hate.

A medium-height brunette came through, a clipboard in her hand. Paul said, 'Can we get a copy of that executive order? And bring a requisition for Mr McQueen to sign, okay? It's McQueen, Alan.'

Anthea dashed out of the room. Paul stood his ground and Garvs straightened up, a bead of sweat on his top lip.

'*Davis* is going nowhere, 'cept on a plane into Darwin. Townie, if he's lucky,' said Garvs.

'Ten days ago your government resourced us to requisition from all coalition partners as part of our joint CT sweep. So I'm requisitioning,' said Paul.

Garvs tried to stare him down. But Paul didn't seem to mind. He stared straight back.

Anthea came back, gave Paul a piece of green paper, the last or second-last sheet on a triplicate form. The whites, reds and blues were sitting somewhere else, probably in Canberra and the British Embassy. The green paper had a man's handwriting in the tasking section. Some boxes were ticked, N/A was written in other places. The signature was looping but you could read the name: the Australian Minister for Foreign Affairs.

Mac had never seen an EO before, but he remembered the low-level circular that had accompanied the agreement between the UK, Australia and the US to share intelligence and assets in the latest CT operations.

Mac handed the order to Garvs, whose breathing was stiff as he went all out on the chewing gum.

'We'll see about this,' said Garvs, heading for the other side of the room, where he grabbed at a phone and hunched over it.

'What made you cotton?' said Mac to Paul, keeping his voice soft.

Paul looked over at Garvs remonstrating into the phone, whispered 'I was walking around the long way to get to Hasanuddin Airport,

287

and I realised something. In all the years I'd been observing you, writing field reports on you, I'd never seen you anything except cool.'

'Thanks.'

'So when I finally got to speak with you in that van, and you're a wreck, I thought I should assume something was genuinely up and try to work it through.'

'Yeah?'

'Realised that the CL-20 that Sabaya had –'

'You knew about that?'

'Came from a US Army bunker in Guam. I'd been trying to get a handle on what it was for. So I'm walking along with a bleeding face and remembering that Sabaya had spent a week in Manila. I put that with the VX heist. Realised why you looked so stressed.'

Garvs turned with the phone at his ear and the order in his hand, said, 'Hang on just a minute, you two.'

Garvs rabbited on to whoever was listening in Canberra. But nothing trumped an executive order. Garvs put the phone down, sullen, handed the sheet to Anthea and shrugged. Then he called Nigel through.

As Nigel loosed the irons, Mac signed a British government form, freshly printed out with his name on it.

Mac checked his backpack. The Heckler was still there, so were the passports, cash and visa.

As they left, Mac couldn't work out what saddened him more; Anton Garvey's dejected state, or the chewing gum wrapper that lay on the desk.

Special Mint. Bartook.

CHAPTER 33

Mac sat in the back of a civilian-marked Gazelle helo as it flew in to Singapore at one hundred and eighty miles per hour. It was 9.16 am. Clear skies, medium humidity.

Next to him was an MI6 contractor called Weenie. Despite the crap name, Weenie was the comms version of a safe-cracker. Between them sat two cases with the capacity to lock on to restricted or scrambled frequencies such as those used by the Port Authority, the Singaporean Police or the armed forces. Weenie couldn't promise he'd be able to jam into the Americans' bandwidths, but he'd try. The other, smaller case – the size of a laptop bag – allowed Weenie to find the location of cell phones.

Mac told Paul all he could remember about where the VX might be and what, precisely, had been in Sabaya's message to Hatfield. However, his mind was so exhausted he was having trouble focusing. Paul wasn't in great shape either. When they pulled him out of MMC, he'd had a shot of morphine just an hour earlier. They were a right pair.

'The thing we have to remember is that Garrison or Sabaya – whoever's running the show – asked for Hatfield by name,' said Mac.

'Clever,' said Paul.

'Well, yeah. Ensure conflict and confusion in the other camp before you make a single demand.'

They flew over the Pasir Panjang terminal, the western-most of the four major terminals at the south end of Singers. To their right, more than twenty large container ships sat at their berths in the other three terminals: Brani, Keppel and Tanjong Pajar. Keppel and Pajar clung to the main island but Brani was a small island in the Singapore Strait, just in front of the larger island of Sentosa.

Paul trained his binos on the ships below, picked out a name plate.

'Second away from us on the mainland quay,' said Paul into the mic. 'That's our *Golden Serpent.*'

Activity around Keppel Terminal seemed to have stopped. The rubber tyre gantries and portainers were stationary.

'The MPA has finally gone to Em-Con. Or the cops have done it for them,' said Mac.

'Em-Con?'

'Emergency contingency.'

The pilot crackled into their two-way radio chat, 'I'm being asked to divert. It's controlled air space.'

'Circle back, mate – go to Plan B,' said Mac.

The Gazelle banked hard, dipped and accelerated downward before tearing back along the path it had come. Diving to a very low flight path, they zapped back into the Malacca Strait for two miles and then banked hard left at ninety degrees. Mac was convinced the rotor was going to hit the sea and the pilot was not backing off in the speed department.

Mac swivelled to his right and checked out the two eastern terminals. 'They've shut down Brani and Pajar too. The media will be on it soon.'

They flew low behind Sentosa Island, the peak of the island's hill hiding the Gazelle from anyone on *Golden Serpent.*

The pilot dropped to the beach behind the plush greenery of the Sentosa Golf Club. Paul and Mac checked radios, watches, weapons and cell phones. They threw two black Cordura gear bags onto the sand and jumped out. The pilot and Weenie gave thumbs-up as the Gazelle lifted away, and Mac realised it had dropped a large webbed sling on the beach from a release-hook beneath the fuselage.

Mac walked over, grabbed the sling and dragged it up the beach beneath a stand of trees and undergrowth. Then went back for the black bags.

Paul checked radio contact. Ran some tests and redundancies with Weenie.

Mac got the three gear bags to the undergrowth, unharnessed the four points of the sling, let it fall open and saw a bunch of equipment. In its own light canvas bag he saw a folding kayak, known as a Klep. There were black nylon webbing sacks which contained goggles, fins, weight belts, snorkels and rebreathers. Two of everything.

Mac exhaled, stared. He knew this stuff from the Royal Marines. The thirty-two-week basic commando course had given way to another six months of what they called the 'canoeists swimmer' program, the selection course for the Special Boat Service, or SBS.

It was hell, especially the nocturnal frogman sections. He had learned how to be very scared yet put the fear aside by focusing on a mission. But it didn't mean he was comfortable having a frogging exercise foisted on him with no warning.

'We okay, mate?' asked Paul, who had moved up to the stand of trees.

'You ran a database, found my military listings, didn't you?' said Mac. 'And then you dreamed up this shit!' Mac kicked the Klep.

'Mate, watch the boat,' said Paul.

Mac saw confusion and he pulled himself together. The guy was just trying to do his job, and picking another bloke with a military background was the smart thing to do.

'Sorry, champ,' said Mac, smiling. 'I walked up, saw that rebreather, and *woah*!'

'I see.'

'It's okay. I just have to get psyched into the frogman bit. No more surprises, okay?'

Paul laughed. Shook his head at the joke of it all. 'Mate. Glad I'm not the only one.'

'You what?'

Paul eyeballed him. 'Let's just say that if we can do this during daylight, that'd be out-fucking-standing. Know what I mean?'

CHAPTER 34

They made it to the top of Sentosa Island in three and a half minutes, through the golf course and skirting the buildings on the top of Serapong Hill. No one from the golf club stopped them. In their ovies they looked like contractors or tradesmen, which was why the British military trained intel and special forces to wear them. They took the shape away from a man, made it harder to see gait, and created a sense that the person must be where he was for a reason. More importantly, the block-colour of the overall took all the observer's attention, making the face retreat. Add a cap and you became the grey man. For people like Mac and Paul ovies were about the cheapest and most basic building block of fading into the background.

They edged through trees to reach the top of the hill. To their right they looked down five hundred metres to a new canal residential subdivision. In front of them was Brani Island, sitting in the harbour channel. Beyond that was Keppel Terminal on the main island of Singapore.

They perched behind a fallen spruce, panting. Paul pulled out the binos, had a quick look. Handed them to Mac. 'You know what we're looking for, mate. I'll get Weenie working for his dough,' said Paul.

As Paul keyed the radio and spoke to Weenie, Mac put his eyes to the rubber-coated Leicas. He touched the auto focus a couple of times to make sure there wasn't a sharper position, then he looked. The first impression was total stillness. Port of Singapore was a 24/7 business and Keppel Terminal was *never* still. Mac swept from left to right, moving from the massive truck/rail freight interchange depot on the far side of Keppel Road to the end of the terminal beside Keppel, Tanjong Pajar. At Pajar the apron squared off and suddenly fell into open sea and the Singapore Strait.

No movement.

He dipped the binos to the foreground. In front of him, on Brani Island, the activity on the container terminal had stopped too.

To the left of Brani Island Mac saw the causeway that linked Sentosa and Brani islands to the main island. It was chocka, all the vehicles heading in one direction.

A blast of noise behind them caused Paul and Mac to duck reflexively. It was the Singapore cops telling people to get the hell out of the buildings and the car parks and move across the Gateway Avenue causeway.

They listened to a man in the car park at the top of the hill argue with the cop. A tense police officer snapped back, 'Get in the car, get across Gateway, and there's no right turns into downtown today, sir. Get on the Ayer Rajah Expressway and go to Malaysia for the day.'

The cop car moved off down the drive towards the golf club, and Mac heard the man whining to his family, heard the wife say, 'Let's just do what he says.'

Paul continued on the radio while Mac went looking for *Golden Serpent* through the Leicas. It was a red-hulled vessel, perhaps three years old, with its deckhouse two-thirds of the way down the ship from the bow. It belonged to a Korean shipping company, Golden Dragon Line. All of their ships started with 'Golden'.

Mac had her as a nine-thousand-container ship, what they called a Post-PanaMax because it was too big to fit through the Panama Canal's locks. It looked fully laden, an absolute shitload of containers to search.

He scanned back and forth. No movement. Sitting stock still he scanned for any reflections from inside the bridge. The cloud cover hadn't arrived yet so there was every chance he might catch a glint.

Nothing.

He switched to the cargo decks, looking for any sign of the VX bomb. It had been shipped in a forty-foot red container box that looked completely standard, except for a smart box on one end. A smart box would stick out like a household fusebox about halfway up the height of the container. Mac knew what to look for, but couldn't see it.

He gave the Leicas back to Paul, who said into the mic: 'Yeah, mate, get back to me in ten, huh? Cheers, mate.'

Weenie had jammed into the radio chatter on the Singaporean side, said Paul. 'Something called the EOC?'

'Yep,' said Mac. 'That's the Emergency Operations Centre. I'm betting it's down at Tanjong Pajar. It'll be in the MPA ops centre.'

Paul shook his head. 'How do you know all this?'

'Mate, while you were running around with Aldam Tilao, I was pretending to be all sorts of things. Don't you worry about that.'

'Okay, well they're fully panicked. Weenie says there's lots of screaming and blame mongering,' said Paul.

'Glad to hear it. Any word on what they're doing?'

'Evacuating the whole city. Apparently there's no safe levels of this stuff. You can't have people wandering around. There's arguments about that, but a fire chief has stepped in.'

'That'd be right.'

'Weenie wasn't sure. He thought the word was Hazmar, or something. Said it sounded Arabic.'

Mac laughed. 'It's HAZMAT.'

'Shit. Sorry.'

'The arguments are jurisdictional. In most EOPs –'

'Speak English, mate.'

'In most Emergency Operations Plans there's a command and control chart for who makes the final call. But once it goes to HAZMAT, the fire chief – in most countries – has control of the ground.'

'Thought you said the Yanks had brought in some classified cavalry? Yanks going to let a fire chief run the show?'

Mac didn't know quite how to explain it. 'Mate, the bottom line in emergency management is who runs the cops. You can't run an evacuation without them. And when things get stressed, and people are talking about nerve agent and evacuations, the cops will work with who they know and trust. And that would be the fire department, not some American general.'

Paul nodded. Made sense.

'Has Weenie heard anything about what Garrison and Sabaya want? We need to work out where this is going, maybe get there before them,' said Mac.

'I'll get back to it.'

'Mate, didn't bring any tucker did you?' asked Mac.

Paul pulled out a couple of protein bars from his breast pocket, chucked one. 'What, they can't feed you?'

'Mate, I thought the Australian Air Force was going to personally attend to me. Till you turned up.'

Munching on the protein bar, Mac looked down on *Golden Serpent* and, seeing Brani Island between themselves and the ship, made a decision.

Paul got off the phone. 'Weenie says he picked up a conversation between a cop and a politician. Something about prisoners? The politician told him he had no jurisdiction over Philippines prisons, let alone over Moro separatists. Weenie's still on it.'

Mac stood, looked down at Brani Island. 'Moros, huh?'

'It's what he's hearing,' said Paul.

'You believe that?'

'Mate, looks like you saw a ghost.'

Mac nodded. 'I don't buy it.'

'What?'

'You know these guys are pretty smart. They heist a couple of rare birds: VX and CL-20. They hijack a huge container ship and sail it into Keppel Terminal. Right beside the city that's alongside the busiest port in the world.'

'Pretty smart, I guess.'

'Then the first contact they make is to a US Army general who hasn't even arrived yet, a move guaranteed to cause confusion and dissent in the Singaporeans.'

'Uh, yeah.'

'You know, Paul, those two blokes made everything so much harder for the Singaporeans by first making this a terrorism issue, and then compounding things by making it HAZMAT. Think you'll also find that Interpol have probably listed VX as a weapon of mass destruction. These guys down at the MPA are opening their ring binders at pages they never thought they'd be opening.'

Paul nodded.

'But the third complicating strategy would have been surprise. That would have sealed it. They could have berthed, been picked up by helo, by speedboat, frogged out of there, whatever. And then triggered the bomb with a Nokia as they flew off to their suite in the Maldives. *Voomph!* One hundred and eighty VX bombs aerosoling five hundred metres into the air. Take about two hours for that vapour to descend all over Singapore.'

'Okay. So they didn't do that.'

'No. They've been sitting there.'

Paul took a moment. 'What about the Moro demand?'

'If you were Sabaya, would you go to Singapore?'

'Nah, just raid the prison. He's done it before.'

'Precisely. So what's he doing in Singers fucking round with namby-pamby political demands? He's some Brigadi Rossi uni student all of a sudden? That sound like the Abu Sabaya we know and love?'

Paul nodded, agreeing. If Sabaya wanted someone out of prison, he'd do it Filipino-style: bribe some guards, kidnap the governor's daughter, show up with some firepower and walk out of the joint with whoever he wanted.

'Secondly,' said Mac, 'have you ever heard of Sabaya making a demand that didn't have a dollar sign at the front and a handful of zeroes hanging off the back?'

Paul laughed. 'Oh mate. You're good.'

'Well?'

'No, you're right. You're right.'

Mac put the rest of the protein bar in his mouth and looked across at *Golden Serpent*. The Singaporeans would have to negotiate with Sabaya and Garrison, but Mac and Paul weren't under those constraints. They had to get aboard that ship.

CHAPTER 35

They swam fast to Brani Island, both happy for the daylight. Mac led, keeping to a depth of five metres. Though hard on the lungs, the rebreather wasn't as bad as Mac remembered. He focused completely on where he was trying to go to make the fear go away.

They frogged to the south side of Brani Island where they were expecting no surveillance. The cars were already flooding off Brani, and the Singapore Coast Guard were on the water.

They were naked, dry clothes sealed in their backpacks.

Mac brought them up beside the stern washboard of a moored mid-sized roll-on/roll-off ship. To their right was the large slipway for ships, and further on was the Coast Guard depot. No cops. No boats against the quay.

They went up a galvanised iron ladder onto the wharf. To their left was the western extreme of the Brani container terminal. None of the rubber tyre gantries were moving, there was no one to be seen.

They kicked off the Turtle Fins, looped them over their elbows. Shook off the waterproofed backpacks and made for an area where forty-gallon drums had been stored against the side of a wide, squat security building with a central roller door entry.

Pulling off their nose clips and small swimming goggles they tore the velcroed rebreather bladders from their chests, breathing shallow in the morning sun, not talking. Each man pulled the double seal-lock bags from his backpack and retrieved dry clothes. They wiped themselves dry with a chamois, pulled on undies, put on hip rigs then ovies over the top. Put watches back on, turned them inside their wrists.

Mac checked the Mark I injector kit: a nerve agent antidote that neither of them had any faith in.

Paul pulled the radios out of a seal-lock. Booted up.

Mac pulled the Heckler out, pulled on his Hi-Tecs and did a quick recce, looking for eyes.

There were several buildings on Brani but the only movement seemed to be the cars of the employees trying to get off the island and onto the Gateway bridge. He couldn't see to the north side of Brani so he couldn't see *Golden Serpent* across the channel.

Coming back along the southern quay, he looked up at the ro-ro ship. It was white with blue and green piping, no evidence of a shipping line and no name. It seemed out of place amidst the behemoths on the other side of the island.

He froze as something caught his eye. Thought he saw movement on the upper decks, but couldn't catch it again. Must have been a bird.

He kept moving, saw that the ship's rear tail gate was down on the quay. But no people.

'Place is deserted,' said Mac, returning. 'Can't believe this is what they wanted.'

Paul nodded. 'I see your point. It seems like a whole lot of trouble to go to and not push the button.'

Mac had talked Paul into the minimal approach if the bomb was detonated: jump into the water with rebreathers. It might not be foolproof, but VX was water-soluble and if they stayed in the water with their closed-circuit rebreathers they at least wouldn't be breathing the stuff.

Paul got through to Weenie, nodded, signed off. 'Development. Our terrorist mates are broadcasting on maritime frequencies. They're telling other captains what they've got and what they're gonna do with it. They're giving them an hour to get out of Dodge.'

'I guess they're still on the bridge, trying to create confusion, huh?' said Mac, not entirely convinced.

'Weenie reckons the message started going out about five minutes ago.'

They looked at each other, puzzled. It was the weirdest terrorist incident they'd ever heard of.

Putting their dive gear into their webbing backpacks, they stowed them and readied themselves to speed-march a route north that would take them through the small forest in the middle of Brani and across the huge city of containers on Brani's north shore.

As they set off, Mac thought he heard movement in the security building. Couldn't be sure because at the same time the still air started vibrating as helos came into view. Two dark Singapore Army Apaches swept low over their position and headed north for the tip of Brani Island. Boeing's AH-64D was one of the most heavily armed helicopters ever built and their mushroom pod above the main rotor gave them a sinister appearance. But with all their rockets and air-to-air missile capability, Mac knew they'd be pulling up well south of *Golden Serpent*. There wasn't much that air power could achieve in the current situation. It would boil down to a couple of men getting onto the ship and doing what they had to do. It would be close-range and Mac was already nervous.

He got his mind focused on what was ahead. Tried to blot out the fear.

CHAPTER 36

Mac and Paul jogged down the forested knoll in the centre of Brani and into the vast boulevards of the terminal, where container stacks took the place of buildings. Mac had lost the thread on *Golden Serpent*, wanted to get a closer look before he decided what to do.

'Mate, Port Master is letting them go,' Paul panted, putting his hand up to his ear.

'Who?' said Mac.

'Ships, mate. Weenie says the Port Master just cleared a bunch of ships to leave, they've been threatening legal action.'

Mac kept hauling.

'How they going to get out without tugs?' asked Paul.

Mac thought back to the way those seamen looked on *Hokkaido Spirit*. 'Mate, they'll find a way, believe me. They've all got bow-thrusters.'

They kept good pace. The wet frog gear dripped down Mac's back, blending with the sweat.

They stood panting, hiding beside a stack of containers. Humidity was getting up. They shared a bottle of water.

Before them stood an eighty-metre stretch of concrete apron. Big rail lines sat lengthwise in the apron and the enormous portainers that ran along the rails sat idle. Across the channel behind Keppel

Terminal was the city and the leafier residential areas of the city-state. Garrison and Sabaya had picked a good spot to blow the VX.

Paul worked the radio with Weenie. 'Mate, can we get anything from the Americans? Yeah I know, mate, but . . .'

Mac looked through the Leicas. Scanned the *Golden Serpent*. No movement.

He held on the bridge as long as he could without getting eye-strain. The windows on the bridge were tinted so that the brighter the sun, the darker they got. He couldn't say there was no movement. But he couldn't see anything that would count for people either. He had no confirmation that they were on the bridge.

They needed confirmation on whether the hijackers were even on the ship.

Further down the Keppel quay two ships cast off, their bow-thrusters boiling, pushing them out from the container terminal. Another ship was already making way up the channel and was about two minutes away from *Golden Serpent*.

Paul and Mac looked at one another. Neither of them wanted to be frogging across that channel with some of these three-hundred-metre giants in a race to get out of town.

'What's Weenie up to?' asked Mac.

'Been watching CNN. Reckons the place is in lock-down. Changi's shut, railway stations closed down. Only things open are the causeways into Malaysia, which are packed. Total panic. Media's not reporting what the stuff is but the assumption is that it's serious.'

'How's that?'

'An amateur grabbed footage of the US Army in their bio-hazards. CNN were running it for a while, but it's stopped. Government probably asked them to take it off.'

Mac nodded but something felt wrong. 'Isn't it time you got on to your military attaché people? They got us into this game. They're a part of the coalition, aren't they?'

'I don't know if our people are down there. But you know what happens when the Yanks turn up. They control all out-bound comms. It's their protocol, you know, because of the Nokia detonators.'

Mac hadn't worked with the Americans at this sort of police-action level, but he'd heard they jammed all comms other than frequencies they approved to prevent the two most obvious ways a bomber detonated an IED: by Nokia phone or a simple radio switch. Bombers could also use on-site detonation – made famous by suicide bombers – or a timer. If you wanted to make it really difficult, you put in a chemical tilt-switch which closed the detonator circuit when someone messed with the IED.

The Americans didn't jam frequencies so they could show off. They did it so bombers didn't lure law enforcement and military on site and then detonate something right under the Emergency Operations Centre.

Mac did a three-sixty, put his hands on his hips, walked out onto the apron. Kept walking, down to the waterside. The helos had dispersed: one to the north, one to the south.

Paul stuck his head out from their hiding place beside the container stack. 'Oi! What the fuck are you about?'

Mac stopped and turned. The frogman kit dripped down his left hip. 'Come on.'

'Sabaya said no one is to approach the ship. Aren't we stealthing?' Paul shouted.

'Mate, they're not on that ship.'

'How do we know that?'

'Because they're too smart and whatever else they want, it has nothing to do with blowing themselves up on CNN.'

Paul walked out onto the apron, looking around, and stopped near Mac.

'Just worked this out?' he asked.

'Been gnawing at me. You know.'

'They're not the vest types?'

Mac smiled. 'I was thinking about what that much CL-20 could do to that ship. Those blokes have no intention of going down with it. And they can't detonate remotely, not with the Yanks jamming the frequencies up.'

'So how are they doing this?' said Paul.

'The same way they did Minky and the manager of the MPS store.'

'Hostage?'

'Or threat of it,' said Mac. 'You worked for Sabaya. Think it through, how would he be handling this?'

Paul looked to the horizon. 'He'd have the captain and the XO really scared. Shitting themselves. They'd be reading from a song sheet.'

'Literally.'

'Well, yeah. Don't you reckon?'

'Yeah,' said Mac. 'I think you're right. They're shit scared and they have a script they're reading from. They're making their calls at the intervals Sabaya instructed. And Sabaya is listening in.'

'How's he doing that?'

'Reckon he's changed the settings on the Universal AIS.'

'The what?'

'The Universal Automatic Identification System. It broadcasts a whole list of information to all other ships all the time. Helps them calculate time to collision, that sort of thing.'

'What are these guys doing with it?'

Mac thought about it. 'I think *Golden Serpent*'s AIS is broadcasting a whole lot of info that Sabaya input. I think these other ships know exactly what's on board because it's coming up on their screens. Sabaya wanted a stampede. He wanted it in the world's busiest port,' he said, pointing at the channel where five ships were now vying for exit room. 'And he's got it.'

'So how is Sabaya hearing the captain do his thing?'

'The AIS is broadcasting from the bridge, Sabaya just opened the mics. It's on the maritime VHF band and Sabaya is betting it's one of the few frequencies the Americans would never shut down. Sabaya's listening from somewhere and he's running a watch on the poor bastards who are reading this stuff.'

Paul walked around in front of him, sceptical. 'You heard that message from Sabaya. He warned about approaching the ship, said he'd blow it if we came anywhere near.'

'He knows the Yanks have shut down the airwaves, so he can't detonate remotely. So it's either on a timer or it's a hoax,' said Mac. 'What I don't want happening is the media seeing us. If Sabaya's got hostages, that's when they die.'

Paul accepted the argument. 'If Sabaya and Garrison aren't on the ship, where are they?'

'Dunno. But I know how we can find out.'

* * *

They found an MPA tender craft moored two-thirds of the way down the Brani Terminal quay. It was a thirty-five-foot rigid inflatable design with a small, functional cabin at the front. Paul found the key first time, under the cushion on the skipper's chair. He fired up the two Evinrudes, pushed the throttles forward and banked the craft round as it struggled to get up on a plane. They had their rebreathers strapped to their chests, over the ovies. The dual corrugated rubber hoses fell away over the front of the breathing bags. It wasn't as good as a bio-hazard suit, but it might just save their lives in a scrape.

They motored straight towards the port side of *Golden Serpent*. Mac was pretty sure that if Sabaya and Garrison were not on board, the crew would be relieved to see them. The problem was going to be ensuring that Sabaya was not listening in, that the place wasn't bugged and that there were no Sabaya-friendly crew on lookout. Paul and Mac also had to make sure they didn't show up on CNN because Sabaya and Garrison would be watching. The bomb was another matter. It was obviously on a timer, but neither of them wanted to dwell on that.

Midway across the channel Paul keyed the radio again to speak with Weenie. But the connection had gone. They'd moved into the jammed airspace and for the rest of the mission they'd be operating unsupported. They came alongside the huge ship. Helos thromped somewhere but were still standing off. Mac couldn't see them. Paul cut the engines and they drifted until they touched, then he put a pole out, pushing off slightly to stop a thunk. As the tender wallowed, Paul pulled an eleven-millimetre grappling rope from his backpack. The line was thin brushed nylon with a small, heavy three-point hook on the end.

Mac looked up, doubted they had enough rope, doubted he had the ticker for this climb. The last time he'd done something like this he was in his twenties and now he was closer to forty than thirty. Still, there was no way he was going to whine about his wrist. Paul's face was still a mess and he hadn't heard a peep out of the bloke.

Paul couldn't get a bite on the hook, so Mac had a crack and got it over the railing on the third go. It seemed to be a solid hold, but you never really knew about these things until you were halfway up the wall. They pulled on black fingerless gloves and Mac wiped the soles of his Hi-Tec Magnums by rubbing each on the opposite ovie leg.

He made a trial squeeze on the rope and the wrist didn't feel too bad but he reckoned he had about forty seconds to do the business before he ran out of gas. It could be a wet ending.

Mac swung to the side of *Golden Serpent*, letting his knees bend as he hit painted steel. He felt his arms and wrists take the weight through his back, and he consciously kept his feet soft. Then he started to climb, right hand over left, small steps, trying to get the weight pushing out and letting the knees do the bending.

Two-thirds into it his arms started to lock out. His normal workout regime revolved around the boxing bag, and that kind of fitness was pretty hopeless for a rope climb. He groaned it out, trying to relax the crook of the arms slightly. But he slipped back down the rope.

He got his feet on the steel again and pushed out, his arms and stomach crying out for respite. He started up again. Got to four-fifths, and the arms were totally locking out at the elbows. Like the forearms and biceps had set solid and would never open again, and as he hissed through the agony his arms went into a full cramp. He gritted, mumbled, blew spittle and turned the word fuck into a very simple but long prayer.

He ground it out: three steps to go, two steps, one step. His mantra became the Royal Marines' combat course instruction: *Don't let go of the rope until you're over the edge*.

But he was in too much pain, his arms needed rest and he reached out for the bottom rung of the railing in front of him. Like a whisper of hope.

He wasn't past the edge.

In an instant, his legs fell out from under him, his rebreather on his chest bouncing him off the ship's side so he was stretched out to a full traction position, his hands locking around that bottom railing.

Flying like a flag.

From the corner of his eye he saw the rope go taut again. Paul's turn. Mac swung his legs side to side, then threw his right leg upward, catching a toe on the deck. Dragging his knee up, he pulled himself up to the iron bulwark, rebreather getting in the way, and willed himself over the railing.

He fell in a heap, caught his breath on his knees. Felt sweat dripping beneath the rebreather unit. Looked around. No one having a nosey-poke. Reaching into the side flap of his ovies, he pulled out the Heckler, checked for load, checked the breech, ejected the magazine, double-checked.

Mac looked at the decks above him. Still no movement from the bridge and no security detail like you'd expect if Sabaya was around the shop.

Paul came over the side. Collapsed with a groan. 'Too old for this shit.'

They crouched there, got their breathing under control, got circulation back in their arms and hands. Paul pulled out his SIG, checked for load, checked the mag.

They'd landed almost directly below the bridge wings and were probably in the best place on the ship not to be seen.

They moved to the hatchway door that would lead into the deckhouse where they discarded their rebreathers. If the VX blew, it would wipe the ship out anyway.

After jiggling their ovies to check for change or keys, Mac took three strides to the hatchway door. Turned the lever handle.

Pushed in.

CHAPTER 37

The ship hummed softly. The lights were on and Mac smelled breakfast. Eggs, toast, coffee.

But no people. Nothing.

They were in a lobby, much like that of a mid-sized apartment building.

Paul pulled the hatchway door behind him, closing it silently. Didn't want to leave it flapping and have some do-gooder come down for a nosey-poke.

Paul pointed downstairs; he wanted to check the troops before he stormed the bridge. Like Mac, he liked to know the numbers.

They went down a flight of stairs and into a storage area. From here, most of the food that ran a ship was kept cool till it needed to be freighted up the service elevator to the kitchens. The stewards' area was down there too: all the toilet paper, the laundry, the cleaning gear.

They walked through the area, both breathing shallow, shit-scared about when that VX was going to blow. The silence was eerie.

They came to a cool store at the end, pushed through the clear plastic curtain and stood there in a room that was the size of a one-bedroom apartment. Five men, aged about nineteen to mid fifties, lay on the floor. Filipinos by the look of it.

A carcass had fallen on one. Some were dressed in whites – kitchen guys probably, getting the provisions for the evening meal when the pirates hit. Two of them were in orange overalls, bullets in foreheads, behind ears. Blood across the floor, set like a dark carpet.

Mac tasted that metallic blood thing. Some people smelled it; he tasted it.

They pushed back out and went further into the ship. If Garrison and Sabaya had wanted this whole thing to go smoothly they would have needed most of the crew onside going into Singers. You couldn't run a nine-thousand-container ship without engineers, general seamen and the officers. They'd waited and then executed the lot of them.

He needed to check the engine room. Even on ships this large there was only one engine and one screw shaft so it should be straightforward.

Mac accidentally knocked the claws loose on his wrist bandage, thought *Bugger* it and unbound the crepe. Chucked it.

They came to the hatchway door, AUTHORISED ACCESS ONLY written in several languages, Korean at the top. Paul couldn't open it. There was a keypad on the wall beside it with a solid red light on top and a green light beside, but not on. Even large ships had manual overrides on their engines, so the last thing ship owners wanted was some seaman getting drunk and deciding it would be fun to fuck around with an eighty-thousand horsepower MAN B&W straight-14.

Paul turned to Mac. 'Any ideas?'

Mac shrugged. 'Someone's birthday?'

'Anything else?'

'Four zeroes – always works for mobile phones.'

'Let's forget it,' said Paul.

They walked back across the vast storage bays, noticing how many nooks and crannies and smaller offices and rooms there were. They could have searched the lot, but it didn't seem like a lively place.

They hit the stairs to go back up. Paul stopped, brought his SIG up. Mac followed his gaze. Brought his own Heckler up.

Paul moved to his right, angling towards the stack of boxes that said Kleenex on the side. Mac hooked left. Moving in an arc, his breath was rasping now. He could feel the adrenaline pumping blood into his brain and ears. Everything roared. He couldn't get enough air. Wiping the wetness from his forehead he tried to concentrate.

Mac found a half-wall, propped against it, aimed up with a cup-and-saucer and flicked the safety. Paul looked over and, happy with the cover, walked further forward, looking, looking. Mac tried to keep his breathing down. A shoot-out in a confined space like this left no room for retreat. Someone was going to drop. He didn't want it to be him.

Paul moved forward slow, keeping the head, arms and shoulders absolutely still. His heavily muscled upper body flexed against the grey cotton overall fabric, his legs moving beneath like they were independent of his body. His sleeves had two turn-ups; Mac could see his wrists flexing.

Suddenly Paul leapt back, could barely get his SIG down fast enough. Hyperventilating.

Mac came out from the wall, ready for it, shooting stance going haywire, back and forth, up and down. Breathing all over the shop.

Paul held the stance, chest heaving. Then Paul's SIG was at his side and he was laughing at the ceiling.

Mac walked over. Looked around the Kleenex stacks and saw a West Highland terrier panting back at them.

White.

They found the biggest pile in the kitchens. Mac counted eleven Filipino sailors, most of them in pale blue ovies. They were lying across each other, under the stainless-steel kitchen tables, along the lino floor. One sat in a chair in an office, slumped, tongue out slightly, eyes open, bullet hole in the forehead. A psychedelic screensaver pattern repeated on the laptop in front of him.

Paul and Mac avoided each other's eyes. This many corpses, so well organised, meant there'd been a decent-sized posse on this ship at some point. The signs were not of struggle: no tracked blood, the bowls and knives were undisturbed on benches.

'Mate, let's stay out of the blood, eh?' said Mac.

'Yeah, and no touching.'

If they could defuse the bomb and save this ship Mac wanted the Singapore cops all over this, wanted a proper crime scene, wanted

Garrison and Sabaya sitting in a courtroom, getting nagged to death by a public prosecutor. One charge of murder after another would be harder on a couple of egos like theirs than dying of lead poisoning.

They went back out into the lino-floored dining room, took a seat at a table. The officers' was on the other side, with mahogany panels and big crystal decanter sets. The place was set for a meal.

Paul grabbed a bottle of mineral water and they both slugged on it.

'They must have had at least ten guys in here to do this lot so fast,' said Paul.

Mac hoped they weren't still aboard, hoped they didn't get to the bridge and find a greeting party. He was starting to have these weird feelings, as if Garrison and Sabaya had been expecting him to come here all along. Like it was some kind of game. He was so tired he could no longer judge if what he was thinking was sensible or not.

The next step was going to be tricky. Mac's assumption was that Sabaya had someone in the captain's family and had him making contact with the Emergency Operations Command at set intervals. He'd also be watching on CNN. Would have told the captain that.

'You know, Sabaya does kill these people. He's serious. So how are we going to do it?' said Paul, worried.

'I have an idea for that,' said Mac. 'But first, let's see that song sheet.'

The bridge wasn't secured, even though it could be locked in the same way as the engine room. There were two stairways into the bridge. Paul and Mac took the port side one. They were assuming whoever was on the bridge would have all their attention focused to starboard and the Emergency Operations Centre behind the pile of containers on Keppel Terminal.

The port bridge door had a large glass window in it. Looking through it, Mac saw one man in a white shirt slumped in what looked like a huge La-Z-Boy. It looked out through tinted glass along the entire loaded deck of *Golden Serpent*. The man seemed to be gnawing on his fingers.

Mac craned his neck to the starboard side of the bridge, couldn't see anyone else, and looked at Paul. 'One there at the moment. Want me to take him?'

Paul gave thumbs-up and Mac eased the door inward. It made no sound. Still a relatively new ship.

Glancing behind him, he saw that Paul had stowed the SIG, had a small pad of lined paper and a pen.

Mac pushed through, took two strides, cupped his hand over the reclining bloke's mouth. Paul moved to the starboard end of the bridge. As he did, a face poked out, white-haired, middle-aged, a steel teaspoon in his hand, mouth open, confused.

Paul didn't blink. Veered straight into him, hand over the mouth, swung him round into a half-nelson.

Mac brought his mouth down to his bloke's ear. Whispered, 'No sound. Okay?'

His head nodded.

'Speak English?'

Nodded.

'They got your wife?'

Head shook.

'Kids?'

Nodded.

Mac felt a gulp.

'They're listening in, right?' whispered Mac.

Shoulders shrugged, then head nodded, a *yes, maybe*.

'My name's Mac, Australian intelligence. That's Paul, British intelligence. We're here to help but they can't know we're up here or they'll kill the hostages. Okay?'

The head nodded. Another gulp.

'We're going to communicate by writing, okay? Talk to the other guy, but not us. We'll try to sort this. Okay?'

Nodded.

Mac let him go and he turned slowly. Dark hair, fortyish, long face, eyes red. Been crying a lot.

Mac offered his hand and they shook.

Paul let the other guy go and they walked over to Mac. All shook hands. Silent. The two ship guys looked hollowed out with stress and lack of sleep.

Paul got to the map table behind the big recliner chairs, put the pad on the map table. The older guy put on half-glasses.

Where's your song sheet? Mac wrote on the pad.

The older guy walked to the starboard wing of the bridge, picked up a piece of paper, came back.

They looked at it. The last announcement had been and gone at one pm. The next was for one-thirty. They looked to the last page. The final demand was at 6.05 pm – essentially, a long screed of Moro invective and praises given to Allah.

Mac flipped back. The next demand to be broadcast was going to be: *We demand the fourteen Moro separatist prisoners being held illegally in Manila be released before six pm local time tonight and brought to this ship, or we will detonate the VX nerve agent.*

Mac looked at his G-Shock: 1.13 pm.

He beckoned the officers, and they all left the bridge, moved down two flights to the dining room where they introduced themselves. Jeremy was the younger one – a New Zealander; Wylie was American and the captain. They were both based out of Singapore, where their families lived.

Jeremy shook his head. 'How are we, I mean, how can we . . .' His voice broke, unable to go on.

Wylie looked at Paul as if to say: *See what I've been putting up with?*

'No one wants to be here, right Jerry?' said Paul.

Jeremy nodded.

'But here we are all the same. We're gonna try and sort it, but we're gonna need you, mate. Up for it?'

Jeremy nodded. Looked away. Embarrassed at his state.

'We're betting these guys have gone into the AIS system and switched on the bridge broadcast system,' said Mac.

'The one that only cuts in after a collision?' said Wylie.

'That one, yeah,' said Mac, liking Wylie already. 'We think your conversations are broadcasting to all ships, and that's how Sabaya and Garrison are listening in.'

'Is that their names?'

'What are they like?' asked Mac.

Wylie grimaced. 'Well, they know how ships work, they knew what we were doing and where we'd be. I mean, they weren't like what you expect of a pirate or a terrorist.'

'What were they focused on?'

'The American kept talking about clarity, kept reminding me that anyone who commanded a vessel this large had to have an adult grasp of clarity.'

Wylie exhaled, grabbed at a glass of water. 'Then he put that sheet on one side of the table, and the photo of my wife on the other, said, *Here's how it works.* And we've been up here ever since, broadcasting this rubbish.' He slapped the song sheet against his thigh.

Jeremy sniffed. Paul eyeballed him, said, 'Come on, mate.'

Mac wanted more. 'They tell you they'd be watching on TV?'

'Yes, sir. Told us that this was a tailored CNN incident.'

Mac's ears pricked up. Didn't know why. 'The American. He said *incident?*'

'Sure did. Said it several times. Said he'd be watching it on CNN and if we got stormed before the set time on the sheet, he'd blow the place up and kill his hostages.'

'You know which one is the VX?' asked Mac.

'The what?' said Wylie.

'It's nerve agent. They stole it, got it on this ship.'

'Oh that. Is that what they call it? Yeah, they hauled these big black bags down to twelve –'

'Twelve?'

'Bay Twelve. It's the twelfth container from the stern. About halfway between the bridge and bow.'

'Then what?'

'We worked out it was twelve eleven eight-six.'

'What was?'

'The container they were working on. They knew all about the bridge gantries and ladders and lashing. They seemed to know their stuff.'

'What's twelve eleven eighty-six?'

'It's the container position,' said Wylie. 'It's bay twelve, row eleven, tier eighty-six.'

Paul frowned. 'In English that would be?'

'It would be halfway to the bow, on the outside – starboard – side of the stacks, and high up. About second or third from the top of the stack.'

Mac mulled it. Twelve eleven eighty-six, exactly where the officers on Hokkaido Spirit said you'd have to put a container if you wanted to open it en route.

Mac beckoned Paul to another table, whispered, 'We can't pull the cops and the Yanks in here to do the bomb or these guys are going to lose family, right?'

Paul nodded.

'So we have to get the TV cameras shut down. Make it look like the Singaporeans have moved to a new Em-Con level.

'Once we can get those helos and cameras out of here, then Sabaya and Garrison are blind. They can hear those demands going out every thirty minutes, and they think it's all going on. But they don't know the Twentieth is crawling all over Golden Serpent trying to disarm their bomb.'

'Sounds like a plan.'

Mac went back to Wylie and Jeremy. 'Mate, think we might have an idea,' Mac said to Wylie.

Paul wanted to know how they'd been speaking with the Americans, and Wylie said, 'The ship-to-shore phone.'

'Where is it?' asked Mac.

Wylie pointed at a table next to the starboard window. There was a heavy white handset face down on a white plastic cradle.

'Got a number?' asked Paul.

Wylie pulled a folded piece of white paper from his shorts.

Mac and Paul swapped a look. With the ship-to-shore phone not jammed it might be possible to get through to Sawtell or the Port Master or Hatfield. Mac wasn't hopeful on that score. Once the EOC starts its business – especially a US military one for a terrorist threat – the lines of communication go so high that outside calls are not taken. Hatfield would be sit-repping as high as CINCPAC, Joint Chiefs and maybe the Oval Office. There wouldn't be too many rubber-neckers getting through.

Still, it was worth a shot.

Mac checked his G-Shock: 1.25. He looked at Wylie, whose face fell off him like a flesh waterfall. 'Guys, you're up again. Do what they tell you, all right? Don't talk about us. We're trying to get this sorted. Do it by the book, right?'

The two officers nodded, gulped down some water and walked back upstairs, dragging their feet. Mac sat back. According to the Sabaya sheet, the whole thing timed out at six that evening. It gave them about four and a half hours to come up with something. If they couldn't alert the Singaporeans and the Yanks within the next half-hour, Mac was going to slip back into the water and stealth round there himself. Or even better, get Paul to do it. He got out of Hasanuddin, piece of piss. He could try getting into a US Army EOC.

Mac walked to the starboard window, looked out. He could make out the flash of a rotor or a truck at intervals where you could see through the mountain of container stacks. There were black-clad Singaporean SWAT teams lurking between the containers. Mac wondered what they thought they were going to do: storm the VX consignment? Intimidate the CL-20?

The EOC had been mounted back from the apron. Tucked among the container stacks.

Mac could see broadcast trucks along the raised Ayer Rajah Expressway. There were at least thirty of them and there seemed to be a roadblock of more trucks and vans trying to get the circle seats. Even without binos Mac could see their satellite dishes on the roofs, uplinking with a continuous feed. They were getting used to the thirty-minute spacing of the demands, perhaps. The AIS broadcasts meant CNN and Fox News could be getting their feeds from any one of the ships. Could even be getting it from a hobbyist with a VHF receiver who could hook into the maritime bands.

There seemed to be a flurry of activity, then *voomph*, along the rows of OB trucks the klieg lights and reflector brollies lit up and the row looked like something out of a sci-fi movie.

Mac wondered why the lights had gone on now, in the middle of the afternoon, then looked at his watch: 1.29. *Golden Serpent* had become the news cycle. Bottom of the hour live feeds to the anchors. Lots of reports starting sentences with things like 'We're hearing', and 'There's a real sense', in lieu of having any information.

The next thing to arrive was going to be the anchors. They'd be coming in from Honkers, Sydney, KL, Manila, Jakarta and Bangers. They'd want their own trailers. They'd want higher platforms than the others, better lighting, better synergies with the EOC. They'd need bigger OB trucks so the anchors could broadcast their shows out of Ayer Rajah, with *Golden Serpent* in the background. They'd need more producers, more lights, more make-up. They might even bring the weather girl and the sports guy.

They'd be clamouring for the Twentieth or the Singapore cops or the MPA to appoint a PR flak to manage the media. The PR flak would be so inundated with requests and demands from the producers and reporters that she'd have to requisition time, real estate and resources to create constant cycles of press conferences. People like Hatfield and the Port Master would tire of saying no. They'd finally drag themselves into the press conference, become annoyed, mumble something like, 'Who ordered this gaggle-fuck?' Which would become the next news cycle.

Mac wanted to short-circuit that process.

Standing back from the window, he looked up at the wall, saw a TV. He found a remote beside it on the wall-mounted platform. Switched it on, found CNN, kept the volume low. There were panning shots of *Golden Serpent* with American voices narrating, bringing audiences up to date. *A large container ship has been hijacked by terrorists and is currently berthed at Port of Singapore with what is believed to be a large amount of nerve agent rigged to a very large bomb.*

The voices went on, talking about demands and Moro prisoners, had experts talking about what nerve gas does to people. The nerve gas guy kept trying to make a point, but he got talked over so they could seg to the OB. Mac thought he heard the nerve gas guy trying to say, 'Are your people suited up?'

CNN cut to the OB. The reporter had a helmet of hair, a Banana Republic photo-journalist uniform and a beautiful delivery. But she wasn't suited up and would have a major problem if she was still standing on Ayer Rajah when the VX blew.

The final demand was at six o'clock. It was going to be a prime time nerve gas attack.

CHAPTER 38

Paul dialled the number and handed over to Mac, who was now watching Fox. 'You want to do this?' he said.

Mac nodded, put the phone to his jaw. When the phone picked up, it immediately auto-switched to a recorded message telling Singaporeans to make for the causeways, get into Malaysia. It gave bus pick-up points and told foreigners to get out of Dodge, phone their embassies . . .

Fuck! The Americans had outsmarted themselves. To open a clean line between the ship and the EOC they'd diverted everything else, including all other ship-to-shore phones on *Golden Serpent*.

Mac had an idea.

'Mate, what's Weenie's sat-phone number?'

Paul called it out and Mac dialled the handset. Weenie answered in two rings and Mac told him what he needed. Weenie's laptop connected to the sat-phone and made him a travelling PABX switchboard through which Mac could be connected anywhere in the world.

'Don't worry about MPA,' said Mac. 'They'll be off their feet. Get me Camp Enduring Freedom in Zamboanga.'

Mac waited for Weenie to go to the US Department of Defense directory and dial.

'Through now, Mac,' said Weenie.

The line rang and rang. Finally someone picked up. Mac recognised the voice. His old mate.

'Alan McQueen, Australian Embassy. In a jam down here in Singers, mate. Could you get me through to Captain Sawtell quick-smart?'

There was a long sigh. 'Captain Sawtell is operational, Mr McQueen.'

'Yeah but – '

'I would have thought you'd be quite aware of that if you're in Singapore.'

Mac didn't have the time. 'Look –'

'So I'll just have to take a message.'

Mac breathed long. 'Look, Craig is it?'

'Corporal Craig, yessir.'

'Watching Fox News?'

'Mr McQueen, I can't –'

'Have a look at the deckhouse,' snapped Mac. 'Can you see it? Big white thing rising above the containers. Got it?'

'Mr McQueen, I don't see –'

'Count two windows below the bridge. The starboard bridge, the one you're watching. See the window? Big square number?'

'Yes sir, Mr McQueen, I see it. I'm sorry, I have to go –'

'Keep your eyes on that window, Corporal.'

Then Mac did what he had to do, before a worldwide audience.

'See it, Corporal?'

There was a silence, then, 'Oh my God!'

Mac composed himself. Tried to keep the anger down. 'Now listen, Corporal Craig. Don't make me say this again, okay? I've been on the go for six days chasing the people who are doing this. I'm working on secondment with the British government and I was previously on secondment to General Hatfield's Twentieth Support Command. At this very moment I'm on *Golden Serpent*, which means I'm sitting on top of a nerve gas bomb that could go up at any second. I'm tired, I'm emotional and I'm scared, mate. I need to talk with John. I need to talk with him now! So. Patch. Me. Through. *Now!*'

'Through now, Mr McQueen. By the way, it's a party line.'

The line buzzed and whined, then clicked.

'Sawtell.'

'Darling! You don't phone, you don't write!'

'That your lily-white, McQueen? Damn, that thing's whiter than a Republican Christmas.'

It was always the way, using humour to defuse things, kid yourself that your life wasn't on the line. They got to the business. Mac gabbled, Sawtell wanted lots of sit-rep but Mac didn't have the time to go over everything. 'Look, most of the crew's dead except for two officers. They're reading off a sheet Sabaya gave them . . .'

'McQueen, this is Hatfield. Twentieth. I've been listening to your account.'

'Sir, I need you to promise me that when I finish the briefing, no one comes aboard until we can shut down the media. Please, these guys are beside themselves. You know what Sabaya's like with hostages.'

'I can't promise that, McQueen. VX is at a level that takes us to algorithms. You understand what I'm saying, right, son?'

Mac understood. When you got to the higher echelons of CBNRE you had a set of algorithms that you had to work to. The lives of the three people related to *Golden Serpent*'s officers would be netted off against the potential harm of a mass VX device being detonated to aerosol over the city-state of Singapore.

So Hatfield wasn't about to promise anything to anyone.

Mac felt sick but he had no choice. If Hatfield was mentioning algorithms, at some point they were all going to have to confront the old argument known as Greater Good.

'General, there's no tangos on this ship. And the list of demands these guys are reading from runs through to eighteen hundred hours. We've got till chow to find it, disarm it.'

Mac had barely got it out before the yelling started up and down the US Army party line. It was like a room full of dead clocks had started ticking. He heard Hatfield muttering a list of orders at his people. He was going so fast that Mac could only pick up snippets of information.

Mac cut into the din. 'General, please shut down the media first. I mean, before you bring the bomb teams on board. These guys have family being held hostage.'

Hatfield couldn't disguise his relief. He had roughly four hours to dismantle a nerve gas threat – and he had a tango-free environment in which to do it.

Hatfield had taken the information and done what good generals do. He'd made a decision.

Paul came down from the bridge having asked Wylie to open the gangway doors. Mac didn't want to go up there and look at those blokes after he'd promised them the kids and wife would be fine.

Paul sat, gave Mac a look. Mac knew what he wanted. 'What?'

'What?' said Paul, cocking an eyebrow.

Paul wanted to rescue the hostages, Mac just knew it.

'Fuck's sake, mate, I'm not Rambo,' said Mac, looking away. He was so tired.

Paul laughed. 'Come on, Tiger. Let's give it one last roll. See if we can't bag these cunts.'

Outside Mac saw the gangways being dragged by tractors to the side of *Golden Serpent*. SWAT teams, fire fighters and lots of US Army were milling on the dock clad in either white, yellow or green bio-hazard suits. There were helos in the air, the clanking sound of Black Hawks, the throb of Apaches.

'Okay,' said Mac. 'So we have one Moro terrorist and one CIA black sheep. They have a five-hour head start. Where do you want to begin?'

'Back on Brani you told me you might have an idea about that,' said Paul.

Mac thought about it. 'We'll need Weenie. We'll need a helo.'

Paul slapped Mac on the shoulder. 'That's more like it.'

Mac rose, almost lost his balance.

Mac slipped up to the bridge to have a word before the Yanks and Singaporeans came aboard and threw everyone into a three-day debrief.

He leaned in the door, silently beckoned to Wylie.

Wylie saw it in Mac's eyes immediately. 'We're still on air, aren't we?'

'Mate, as soon as I told them there was a timeline on this thing, they moved in. Couldn't stop it,' said Mac. 'I'm sorry.'

Wylie clenched his fist, looked at the floor. 'Fuck it! You promised us. You both promised us. We've done everything your way.' His bottom lip trembled.

'We're going after them now,' said Mac. 'No promises, but we're going to try.'

'Really?'

Mac nodded. 'I'll need photos of Jeremy's kids and your wife. Need names, nicknames, cell phone numbers. Anything that could help us.'

Wylie went into the bridge, came back with Jeremy. They emptied their wallets of pictures. Jeremy had two dark-haired daughters, about five and seven.

'The younger one's Rachel,' said Jeremy. 'The older one's Fiona, but she answers to Feef.'

Mac wrote it on the back of the pic. Pulled out Wylie's wife: slim, attractive, well dressed. A sort of 1980s blonde hairstyle with big Farrah flicks down the side.

'Her name's Karen. She's amazingly calm in a crisis. She'll do what you ask her,' said Wylie.

Mac saw Jeremy's hands going to his face, freaking out. Ignoring it, he brought it back to Wylie.

'Tell me more about what they were doing. They drop any hints about where they were going?'

'They didn't kill everyone. They took Irvine, one of my officers. Someone belted him in the face and one of the guys in charge – the Filipino – said something like, "Don't damage the goods, I don't want him useless for the next leg." I thought it was a strange thing to say – the next leg – like it was a tour or something.'

'Irvine?' asked Mac.

'Yes, Peter Irvine. Canadian. Highly experienced in these waters.'

'Anything else?'

'Not that I can recall.'

'How did they leave the ship?'

'By tender. Rigid inflatable thing. Might have been from Brani Terminal.'

'Which way did they go?'

Wylie pointed over the port side, across the channel to Brani Island.

Mac nodded. 'Three of them, huh?'

Jeremy leapt in. 'And the woman helming the tender makes four.'

'Sorry?' said Mac.

'The woman,' said Jeremy. 'I went out on the deck when they left, had a look. There was a blonde woman driving the tender.'

Mac's ears filled with blood, heart pumping behind his eyeballs. 'Woman?'

'Yeah. Mid thirties, very attractive professional type. Couldn't work out what she was doing with these scum.'

'How was she dressed, mate?'

'Jeans and a shirt. Pale-blue polo shirt thing.'

Jeremy moved closer, as if something had occurred to him. 'Umm.'

'What else, mate? Could be important,' said Mac.

'Nothing really. It's nothing.'

'Come on.'

'Well, she looked up and saw me watching.'

'Yes?'

'And didn't tell the blokes.'

CHAPTER 39

Mac and Paul came off the gangway, onto the quay, holding newspapers over their faces to stop any unfriendlies identifying them on TV. Don and his sidekick from the Chinook swooped on them and another pair of men in bio-hazards walked past them towards Wylie and Jeremy.

They made straight for Hatfield's Chinook and sat in the aft freight area. Hatfield's voice boomed clearly through the bulkhead. Don thanked Mac and Paul for the work, and Paul asked if he could use the Chinook's radio-telephone. He called Weenie and requested the Gazelle.

Mac briefed Don. 'Mate, you can get this to your guys: the container's at twelve eleven eight six. It's about halfway between deckhouse and bow, on our side – starboard – and it's high up. The eighty-six position is two or three from the top of the stack.'

Don touched his throat mic. Relayed the information exactly.

'Was anyone exposed?' asked Don.

Mac shook his head. 'Not that we know of.'

'Did these guys remove any of the VX?'

'Couldn't tell you, mate,' said Mac.

Don mulled it over. 'Where are Garrison and Sabaya now?'

'We've got an idea. Might need some of your special forces,' said Paul.

323

Don looked sideways at Paul. Clocked the muscles, the broken nose, the steady eyes. Looked back at Mac. 'Worked with Sawtell's unit before?'

Mac nodded. 'Good outfit.'

'They're not needed here. But we'd like a chat with the thieves. Understand?'

Mac nodded at that. 'We get access to the comms stuff?'

'Depends what it is, McQueen, you know that.'

'How about a lock on a satellite phone?'

'Can do.'

'What do you need, Don?'

'I need Garrison and Sabaya. Can do?'

'We'll try.'

They swept south-east at one hundred and seventy miles per hour, Gazelle in the lead, US Army Black Hawk taking the sweep. Mac and Paul spoke with Sawtell over the radio system as they headed for Jakarta.

Sawtell wasn't buying it. 'I don't get this – must be some mistake, Mac.'

'You saw the lock. It came from your guys,' said Mac.

When they'd been jogging across Brani Island that morning, Mac had wondered if the bank account number he'd retrieved from Mister Turquoise in Makassar wasn't in fact a sat phone number. A sat phone belonging to Garrison. Back at the EOC Mac had phoned the number stored in his Nokia – just given it a blip – and that had been long enough for Brown to get a lock on it from space.

Mac had the coordinates of the phone on a sheet on his lap. They pointed to a part of north Jakarta, near the port and Soekarno-Hatta airport. It was home to warehouses, industrial parks and huge freight forwarding depots.

Sawtell crackled in again. 'Why would they head back to Jakarta? What's there?'

Paul cut over. 'Could be where they're hiding the hostages.'

Paul was now running the op. Whatever he'd been in a previous life, he sure knew his stuff on the basics of hostage rescue, what people like Mac called a snatch. Paul had also made sure POLRI were in the loop. The British had a liaison bloke clearing the way and the Indons were offering backup.

Sawtell and Paul had decided that the way to approach the Garrison clubhouse was from the Java Sea end of Jakarta, coming in via the reservoirs, water retention tanks and canals that criss-cross that part of the city. Staying low would keep them hidden and would confuse any noise.

They'd picked a spot, a wooded area on the banks of a large reservoir. The reservoir was joined to the sea by a canal. About ten blocks south of the wooded area was the last lock on Garrison's position: a warehouse complex.

Mac looked at the map on his lap, directed the pilot into the landing zone. They dipped, found the canal and hovered along the waterway between one- and two-level warehouses. Lifting slightly over a lock, they came down again and then they were hovering over the wooded area. It was four pm, humidity building, skies becoming overcast. Picnickers stood up, held onto hats and scarpered as the down draught from the helos tore leaves off trees.

They hovered to the park between the trees, touched down. De-powered.

Sawtell's four-man unit spilled out of the Black Hawk in their in-country clothing: olive drab overalls, bullet-proof vests underneath.

Mac saw Spikey. They greeted, thumb shake.

"Zit going, champ?'

'Man! That you in the window?' asked Spikey.

'That's me.'

'Man! No wonder you're called Chalks.'

Paul walked over from the Gazelle with two white kevlar vests. Pulling down their ovies, they strapped the vests in place.

Crouched beneath a banyan tree, they peered at Mac's map. Paul put down the pictures of Rachel, Fiona and Karen, made sure he said their names. The Special Forces guys soaked up the images like they were drinking. Mac knew the kind of exercises these boys would be doing day after day on their base: rego numbers, photos, phone numbers, website addresses, email addresses, log-ons, PINs. Seven photos of the same person in different disguises over a fifteen-year period. Information fed to you in flashes, information that in the field could be the difference between life and death. Exercises under extreme pressure where you had to force your mind to resemble a photographic memory.

Sawtell and Paul talked in military acronyms and short cuts. Mac was relieved they wanted to take a stealth approach rather than a 'dynamic'. Dynamics could work when you had intelligence, via thermo sensors, listening posts and fibre optic eyes, but if you didn't have that intel, and you were rushing, the dynamic approach was riskier for the hostages than the hostage-takers.

The two agreed on everything except the closing scene. Sawtell's mission was to render Garrison and Sabaya. Paul made it clear that if something made him jumpy, he'd shoot it. 'I'll give myself plenty of time to figure out which way to point his arse.'

Sawtell eyeballed him, laughed. 'They teach you that shit too?'

'Bear jerk off in the woods?'

They jogged the nine blocks to the target carrying Beretta handguns, no rifles. With the bullet-proofs, they all sweated heavily.

The warehouse covered half a block. Perched on a corner hidden from the warehouse's view, they could see across the road that the Arrow freight depot and warehouse had two entrances: one from the cross street and the other from the main street. A three-level administration block fronted the building, set back from a forty-metre apron. To the right of the office section was a large dark-red roller door. Closed. A pedestrian door was set in the main door. Also closed. Behind the door, the warehouse roof stretched one hundred and twenty metres.

Down the cross street side of the structure, there was another large roller door and an open parking lot.

Sawtell double-checked the location. Wouldn't pay to be stealthing around the wrong building.

Sawtell turned to Paul. 'Looks to me like two sections to this; that office section and the warehouse section. We'll take the office. You two take the warehouse. Copy?'

Paul nodded.

'Right, ladies. Check radios,' said Sawtell.

Hands went up to earpieces while Sawtell rattled off the alphabet in Alpha Bravo Charlies. Got six thumbs-up.

'Check clocks: on my marks . . .'

Everyone started their mission clocks.

'Check weapons.'

Slides slid, mags dropped out and eyes looked down spouts. One of the Green Berets pulled the zip on his ovies down and checked the smoke grenades on his webbing.

Sawtell checked his own Beretta, took a breath, said, 'Ladies, you never get a second chance to make a first impression.'

'Fucking eh,' came an American voice in reply.

Mac checked for cameras, saw a dome protruding from the wall above the side entrance. Looked to the main entrance. Saw a dome there too. He pointed them out to Paul.

'If we go through the official entries someone's going to know about it,' said Mac.

'Ideas?'

'Just the oldest one in the book.'

'Rough but effective,' said Paul, keying the mic and asking Sawtell if their first stop might be downstairs in the fuse box room.

'Found cameras?' said Sawtell.

'One over each entrance.'

'How long you need?'

Paul looked at Mac, who said, 'Twenty seconds.'

'Stand-by,' said Sawtell.

Mac and Paul started down the cross street, hands in pockets, eyeing the warehouse door from across the road as they walked. In his pocket Mac felt the two thin wire jiggers from Spikey's bag of tricks.

They crossed the road, catching glimpses of the warehouse door through mid-sized trees. The pedestrian entrance was locked with a standard Lockwood device and if it was the type Mac had trained on, he'd only need ten seconds. If he sweated, slipped and screwed it up, he'd need the twenty. Twenty seconds was an optimum time to pull the power down in Jakkers. It was long enough that when you started it up again the bad guys might assume it was the unreliable power supply on the blink.

Sawtell sit-repped: Spikey had walked straight in the front entrance, and dipped down to the basement.

Mac and Paul veered left and walked towards the side entry door fifty metres away, their eyes locked on the fluoro lights under the awning over the side entrance. Their breathing was ragged now, their hands sweaty in the afternoon humidity. It had to be thirty-five degrees. They closed on the door, waiting for the power to be killed.

The lights went down and Mac and Paul ran the last five strides to the door, Mac dragging out the jiggers. First one in, holding the barrel where you want it. His fingers slid on the wire. He jigged the second piece of wire over the top of the first, twisted and pushed upward from the front to the back of the lock. The second part of the mechanism turned and Paul's pressure on the door made it click inwards.

Paul held his SIG in his right hand, pushed through with his left. Mac followed. The fluoros flashed on again. Paul shut the door gently as Mac moved into the interior.

The lights in the warehouse were flickering back to life too.

They swept with their guns. It looked like they had the place to themselves. There was a large empty indoor space in front of them, obviously where traffic passed through. To the right were lanes of stacked containers.

Suddenly they heard voices and slid to the right four paces, crouching behind red containers stacked two-up.

Indonesian voices echoed around the warehouse, coming closer.

Paul stuck his head around, pulled back. 'They're just checking the place with a flashlight. What the fuck you need a flashlight for when the lights have gone back on?'

Paul looked again. 'Okay, so now they're looking at the ceiling. And wouldn't you know it – lights!'

Paul turned and looked down the narrow alleyway where the containers didn't quite touch the steel side of the warehouse. It ran to the end of the building. 'Better recce, eh mate?'

Mac nodded. If there was an office or a van at the other end of the structure, they'd better find it. The girls and the woman were not going to come to them.

They jogged fast, jumping old brooms, Coke cans, dead spiders and porn mags: the detritus of warehouse life. At the end of the container row, Mac poked his head round the corner. There was another roller door entrance at this end of the building. Blood pumped in Mac's ears, his kevlar vest swimming on a layer of sweat.

There was an office perched up on a mezzanine at the far corner, set up so it could look down on the warehouse. There was also a ramp leading down to a sub-level.

Paul gestured. He'd go into the sub-level. Mac should check the other side of this level and the raised office.

Mac made across the rear roller door area, veering left in an arc to avoid the static camera over the inside of the door area. Heading for the raised office he looked down the corridors between the container stacks. His stance was perfect but there was no one to aim at. There seemed to be tons of freight in the joint, but no work being done.

The stairs to the office were single helix. He stopped for two seconds, caught his breath. Paul crackled on the receiver. 'Okay, Mac?'

'Right as rain.'

He took it easy up the stairwell. It was open so he could see straight to the top. It also left him exposed should anyone walk into the warehouse.

The door to the office had a glass panel in it. Mac peeked through: couldn't see anyone. Pushed through the door. Walked across the floor area to what looked like a storage area.

A bang.

Mac froze. Lifted the Heckler.

More bangs, different tones. A gunfight. Mac ran down the stairs, trying to get his breath, not panic. It took an effort to run towards a gunfight rather than away from it.

The gunshots were coming from the other end, up in the office area. Sawtell's boys getting stuck in. Mac sprinted down the central corridor of the containers, an area large enough to get two trucks past at once.

Then the noises started coming from below him, the concrete almost shaking with the blasts. There were shouts, adrenaline-soaked male voices, crazed with anger or fear. Hard to tell.

Radio crackled. Paul, panting, 'Mac. Get here now!'

Mac doubled back at a sprint, flying right into the curved downward ramp to the sub-level, face to face with Peter Garrison, fifty metres away at the bottom of the ramp. They stared at each other, mouths open, panting, confused. Garrison raised his M4 with both hands. Mac was about to squeeze off when his leg gave out from under him. He spilled forward, lost his sights. His groin made a tearing sensation, his inside left knee hit concrete. Garrison fired over the top of him, chipping concrete all the way up the ramp.

He hadn't shouldered the M4 properly and it recoiled upwards and away to the right.

Mac rolled to his right. Garrison got a better shoulder. But assault rifle fire sounded close behind him and Garrison turned, tried to run back to his cohorts. Mac squeezed off, hitting what he thought was the American's right calf. Garrison staggered a bit, but veered to his right, firing back into the sub-level as he went.

Mac limped down the ramp, his knee agony, breathing at thirteen to the dozen. Coming down to the flat level, he saw Garrison and two other men with assault rifles get to a stairwell against the far wall. Mac took a stance, squeezed off two rounds. They kept running. That was the trouble with a short-barrel handgun: no range.

He ran towards the stairs, five shots left and three men ahead of him, all armed with the latest assault rifles.

To his left he saw Paul, lying face down, blood around him on the concrete.

Mac's blood drummed in his ears as he got to the stairs. Standing to the side, he looked up quickly, pulled back, looked up again and threw himself flat against the other wall at the foot of the stairs, Heckler pointing up in a cup-and-saucer. His breathing was out of control, his eyes blurring with sweat. There was no air in the sub-level, and with the humidity it was making him gasp for oxygen.

He made up the stairs. Slow. In the movies, people giving chase always ran up stairs after the bad guys. In Mac's world, the stairwell was where people were shot.

He got to the double-back in the middle of the stairs, suddenly realising the stairs went back to the street-level warehouse.

Sticking his face around quickly, he pulled back, stuck it out again and kept it there. Heard something, a rumbling sound. Moving up, he came to the top, stayed low, looking for the shooter. He came out of the stairwell, homing on the rumbling sound. Across the warehouse, the roller door was going up.

A roar sounded as an engine fired. Mac started running. Coming around the last stack of containers, he aimed up. Forty metres away the last guy was shutting the rear passenger door of a blue BMW 5-series. As the engine gunned, the roller door went up further.

A back-seat passenger pointed his M4 at Mac, the fire coming in three-shot bursts. Mac ducked behind the container as paint chips flew. More carbine gunfire chewed up the steel he was hiding behind. The BMW accelerated through the doorway and Mac came out of hiding, squeezed off, took out the rear window.

He ran to the door, caught the last part of the rego – 452.

Struggling to get his breath, he bent over, hands on knees. He felt so old – way, way past his prime for this shit.

Voices sounded behind him and he swung around and went to his knee in one motion, ready to squeeze off.

Sawtell, jogging, yelled, 'Don't shoot.'

Mac sat down on his arse. Resting arms on knees, he looked at the ceiling.

He wished he hadn't seen it. But he had. The driver – a blonde woman – had looked him in the eye.

'You okay, Mac?' asked Sawtell.

Mac tried to respond, but vomited between his legs.

CHAPTER 40

They found Paul leaning against a large blue plastic dumpster bin clutching at his left side. The blood trail from where Mac had seen him lying was thick and dark.

'Shit, Mac,' he grinned. 'What is it with Aussies and trouble?'

'Follows us round like a bad smell. Didn't I warn you?'

Sawtell knelt and lifted the left wing away from Paul's body. Paul winced, gasped.

Sawtell whispered low, looked under there. Dark blood oozed through layers of clothing and kevlar.

Sawtell keyed the mic, ordered his medic guy to come immediately, then had another thought. 'POLRI there yet?'

Sawtell listened, then said, 'Negative. Stay with the hostages until POLRI get there. Secure the area. Over.'

The Green Berets had rescued the hostages with no injuries.

Sawtell unzipped the top of Paul's ovies and looked at Mac, who came around behind Paul, held him up and forward while Sawtell stripped down the top of the grey ovies. Unclipping the fasteners on the kevlar vest, Sawtell pulled it over from the right-hand side then peeled it downward along the left arm.

The slug had grazed straight down the left side of Paul's ribs in the area where there was no kevlar, only an adjustable gusset. There was another slug embedded in the kevlar, folded back on itself like a rosette. The flesh wound looked like Paul had leaned against an iron someone had forgotten to turn off. There was bone showing and a lot of blood – five-inch wet scar peeled back like a madman's laugh.

Paul was trying to keep his breathing under control, but the shock and the pain were pushing him towards hyperventilation.

Mac stripped down and handed over his white undershirt to Sawtell, who used it to stem the blood in Paul's ribs.

Sawtell looked up at Mac. 'Get 'em?'

Mac shook. 'Nope. M4s versus a pea-shooter.'

'Gotta get you something with a bit more authority.'

'They're in a pale blue 5-series Beemer. Last numbers on the rego are 452,' said Mac.

Sawtell shook his head. 'This Garrison is starting to irritate me. A bad advertisement for Americans.'

'What?' deadpanned Mac. 'They're not all like that?'

Paul laughed.

Sawtell eyeballed Paul. 'What are you laughing at? The dude just shot you!'

'He'll keep, mate,' said Mac.

The adrenaline slowly washed off them as they spoke. Even whispers sounded like screams when you were coming down from the kind of adrenaline squirt you got from a gunfight.

Mac kept a close watch on Sawtell. Watched the way he talked soft, drew Paul back into the game, not wanting him to lose consciousness but also not scaring him.

The blood kept coming and Paul needed a fresh staunch.

'Here, take this,' Sawtell said to Mac.

Mac held the bloodied shirt as Sawtell tore down his own ovies, unfastened the bullet-proof vest and used his undershirt on the wound. Got Paul to hold it in place by relaxing his left arm on it.

The smell of cordite was still fresh in their nostrils. It hung around in the sub-level.

'Sabaya here? Anyone see him?' asked Mac.

'He wasn't in the office section,' said Sawtell. 'Thought he might be in the warehouse.'

Mac shook his head.

'He wasn't down here,' said Mac.

Sawtell stood, fiddled with the radio and couldn't get a signal. He pulled it apart, blew on every connection, then slammed the transmitter box between his hands a couple of times. Turned the thing on again and gave thumbs-up.

'Roger that. Copy,' he said, after a pause.

Sawtell demanded to know if anyone had a handle on Garrison and the girl.

The reply wasn't what he wanted.

'Listen, McQueen chased them to a blue 5-series BMW. Registration includes the numbers four, fiver, two. Four fiver two. Got that? Blue BMW, 5-series.'

By the sounds of it, the troop had lost their trail. Sawtell snapped like someone who was way over the whole thing.

'Okay, okay. Manz and Spikey get down here now. We're on the sub-level of the warehouse. Bring the medic pack, okay?' he ordered, and signed off.

He looked at Mac, who was taking in their surroundings. There were forty or fifty shipping containers around them that by Mac's reckoning would be stuffed with books, furniture and ceramics from all over Asia. Amongst them would be gold, drugs, counterfeit US dollars, cigarettes and whisky, maybe even some bunkered crude oil. Who knew what was in these things? He was quietly amazed that customs and the cops ever found a damned thing in such a secret yet ubiquitous form of moving goods.

Sawtell came over, asked if Mac was okay.

'Yeah, mate,' said Mac, thinking about how Garrison had been cropping up in chatter, briefings and intel gossip for years. He wondered what role he really played and who protected him. Was it someone actually in the Agency, or was it political? Someone from State or the Oval Office?

Sawtell took another blast on the radio. This time it sounded like POLRI. 'Captain John Sawtell. US Army. We got one down, officer. Need an ambulance down here. The fugitives are driving a blue BMW, 5-series . . .' said Sawtell.

Sawtell never seemed to get tired, thought Mac. He operated like a machine and it was pretty obvious why the US Army had tagged him for leadership. Mac liked that he never identified himself as being Special Forces. You could always tell the genuine article in the US military because they'd tell you they drove a truck, shovelled chow.

The cordite smell wasn't getting any better. Mac wondered if Garrison was using experimental rounds. It wasn't like any kind of firearm discharge he'd ever smelled.

Behind him, Sawtell signed off.

'Smell that? That cordite?' asked Mac.

Sawtell chuckled. 'Shitty loads. Not yours, are they? That pea-shooter powder?'

Paul laughed too.

Mac walked forwards, sniffing. Something wasn't right. One of the few things he could remember from his trips to Aberdeen Proving Grounds was to do with the smell of bitter almonds and freshly mown green grass. He couldn't remember what they corresponded to, but they were listed as the two biggest giveaways that there was some bio-chem nasty lurking around the shop.

He walked along the containers: forty-footers, white and red mostly. The smell got worse. It was like he could taste it. His Hi-Tecs squeaked on shiny concrete, echoing around the sub-level. Sweat trickled down his back. It wasn't bitter almond, it wasn't mown grass. It was putrid and sweet. It was human and chemical.

Most of what Mac knew about containers, he knew from Jenny Toohey. And the vivid memory he had of the work she did was the telltale sign that there was a container of slaves in the vicinity. Jenny once told him, *It's a smell you never forget. I smell it in my nightmares.*

Mac froze to the spot, gulped, stomach churning. Couldn't deny what he was smelling.

Shit and bleach.

CHAPTER 41

Sensing something was wrong, Sawtell joined Mac. Paul rose from his sitting position, awkward but silent, checked for load in the SIG.

Sawtell pulled the slide back on his Beretta, the noise filling the sub-level space.

Mac shook his head.

They crept forward silently, Mac's breathing ragged.

The smell got stronger.

They moved down a corridor between pods of containers, the dark intensifying the atmosphere.

Mac stopped, his ears rushing with his breathing and pulse.

He tried to remember Jenny's conversations about a particular case: holes hidden high up in the box, right under the top beam; holes in the floor of the container. He'd found her work fairly distasteful, always tried to change the subject.

Sawtell's eyes were wide now, troubled by the smell. 'You sure this is okay, McQueen?'

Mac nodded, gulped. Wished he had a neckerchief.

'Don't smell okay,' said Sawtell.

They turned into another avenue created by containers where it was darker and tighter. The smell was so intense that the three men could taste it in their mouths.

'Holy shit!' muttered Paul, then retched.

They stopped beside a red forty-foot container with white ID markings but no shipping company logo. Mac tried to control his breathing, put the back of his hand to his mouth not knowing whether to retch or cry.

Sawtell and Mac looked at each other. Neither wanted to be the first to puke.

'Fuck!' complained Paul, wiping dribble from the side of his mouth.

Sawtell squinted at Mac. 'That the smell of . . . of *people?*' he said.

Mac unholstered the Heckler out of its rig, his legs shaking and sweat running down his face from under his cap. His feet swam in his Hi-Tecs as he stepped forward and tapped on the steel side with the Heckler.

Nothing.

They looked at each other, their breathing crashing like Bondi surf.

Mac was about to go to another container. Then they heard what sounded like a squawk.

They waited a few seconds. Then came some murmurs. Muffled. Indistinct.

Sawtell grabbed Mac's bicep.

Then screams, cries.

'Hello,' Mac shouted, tapping on the steel side again.

Voices were now obvious. Young voices.

Sawtell almost wrenched Mac's arm off, his face aghast. 'That's – That's . . . That's kids. Fucking *children!*'

Mac tapped the side again. Shouted, 'You okay?'

The noise rose to the sound of a playground of yelling kids from a block away.

Sawtell ran down the side of the box, bare-chested, panicked, sweat pouring down his back. He took the corner around the container so fast he had to grip on the pillar to stay upright. Mac was behind him. Sawtell stopped, fumbled with a huge padlock on the locking handles of the door and then shook at it like a madman, gripping on it so hard it looked like his fingers could knit into the padlock hook.

Sounds from inside the box got louder.

Mac yelled, 'It's okay – we're getting there.'

Then he stepped back, pulled out his Nokia and dialled Jenny, who was having lunch with her crew. Mac gave her the address, asked, 'Could you give us a hand?'

Sawtell keyed the radio, yelled for someone to get the angle grinder from the helo and bring it.

The sounds of screaming and pleading from the container were now joined by a drumming sound – scores of tiny hands banging on a steel box.

Sawtell was losing it. He stood back, levelled his Beretta at the locks on the door until Mac stepped in, stopped him. Not such a good idea.

Sawtell looked at Mac, shaking his head slowly like *This is not happening*. 'Kids! What the fuck is a bunch of kids doing in a fucking container?!' he shouted, slapping on the container door with a big open hand.

Little hands banged back from the inside. Tiny voices screaming *Maa, Maa, Maa*.

Sawtell was crying as he zeroed in on Mac. 'Well?'

'Mate, they're . . . um.'

'*Yes?*' yelled Sawtell.

'They're, probably, you know, sex slaves. I can't be sure . . .'

'*What?*'

'They're probably being shipped to, you know . . .' He cleared his throat. 'Umm, paedophile brothels, private clients – or owners, whatever they're called.'

The din of children got worse. Crying, pleading.

The smell and sound warped the air.

Sawtell seemed to look straight through him and for a split second Mac thought he was going to have his head torn off.

Suddenly shouting echoed in the sub-level.

'Over here, guys,' yelled Mac.

The Green Berets arrived with a big green canvas gear bag and pinch bars.

Sawtell pointed at the container. 'Open it. Now!' he ordered, beyond fury.

The two forced-entry guys set up their stuff. One ran to find power, the other guy set up the angle grinder.

The medic team arrived too, got to work on Paul.

Sawtell stood over Jansen, the angle-grinder guy, whispering like a maniac. 'This is going to be the fastest forced entry you ever pull, Jansen. You hear me? They'll give you a goddamned gold medal for this.'

Jansen nodded, put on his protective visor and gloves then busied himself with the machine, ensuring that nothing could go wrong.

The other guy reappeared with orange cable for Jansen's angle grinder, and then picked up the pinch bar.

The children still banged and yelled.

Jansen powered up and stepped over to the door bolts. Sparks poured like an orange waterfall as he went to work.

The two doors had big handles which folded inwards where the doors met. When the handles were folded down, they locked in place security bars that extended from the top to the bottom of each door. Each door had two vertical locking bars and there was a massive German padlock securing the handles over one another in the centre of the doors. Jansen had to chop out the centre sections of the security bars; the German lock would be hardened steel and would take too long.

The noise and smell were too much for Paul, and the medic guys escorted him away. Mac went with them and pulled out the phone, hitting redial. Jenny picked up and said, 'Almost there.'

Mac jogged up the service ramps to the main warehouse entry, pressed a button and the huge roller door went up. The scream of the angle grinder burst out into the sunlight.

The frontage apron of the warehouse now hosted a Gazelle and a Black Hawk, the pilots chewing the fat.

After three minutes a blue Commodore wagon raced onto the front apron area, a POLRI light truck behind it.

The Commodore stopped beside Mac, Jenny in the front passenger seat. Mac just said, 'Sub-level, you can drive down.'

'You okay?' said Jenny.

Mac shook his head, pointed into the building.

They squealed off, the POLRI truck following. A third vehicle parked on the apron. It was a mid-sized, unmarked bus. Empty.

Two POLRI women got out and opened the side storage areas, pulling out piles of blankets, white towels, portable shower stands and large blue plastic bags. One bag fell over, spilling children's gear on the concrete apron. There were dresses, undies, sandals.

Soft toys.

Mac waited for the ambulance and directed it down to the sub-level. As he walked down he felt his pulse increasing again. He gagged on the smell, flinched at the screaming noise, feeling the fear and pain in the people down there.

The door was almost off when Mac arrived. Sawtell stood behind his team, eyes huge, a mix of fear and rage, his body poised like a professional wrestler about to clinch.

A POLRI woman videotaped the proceedings, while Jenny yelled into a radio handset, one finger in her left ear. After she got off the radio she conferred with her POLRI colleagues.

A decision apparently made, she walked over to Sawtell, who turned to her. For a second Mac saw a scared boy under that machine-like exterior.

The angle grinder suddenly free-revved for a split second and Jansen shut it down. Smoke hung, mixing with the container smell. Hideous.

The kids started up again as Jansen's offsider pulled back on a pinch bar. Metal twisted and ground against itself, and the right-hand door swung open like the scene in a ghost movie.

Mac felt bile coming up as the stench flooded the enclosed space.

A small dark figure was the first out. Cambodian. Five years old. Big eyes. Naked. Shit all over her.

Looked around. Confused.

'Maa?' she said.

CHAPTER 42

Mac, Sawtell and Paul sat speechless outside the office section of the warehouse.

Paul had been cleaned, stitched and given a morphine needle. He didn't want to be in the ambulance. Wanted the more critically ill kids in it.

Sawtell was blanked out. Thousand-yard stare into nothing. Even his own men were leaving him alone.

Mac had cordoned off the far-end ramp to the sub-level, hoping the POLRI might find some Garrison blood samples down there. He wondered what was happening in Singapore and tried to understand the situation now that he'd actually seen Garrison and Diane together in a getaway car.

Mac was so tired he could barely keep his eyelids up, even with the circus that had descended around them.

To their left, the POLRI women scrubbed down the healthier children in the portable showers, dried them off, photographed them, booked them. Then they dressed them and put them in the bus with an orange number tag on their new clothes.

Aged about four to ten, there were about seventy of them, boys and girls.

Beside the bus Jenny spoke into a mobile phone, her offsider beside her with a clipboard. Every few seconds Jenny leaned over to read out numbers: probably relaying container ID to someone at United States Customs and Border Control or the Jakarta Container Port.

A POLRI Criminal Investigation Division team dealt with the two dead Garrison guards upstairs. Another team processed the rescued hostages from a POLRI van by the helos. Jeremy's kids stayed inside, but Wylie's missus emerged and sat on the step box, lit a smoke, inhaled deep, lucky to be alive.

More teams from POLRI, FBI, Scotland Yard and AFP appeared ready to box-scan every container to see if there were more kids down there. They could do it with heartbeat detectors or thermo imagers. Mac found it shaming that while sexual-servitude trafficking was a crime that happened mostly in South-East Asia, it was driven by demand and money from Western countries.

Apart from the sheer horror of what he'd witnessed, Mac had never realised what a logistical nightmare the whole thing was. Now he could see why Jenny was gone for days and weeks at a time, working herself to a standstill. Once you found a container like this, you had to work back to the ship, back to the freight company, back through the terminal gate-logs, back to the trucking companies and the clients in order to see where it came from and whether there might be more like it. And then you had to work forwards, too, try to find where other containers from the same source might be going, where another box full of children might be sitting, waiting for the paedophile industry to hand over the money.

It was a harrowing detail for cops and Mac knew it chewed them up at a hell of a rate. Not only did they have to make arrests and have an evidence bag at the end of the process, they also had child victims in the most appalling and distressed states. There were only so many hours in the day; only so many resources. Only so many containers you could search.

In front of Mac the liaison people from various embassies attempted to straighten out the in-country cooperation angle with the POLRI. The way it usually worked was the police had a job to do and wanted to take statements from those involved in, or witness to, the incidents, regardless of their nationality. The liaisons' job was to insist that that was not in the spirit or the letter of the agreement between the countries.

The Yanks had no interest in allowing a Special Forces captain to make a statement to Indon police. And the British weren't even acknowledging Paul. A Pommie liaison woman's voice rose over the pack. 'If there was a British national involved in this incident – and I'm not confirming there was . . .'

Mac saw a Javanese BAIS operative he knew, Edi Sitepu. He was listening in on the diplomatic hoo-ha. He caught Mac's eye and came over.

They shook and Edi sat down. 'Can't work this one out,' said Edi to Mac. 'Lots of talking about Abu Sabaya, but was he here?'

Mac shook his head, sipped some water. He hoped at some stage during his lifetime that smell was going to get out of his mouth. 'Garrison and Sabaya must have split. Don't know where either of them are.'

'That Peter Garrison. Bad news that one,' said Edi, shaking his head. 'You know we tipped off the Americans about him last year?'

Mac didn't know.

'But it turned into this.' Edi nodded at the British and American embassy folks doing their thing.

Mac remained silent, exhausted, over it.

'The thing to do was to get us in a loop, hey Mac?' said Edi.

Normally Mac loved the way Indons got Western phrases slightly wrong, but his mood was too bleak. 'Would have been great before Bali, too, eh Edi?'

Mac shouldn't have said it.

Edi's face darkened. He and Mac hadn't always seen eye to eye. The Timor thing and Mac's involvement in some aspects of it had created a stand-offishness between them, even though they could have shared some more basic operational chatter over the years. Thing was, Mac's legacy in Timor saw him gravitate closer to the old President-controlled BAKIN – now BIN – at the expense of the armed forces-controlled intelligence organisation, BAIS. So it was hard for Mac to simply make a call to Edi and get him in the loop on something like Garrison and Sabaya, even though he wanted the Indon perspective.

'Look, Edi, why don't I tell you what I know and you tell me how we're going to catch these pricks – fair?'

Edi shrugged.

'So what are the cops saying about the bodies up there?' asked Mac.

'Dunno, Mac. They not talking with us.'

Same old same old, thought Mac, wearied by it all: cops, spooks and military refusing to speak to one another.

He reckoned a solid police ID on Garrison's thugs – the ones who didn't make it past Sawtell's boys – might be useful.

'You got anything on the BMW?' asked Mac.

'Corporate registration in the name of a shelf company. Import/export. All the usual shit. Nothing linking it with Garrison, but we're following up right now.'

'So, how'd it go down in Singapore?' asked Edi, pushing for his own information.

Mac felt like Edi was going too far.

'It was a decoy, mate. Sure of it.'

'Decoy for what?'

Mac shrugged. 'Just didn't feel like real terrorism.'

Edi made a humming sound deep in his throat. 'Funny timing though, eh Mac?'

'Timing?'

'You know, with Xiong in Singapore the same morning.'

Mac looked at him, his interest aroused by the Indonesian perspective. 'Tell me.'

Edi shrugged. 'Probably nothing. What do the Americans call it?'

'What?'

'Inciting incident? Something like that?'

Mac was so tired, but he smiled. 'Inciting incident?'

Inciting incidents were what the CIA created in order to justify a response, usually of a military nature. They'd get their contractors to stage an atrocity somewhere and then false-flag it – get the media and other governments to pin it on the government they wanted to invade or launch a coup against.

Mac was running flat-out trying to see where Edi got Singapore into the mix. 'You're not telling me the CIA is in this? Garrison is a black sheep, far as I can tell. He's not with the program – is he?'

Edi smiled. Big Javanese smile. 'Mr Mac, inciting incidents don't have to be Agency. Just see this from Asian eyes. Which country wants

344

a reason for Singapore to embrace its military? Perhaps in the form of a naval base?'

Mac clicked. 'So the Chinese get an incident that focuses the need for their military presence in Singapore. What do Garrison and Sabaya get?'

'Don't know,' Edi mused. 'Some of that Chinese gold?'

Mac thought about it. The Chinese economy was the world's fastest-growing, but at the highest levels of its government, everything was still transacted with gold.

'You saying the Chinese paid Garrison and Sabaya to pull that thing on *Golden Serpent*?'

'Sure. Does the CIA use its own people or official budget to pull its stunts? Remember Irangate? That was an off-the-books funding operation to get money to paramilitary contractors in Central America.'

Mac nodded. 'I guess it was.'

'Garrison is probably tolerated in the Agency because he's their funding guy,' said Edi.

'Know what, Edi? You in the office tomorrow morning?'

Edi shrugged.

'I might call you,' said Mac.

'You do that.'

Mac noticed one of the POLRI women had given Paul a bottle of water, but he wasn't drinking it. Mac opened it, gave it to him. 'Keep the fluids up, mate.'

Paul had been strapped by the medics and was referring to his rib-wound as a 'nick'. He drank, his face a mask of impassivity. Mac wondered if everyone still had that taste in their mouths.

'I've been thinking,' said Mac. 'We've forgotten about something, haven't we? The other hostage, the officer from *Golden Serpent*.'

Paul shrugged.

'Well, what's that about?' asked Mac.

'Either they're going to make more demands, or they've got another ship,' said Paul, then looked away, wincing with the pain in his ribs. 'You saying that there's no more demands? What they came for is actually on a ship somewhere?'

'Makes sense, doesn't it? I mean, if we agree the Singers thing was a hoax?'

'A decoy.'

'Okay, decoy,' said Mac.

'So why did Garrison come to Jakarta?' said Paul, suspicious.

'Don't know, mate. Take care of business? It's where his hostages were.'

'And where's Sabaya gone?'

'What if where he's gone has nothing to do with it? What if the key to this is what's on the ship he's hijacked?' said Mac. 'Remember Wylie saying the third hostage is a Canadian bloke with a lot of experience in these waters?'

'And Sabaya referred to the Canadian as the "asset",' said Paul, his face lighting up. 'You know, there *was* that strange thing in Singers. Remember, when Weenie came on the radio and told us that all those ships were demanding to get out of the port?'

'Sure do.'

'And you called it a stampede.'

'Yeah.'

Paul looked into the middle distance, thinking. 'You know, you create a lot of confusion by getting that kind of exodus in a major port. But Garrison and Sabaya weren't pulling a real hostage crisis, were they?'

'Nah.'

'So why did they need that chaos?' asked Paul.

'That's what I'm getting at,' said Mac. 'I think they staged that thing to get hold of a ship. They knew the MPA would be looking elsewhere. The Coast Guard were obviously focused on one thing. US Army could only think of nerve agent. Same with the cops.'

'Get the attention on one thing . . .'

'. . . steal a totally other thing.'

'Then, once they were standing on their new ship, they trigger a race for the exits, give themselves a head start,' said Paul.

'No ship owner is really going to know what's going on till this dies down,' said Mac, 'and it won't be over for another two hours or more.'

Paul swivelled, eyes ablaze. 'If your theory's right, they've given themselves a head start of – what? – ten hours, eleven hours?'

'Depends on exactly when they left Golden Serpent and went to Brani

Island with –' Abruptly, the last few days tumbled over and things fell into place. Mac sifted his subconscious.

'What is it, Mac?' asked Paul.

Mac shook his head slightly. 'This may sound crazy, but I think we saw the ship they hijacked. I think they were on it.'

'When?'

'When we came out of our swim to Brani and came up alongside her.'

'That white thing?'

'Yeah – roll-on/roll-off. I thought I saw something on the upper decks but I couldn't confirm it. What I remember now is that the tailgate was down on the dock. Remember that?'

'Yeah, I do.'

'When we were taking off, there was a sound in that building, remember?'

'No, I don't. You saying they were in there?' said Paul.

'I think they were waiting for us to go so they could continue loading it up. They'd already put out the scare story to all the ships. We stumbled into the middle of it.'

'So that's our ship?'

'Dunno. Might have to tip the Singaporean cops to it.'

Paul looked at Mac. 'Not our fight, mate.'

'Not our fight,' echoed Mac.

Mac thought about finding a cab, going south, booking into the Marriott or Regent with his DBS Visa card, and sleeping solid. If he could get through on a phone call first time, he might tip the Singapore cops off. But he doubted they'd listen. He'd play it by ear.

He couldn't see anyone from the Aussie Embassy. Looked like he'd got lucky, sidestepped the paperwork. He'd catch up with all that later. Pop in on his way to Soekarno-Hatta.

As he eased weight on to his legs to test how his knee was doing, Jenny came over, sat between Mac and Sawtell.

'You okay, Mr Macca?'

'Way better than those kids. That's for sure.'

'Believe it or not I've seen far worse. No corpses this time,' said Jenny. 'The guys are pretty happy about that.'

Mac nodded absently, no idea how to express what he was thinking.

'Back to Sydney?' asked Jenny.

'In a couple of days. Gonna sleep first.'

'Where?'

Mac shrugged. 'Marriott. Regent. Wherever the cab stops.'

Jenny looked at the bus. 'Why don't you sleep at the apartment?' she said, voice light, just doing a mate a favour.

Mac nodded. 'Sure,' he said, keeping it light too.

'Hang around for half an hour while I finish up here and I'll drive you over.'

Mac went to say 'Thanks' but no sound came out.

Jen was about to get up when she noticed Sawtell, slumped between his knees, face in his hands.

Jenny put a comforting hand on his back, said, 'Hello.'

Sawtell sat up like he'd just woken up, rubbed the heels of his hands into his eye sockets. His lips were a bit swollen.

'I'm Jenny,' she said, putting out her hand. Sawtell took it, mind elsewhere.

Jenny got him talking, about his wife, their plans to have kids, how he wondered if he could do that now. He talked about growing up in a wealthy country, taking everything for granted.

Sawtell gradually regained some of his colour, and asked Jenny how she could spend her life doing this.

'See that container?' said Jenny.

'Yep.'

'You want the bastards who did that caught?'

'Damned right.'

'You want the men who pay to rape those kids caught?'

'Damned right I do.'

'You want to know that a few kids of the thousands get saved from that?'

Sawtell nodded.

'So do I,' said Jenny, using Mac's right shoulder to push herself to her feet.

'Bye, John.'

'See ya, Jenny.'

They shook.

'And don't let this joker lead you astray, okay?' She pointed at Mac. ''Cos he will.'

She smiled, gave Mac that look. 'Something about your arse? On CNN?'

'Fox News.'

Jenny shook her head, moved back to her crew.

CHAPTER 43

Mac lay in the bath, let it soak, the sound of CNN echoing through the apartment. It was all *Golden Serpent*, with an ever-increasing roster of experts being dragged in from think tanks, universities, government and police to give their opinions. Mac felt wearied by most of the comments. The experts didn't seem to know what they were doing on air any more than the anchor did.

It was five-thirty pm in Singapore and the authorities still hadn't declared the emergency over. The city was evacuated, Changi was closed and the port was locked up.

Coiffed reporters did live crosses from as far north as Tokyo and as far south as Sydney. Without a press centre to spoonfeed them, it was mostly only conjecture making it onto the tops and bottoms of the hour.

CNN was trying to link the Jakarta shoot-out with *Golden Serpent*. A good leap, but no one was confirming it. And POLRI hadn't confirmed anything except the presence of two deceased males in a north Jakarta warehouse.

The whole thing was still in play, even though Mac knew almost for certain that the Twentieth would have had enough time to do what they did better than anyone else.

All the media had were two officers and two 'engineers' being escorted off the ship. They were still seeking confirmation regarding the number of deceased still on board. The media would have to wait for the detectives, and the detectives had to wait for the CBNRE guys to give the all-clear. In the meantime, they had scores of shots of bio-hazard suits swarming over *Golden Serpent*'s container stacks.

Mac wondered about Edi's inciting incident theory. Indonesian intel types tended to see Chinese motivations that Westerners might miss. But then again, some of the inciting incidents staged by intelligence organisations over the years were hardly in the realms of common sense. If nothing else, Edi's outlook made a good fit with what Wylie had told him on *Golden Serpent*, about Garrison referring to the VX bomb as an incident tailored to CNN.

Back in Sulawesi, Cookie B had gone immediately to the money. As in: where's Garrison's payday? Now another Indonesian spook had bypassed Mac's entire carefully assembled scenario to state the obvious: that someone stood to gain from making Singapore look insecure and easily attacked, and from a maritime source.

Mac ducked under the water, the taste of shit and bleach still in his mouth, gunfire still ringing in his ears.

The knee didn't feel too painful as he dried off. If it was going to be a problem, it would flare up by morning.

Pulling the curtains, he turned off his mobile phone and crawled between clean sheets.

He mused briefly about how strange it was to lie in Jenny's bed thinking about Diane. Then finally, mercifully, sleep came.

Bacon, coffee and eggs filled Mac's nostrils. He opened his eyes, not knowing where he was for a few seconds. The bedside clock said 7.20 am but he felt like he could sleep for another twenty-four hours.

'Hey, sleeping beauty,' said Jenny when Mac appeared in his undies. He went for a cheek kiss but she took it on the lips. Tasted of Close-Up, the red one.

Jenny was about to leave for work and there was a cooked breakfast for Mac ready on the table.

'You know,' she said, pulling back. 'I liked coming home to a man in my bed, even if he was dead to the world.'

They stared at each other for what felt like an eternity. Then Mac said, 'Umm, I liked it too.'

They both drew breaths. Six years of sex and so much not said.

She play-slapped him, laughing. 'You!'

'Me?!' he said, laughing too.

'Yes, you!'

'I never done nothing.'

She gave him a look, like *That's the point, stupid.*

'Are you okay?' she asked.

Mac nodded. 'Still in one piece, can't complain.'

'That's not what I meant,' said Jen.

Mac didn't know if he was ready to talk about the children. 'You know, what happened down there . . .' He shook his head, the words not coming.

'There could be a happy ending for this lot,' said Jenny. 'We think they're from northern Cambodia and southern Laos, so there's a chance of getting them back to their families.'

Jenny was probably putting a gloss on it to make him feel better, thought Mac, but he didn't care. He wanted to believe there was a happy ending for those kids.

'I'll tell John. He'll want to know that,' said Mac.

Jenny's eyes softened. She fished in her holster bag, came out with her spare keys. Put them in his hand, seeming a little embarrassed. 'I, umm . . .'

Jenny Toohey was not a woman who gave her house keys to a man. She started to say something, then rubbed at her eye, looked away.

'Bloody pollen,' said Mac.

'It's a shocker,' agreed Jenny, then paused. 'All that drama yesterday. I forgot to tell you . . . I wanted to say to you, 'cos if you ever, you know . . .'

Mac couldn't tell her to forget it. Couldn't bat this one away.

'Umm, when I saw that bloke Paul and that bullet wound. And I realised what had happened down there, I . . .'

Mac put his right hand out. Took her left. She looked at the ceiling, took big gulps.

'The life we choose, right?' said Mac.

'Or did it choose us?' she said lightly, like it was meant to be a

352

joke. But her heart wasn't in it. Truth was, the protocol for people who ran the danger of being killed in their line of work was to gloss over the obvious. You made endless jokes about farts, penises, crossdressing, gay sex, masturbation, constipation and incontinence – all of it to bring people closer without having to say, *By the way, in case you're shot tomorrow* . . .

Mac didn't know what to do, so he hugged her, feeling her wet nose and eyes against his neck. She burrowed in, sniffled. Held tight. Then she moved her mouth up to his ear.

Wasn't till she was out the door that he realised she'd said *I love you*.

The bacon and eggs were Nirvana, the toast bliss, the freshly brewed coffee outstanding. Mac wolfed the lot and chased it with an orange. He turned on the television and saw the Singapore story still unfolding, but he muted it – still a bit lost in the moment with Jenny. Then he rinsed plates and put them in the dishwasher, wiped down the breakfast table and the benches and cleaned the sink with some Ajax. Jenny was a great cop but a lousy housekeeper.

He took a long shower, pulled his ovies out of the washing machine and put them in the dryer. If he got on a flight that day, he might buy some threads. But if he was kosher with the embassy, he would see what he had lying around in his locker in the compound. For the first time in weeks he had a sense of time and ease and it felt good to have some tucker in his belly, some sleep under his belt.

He hit the sound on the TV and saw the cable news services still hadn't finalised the *Golden Serpent* story. One of the terminals at Singapore had reopened for a few exceptional shipments, but Keppel and Brani were still locked down and the city was evacuated with martial law in force. Sixty or seventy ships were standing off in the Singapore Strait. Changi was only dealing in government and military aircraft.

Something was holding up the declaration that the emergency was over. The Singapore government would be climbing the walls with frustration, thought Mac.

Then it came. Fox News had found a Singaporean politician who was lambasting the government's lack of preparedness for a maritime terror incident. And the clincher . . . *Singapore needs closer military ties with its friends*. And he wasn't talking about the Americans. The biggest trump that the pro-China lobby held in Singapore was the fact that the US Navy had a policy of not informing host countries of arrival times for their ships. It made it easy for the pro-China lobby to typify the Americans as arrogant and interested in their own geopolitical game rather than the wellbeing of Singapore's economy.

Another Singaporean man came on, from a commerce association, talking about a *realistic defence policy*.

To Mac's ear it sounded rigged. The words 'friends' and 'realistic' – when they were used in the Singapore context – were terms straight from the MSS propaganda manual. The Chinese had spent thirty years infiltrating all layers of Singapore's political, bureaucratic, military and commercial elites. Which was why the Americans found it impossible to get Singapore to become a full client-state.

Edi had been right, thought Mac. *Golden Serpent* was starting to look like an inciting incident.

Catching sight of Jen's phone charger, Mac grabbed his Nokia from the bedroom, brought it through and plugged it in. Booting up, the envelope graphic appeared. He sat on the sofa, hit 'messages'. The first one was a text: *Call me urgent. Paul.* It had been sent at 10.30 the previous evening.

The next message was an invitation to call his service provider's voicemail service. Mac dialled in. It was from Don, the DIA guy, wanting to talk quick-smart about 'our friends'. He left a number, said the secret handshake was 'firefly'.

Mac started with Don. The number was a global-connect free call that took him to what sounded like the Pentagon.

'It's Richard Davis here, Southern Scholastic Books. Could I speak with Don in Defense Intelligence Agency, please?'

'What's the time there, Mr Davis?' said the woman.

'Firefly.'

'Thank you, sir. Connecting you now.'

The connection buzzed and clicked.

'Don? It's Mac.'

'Shit! Thanks for getting back to me, McQueen.'

He sounded like crap, like a man who hadn't slept.

'How can I help you?' asked Mac.

'We clear?' asked Don, meaning were they on a secure line.

'Personal cell phone,' said Mac.

Don hesitated.

'I bought it three days ago from a convenience store. It's clear,' said Mac.

'Listen. Okay. So . . .' started Don, clearly jangled.

'Everything okay?' asked Mac. 'CNN's not saying it's over. It is over, right?'

'Umm, our friends.'

'Yep.'

'They got into the container.'

Mac assumed they had, to wire their IED. 'Yep?'

'And we've disabled the device.'

'Yep?'

'And we've secured the agent.'

'Yep?'

'Umm – you sure this is clear?'

'It's clear.'

Don cleared his throat. 'McQueen, we shipped one hundred and eighty bombs.'

'Yep?'

'There's only a hundred and seventy-nine bombs in that container.'

There was a big pause.

'Shit. You know where it is?' asked Mac.

There was a sudden commotion, Hatfield bellowing in the background. Mac could envisage the Chinook's situation room: incoming calls from the Oval Office, the Singapore President and the Pentagon. Soldiers, spooks and scientists wincing at having the paint stripped off them.

Mac thought fast. 'Have you searched the seabed? They may have tossed it, trying to extend this as long as possible.'

'We're got divers down there. But once you start on that, you have to retrace its route. We've got the SONAR birds doing that as well. It's not there. We're assuming our friends are travelling with it.'

Mac exhaled. 'What about the ship? It's a big tub, lots of areas to conceal something like that.'

'All over it with explosive detectors. Been going all night with revolving shifts. We've got our Europe team here too. Nothing. It's with them.'

Mac thought about the ro-ro ship, the one he and Paul assumed had been hijacked by Sabaya.

'Look, here's a left-field one, okay?' said Mac. 'On our way into Singers yesterday we came through Brani Island and there was this large unmarked ro-ro ship on the south side of the island.'

'We searched that area, I think,' said Don.

'I don't think they dropped the VX bomb there. But my hunch is they stole the ship. They were last seen motoring for Brani Island on a tender boat first thing in the morning. The *Golden Serpent* officers told us that,' said Mac.

'Could have been getting a helo from Brani or Sentosa,' said Don.

'In that case you'll have to check flight logs. They were going to controlled airspace that morning because of Xiong coming in so air traffic control would have been noticing everything.'

'You said the ro-ro ship was unmarked?'

'Yeah. No name, no shipping line, couldn't see any flags. If it's unmarked then there's something fishy about it. Like your transporter for the VX, right?'

'Okay.'

'The thing to do is get the Singaporeans to tell us exactly what the ship is for, who owns it and why it was docked there. We have to get access to that warehouse, too.'

'Warehouse?' asked Don.

'Yeah, the tailgate of the ship was down and I heard sounds in this security building. It's built like a bunker. You'll know what I mean when you see it.'

'Okay.'

'If we can identify the ship then we have something to chase. And if we know what's in that warehouse, we have some kind of clue about where they're headed.'

'Think I can swing that,' said Don.

'The thing to remember,' said Mac, 'is that these guys had the chance to do what Garrison did and just fly away to another country.

But if I'm right, they've taken the most conspicuous escape they could have taken.'

'See what you mean.'

Mac felt he'd done his bit, helped out a fellow professional. But Don wasn't finished with him.

'Look, I thought we could use a Sabaya expert. Most of your calls have been correct so far,' said Don, almost sheepish. A big change of attitude.

'What, you want me by the phone for the next couple of days?'

'Umm, no. I was hoping we could get you on the bird with Sawtell's unit?'

Mac hissed air, neither body nor mind up for this. 'I would, but I've got things to sort out with the embassy, and –'

'All done,' said Don.

'All done?'

'Yeah – sorry, McQueen. I took the liberty. Forgive me, willya? I'll buy you a beer sometime.'

Don was in a tough place, to be throwing a beer into the deal.

'You took the liberty?' asked Mac.

'Umm, yeah. You're seconded. Call it a specialist rotation.'

Mac laughed. 'Where?'

'Halim. Noon. Firefly.'

CHAPTER 44

It was 8.36 am. Mac had a few hours up his sleeve before he had to make for Halim on the outskirts of Jakarta. He dialled the number Paul had left and waited. It went to voicemail. He rang off and checked on the ovies to see if they were dry.

Mac's Nokia rang as he was looking for a wayward sock in the dryer. Jogging into the kitchen, he leaned over and grabbed the phone.

'Davis.'

'Hi sweetheart, get the flowers?' It was Paul.

'Oh those were flowers? Sorry, just wiped my arse with them,' said Mac, thinking Paul was sounding alert for a guy with a gunshot wound.

'Mate, thought you might like to come down and have a chat with a new addition to the team?' said Paul.

'Voluntary new addition?' asked Mac.

'Haven't decided yet, mate. Come down, have a natter.'

The address was four blocks from Jenny's. Paul had a subject in what they called a 'cabin'. It was like a safehouse, except in a cabin you generally interrogated people. There was nothing safe about it.

Mac stretched out as he walked. He had his ovies and Hi-Tecs on but no Heckler.

The address was a duplex on a quiet, tree-lined sidestreet away from the main boulevards. Mac knocked, saw an eye flash over the peep hole. Someone had been standing or sitting right there.

The door opened. A burly bloke with a holster pouch around his middle stepped out and gestured for a pat-down. Mac submitted. Bloke checked in and behind his ears too then ushered him through. 'They're in the living room, sir.'

Mac clocked Paul and two other men: trop shirts, hip rigs. Clean-cut, athletically built. Sitting on coffee tables and chairs, they were gathered around something of interest. Not a TV, but a blonde woman wearing jeans and a pale blue polo shirt. Very good-looking, curvy. Big black eye. Bruised neck.

All eyes turned to Mac, his eyes on Diane.

She smiled up at him, embarrassed, then looked away. It was obvious she hadn't had much sleep last night. He wondered if the lads had been taking turns winding her up, getting her to slip in her story.

Paul stood, hooked Mac by the arm. 'Time for a cuppa, yeah?'

'What's the story?' asked Mac after Paul closed the kitchen door. Paul's nose strap was new, the black eye was subsiding and he was moving freely despite the rib wound.

'Her name's Diane,' said Paul. 'Been working for us on the Garrison thing. *Allegedly.*'

'What's she doing here?'

Paul gave him the look. The *don't shit me* look. 'This is the bird you were asking me about, right?'

Mac shrugged.

'You asked me if our side had someone infiltrated to Garrison, remember? I said I didn't know,' said Paul.

'Yeah, got ya,' said Mac.

'That's her, mate,' said Paul, jigging his thumb over his shoulder.

Paul and Mac looked at one another. At every meeting of even friendly intel types, there was a point where you had to decide if you were going to divulge, or bullshit.

Mac's brain spun. He decided to half-divulge, see what it would flush out. 'You know, I thought she was a double,' he said.

'For who?' asked Paul.

Mac smiled at him. The Poms knew Mac had been sleeping with her. Must have. They had him logged going into the British compound, they had Carl to debrief, they had tapes logged of Mac's night in the cottage. They had prints and DNA, if that's what they wanted.

'Well, put it this way, mate,' said Mac. 'She was enlisting me but actually working with Garrison.'

'Coincidence. I mean, you're gorgeous. Not that you're my type.'

Mac sniggered. 'She was enlisting me while I was being stalked by Garrison and Sabaya.'

Paul nodded. 'She was driving that BMW, too, right?'

'Didn't see her struggling to escape her captors,' said Mac.

'And according to Wylie, she was driving the tender craft that took Garrison and Sabaya and the Canadian hostage to Brani.'

Mac had said enough, now he wanted answers. 'So she's working for you lot? What capacity?'

'Then I'd have to kill ya.'

'Where'd you pick her up?'

'POLRI found her wandering around on the road to Bogor. She was disoriented.'

'Beaten up you mean? You guys do that?'

'Nah, mate. Sri – the big one with the white shirt – he reckons it's scopolamine. Something like that.'

'That's what they did to Judith Hannah,' said Mac.

Paul poured the tea. 'Thought you might like a chat with her?'

'Why?'

'She might open up to you.'

'Why? She was just playing me.'

'Never know, mate.'

The fact Paul had even got him down to another outfit's cabin was a big first step. The way it worked was Mac was supposed to reciprocate. Show good faith.

Mac jiggled his tea bag. 'What are we trying to find out?'

Paul shrugged. 'Usual. Is she one of ours? Is she doubled? What does she know about Garrison and Sabaya's plans that we should know? Just a reminder that that's what she was sent out to do.'

'What do we know so far?' asked Mac.

'You're right about Brani Island and that ship. Something is going on there. She said they called it 'the stuff'. She doesn't know what they've

360

taken off with. But they did take off with something from *Golden Serpent*, according to her. They called it the insurance policy.'

'She's telling the truth in one regard. The US Army has lost a VX bomb during the hostage drama.'

'Okay. That's one tick for her. She says she was a hostage after that.'

'She didn't look too scared in that BMW,' said Mac.

'Well this is it, mate. She reckons they injected her with the scopolamine and interrogated her on the road to Bogor. The goons wanted her dead. Garrison saved her. Had some theory about how he doesn't kill his lovers.'

'Man of integrity.'

'Real gentleman.'

'Sounds like you got it all, mate,' said Mac.

'It's not adding up for us. Have a crack?'

'Can I do it without an audience?' asked Mac.

'Sure. We'll be on the patio.'

Diane curled her legs under herself and turned to Mac on the sofa beside her. 'So, don't tell me – you're the good cop, right?'

Mac looked at her, stony-faced.

'This is shit. I should be in a hospital, Richard. Not putting up with this sexist *crap!*'

She yelled it so the blokes on the patio could hear. The one called Sri turned, looked in through the glass and went back to his tea.

Mac realised he still liked her. 'Sexist?'

'They train us up, just like the blokes. They assign us, just like the blokes. They even pay us the same. But when it comes down to it, as soon as they ask you to *infiltrate* a man' – she curled her fingers over, making inverted commas – 'then you're a slut.'

Mac raised his eyebrows.

'But wait, there's a catch,' said Diane. 'You're this special breed of slut who's actually virginal and innocent. So you sleep with a man once and you're so overcome by the amazingness of the experience that you become a double agent just to be with him forever.'

'Didn't know I was that good,' said Mac.

Diane laughed, shook her head. 'Not you. Bloody hell! You were a mistake.'

'A mistake?'

'I didn't know you were who you were, okay?' she said.

'Until when?'

Diane gave him the look. 'Don't get cheeky.'

Mac looked into his tea. 'You telling these blokes everything?'

'I'm doing what I can. You ever been doped up?' she asked.

Mac thought about it. 'No. Don't think so.'

'Well it blots things out, leaves some things clear. That's why I've been telling them I need some medical care, get detoxed from this stuff. But I've been up all night going over it. I need rest, not interrogation.'

'What can't you remember?'

She rolled her eyes, like *duh*!

Mac thought about it. 'Let's see if I can jog your memory. That souvenir Garrison and Sabaya took off the ship?'

'Yeah. The comms gear?' she said.

Mac shook his head. 'They've got a VX bomb. Took it from the container.'

Her hand went to her mouth. 'Why? Why would they do that?'

'I need you to tell me.'

'Shit!'

'Well, yes. It's a hundred-pound bomb, so it can be lifted by one strong man. You can drive around with it in the boot of a car, walk it onto a train, hide it in a sports stadium, leave it in a mosque . . .'

Diane was silent, a blank.

'So where are they headed?' asked Mac.

She shrugged. 'Don't know.'

'Diane, you have to think about this. *Where* are they going?'

She shook her head. 'North? Maybe? I don't . . .'

She was synthesising, trying to please him. In Mac's experience, when an interrogation got to this point you either went straight to the hard stuff, or you let them rest. He'd try to get something from her, maybe spare her the unpleasantries.

'Okay, what do they want with the VX bomb?' he said.

'I didn't even know it was a bomb until you told me,' she complained. 'Stop trying to trick me, okay? I've been up all night with that shit.'

He couldn't tell if she was lying. She was tired, there was a drugs component and Sabaya and Garrison were not the kind of people to tell their secrets to a floozie. There was no reason to tell her they had a VX bomb or where they were taking it. On the other hand, Diane may have been turned by Garrison and been planted back in the British camp to keep an eye on things. It had happened thousands of times before – it was the basic building block of counter-espionage.

He went for the easiest question of the day. 'Diane, what's on that ship?'

Her eyes sparked up. 'Gold!'

'Gold?'

She nodded. 'Thousands of tons of the stuff.'

Mac continued on for a while but didn't get any further. He was a pro, she was a pro. They both knew the game and they weren't getting anywhere.

He wanted to talk about them, work out the real stuff. The cabin was wired for sound and Mac knew the boys from Six would have a great old laugh about McQueen grovelling to a bird. But he didn't give a rat's. 'I thought you were the one. You know that, don't you?'

She shrugged, offhand, her beautiful pale eyes suddenly looking cruel.

'That it?' asked Mac. 'A shrug?'

Diane gave him an impassive look. 'Guess it's wrong girl, wrong number.'

Mac didn't get females sometimes.

CHAPTER 45

Mac opened the patio doors. The bloke called Sri looked him up and down, exhaled smoke and flicked the butt over the edge without looking where it would land. Mac hated that.

'She needs sleep, guys. Get her down to MMC,' said Mac.

The blokes glanced at one another. All Poms, but looking like a spectrum of Asia: Paul Filipino-Mex, the other bloke Chinese and Sri with his southern Indian fizzog.

Sri was obviously in charge and seemed like the guy who looked after the pliers and crocodile clip department. Mac clocked his big wrists and forearms, had a flash of what he'd do to Diane.

Mac may have just been played by a beautiful woman, but he also felt disgust at what Sri might be planning to do next. Maybe his lust and love for Diane were still there. Couldn't work that one out. What he knew was that torture and bashing were the lazy spook's way of doing his job.

Sri and Mac stared at one another and Paul stood, grabbed Mac by the arm. They walked back into the kitchen.

'Watch it, mate,' said Paul.

'What? That wanker?'

'Not in the Marines now, tough guy. I'm telling ya, friendly like, don't fuck with Sri.'

'Diane's lost it, mate. Drug-fucked. Detox her and let it come back. Do it natural,' said Mac.

Paul nodded, smiled.

'What?' said Mac.

'Oh, nothing.'

Mac felt a blush start. 'You've got a filthy mind, know that?'

'Oh, come on, mate.'

'Me come on? Would Sri be so keen for the wet work if Diane was a bloke?'

They stared at each other.

Paul looked away first. 'So what did you get?'

Mac thought about it. 'Well she had no idea they'd taken nerve agent off *Golden Serpent*.'

'Okay.'

'And that white ro-ro ship on Brani? They did steal it. And it's loaded with gold.'

'Fuck me!' said Paul. 'How much?'

'A lot, she reckons. Starting to see a motive?'

Paul shook his head. 'The greedy cunts!'

'Not what I'd write in my report, but you're getting there.'

Mac noticed something. Looked down at Paul's chest. 'What the hell's that?'

Paul looked down, pulled apart the dome fasteners on his new grey ovies. There was a massive black and blue bruise on the right pectoral. An egg yolk was developing in the middle.

'Christ, mate!' said Mac.

'Yeah, imagine it without the kevlar.'

'Spaghetti bolognaise,' said Mac.

'Fucking paella with Tabasco.'

Mac saw the oven clock. 'Mate, gotta be somewhere at noon.'

'Where you going?'

'Man about a dog,' said Mac.

'You too, huh?'

They got out of the Humvee, into the intense heat and humidity of a late morning at Halim Air Base. Mac had it at thirty-seven degrees.

The MP got out of the driver's seat, came around and gave Paul his SIG and Mac his Heckler.

A bunch of Army guys toted bergens to a Black Hawk and John Sawtell appeared out of a hangar behind them. Back in his BDUs and wearing a boonie hat and sunnies, Sawtell greeted the spooks. Mac wondered if he'd been drinking last night, trying to erase the memory of the kids in the container.

Mac kicked it off. 'Mate, need a detour to Brani Island. Can do?'

'Can do, my man. Didn't DIA tell you? You guys are calling the shots.'

They hugged the coast back up to Singers, Sawtell sitting behind the pilot. The other six sat in webbing hammock seats in the back. Mac keyed the mic and asked Sawtell why they appeared to be going a slower return route. They'd come straight over the sea on the way into Jakkers.

'Asymmetric routes,' Sawtell shouted above the din. 'Never fly an exact return route. Never know who's down there with a SAM, waiting for you to come back the way you went.'

The flight would take an hour and a half. Mac relaxed, trying to put pieces of the puzzle together. See how it worked out.

It looked like Garrison and Sabaya had planned the *Golden Serpent* to heist a shipload of gold. It seemed like a lot of trouble to pull a heist. Maybe it worked if you saw it through locals' eyes? If Mac took the Edi approach – that Sabaya and Garrison were carrying out an inciting incident to give the Chinese naval base more leverage – and added that to the Cookie theory that wherever Sabaya and Garrison went, there was loot, then what you had was a unified theory. Sort of.

Mac wasn't going to buy it just yet. If it was that simple, then where did the stolen VX bomb fit in? Just a decoy to keep the port closed down a bit longer, to get the Americans and British and Singaporeans searching for WMDs rather than a shipload of gold?

Maybe.

Other things pulled at Mac's mind. Who did the gold belong to? What was it doing on Brani? How did they heist the whole thing? An inside job? Pretty big inside job – Diane had said there was thousands of tons of the stuff. He wondered what that looked like.

* * *

Mac joined the hook-up to Don as Brani Island came into sight. Don had satellites, AWACS, Unmanned Aerial Vehicles and the US Navy sweeping for the stolen ship, but finding it was not proving easy. They couldn't get a proper ID on the thing and the Singaporeans were proving cagey about why it was unmarked, who owned it and who was operating it. Basic stuff but no response.

'Can you get the State Department to insist?' asked Mac.

'Already asked,' said Don.

'Have you told the Singaporeans that it's transporting a stolen cache of VX nerve agent?'

'Sorry, McQueen. That's classified. It's not the kind of thing we discuss.'

'Well, around in circles we go again. Just like nine-eleven, huh?'

'Oh, come on, McQueen.'

'Looks like it to me. The Singaporeans won't tell you about the ship. You won't tell about the VX. Same old same old. Just like the Agency and the Bureau.'

There was a pause. Mac leaned over, pointed out the southern point of Brani where he wanted to land.

'Look, I'm about to talk with them again,' said Don.

'I've got an idea,' said Mac. 'Tell this Singers bloke, tell him from me that that's the last time I show my arse on global television to save his crummy container port.'

Don laughed, wearily. 'Think it'll work?'

'Chinese sense of humour, mate. Might do the trick.'

Mac felt the Black Hawk descending. To the right, *Golden Serpent* was still in port, bio-hazards swarming her like an army of white ants. The portainers removed containers – probably to work out what else was on the ship. It's what the Twentieth were known for. They'd take that thing apart like they were watchmakers, and the delay would be driving the Singaporeans nuts.

Mac had been thinking more and more about how and where the Chinese fitted into this. He was leaning towards the Indonesian interpretation and decided to twig Don to a possible Chinese angle. 'Don, mate, have a good think about this: is there an alternative you can talk to in the Singapore government?' asked Mac.

'What do you mean?'

'Well, you may be dealing with someone who's stonewalling, perhaps on behalf of the Chinese.'

'What, you mean that whole conspiracy about whether CIA or MSS is running Singapore?' said Don.

'Well, yeah,' said Mac. 'The Singapore power structure is split between being generally pro-China on security grounds, and totally anti-China on Commie grounds. When it comes to this ship, I'd be trying to speak with someone who doesn't trust the PLA as far as you could spit them. Reading me?'

'Copy that. I know just the man.'

The security building was partially sunk into the ground, like a bunker – as if the thirty metres it rose into the air had been pushed up out of the surrounding quay apron.

Mac, Paul and Sawtell walked the perimeter while the troopers stayed by the Black Hawk. After one full circuit Sawtell stopped at the front, said, 'Well that's it, ladies. Two entry points: security vehicular roller door – high-tensile steel, custom fabricated by the looks of it. And a security pedestrian entry which looks like one of those Austrian vault doors.'

'Security building,' said Paul.

'Locked down tighter than a Q-store,' added Sawtell, smiling.

Mac looked at the concrete driveway, saw faint dirty tyre marks in a line between the roller door and the rear of where the roll-on/roll-off ship had berthed. He looked at Sawtell. 'Gotta get in there, John. Can do?'

Sawtell shrugged, called to Jansen, said he wanted guys on the roof too, checking any entries through the air-con or a ceiling window.

All around the island the thromping sound of helos filled the air. The DIA and Twentieth were still looking for their VX in the most obvious places: in a line between *Golden Serpent* and Brani Island. They dangled huge alloy pods below the aircraft and flew at about ten miles per hour along the top of the water. They'd be picking up every old anchor and car wheel that had ever gone to the bottom, but that was going to have to be part of the process.

Jansen and his sidekick started on the pedestrian door. Spikey made quick work of getting onto the roof and came back almost immediately, looked over the roof line, and said, 'Ducted air-con. Send up the jockey.'

Special forces spent a lot of their time training to get into places they weren't supposed to be in. For that reason, most units had their unofficial 'jockey' – a smaller man who could pull the kind of break and enters someone like John Sawtell was not built for.

A sinewy little bloke Mac recognised as Fitzy ratted up the rappel rope in three strides and hauled himself over the edge sideways like he was on a pommel horse.

Sawtell looked up. 'Make it fast, Spikey. I'm running a watch on ya.'

The other troopers abandoned the security door, tied Spikey's canvas gear bag to the rappel rope and it was pulled up to the roof. Almost immediately the sounds of renovations filled the air.

After nine minutes there was a clunk, and a jerk. And then the roller door was rising. It went up very slow, obviously heavier than your average warehouse door. As it came up, Fitzy was exposed, standing with one hand on the door control knobs, wearing nothing but undies and axle grease.

Paul and Mac pulled their guns and checked for load as Sawtell beckoned Fitzy out and stationed one of the troopers with the Black Hawk. Then they moved forward into the building.

It was eerie and warm inside. The air-con had been off for a while and the heat and lack of air made for a musty smell.

Mac looked up and saw Fitzy's rope dangling from a duct in the ceiling. Someone was hauling it back out.

Stretched out in front of them was a standard concrete-slab warehouse. In the middle was a down-ramp to a sub-level. To their left was an admin office. The office closest to the in-door was a controller's desk. Then there were three other offices behind it. And behind those offices was a large white demountable.

They moved along the demountable, passing tubs and gas cookers and underwear hanging out to air. People lived here.

Sawtell pushed the door to the demountable with his M4 carbine, leaned back and poked his head round. He leaned back again, and motioned with his head for Paul and Mac to take a look.

Paul walked in first. Hit the light. Froze. Mac looked over his shoulder. There were four cot beds down each side of the demountable.

Wood-veneer finish on the inside. You could see clothes trunks fitted beneath each bed. On the beds were five men in various states of dress. Dead. Pools of dark blood, set and dried.

Paul stepped forward, making a show of avoiding the blood. Stowing his SIG, he knelt beside one of the men, who looked about twenty-one. Chinese, probably southern coastal provinces, his eyes open, tongue slack and face still lively, except where the slug had exited below the right cheekbone. Paul pushed the man's face back, twisted it slightly, found what he was looking for. The entry hole was just behind the left ear.

Paul gently parted the dead man's hair around the entry wound. There was a dark charcoal-like marking on the scalp around the hole. Paul scratched at it and the dark stuff came straight off.

'Executions,' said Paul, standing. 'They used suppressors – don't scorch but they leave a sooty residue. Shot at close range. Maybe knew the killers?'

Mac looked from corpse to corpse. 'What the fuck happened here?'

They fanned out. Sawtell's boys heading down the right side of the top warehouse level, Mac, Paul and Sawtell taking the left side.

The containers were mostly open. Sawtell pointed the M4 into them, the Maglite on the bottom of the barrel illuminating the interiors. Lots of wood shavings and polystyrene balls. In one container they found Ming vases still in their wooden cases. In another there were racks of paintings – maybe two hundred of them.

Before they went downstairs, Mac found a locked forty-foot green container. Sawtell held up his hand and they walked the box, tapping on the steel, asking if there was anyone in there. Asked Paul what hello was in Tagalog.

Without kids to worry about, the Berets had the doors off in twenty seconds. Mac poked his head in. It looked like two large objects arranged end to end, covered in tarps. Mac asked for a Ka-bar and slashed the first tarp off, peeled it back. A red car with a black horse on a yellow badge. A Ferrari.

He slashed the second tarp back. A white sports car with a sky blue stripe over it, end to end. Mac, Paul and Sawtell looked at one another. Shrugged.

'Must be flash, I guess,' said Paul.

'I guess,' said Sawtell.

Sawtell yelled at Spikey and Spikey jogged over.

'You know about cars,' said Sawtell. 'What's this?'

Spikey's face lit up. 'Oh man! You are freaking kidding! This red one here is a Ferrari Enzo. Worth over a million bucks. Hard to tell because every time one sells, the price goes up. Only four hundred made.'

Sawtell asked about the white one.

'That is the finest grain-fed all-American sports racer ever built.'

'Oh really?' said Sawtell.

'That's a Ford GT40. Won Le Mans three years in a row. Kicked Ferrari's ass.' He nodded at it. 'Looks original. I'd say a '68 prototype.'

Sawtell asked if it had a price on it.

'Hard to say,' said Spikey, like he was a medical specialist giving an opinion. 'You can't buy 'em. They swap hands privately. God knows what this is doing in a container in Singapore.'

Mac was starting to get the picture. Diane had told him that Sabaya and Garrison had taken off with thousands of tons of gold. What they were looking at was the stuff left behind.

Mac was getting the creeps. He wanted to search the sub-level and do it quick.

Going down the ramp Sawtell asked if Mac was all right. 'Yeah, mate. Just got the willies.'

'Why?'

'Those dead blokes.'

'Yeah?'

'Clock the haircuts?'

'Aah, yeah . . .?'

'Worse than a para's, mate.'

Paul laughed.

'I'm serious,' said Mac, his breath coming faster. 'And did you see those beds?'

Paul nodded, knowing what Mac was getting at. Mac turned to Sawtell as they got to the sub-level. 'See those beds, John?'

'Sure did, my man.'

'Only one place in the world where a man has such a bad haircut, and a perfect bed,' said Mac, checking for load.

'And I don't need to tell either of you shit-kickers where that might be, now do I?'

CHAPTER 46

They found the other Chinese soldiers in the far corner of the sub-level. All three of them had been shot in the head with suppressed handguns. Paul reckoned standard 9 mm loads – NATO Nines. Mac knelt, had a look at the assault rifles that were on them or scattered around: Type 95s, the standard PLA assault rifle. They were standing in a People's Liberation Army facility.

There were no containers on this level and Mac could see this was where most of the recent vehicular movement had come from. There were tyre tracks around the sub-level and up the ramp and a diesel tug sat where it had been turned off. Big steel trolleys were in various states of use. They had collapsible sides and large-diameter rubber tyres. In other places there were steel pallets designed for forklifts.

The troopers ambled around as if in a trance. On a dozen or so of the pallets that had been left abandoned there were stacks of gold bars. Huge bricks of the stuff. The four hundred troy ounce monsters that alone were worth about US$160,000 a piece. Spikey tried to pick one up with one hand and failed.

On one of the transport trolleys there were at least eighty of the bricks. As if they'd been loaded up but then they couldn't quite fit them in the ship.

Mac was getting very, very paranoid. The amount of wealth that had walked out of this facility in one go was beginning to feel like an astronomical number that would have to be countered. One of those cosmic actions that needed a reaction. And the Chinese military was a big enough pendulum to swing back and create the counter-force.

Based simply on what he was looking at, there was US$50 million in leftovers. What had Cookie Banderjong asked him in Sulawesi? Where did the gold always go? The Chinese! *Well done, Mr Macca!*

Looking over at Paul, Mac could see fear there too.

'You thinking what I'm thinking?' asked Mac.

'I'm thinking that this is a PLA facility,' said Paul. 'I'm thinking someone stole a shitload from here. And I'm thinking that the last thing any of us need in our lives is to have the PLA believe that we are the thieves.'

'Bingo.'

Paul shook his head. 'How much is here?'

'I reckon about fifty million, US.'

'If they left fifty million as the crumbs, what the fuck did they take?' said Sawtell, joining them.

They all looked at each other. Enormity dawning.

'Well?' said Sawtell.

Mac didn't want to exaggerate the haul. 'Well if they took twenty bars for every one they left . . .'

'You saying Garrison and Sabaya are floating around out there with a billion dollars in the hold?' interrupted Paul, clearly alarmed.

Mac shrugged. 'I don't know. What I *do* know is I don't want to be standing here when the Chinese generals turn up.'

Sawtell and Paul nodded at each other.

'I need my teeth pulled,' said Mac, 'I'll see my dentist.'

The headsets crackled with urgent yells from topside. They ran up the ramp, troopers leading the way, emerging with M4s at the shoulder, covering one another.

Swivelling to the left they saw three Asian men in suits with their hands up in front of the Black Hawk. The Green Beret who'd been left to guard the helo was yelling at them to get to their knees. The pilot had an M4 at his shoulder too. The guys in suits were reluctant to drop.

Mac and Paul jogged behind, nervous, breathless. The troopers went straight up to the suits. Spikey butted the first one he saw, swinging and landing the black rifle butt square behind the first guy's left ear. The guy dropped like a sand bag.

The leader of the men said, 'Okay, okay,' and got to his knees.

Mac was panting when he got in front of them. He scanned the area to see where the rest were coming from. Sawtell was already checking that.

The suits were Chinese. Paul jabbered in Mandarin. Their leader – about forty-five, solid build, charcoal suit – jabbered back, forceful. Paul asked him something. The guy shrugged, spook-style.

Paul turned to Mac. 'They speak English. Not saying who they work for.'

Mac leaned into Paul's ear. 'MSS?'

'I'd say General Staff intelligence,' mumbled Paul.

'This is ridiculous,' said the head guy, shaking his head at his friend. 'He needs an ambulance.'

'Who are you?' said Mac.

'Who are *you*, might be a more appropriate question,' the guy replied.

'Really, champ?'

'Ah. So we have the Australian,' said the head guy with a knowing smile. 'You must be McQueen?'

Mac didn't like that. In the intel world, it was plain rude. 'Don't worry about the Australian, mate. Didn't someone tell you never to creep up on the US Army? Might get the whole wrong idea.'

'Can we get up now?' the guy said, almost haughty.

Mac nodded and the Chinese bloke stood, brushed off his pants, held his suit jacket open. Sawtell sent off Spikey and Jansen, who came back with a couple of handguns.

The Chinese bloke held his hands open.

'What's your name?' said Mac.

'Call me Wang.'

'I'll call you wanker, you keep on like this,' said Mac, moving his Heckler up a fraction. 'What are you doing here?'

Wang chewed gum, arrogant, not in the least intimidated. 'I'm the managing director of Kaohsiung Holdings – the owner of this facility,' he said, hands on hips.

Mac was getting the creeps. Big time. He turned to Paul. 'Mate, can you run that with Don, at the Chinook? Kaohsiung Holdings.'

Paul got straight on it.

Mac turned back to Wang. 'Where you registered, Wang?'

'Singapore, of course,' said Wang, looking at the open roller door. 'So you broke into my company's premises?'

Mac could see how this guy got his start in life. He'd bet it was secret police. The whole answer-in-a-question thing.

'Just needed to take a shit, actually,' he said. 'Found a great little dunny. Red car. Nice leather, comfy little throne room.'

'I suppose you realise that this is technically a diplomatic zone?' countered Wang, smirking.

'I suppose you realise this is technically a crime scene?' Mac snapped back.

Wang rolled his eyes, like he was tired of these games. 'You are not going to like the diplomatic consequences of what you are doing, Mr McQueen.'

'Really? The orange ovies and paper slippers might not suit you either when the United States government fingers you for thieving their nerve agent.'

'What?!'

'This is the last known transit point for a consignment of VX nerve agent that was stolen from the Department of Defense yesterday. I'm just running your bona fides through DIA right now.'

'Oh, come on. We just got here,' said Wang.

'I have eyewitnesses who will swear that you turned up and took responsibility for the whole show.'

Paul interrupted, got in Mac's ear. 'Kaohsiung Holdings is a front company for the PLA General Staff. DIA have them as primarily an arms dealing group.'

Mac glanced at Wang, who was starting to look frazzled.

'Look, McQueen, I'm under time constraints. What do you want?' said Wang.

'I want to know what connection your company has with the *Golden Serpent* terrorists,' said Mac, unsmiling.

'That's ridiculous.'

He was too pompous too quickly. A liar's tell. An honest man would have answered with confusion, slightly mystified. Wang had been ready for it.

'Okay, Wang. Tell me. There's a bunch of PLA lads down there. Dead. They've been shot at close range. Why would they have allowed their killers to get so close? Maybe they knew them, huh?'

Wang was confused now. 'Dead?'

'Sure. Young lads too.'

Wang rabbited something at his offsider. The bloke shrugged.

'What's happened in there?' asked Wang.

'Well, put it this way, Wang. There's a lot of open spaces where the gold bars used to be.'

Wang's chest seemed to deflate in front of their eyes, his breath catching like a man with angina. He just managed to stop gulping long enough to croak at Mac, 'The gold?'

'There's about two hundred bars left.'

Wang turned pale, looked like he might keel over. He shook his head absent-mindedly, possibly wondering how quickly he could get his immediate family to a new country. Fixing Mac with a stare which was no longer arrogant, he said, 'Um, how? How did they – ?'

'Well that's what we have to talk about, Wang. See, we need to find your ship too,' said Mac.

Wang spun on his heel and looked back at the quayside as if to say, *I knew something large should have been there.* He gabbled at his offsider, who shrugged again.

Wang turned back, totally panicked now.

Mac winked. 'Now we're in the diplomacy zone, champ.'

Mac and Paul spelled it out very clearly to Mr Wang and his associate: the VX was non-negotiable.

Sitting on the side of the Black Hawk they watched Sawtell's boys get the butted Chinese suit on his feet again, vomit all down his jacket.

Wang was still in a state of shock. They'd taken him into the building, shown him around. Mac was disappointed with his priorities. He'd winced at the dead boys upstairs, but when he got down the ramp and saw the space almost empty, Wang put his face in his hands as if he was going to cry.

So they'd talked it through. Mac wanted the name and codes and IDs for the ro-ro ship. He wanted them quick so he could get DIA tracking the thing.

'What do we get? Where's the gold?' argued Wang.

'Mate, the gold's on the ship. Take the frigging gold – we don't care. We have a couple of very bad blokes running around out there and they're armed with VX nerve agent. You want that being detonated in Shangers?'

Wang shook his head.

'So let's hear it.'

Wang stammered, made a few false-starts – classic liar stuff. 'Um, the ship is called *Hainan Star*.'

He looked pained.

'Come on, mate,' said Paul. 'Time is money.'

'I can't talk about these matters,' stammered Wang.

'You'd rather I ask than you tell?' asked Mac.

Wang nodded quickly.

'*Hainan Star* got all the satellite tracking gear on it?' asked Mac.

'No comment.'

'*Hainan Star* linked into that AIS maritime broadcast band?'

'No comment.'

'Any of that gold come from Burma, Iran, Syria, North Korea or al-Qaeda?' said Mac.

Embarrassed, Wang whispered, 'None of your business.'

Wang was right about one thing. The south end of Brani was a diplomatic zone. By the time Mac and Paul were out of the Black Hawk and hauling Wang in to meet Don and Hatfield, the Singaporeans and Chinese had a posse of chiefs doing their rain dance on the Keppel Terminal apron.

Mac couldn't believe what he was seeing: it was classic office guy stuff. There was an emergency with stolen nerve agent, but a certain type of man could always find the time to make his little office empire the priority. Mac and Paul twigged early: the Kaohsiung Holdings property was a clearing house and repository for the PLA General Staff. Singapore had the security, had the huge throughput that would hide an 'invisible' ship, and it had small armies of brokers, bankers, solicitors and accountants who could turn gold into all sorts of legitimate assets. Singapore was set up to do business, and the amount of business Kaohsiung Holdings did in the city was probably too great to allow legalities to get in the way.

There was another reason for Singapore's pre-eminence as a gold and cash repository for the Chinese. It was the global centre of an underground gold-clearance and banking system called *fie chen*. Similar to the Muslim *hawala* that operated in the Middle East, *fie chen* was outside government or regulatory control and operated on a transnational basis of trust. It was racially exclusive, too, and family-delineated. You couldn't partake in *fie chen* unless you could show a multigeneration connection to it. One of the worst arguments Mac had ever had with Jenny had been about *fie chen*. He'd said it was like the freemasons. She'd said bullshit, that secret transnational banking systems were one of the reasons slavers got away with it so easily.

Mac and Paul watched as Wang was caught by his people as he was trying to get into Hatfield's Chinook. Don came out, but he was powerless. The People's Republic of China was reclaiming the bloke, and the Singaporeans were backing that.

Mac gave Wang the wink. 'There goes the gold, mate. Looks like it's going to get split seven ways, huh?'

Wang tried to say something with his eyes, but the MSS thugs dragged him away for one of those dentist appointments where you never have to wait.

Mac followed Don into the Chinook. Hatfield was laid out snoring on one of the airline seats. Like spooks, army blokes had to take sleep where they could find it.

Don sat down at the map table. 'Want coffee?'

Mac shook. Paul nodded. Don asked Brown's sidekick for coffee. Brown turned, said hi to Mac.

Don looked like shit. Pale, drawn, unhappy. 'So, what have we got?'

Mac felt sorry for him. All his DIA guys were probably on *Golden Serpent* or with the naval SONAR birds. Mac and Paul were still a sideshow – although the briefing they'd given Don over the radio was bringing Kaohsiung Holdings and the PLA further to the centre.

'Mate, we've had an idea,' said Mac. 'The PLA General Staff have been running this ghost ship around Asia for years. Probably got others too.'

'It's highly illegal,' said Don. 'Not to mention incredibly unsafe.'

'Not so different to the unmarkeds that go out to Johnston.'

'That's different, and you know it,' said Don.

Mac was glad Jenny wasn't present.

'Anyway, the idea,' continued Mac. 'Let's say we can't get any satellite bounces off this tub. It's not on the AIS, so we can't trig a position, right?'

Don nodded. As the coffee came, Paul reached forward.

'But we still have imaging, right?'

Don nodded.

Mac looked over at Brown, who was in front of his panel of screens and keyboards. 'That right, Brownie? We can find an image of *Hainan Star*?'

Brown turned and looked at Don, who said, 'Go ahead.'

'Can I get a better idea of what you want?' asked Brown.

Mac got up, walked over to the panel. 'Okay, so once there was a terrorist emergency in Singapore, the satellite cameras would have been going overtime, right?'

Brown nodded, looked at Mac with a dawning smile.

'And it was in the morning, clear morning, right?'

Brown broke in, lightbulb going on in his head. 'So there's going to be a shot of *Hainan Star* logged somewhere.'

'Bingo, Brownie.'

Brownie tapped on keys, mumbled things into his headset. He scrolled databases, input searches, manipulated dates. He played multiple keyboards like Rick Wakeman. Finally, the big black SGI screen came up with an astonishing image: Port of Singapore with a time and date log on the bottom right. On the top right were coordinates in the nautical format. A ghosted cross-cursor floated in the middle of the screen and the imagery was amazingly clear.

'Shit. Guess they dropped the Polaroids, huh? Got some new gear?' said Mac, impressed.

Brownie laughed. 'It's pretty good stuff.'

Mac took a seat, pulled it up close. Paul and Don leaned over the back of both of them. Mac asked for a closer pull on Brani. Brownie shifted the cross, double-clicked on his mouse. The image got closer over Brani.

'Again, mate.'

Brownie brought them in close, then Mac asked him to go further south. They zeroed in over the Kaohsiung Holdings building and *Hainan Star*.

The time code said they were looking at an image from seven-thirty am, the day before.

'Can we take the time series forward, say ten minutes at a time?'

Brownie brought a smaller box up on the screen, changed a setting and got rid of the box, then took the time series of images forward by ten-minute increments by hitting an arrow key on the SGI keyboard.

The men watched the tailgate come down at eight am, watched the tug from the facility drive into the ship's hold at 8.10. Brownie stopped the series. Let real time run. You could see the tug moving into the ship, with no trailers.

Mac smiled at Paul and Don. 'It was being offloaded.'

The time series jumped forward again. Tug taking trailers out of the hold, soldiers in plain clothes lounging on the quayside with assault rifles over their shoulders.

At eight-thirty, the emergency started. Brownie ran the real time. People out of the building, looking around. Pointing into the building. People up and down the gangway of the ship. Confusion.

Brownie took it forward in jumps again. At 8.50, a tender boat arrived at the quay. Brownie took it back to real time. A group of people walked up to the Kaohsiung building. Two peeled off, placing a large bag on the quay beside the ship's gangway. Then one went up the gangway, the other joining a group of people. They went into the building and about three minutes later the tug was moving trailers again, this time out of the building and into the ship.

Paul laughed. 'Holy shit, Mac. Ever get the feeling you're in the wrong line of business?'

Mac was quietly astonished at what he was watching. 'Tell ya what, if we find these blokes we'd better bring the cavalry. Know what I mean?'

Don and Paul nodded.

Brownie took the time series forward again. At 9.20 am, a person who looked to be in charge suddenly walked onto the quay. The tug reversed into the ship and soldiers disappeared into the building.

They waited. And waited. Mac was about to ask Brownie to go back to the time series, but then there it was. A naked man – Mac – emerged on the quayside, right behind *Hainan Star*, holding a black box to his chest. A smaller bag was on his back. He paused, looked around.

Mac turned to Brown. 'Beautiful one day. Perfect the next.'

Another man appeared on the quay, carrying the same accessories as the first man. Also naked. Paul.

Mac winked at Brown. 'Not true what they say about Asian blokes.'

Mac made a sign like he was awarding a goal at the MCG. Felt a clip over the ear.

Onscreen the men moved to a position beside the building, dressed in overalls. One walked out of the picture. The other stood there, maybe making a call. The other man came back, they stowed their stuff and jogged away.

About forty seconds later, the loading operation began again.

Mac looked at Brown. 'Now what we need is to get a still shot of *Hainan Star*, load it into that tricky NSA neural net stuff, and run a real-time matching exercise. All ships have distinctive dimensions and features. If we can find the same size, same shape, we've got a target.'

He turned. 'Right, Don?'

Don looked at the SGI screen. 'I like it.'

CHAPTER 47

Mac got nasi goreng from one bain-marie and some stir-fried vegies from another. Grabbing a bottle of water, he walked over to the plastic table where Don, Paul and Sawtell were seated in the makeshift chow line.

Mac put his plate on the table, ready to dig in, noticed the others had barely touched theirs.

'Problem, boys?' he asked.

'Shit, what happened to the food?' said Sawtell, pushing it around his plate.

'Have to get Michelin in here for a quick chat, eh John?' joked Mac, but Sawtell wasn't smiling.

'I'm with him,' said Paul. 'Bloke's gotta eat.'

Don smiled, rolled his eyes. 'Singaporeans doing the catering,' he said, like that explained everything.

Mac couldn't believe it. 'What, you want to get McDonald's and Pizza Hut in here? Shit, guys, we're in Singers. When in Rome – all that shit.'

Mac looked into annoyed, peevish eyes and got up. He went over to the chow line, grabbed the fruit bowl, came back with it. Hands went out, grabbed oranges, apples and bananas.

'Just been having a chat with John,' said Don. 'It's going to have to happen in two sections. The boat in one section and the fugitives in another. Copy?'

Mac and Paul nodded.

'So there's going to be a pursuit by Special Forces, with some SEALs in there too,' said Don. 'Then there's the matter of securing the stolen substance and securing the ship. There's going to be an overlap there, obviously.' He cleared his throat.

Mac scoffed his nasi goreng, ravenous.

'I think we've all been very lucky so far with the VX,' continued Don. 'But these guys are running around with a warhead of the substance, and it's sitting on a bomb. Please, *please*, leave the scene if there's any doubt, okay?'

They looked at him, silent.

'I'm serious, guys. I know you've all got the Mark One pack, but you can only do so much with the antidote. Believe me, this stuff will finish you in five minutes. You won't even smell it.' He looked from face to face, making sure they all understood there were to be no crazy heroics. 'So leave the ship to the Twentieth – just leave it – and if the fugitives have the stolen item on their person, or in proximity, stand off, okay?'

The call came at 1.58 pm local while Paul and Mac were running through the ins and outs of the M4 carbine, the Green Berets' official assault rifle.

Brownie leaned out of the Chinook door and yelled for Mac and Paul to come into the command Chinook. Don was speaking into a phone as they entered, spittle flying. There were two images on the SGI screen. One was of the *Hainan Star* from the earlier images, the other at a different berth.

Mac got closer, amazed at the comms and imaging gear the Yanks took for granted.

'Got a match,' said Brownie, clearly proud of his work.

'They the same? *Hainan Star*?' asked Mac.

'No name coming up. But, yes sir, the computers say it's a match,' said Brownie.

'Where's this one?' Mac pointed at the second image.

'Don's double-checking, but the grid says the Sulu Islands.'

Paul and Mac looked at one another. Behind them Don was rousing resources from wherever he could find them. The satellite imagery was being shared from Guam to DC to Manila.

Mac pointed at the time coding on the bottom right of the second screen. 'Is that real time?'

'Sure is,' said Brownie, 'we're live.'

'Holy crap,' said Mac.

'Back into Mindanao. Same old same old,' said Sawtell.

The Black Hawks pulled out before the Chinooks, Sawtell right behind the pilot. 'Buckle in, ladies. It's going to be a long flight.'

The two Army Black Hawks lifted off. The Navy SEALs were still getting their divers out of the water. As the helo pulled away Mac saw Hatfield standing outside his Chinook, dressed in T-shirt and BDU pants. Tired, stressed.

Mac sat back, taking occasional sit-reps from Sawtell as it was relayed to him from Brownie. There was a special Marines recon team out of Zamboanga being saddled up to get into the Sulu Islands quick-smart. But they'd been rostered on base duties and hadn't been prepped for quick-reaction so half of them were in the gym or at the movies in town. The two QR forces – SEALs and Green Berets – were in Singapore.

The Black Hawk chugged on over the Java Sea. Their first stop would be Balikpapan on the east coast of Borneo. Then they'd hop straight into Sulu, the chain of islands joining the south of the Philippines archipelago to the top of Indonesia. Zamboanga City poked southwest into the Sulu Islands. It was darkly familiar to all of them.

The Sulu Islands had been a haven for pirates and bandits for hundreds of years. It was to this remote and inaccessible chain that Abu Sabaya had always withdrawn when there was too much heat on Mindanao. One of the biggest battles Sawtell's Alpha team had fought was on the Sulu island of Basilan. Other sorties had taken US Special Forces and their Filipino counterparts down to Jolo, another pirate stronghold island in the chain. It was tough countryside with dense jungle and locals loyal to Sabaya. Just getting helos onto some of the Sulu Islands was perilous in itself. Locals with SAMs and belt-fed

.50 cal machine guns were not afraid of a bit of target practice at Yankee birds.

Mac leaned back, thought about how things went in circles. Thought about that night in Sibuco Bay, just around the point from Zam. Thought about the hoaxed death of Sabaya, how he must have been laughing somewhere on Jolo or further down the islands at Balimbing, biding his time, counting his money, until that chance meeting with Peter Garrison. He could just imagine Garrison: 'Boy, have I got a deal for you!'

Now they were going back in. The coordinates translated to an island between Jolo and Cabucan. The area was so isolated that Filipino legend had it that the Japanese generals hid a lot of their Yamashita Gold in the highlands.

Mac caught Paul's eye. Held it. Both of them thinking, *Two helos of special forces will not be enough.*

Mac looked out over the Macassar Strait while the Black Hawks were refuelled at Balikpapan Air Base. He'd done as much mental prepping for their assignment as he could for the moment, and now his mind wandered to how things had ended with Diane, which still rankled with him. *Wrong girl, wrong number?* What was that about?

Giving it up as a distraction, Mac refocused.

It was late afternoon, clouds built high in the sky. They'd release in about three hours, but in the meantime there was a breeze that worked on the humidity.

In an hour they'd be in the Sulu Islands, and Mac was dreading it. Sawtell had tried to remain calm as they landed in Balikpapan. The early reports from the Marines recon guys was a big zero. No one on *Hainan Star*, no trace of gold. No VX bomb. The US Navy was getting people in there too. But the Marines were being asked to stand-by, not engage.

'You know, you have to put that gold somewhere, right?' said Mac to Paul. 'It's a physical thing, takes up space. It's not like electronic money between computers.'

'Well, yeah. You'd need trucks, need loading gear, need people to do it,' said Paul.

'Absolutely. Then you need a safe little hidey-hole to stash it.'

'Any ideas?' asked Paul.

Mac turned, looked around. 'I've only got one idea, but it's pretty far-fetched.'

'Try me.'

Sawtell wandered over. Tossed them a water bottle each.

'You know, this is Yamashita country.'

'The Jap guy. General. Hid all that gold in caves round South-East Asia?' said Sawtell.

'That's the one,' said Mac. 'It was stolen from their occupied territories. The OSS came through after the Japs were driven out, grabbed a lot of it.'

Paul laughed. 'Man, I grew up on that stuff. My mum? Forget it, brother! The Filipinos love stories of hidden caves filled with gold.'

'Yeah, some of it's bullshit,' said Mac. 'But there *were* some caches found.'

'So what's it got to do with us?' asked Sawtell.

'Yamashita's engineers found real mines and pretended to be exploiting them. That was cover within cover. Most of the Japanese Army had no idea what they really were.'

'Yeah?' said Sawtell.

'The locals thought they were working in a mine,' continued Mac. 'But they were building gold repositories. Had false walls, booby traps, secret tunnels. They'd stash the gold, put in the false wall and drop a part of the old mine in front of it with dynamite. They'd come up with a story that the mine had collapsed, and there was no more tin or copper in there.'

Mac opened his bottle. 'The idea was they'd go back and dig out the gold when the dust of war had settled.'

Sawtell stared at Mac, thought dawning. 'So, that mine at Sabulu? That what we're talking about?'

Mac nodded. 'I reckon we blew their Plan A. I think Sabaya and Garrison had prepped that one for the gold but we found it. I think they've gone to Plan B.'

Paul scoffed. 'What, a whole separate set of trucks, forklifts? A whole new mine prepared?'

'Sure,' said Mac. 'If the haul is a billion dollars US, why short-change yourself on an exit plan? When you pull a job, you have a Plan B?'

Paul nodded.

Mac swigged the water. 'And remember, the Japs have already done your hard work. Some of these storage mines were very well engineered.'

A shout came from the Black Hawks and the whine of the starter motors began.

'So what are we looking for?' said Sawtell.

'I reckon we fly across the interior, find the mine opening and see where the recently used roads are. Shouldn't be hard – it's been raining every arvo.'

Mac paused, looked from Paul to Sawtell. 'I reckon they're already inside.'

'You know where most of that Yamashita Gold came from, right?' said Paul, chuckling, as they headed for the Black Hawk.

'No.'

'Fucking China.'

CHAPTER 48

The Black Hawks swept down into the Sulu Islands – the Wild West of South-East Asia. Sawtell and the SEALs had sit-repped. The SEALs were about to relieve the Marines at the *Hainan Star*, then they were going to work inland to a small township and secure it, ask some questions, see where the bomb might have been left.

Sawtell's Alpha group was going straight into the highlands. Using map databases, DIA had confirmed a mine at the top of one of the island's valleys.

If things turned bad upstream, the SEALs would support. Mac didn't like it, thought the navy could take the ship, the Marines could move into the small town. He wanted those two other Black Hawks filled with SEALs to be right on his wing.

Mac fired up the mic to Sawtell. 'Mate, this is Sabaya country. I'd feel happier if the SEALs were with us.'

'Negative,' Sawtell fired back. 'It's a CBNRE mission so we're tasked for the VX. The Twentieth sets the priorities on this. Sorry.'

Mac sort of understood that you couldn't go chasing the bad guys when the actual item you were trying to retrieve could be anywhere – could be on a ship, could be in a town, could be sitting on the side of a road waiting for a farmer to pick it up, take it home in his cart.

The island was very small but it had to be shut down. And that started with the wharf and the ship.

They flew over the island with a couple of hours of daylight to play with. About three miles across, it was five miles north–south. Mac's gut churned when he saw how difficult the terrain was – mountainous, heavily jungled with jagged peaks and valleys running down to river deltas at the coast. It looked like the pictures they showed candidates at the Duntroon military academy in Canberra. The pictures they put on the wall when they talked about Vietnam and why foreign powers shouldn't fight a land war in Asia. Mac had a second lesson to add: don't fight an island war in the Pacific. The Americans had tried that during the Second World War and suffered casualty rates they were still embarrassed about.

He controlled his breathing. Next to him, Spikey shook his head as he looked out the window. Turning to Mac he said, 'Looks like Basilan. Holy shit!'

'That's enough, Spike,' came Sawtell's voice over the headset.

The other soldiers might have heard about Basilan Island – the Abu Sayyaf fortress – but they hadn't fought there. They were new to this. Sawtell had told Mac what the Basilan campaign had been like and it had sounded like a cross between hell and purgatory: snipers in trees, Claymore mines strung across water sources, poisoned dams, bear traps, hit-and-run guerrillas, and all of that while fighting blind against people who knew every inch of the place.

Now they were back to do it again, with Mac along for the ride. Acid stirred in his stomach as he sensed Abu Sabaya waiting, smiling.

It was going to be a long, long night.

The *Hainan Star* looked intact and under wraps as they swept over it and aimed up the valley leading away from the wharf. Sawtell spoke with the Marines commander at the ship. They were waiting for the SEALs to come in. Waiting for the Twentieth to start their search.

Mac watched Sawtell point his pilot up the valley, thought he saw a glint of excitement. It was funny the way different people were strong, thought Mac. Sawtell had fallen apart in the face of child slaves. But he was the guy you'd follow into a direct confrontation. His courage was infectious.

Mac craned his neck around, saw Paul up and about, stretching, looking out the window in the sliding door, looking down at the terrain. Then he walked to the cockpit bulkhead, shoved his head between the pilot and co-pilot, turned to speak with Sawtell and came back to Mac, kneeling in front of him.

'Only one road up here, mate,' shouted Paul.

Mac gave thumbs-up, and the sweat came down cold and sticky from his forehead. There wasn't going to be any screwing about. One road, one valley, one mine entrance and one Green Berets captain with a glint in his eye.

Sawtell had a set of binos at his eyes as he mouthed something to the pilot, or maybe to Don back in the Chinook. The soldiers around Mac were tuned in to their leader, legs jiggling up and down, thumb-shakes starting along with small whoops, little regimental chants.

Mac concentrated on his breathing.

The Black Hawk gained height as they got closer to the head of the valley. Remembering the thing about SAMs and heavy machine gun fire, Mac realised if there was an anticipated hot zone on this island, Sawtell and the pilot thought they were pretty close to it.

Mac burned inside, desperate to be on the ground – to stand, get running, get his bearings.

The Black Hawk suddenly banked away in a massive loop, like a dipper on a roller coaster. They flew up the other side of the loop by banking in the opposite direction, moving around the peak of the valley to another valley.

Finally they set down. Sawtell roused the troops, checking lists, giving orders, yelling instructions into his mouthpiece to the Black Hawk behind them.

The door slid open to reveal a clearing with jungle rising wherever he looked. Everything around them was flattened by the helo's downwash. Mac hauled his lightweight Army bergen on, tightened it as Paul slapped him on the shoulder and leapt out onto the grass.

The noise was deafening as Mac raced behind Paul to an RV by the ringing trees, keeping his head bowed and stowing his M4 with both hands, his US Army helmet bouncing slightly on his head.

The troopers assembled and Spikey counted heads. Sawtell was the last across, arriving as the two Black Hawks rose into the afternoon sky.

Spikey gave the head-count to Sawtell, then the troopers checked guns, grenade launchers, grenades, rat packs, water and radios. They cammed-up, pissed, took a shit. Some vomited and some prayed. Did what they had to do.

Sawtell pulled the team into a huddle, kneeling in the middle and spelling it out. He looked into faces, zapped people with courage, reminded his boys they were professionals.

He caught Mac's eye, winked, and then said to everyone, 'No heroes on my watch. Okay, ladies?'

The team walked in two groups to create a less-concentrated target. Mac walked with Sawtell in the middle of the first group. The 'jockey' they called Fitzy took point, Spikey swept. Mac felt in good hands. Sawtell's boys had been one of the first special forces outfits into Kandahar in '02, but their real specialty was jungles like Mindanao and Basilan. Tough environments where tiny mistakes were the difference between everyone living and everyone dying.

They moved quickly around the spur towards the head of the valley and the mine entry. Sawtell wanted to do the jungle transit during daylight. Mac liked that, and he liked the way Sawtell's boys maintained total silence while moving really fast. Not quite a jog but more than a march.

Around Mac the men managed to clock the tree tops at the same time as watching where their feet were treading. It was a particularly hazardous assignment for the guy on point. The Sabaya MO – as Sawtell had reminded everyone at the briefing – was to mine and booby trap the approaches to his hide-outs. Fitzy was trying to find a path through the jungle as well as check for Claymores and triplines.

They came into a clearing after twenty minutes, panting, staying low, staying silent. Some drank from water bottles.

When the other team caught up, Sawtell conferred with their team leader, a first lieutenant called Gordie.

Sawtell came over to Mac, got in his ear. 'That's the mine entrance, about half a click at our two o'clock. We're going over the top of it, take out any sentries. Copy?'

Mac nodded.

'You, Paul, Fitzy and Jansen take the ridge right up to the top and check for air ducts or escape routes. Don't engage. Only recce. Copy?'

Mac nodded.

Sawtell gave an RV for six pm, then moved away.

Mac turned to Paul. 'Hear that?'

Paul nodded. Mac beckoned Jansen and Fitzy over. 'Know the mission, guys?'

They gave thumbs-up.

'Fitzy takes point,' said Mac.

'And Jansen can sweep,' said Paul.

The Green Berets nodded. If they hadn't been asked, they would have suggested.

They lined up a point about four hundred metres above the mine entrance and then climbed straight up the spur, making good time. The jungle was less dense than the valley they'd come through, with visibility through the trees as much as one hundred metres in places. They stuck to the Green Beret MO and maintained silence. Mac's advanced hand signals had deteriorated since the Royal Marines but he still had the basics.

They got to a false summit after half an hour and stopped on the ridge. Mac slugged water and looked around. The area was like a small plateau – strangely flat for a piece of ground on a hillside in this sort of country. He did a three-sixty, his M4 already a part of his hands, looking for a chimney-like structure that would alert them to an air vent for the mine. Sixty years ago the dirt was probably excavated and spread around, hence the flat area. Trees had grown up through it and a thick carpet of leaves covered the earth. But it still felt flat, out of place. Maybe.

Paul had the same idea. 'This is the go, right here, I reckon.'

The area was about the size of a basketball court and the vent should have been noticeable. They wandered around the area but no luck.

Mac came back to Paul, who had been doing his own recce, and pointed up the hill. Paul gave thumbs-up – there was a cracking sound and then he disappeared. Vanished.

Mac threw himself to the ground, wondering where the sniper had shot from. Paul groaned quietly, out of sight. Carefully, Mac scanned the flat area and the trees, looking for the shooter.

Fitzy had a sheltered position on the edge of the clearing and Mac could see him looking everywhere at once, pointing his rifle, trying to pick the sniper amongst all the leaves. Facing the other way, with his back to Fitzy's back, Jansen was scoping the ground and trees with ninety-degree arcs.

There were no more shots and Mac's breathing was now ragged. Jansen crawled to Mac on his elbows and they crawled to Paul together, Mac thinking, *Being hit twice in two days – what are the chances?*

Stopping where Paul had gone down, there was no sign of a body. Mac was almost hyperventilating. He had no idea where Paul was, had no idea where the shooter was hiding, had no idea if these were his last seconds.

He cast about, looked at Jansen. Jansen leaned further over and almost disappeared himself, yelping slightly.

Mac heard an echo, grabbed Jansen by the bergen and pulled him back. They moved leaves aside with their M4s. A two-and-a-half-foot tunnel disappeared perpendicular into the ground. Sitting about five feet down was Paul, his right leg jammed into an iron ladder rung, his left leg dangled down into the tunnel, his body wedged against the far side of the tube.

Great if you were into yoga, thought Mac.

Paul was in agony. The painkillers he'd been taking for yesterday's gunshot wound would not be strong enough for the contortion.

Mac dropped his rifle, pulled the bergen off and eased down onto the top rung of the built-in ladder. Putting his hand down, he gripped around Paul's wrist and heaved. After three tries Paul came up like a cork out of a bottle. Jumping onto solid ground and limping around the clearing, he checked his right leg, mouthing the word fuck twenty or thirty times but saying nothing aloud. The slightest human noise in that vent would amplify many times over by the time it echoed into the main tunnel below.

They knelt around the hole and let Paul walk off the twisted ankle. He was in agony.

Mac put his fingers to his eyes, Jansen nodded. They crawled to the hole, dragging leaves away from it so nothing fell down. Leaning over, they stuck their heads in. A breeze came up thick and strong, indicating the mine had some part of it open. But they couldn't see anything; it was completely dark.

It would require patience to hear sounds, evidence of people. Jansen and Mac got comfy and listened while Paul and Fitzy stood guard.

Mac was just about to call it quits when there was a faint clanking sound. Jansen looked up at Mac, then listened again. More clanks, a male voice.

Mac and Jansen crawled into the cover of the trees where they joined Paul and Fitzy. Mac keyed the radio.

Sawtell came on, grumpy with someone breaking radio silence.

'Thought you might like to stealth this?' said Mac.

'Better than storming a steel door,' replied Sawtell.

'We've found the vent. Right up the spur, where you said it was.'

'How long?'

'Take you twenty minutes.'

'See you then. Out.'

Mac and Paul locked eyes. Time to finish this.

CHAPTER 49

Sawtell wanted a man to stay at the tunnel entrance while Fitzy, the tunnel rat, went down first. He wanted Spikey in second for any tricky locks or doors and he wanted complete radio silence.

The men slapped pockets, tucked boot laces into the tops and turned watches inward.

Mac suggested Paul sit this one out, what with the ribs, the face and the ankle. Paul just smiled and downed another handful of painkillers.

The tunnel was steel-lined so the soldiers wrapped M4s in their BDU shirts, tying them over their shoulders like a swag to stop them knocking and echoing. Mac and Paul couldn't use a shirt so they'd need to stick especially tight to the ladder.

Mac was fourth down, Paul after him. They dipped into the tunnel and moved down the rungs. Mac kept looking up to reassure himself there was light above, but after five minutes, he forced himself to look down to make his eyes adjust to the murk.

They made their way further and further into the tunnel. It got so cold the sweat on the back of Mac's ovies started turning icy. The only sound was muffled boots on rungs, shallow breaths. Eleven adult men in a narrow steel tube. Almost one living organism operating to its own rhythm. And it was almost totally silent.

At one point Mac heard a muttered 'fuck' as one of the guys knocked his G-Shock and it lit up.

They travelled like that for what seemed like an eternity, the tension high. All it would take was one tango at the bottom with an assault rifle and they'd all be dead.

Unless Fitzy drilled him first.

Mac didn't know how the US Army Special Forces did it, but in the Royal Marines and the SBS, your designated tunnel rat usually went on ahead. He'd have good night eyes and would be at the bottom of a tube like this, assessing the dangers and opportunities. In the SBS, the jockeys like Fitzy were a special breed. They were also the ones who liked the wet work – the close-in stuff with knives and garrottes.

Mac hoped Fitzy was down there and safe, hoped his night eyes were working better than Mac's.

At last Mac felt a tap on his back – the sign that he was about to touch ground. He eased onto what felt like concrete, put his hand up and touched Paul on the back as he came down. Mac's guide then pulled him back one step by the ovies. Mac pulled Paul back one step. And so it went.

They stood in blackness. Unable to see their hands in front of them. When the entire conga line was down, they pulled each other round in a laager, face in, then knelt down as their eyes adjusted to a low-light environment.

Mac got the feeling they were in a side tunnel. It looked to be curved on the ceiling, running at right angles to how the main mine should run.

'First we find the main shaft,' said Sawtell, almost whispering.

The men pulled their shirts off their backs, unravelled their M4s and put their BDU tops back on. All in silence.

Mac had quelled his nerves to some extent but he was still uncertain about where they were going and how they'd find the VX. He fought the panic urge, breathed it through and looked over at Paul, who was strangely serene.

Without noise, Fitzy arrived back and hand-signalled to Sawtell. Sawtell nodded and they slipped through the blackness behind Fitzy.

After ten minutes they stopped and formed the laager again. Sawtell tapped Spikey who joined Fitzy at a wall. Mac saw there was an iron door set in the concrete side.

Spikey removed his mini-bergen and leaned against the wall while he assembled something. Mac couldn't make it out even though Spikey was only two paces away.

The men breathed gently, excited but patient. Spikey seemed to be cranking something. Mac squinted, strained his neck. Paul whispered, 'Auger.'

The grinding lasted fifteen minutes, the troop dead silent. Then Spikey knelt at the bag and did something with what looked like a texta. He brought a box out of the bag. Fitzy put his hands near the hole Spikey had augered and Spikey flicked a switch. A small black and white monitor sprang to life, so bright that hands went up to eyes. In the glow Mac could see that the tunnel was indeed curved, was about nine feet at its highest point, and had the long lines and grooves indicating where the boards had been all those decades ago when the concrete was poured in – probably by slaves.

The light also showed the door, which was iron, about five-foot tall and much like a hatchway on a ship, with a locking wheel in the centre.

Mac saw an image come up on Spikey's box. They'd put fibre optic through the wall. Spikey looked over his shoulder at Sawtell who stood, knees creaking, and took the box. By the look of the monitor, there were lights on behind that wall. Mac felt his heart rate picking up. Spikey looked at the captain's face, not at the monitor, looking for a sign that they were going to get it on. Do what they'd been trained for, finish Sabaya, grab the VX, get out of Dodge.

Sawtell didn't flinch, his face a mix of concentration, confidence and professional reticence. He went over and over the same stretch of tunnel then looked over his shoulder at Gordie, a big, red-headed, freckly bloke with a Texan accent. Gordie was given the box and he shifted the picture back and forth too. Sawtell whispered in his ear, gestured with his hand. Mac got the impression Sawtell wanted more escape routes. Wanted better odds, rather than just throwing themselves into that lit tunnel and then trying to work out what to do.

Mac liked that.

Mac also had an idea.

He signalled Sawtell and whispered to him away from the hatchway door.

'You sure about this?' asked Sawtell.

'No,' Mac whispered.

Sawtell put his hands on his hips.

'Mate, all I'm saying is that I think that's a blast door. Get behind it if there's blasting down the main tunnel,' said Mac. 'So logically, the blast tunnel follows the main tunnel all the way down.'

'You saying that's not the only door?' asked Sawtell.

'I'm pretty sure.'

'You want to go with Fitzy, check?'

Mac gulped, said, 'Okay.'

Sawtell chuckled. 'I'm joking, McQueen. You look like a rabbit caught on the road.'

Fitzy now moved with a Maglite. The knowledge that there was a concrete wall between the main tunnel and the blast tunnel had eased the caution and they moved quickly, semi-jogging, assault rifles stowed in the almost ready position, past the blast doors that seemed to be spaced two hundred feet apart.

The group moved deeper into the hillside, the cold and damp increasing with every step. Mac sniffled, noticed others were too. The dribbles of water of fifteen minutes before were now running streams down the sides of the blast tunnel. It was getting eerie.

Fitzy suddenly stopped, his hand over the light so it cast a faint glow rather than a beam. Human voices were coming from the other side of the nearest blast door. Sounded like Tagalog.

Sawtell pulled Paul to the front and they listened. Paul whispered something in Sawtell's ear and they listened some more.

Sawtell whispered something to Fitzy, who took off again. The group followed. When they came to the next door, they stopped and listened. Nothing but the sound of water running down the tunnel walls.

Sawtell pulled up Spikey and Fitzy and they did their thing again. Now Mac could see how deft Spikey was with the auger and understood what the texta was all about. Spikey had marked the thickness on the first drilling, so on the second and subsequent goes he'd know where to drill to very quickly. Instead of taking fifteen minutes, it would take three.

What you didn't want in these situations was the auger going too far, and the crushed mortar spilling out onto someone's lap on the other side.

So Spikey was being thorough. He pulled the auger, gave thumbs-up. Fitzy brought the box with the fibre optic camera and Spikey turned it on, got a picture. Fitzy fed it through really slow, until Spikey raised his right hand. Then he manipulated the picture again. To, fro, up, down. Sawtell took his turn. Liked what he saw.

Sawtell pointed at the blast door and Spikey stepped up again. He pulled a mini grease gun from his bag, set to work on the hinges, trying to rub it in with his fingers. Then he greased the locking wheel in the centre of the door and pushed that in with his fingers too.

Wide adrenaline-pumped eyes peered out of cammed faces. M4s were ready all around Mac. Fitzy fiddled with the Ka-bar on his webbing and they all looked at Sawtell, waiting for the go sign.

Spikey stowed the B&E gear, wrapping everything in its own piece of thick felt and putting them carefully in the bag. Then he folded the bag on itself, velcroed it.

Spikey stood and Sawtell nodded.

Mac's breath got shallow and fast. His finger rubbed on the safety.

Spikey stepped to the door, held the locking wheel like he was lifting a twenty-five kilo weight onto a bench press. He put pressure on, his muscles flexing. He put more on but the locking wheel didn't budge. He put shoulder and bicep into it, trying to be smooth but with power, face grimacing.

Suddenly Mac felt relief flow through the soldiers. The locking wheel had turned.

And then Spikey turned to Sawtell.

The wheel had come off in his hands.

CHAPTER 50

They all looked at each other. And then the muffled laughter started. They couldn't help it, with Spikey standing there holding the wheel in his hands like a fucking river boat captain. Sawtell was laughing so hard from the belly that he had to lean on Spikey for balance. People spluttered into their hands, laughed through their nostrils, tears pouring down cheeks, chests heaving. Mac could barely control himself.

It sounded like a bunch of kids in a tent after one had farted – though stifled as if they didn't want to alert an adult that they were awake after lights out.

It took five minutes for everyone to get composed. Then Sawtell put his hands on his hips, wondering what to do with the freaking door. He touched it. And it swung open.

Light flooded in to reveal peeling white paint on curved concrete walls. Adrenaline started pumping and the M4s came up again. Sawtell motioned Fitzy who did the old back and forth hoo-ha with his head a couple of times before putting his head out into the main tunnel. He stepped through. Shouldering the M4, he scanned back and forth and beckoned Sawtell out, who stepped over the bulwark into the light.

When they were all in the tunnel, Spikey pulled the blast door shut and extracted some chewy from his mouth, making enough of a seal to stop it swinging back. Then he reached into his kit bag and came out with the texta, leaving a small red cross over the door.

To their right was a section of tunnel partially closed in, like a room of some sort, with the main tunnel going past it. To their left, the tunnel curved round. Truck tyre marks could be seen on the concrete floor. The gold – and hopefully the VX – would be stored further in.

Sawtell motioned for the group to split. He wanted Gordie's men to go back up to the partitioned areas to clean up, and then catch up.

They looked at their G-Shocks. Sawtell made a cutthroat gesture. The cut and run time was six o'clock, meaning six o'clock back at this door, giving them about forty-five minutes.

Mac wasn't expecting to wait that long. It was a tunnel. What had to be decided would be decided pretty quickly.

Mac and Paul jogged ahead with Sawtell's team, breathing increasingly jagged. The tunnel seemed to go deeper on a huge left-hand spiral. You couldn't see round the corner more than fifty metres. They stopped after ten minutes in front of a large blast door on their right. It ran on ceiling-mounted rails and wheels and it was pulled back as far as it could go. Fitzy and Jansen stepped up. Heads out, heads back, heads out. They walked in slow, M4s shouldered.

Sawtell and Mac came in second, Mac's heart pumping big time, sweat running freely under his bullet-proof vest. All Mac could think of was how this environment lent itself to shoot-outs, not arrests.

The room was large – about forty metres deep and twenty wide – and filled with pallets stacked with four hundred troy ounce gold bricks. One of the soldiers whistled low from behind Mac.

Sawtell ordered a search for the VX bomb. 'You see it – don't touch it. Got that?' he whispered, and stood back while a posse of Maglites moved through the bullion room, the beams bouncing off gold.

Sawtell radioed Gordie's team that they'd found a storage room. He asked them to deal silently with the voices they'd heard.

There was no VX in the room. They kept going, rounded a corner and found a crossroad, both arms of it unlit and tyre tracks down the centre.

Sawtell looked at Paul, then Mac. 'Any ideas?'

'Let's duck in here, wait for this vehicle to go past,' said Mac.

Sawtell deadpanned him, then he heard it too. It was coming from further in the tunnel and was getting closer.

'Wanna take it out?' asked Mac.

Sawtell nodded, said to Jansen, 'You're up.'

They ducked onto opposite sides of the crossroads, an alloy suppressor about fourteen inches long in Jansen's hand. Mac had never seen anything like it. Unlike Mac's suppressor, Jansen's went on in two twists.

Jansen wrapped the M4 strap around his left wrist, shouldered the rifle like it was part of him, brought his eye down to the sights and steadied himself like a rock. Perfect standing marksman pose.

The vehicle noise got louder, travelling at some speed. Mac wondered how fast this Jansen was. He was in a trance. A killer's trance.

Headlights splashed the walls, the noise deafening as the vehicle came into view.

Mac didn't hear the M4. The LandCruiser tore past, Sawtell and the boys running out of their hiding and sprinting after it. Suddenly the LandCruiser piled into the concrete wall. It ground and twisted, the engine whined, someone's foot heavy on the gas. Fitzy was first there. He leapt to the footplate, Beretta in hand, leaned in the window, killed the engine. The rest got to the LandCruiser and Sawtell wrenched the driver's door. A Filipino man in jeans and T-shirt fell out onto the concrete, a single bullet between the eyes.

The lads picked him up and put him on the LandCruiser's flatbed. Spikey got in the driver's seat, started it up and reversed out. Fitzy opened the passenger door and fireman-lifted the other body to the flatbed. Mac couldn't see a mark on him, then realised the M4's round had gone through his right eyeball.

Mac and Paul went through pockets, looked at labels, checked out footwear and dental work. Though soldiers found it distasteful, for a spook it was their trained reaction.

Paul found some money and Mac retrieved a wedding ring on a neck chain. The dead men were both heavy-set, early thirties. Southern Filipino was Paul's verdict.

Mac asked Paul how he knew.

'Teeth like a Maori or Samoan,' said Paul, smiling and tapping on his own front teeth. 'Like all the best-looking blokes.'

* * *

Spikey drove and Jansen rode shotgun, the suppressor still on his M4. They backed up to the crossroad and reversed into the right arm. Dumped the bodies in the dark.

Sawtell keyed Gordie again. Gordie's guys had nailed a couple of the thugs, and had three of them bound and gagged in the quarters they'd found them in. Mac hadn't heard a thing.

Sawtell asked Gordie to secure the tunnel all the way up to the entrance and see if there was a way to open the front gates of the thing. Then he stood on the back of the LandCruiser and said to Mac, 'Might have to split up if this place divides into different sections. You'll take Paul and Fitzy, okay?'

Mac nodded. 'What's the VX look like?'

'Know it when you see it. Olive drab, hundred-pound bomb. Three fins. Oh, and McQueen, no shoot-outs round the nerve agent, huh?'

Mac nodded. He'd prefer no shoot-outs at all.

Sawtell hit the driver's roof and Spikey gunned the diesel, turning right and accelerating further into the tunnel system. After two minutes they drove up to another large door on the right side of the tunnel and Spikey killed the engine, rolling it to a stop short of the door.

Sawtell hit the concrete, finger to his lips. The men followed. Fitzy circled round behind Sawtell to his left and took point, walking through the door with the M4 shouldered. Advancing like that had the practical advantage of being able to pick off tangos as you walked. But it was also psychological; any adversary with even basic training would know this was a guy who knew what he was doing.

Fitzy's gun spat. A three-shot burst at one angle. Then he changed angle like a robot and let blast another three-shot. He leapt back behind the doorframe as a barrage of assault rifle fire burst through the door, taking chunks of concrete out of the opposite wall. Sawtell was on his wrong side, left-hand firing. He called up Manz, a leftie.

More gunfire came through the open door, taking out the light hanging from the ceiling. There was still a light on in the gold room.

Manz was now on Mac's side of the door, Fitzy on the other. They shouldered weapons then Fitzy counted them in: three, two, one . . .

They stepped half a pace into the firing line, executed what to Mac's ears was a perfect symphony of three-shot take-outs, their heads rock-steady, their eyes lined up with their sights. Only their M4s moved up and down, with the shoulders and head following as one whole set-piece. It took huge skill to keep perfect form and composure while you did what Manz and Fitzy had just done.

Cordite hung. Silence.

Sawtell and Spikey moved in between the shooters, weapons shouldered, Mac and Paul in behind them. They fanned out. Five Filipinos lay on the concrete, blood on gold, only one still alive. An older bloke, in orange ovies. He dragged himself up, leaned against a pallet of bullion, blood pouring out of his chest, changing the ovies to purple. He didn't seem to notice.

Magazines were pulled out and pushed in. Breeches cleared, hands checked for load.

Paul walked up. Rattled off something in Tagalog.

'He's ex-army,' Paul said to Sawtell. 'Heard about this gig through his cousin. Pay's okay, food's okay. Could have done without the lead poisoning.'

'He know where our bomb is?'

Paul asked but the guy shrugged, then spoke.

'He says the command is down the end. There's something in a big green tote bag. Takes two men to carry it,' said Paul. 'He says the command complex is another quarter of a mile into the mountain.'

A raised voice came from the door. 'Sir, got company,' said Fitzy.

Mac was glad for the distraction. From the Vietnam War era, the Green Berets had a reputation for an aggressive interviewing style. Mac didn't want Spikey to dip into that kit of his for a whole new set of reasons. Mac had been watching how these guys worked. They were intense and instinctive like a pack of wolves, coalescing round their alpha dog. If Sawtell decided the injured bloke was bullshitting, all it would have taken was a nod from the captain and they'd have torn him up like a two of spades.

They paused at the door, Mac's finger slippery on the safety. Paul's face had a new glow. Through the nose tape and the black eye Mac could see he liked this stuff. Most blokes with a gunshot wound would have been lying in MMC, goosing the nurses. Mac just liked to achieve his end but real soldiers liked the means too.

Sawtell signalled quiet as they listened to another vehicle approach from inside the mountain. Sawtell keyed the mic and checked on Gordie, who was almost at the mine entry.

Sawtell pointed at the LandCruiser and the men leapt to it. Fitzy pulled the wheel round and the other guys pushed forward, then pushed it backwards into the gold room.

Sawtell pulled most of the men behind the LandCruiser then sent Jansen and Manz – a leftie and an orthodox – to the doorway.

The noise got louder. It was slower than the first vehicle.

Jansen's M4 spat. Manz's made more noise. They laid down fire.

Return fire came in, louder than God – thwacker, thwacker – tearing off chunks of concrete as big as loaves of bread. The noise was deafening and dust and mortar filled the air.

Sawtell moved out to support Jansen as someone yelled, 'Fuck! Fifty cal!'

Whoever was out there had brought along a heavy machine gun. Sawtell tried to get beside Jansen but a whole chunk of the sixty-year-old wall just fell away in a cloud of dust. They ducked, covered in grey dust, pebbles and chunks bouncing off their helmets.

The whole troop moved forward and returned fire. Mac decided to switch to his left. He could fire off both hands, even though he didn't like to do it. Kneeling as the concrete burst around him, a chunk flew in his eye. He leaned against Manz's left leg to get the best angle as a beige Ford F100 pick-up appeared about thirty metres away. It had a belt-fed machine gun mounted on a rail over the cab. A Filipino in dark red ovies held the thing with two hands, his forearms bunched up with intensity. Every tenth round glowed white through the air.

Three other men with assault rifles sheltered around the side of the truck. Mac aimed under the truck, at the closest one's legs. He hit a knee on the first three-shot. The guy dropped, but could still shoot. Mac hit him again, in the ribs, and he fell to the concrete.

The air was now filled with gunfire. The F100 looked like someone was trying to paint it alloy colour, patch by patch. The machine gun on the truck swung away from Manz for a split second and Manz put a bead in the shooter's face. The body fell back and down on the flat deck with no fanfare. It wasn't like in the movies.

Another man tried to get to the machine gun. Sawtell shouted, 'Alley oop!' and the would-be machine gun operator got a bullet in his lower leg, then his hip. That stopped him on the flat deck. Manz moved out and along the wall to get a better shot. Aimed up, put a three-shot in the guy's chest.

The last of the shooters turned and ran. Manz took three strides forward, took up the standing marksman and yelled, 'Halt!'

The guy continued and Manz dropped him. It was a small conceit in the military that soldiers never conceded that they had shot someone in the back. It was the floating ribs or the kidneys. That's where Manz hit him. Three times.

Sawtell got them in. Fitzy had a small line torn in his calf muscle. Only flesh, but very painful and bleeding. Manz was the medic on this mission and when he put his medic pack on the ground, Spikey reached in, pulled out saline solution and squirted it into his dusted-up eyes.

Manz pulled Fitzy's legging up, wiped the blood with an iodine pad. Then he squirted grain spirit straight into the bullet-hole. Fitzy gasped, lips peeling back making him look like a werewolf. He kept it tight. Grain spirit was the best thing you could do for a flesh wound in the field, but God, it was agonising. Like you were being cauterised.

Manz bandaged the wound and the unit pushed the F100 out of the way, dragged bodies off the drive, changed mags and checked weapons.

Sawtell got Gordie on the radio, said, 'Open up the tunnel and sweep back through to our position.'

'Copy that,' said Gordie.

Fitzy rose. Tested the leg, gave thumbs-up.

Sawtell pointed at Spikey. 'You drive.'

CHAPTER 51

Sawtell's group split at the Y-junction. The main tunnel kept going straight and the other road veered off to the left. Mac and Paul were led out by Fitzy, who asked Mac to sweep.

They walked down the bulb-lit tunnel at a medium pace. Water was coming down in torrents at intervals. Mac's ill-fitting helmet was becoming a distraction so he took it off, left it on the ground.

A straight section appeared where Mac could see for a hundred metres. There were five or six doorways along the right wall. They got to the first. No door. They peeked around the corner, then walked into a smaller space populated with cot beds. Mac followed Fitzy's Maglite to another door at the back. He'd bet these rooms linked with the main tunnel.

They advanced through the barracks. Mac didn't like the lights being out. It felt like a trap.

Mac caught up with Paul and Fitzy and they paused well short of the internal doorway. Fitzy held his fingers over the Maglite, giving them better sight into the dark of the next room. They edged to the door, Fitzy going first. Mac and Paul shouldered their M4s.

Fitzy did head-out, head-in twice, then left his face there and looked for what seemed about thirty seconds. Taking his fingers off the Maglite, he shone it into the room. Boxes and sacks. Another door on the far side.

It was turning into a rabbit warren. Mac didn't like it. His breathing was irregular and ragged, his instincts on full alert. Paul followed Fitzy into the room, leaving Mac alone.

Shit – I'm the sweep! thought Mac, panicked.

As he turned to check over his shoulder, he heard the first shots whistling through the darkness followed by cracks from the tunnel door. Mac fell to the ground to create the lowest profile for the shooters, then turned and tried to shoulder the M4. Fitzy and Paul yelled at him to get down and get in the door. One of them returned fire. Their shots pinged steel.

Mac looked up at the far door. The shooters had shut them in.

'Sorry fellas,' whispered Mac. He'd been way too focused on what was in front of him to make a good sweep. When Fitzy had his face in that next room, Mac should have been facing the other way, weapon shouldered, covering their arses. Literally.

He'd screwed it up.

They stood, terrified, in the small room as the bolts were slid home on the main door. The small steel door on the other side of this room was now the only way out. Felt like an ambush, Mac couldn't breathe properly.

Fitzy keyed the mic and told Sawtell where they were, what they needed. Sawtell said to hold tight, Gordie's boys were on their way.

Paul looked at Fitzy. 'You wanna wait?'

Fitzy shook his head and they moved to the door. Fitzy knelt, put his hand on the handle. Paul stood straight over the top of him, M4 shouldered, then they counted in: three, two, one . . . Fitzy pulled the lever down, pushed the door in. The corridor on the other side was lit with a bulb. It ran for thirty metres and then turned at right angles to the left. Fitzy pushed the door all the way open, to see who was behind it.

Mac turned, looked behind him. Turned back.

A head peeked out from a turn in the corridor. It looked around, aimed up. Paul shot at the head, concrete sprayed and the head pulled back. Fitzy walked into the corridor, turned right, horror on his face as he threw himself to the ground. Shots rattled over him. He returned fire.

The head down the corridor poked out again, sent lead into the room Paul and Mac were standing in. They ducked behind the doorframe. But Fitzy was still firing down his corridor, stuck in a classic crossfire.

Paul saw it happening. Laid some bursts at the shooter on the corner, then stepped into the corridor, with the open door as cover, turned to his right and tried to shoot from his left shoulder.

Mac tried to look past Paul to keep the corner shooter at bay. But Paul wouldn't get out of the way. The corner shooter came out, Mac yelled and the shooter aimed up and caught Paul in the side. Paul went down.

More rounds came in, tearing up the concrete. Mac pulled back behind the door, then looked out. Fitzy was on his feet and going down the corridor to the right.

Mac ran into the corridor, M4 shouldered, keeping his eye on where the corner shooter had been. He advanced, popping two three-shot bursts into the corner, waited for the shooter's head to come out, waited to blow the thing off.

It didn't come.

Mac got to the corner, heaving, panting. Head-out, head-in. Did it three times. Trying to eat air. Stuck his head round. Slow.

No one.

Heard a voice behind him, spun. Fitzy, with Paul.

Mac's heart roared in his ears, like a 747 taking off, as he jogged back to Paul. It wasn't good. He'd been shot in the side of the chest again, between the kevlar plates. Blood was coming out of his mouth and he was shallow breathing. Usually when a man was shot, hyperventilation set in. Not when you were whacked in the chest. No suction.

Mac knelt beside Fitzy. There was nothing they could do. Mac held Paul's head up. Fitzy pushed his hips back towards the wall. He was limp in the body.

Paul smiled at Mac. He was a good-looking bloke, despite having a busted nose and being covered in concrete dust.

'I'm so sorry, mate – sweep was never my thing,' said Mac.

Paul slurred, blood dribbled out of the side of his mouth. 'Fair's fair, mate. You saved me once.'

Mac thought of how their three-day intense friendship had grown since their first conversation in a hangar at Hasanuddin. Thought that nothing except shit like this could make two people so thick so fast.

Paul reached for the thumb handshake, pulled Mac down, whispered through blood. 'There was someone in Sulawesi.'

'Garvey?' asked Mac.

Paul's eyes rolled back and he slurred, his London accent getting thicker as he tired. 'Then I'd 'ave t' kill ya.'

Paul gripped Mac's hand really tight, like he was trying to feel life.

'Get these cunts, willya?' he whispered.

Then he died.

Mac slumped. Sniffed a bit. It had been a long, long seven days.

Fitzy gave Mac a thumb-shake. Wrapped his left hand over that. 'He's gone, McQueen. But we can keep going.'

Mac nodded.

'And for what it's worth, I don't sweep too good neither.'

They nodded. Mac kept it tight.

'Mate, what was down that one?' asked Mac.

'Another door. Try your way?'

They got to the corner, crept around it. The hallway had no door they could see, it just doglegged in the distance and had several passages off it.

They kept walking, Fitzy's M4 shouldered the whole time.

From the distance, sounds of gunfire thudded and echoed around the complex. It was hard to tell where it was coming from or how many people were involved, but it lasted for a solid forty seconds.

Fitzy and Mac sped up. A sudden commotion sounded ahead as people spilled into the hallway, no doubt urged on by the Green Berets.

Fitzy peeled off two three-shot bursts, dropped one of the men.

Then nothing. Out of load.

Mac picked up the firing, hitting one in the leg. The bloke staggered and a third man turned and fired. It went high, took out a light and rained concrete dust on Fitzy and Mac.

Fitzy had reloaded. The shooters took off and Mac started after them, squinting through dust, keeping his gun on the guy he'd shot in the leg. Saw him pulling out a handgun. Mac put a three-shot burst into him and the guy dropped.

Mac kept walking. Looking behind him he saw Fitzy was catching up. He waved the American through and Fitzy took point. They paused at doorways, looked in. Mac checked behind them. Looking for shooters. They'd given up on the VX search for the time being. The plan now was to clear the tunnel of tangos and then let the Twentieth come through. The first job was to stop these shooters getting out of the place with the bomb.

They followed the shooters up to a larger room and paused. It felt different.

There was a desk and comms gear on the side, some black gear bags, a green canvas bag, a sofa and some chairs. Mac had a sensation up his spine: they were in the command lair.

Mac sensed movement, saw a man on the other side of the room. Peter Garrison smiled straight at Mac and raised his SIG. Mac raised his M4. Garrison shot first, missed. Mac got off a shot but Garrison had already twisted back into the recess he'd come out of.

Mac launched himself into the office, heard Fitzy yell, No! Then Mac's legs were sailing out into midair, his body level with the ground, and as he free-fell his head smashed on the steel ramp that had dropped down beneath him.

Last thought: *Not great at point either.*

He tried to stop it coming but for the third time in as many minutes, Mac vomited into the sack. It hit the cloth right in front of his face and dribbled down to his chest and round to his ear. Vomiting was a normal part of recovery after he'd been knocked cold.

He felt like crap and had no idea how long he'd been out for. He struggled to piece it together. As best as he could get it, he'd run over an old-fashioned spring-loaded bear trap. The legend of the Yamashita tunnels was big on bear traps and sliding walls: all that shit. But Mac might have actually stepped on one.

Now he was on what felt like a quad bike trailer travelling at about thirty miles an hour. He was lying on his side, his wrists lashed in a St Andrews Cross on his chest. When they went over a bump his head banged on steel and his eyeballs ached. The back of his brain felt bruised.

Mac tried to get his mind into gear. Listened for the voices: Tagalog.

Tested his brain for drugs: could count, could rattle off 'Waltzing Matilda'. Tried to sense direction: west? Same direction as the main tunnel. He didn't know.

He'd know soon enough.

Mac woke up to hands pushing him upright, dry vomit clinging to the right side of his face. Someone whipped the sack off his head. He blinked, tried to look around, felt sea air on his face. A Filipino was in front of him, holding a Ka-bar. Lowering it, he cut Mac free.

Blood surged into Mac's hands. It hurt and he rubbed his wrists, looked about. He was sitting on a steel trailer hitched to a Honda quad bike. They were on a spur and down beneath them, to what Mac thought was the north, waves washed into a small bay. It was night, there was an almost-full moon and the thromp of helos sounded from a few miles away.

His hand went up involuntarily to the back of his head. *Sore as.*

'Hit yourself real good, bro.' The voice was Filipino with an American accent.

Standing right there, not three feet away, was Abu Sabaya.

They eyeballed one another and then Sabaya smiled, put his hand out. 'Aldam.'

Mac took it. 'Mac.'

Sabaya laughed, yelling, 'I told you they called him Mac.'

A white man in a polo shirt and chinos spoke from the seat of a quad bike. Peter Garrison. 'McQueen's what the Agency calls him. Thought we'd stick with the program.'

Sabaya was in his trademark black T-shirt, Levis and runners. His black sunnies were pushed up on top of his head. In the moonlight Mac saw what Paul meant by the southern Filipinos looking more Polynesian than Asian.

Mac looked from Garrison to Sabaya. 'This when I die?'

Garrison lit a smoke, pointed at Sabaya, like it was his call.

'Small chat before we get to all that drama, hey McQueen?' He sniggered, sucked on the smoke. 'All Aussies this persistent?'

'All Yanks this greedy?' asked Mac.

Garrison laughed, shook his head. 'Shit, McQueen. You go down there? To Kaohsiung's warehouse?'

413

Mac nodded.

'Don't think they had enough of the stuff?'

Mac shrugged. 'Weren't they paying you anyway, to stage the *Golden Serpent* thing?'

Garrison laughed, slapped his leg. Looked at Sabaya. 'Didn't I tell you AT? Huh? I told you this guy was pure Tintin, didn't I? Hundred per cent boy scout.'

'You honestly thought the General Staff was going to wear that? Write it off to spillage?' asked Mac.

Garrison grimaced, changed the subject. 'Hey, McQueen, you get my present? That fucking dog? Little Snowy? Decided not to shoot it. Just for you.'

Mac nodded. 'Found the dog.'

Garrison giggled, sobered up. 'No, I was happy with the dough. Fifty million US was fair. Chinese have always treated me okay. Good payers.'

'So?'

Garrison pointed at Sabaya. 'So our God-botherer here took exception to certain investments the PLA General Staff is committed to. Went all religious on me.'

Sabaya looked into the American, the way Sonny Makatoa could look into a man. 'Sometimes the only way to control demand is to control the supply. That's economics.'

Garrison laughed. 'Yeah, but economists don't heist the Chinese generals' gold stash just to stop a casino being built. Shit, messing with a Chinaman's gold – that's an unhealthy way to live, bro.'

'Macau isn't a casino. It's an entire zone. It's going to be five times the size of Las Vegas.'

'So it's big?'

'It's an affront.'

Garrison shrugged at Mac as if to say *Silly Muslims*.

Mac thought about what Sabaya had said. The Chinese government had given the go-ahead to develop Macau as a huge 'lifestyle resort' zone. Roughly translated it meant a place where you had casinos, horse tracks, prize fights and poker tournaments, all in the same area. It would be fed by low-cost airlines from around Asia. The deal would be: if you gamble enough money, we'll comp you a flight in from

China or the Philippines or Burma. The General Staff were probably as cornerstone investors, like the mafia was in Las Vegas.

Conservative Muslims thought gambling was against God. Thought it tore apart families and kept poor people poor. Same as what some Christians thought.

Mac looked at Garrison. 'You still Agency?'

Garrison sucked smoke. Exhaled. 'Then I'd have to fuck ya.' He laughed, slapped his leg again. 'It's not what it seems, kemosabe.'

'No?' said Mac.

Garrison shrugged, flicked the smoke without looking where it went.

'Look, Singapore is going to have a Chinese naval base on it regardless of what the Indians like you and I do about it. You may not understand this, Mr Boy Scout, but there are Americans – Agency bigwigs, swinging dicks from State – who think the world would be a better place if the Chinese Navy could deploy in the Malacca Strait.'

Mac couldn't believe what he was hearing. 'Oh, really? The Americans?'

Garrison pointed at Mac with his lighter. 'You gotta stop with the Cold War theory, bro, and think about the future. No nations, just economies.'

Mac shook his head. 'Sounds like something they'd teach you in a third-rate business school.'

'You're laughing, McQueen. But you're just a worker bee like me. I bet there're people in your government who've already decided it's a no-contest if the Chinese want warships in Singapore. Shit, I know a lot of Singaporeans who would sleep easier if the Chinese Navy was camped on the perimeter.'

Mac shrugged. He knew there were those theorists. Knew about the theory that Singapore was too small and vulnerable to control the economic and geopolitical importance it had inherited. That neither India nor China wanted Singapore and the Malacca Strait being the weak link in what would be the world's biggest trade partnership within two decades.

Mac's eyeballs pulsed and he winced. The Big Picture theorising of spooks was a well-worn cliché for Mac. Some spies were never happy just doing their job.

'Look, the geopolitics is great, fellas. But about the VX . . .' said Mac.

Garrison got serious. 'Insurance, bro.'

'Against what?'

'Green Berets. DIA. SEALs. You been asleep?'

Mac looked around. Realised there were three more quad bikes parked on the trail. One had an object the size of a couple of basketballs strapped to its trailer, under a blanket.

Mac looked at Sabaya. 'Please. Tell me that's not the nerve agent.'

Sabaya deadpanned Mac.

'Sure is, bro,' said Garrison.

Mac held Sabaya's stare but spoke to the American. 'You know, Garrison, I may be a boy scout, but that's a frigging warhead.'

'Yeah, so?'

'So, if it goes off it kills everything. Keeps on killing till it dissipates in the sea. And in the sea it becomes harmless in – what – six weeks?'

'Well then, DIA better back off, huh?' said Garrison.

'Think that's going to protect the locals? Any kids live round here?'

Sabaya sneered at Mac.

Mac saw an opportunity. 'Of course, a child's welfare isn't really your concern, eh Peter?'

Garrison looked confused.

'I mean, with all those Cambodian kids locked in that container in your warehouse?'

Mac had a sudden flash of Jenny's strength with those kids.

Garrison gulped, flashed a sideways glance at Sabaya, who stared at him. 'Don't know what you're talking about, kemosabe.'

'Sure you do, Peter. There were about seventy of them, mostly seven-, eight-, nine-year-olds. They were in your warehouse, mate.'

Sabaya talked soft, said to Garrison, 'I told you not to use any place belonging to the Amron brothers.'

'Yeah, but I just needed to get a place with no leasing problems. I didn't know they were still doing that shit. Honest to God, AT.'

Sabaya turned back to Mac, a new look in his eye. 'I've heard enough. Time to move.'

Sabaya put his hand out and one of his sidekicks slapped a Browning in it. He held it up to Mac.

Mac took a breath, closed his eyes. Thought about a cold beer but saw Jenny instead.

There was a gunshot.

Mac was still alive. He opened his eyes, gulping for breath, and saw Garrison slumped on the quad bike. Saw him slip off and hit the ground.

Sabaya gave back the Browning, looked at Mac.

'Here's the deal, McQueen. You get the US Army to get that thing the hell out of my country. And I'll let you do the same thing.'

Mac said nothing, thinking.

A sidekick went to the quad bike, unhitched the trailer with the VX on it.

Sabaya shook his head. 'Never wanted that thing. Just wanted the gold.'

'Pretty large stash to put in one place, isn't it?' asked Mac.

'That's why we've been dropping it all the way up here,' said Sabaya.

It figured. Mac didn't think that what he was seeing in the tunnels added up to what was stolen from Kaohsiung Holdings.

The thugs unhitched the trailer Mac was sitting on and started their quad bikes. The first two accelerated away, along what in Queensland was called a fire trail.

Sabaya found first gear, but didn't let the clutch out. 'I heard you were the one who got the bodies out of the water. Arranged them on the deck?' he said.

Mac didn't know what he was talking about.

'Tino's mum thanked you at the funeral. Gave her a body to bury.'

Sabaya accelerated away, leaving Mac standing there in the jungle.

He walked over to Garrison. Ratted his SIG. Checked for load, checked the spout, made to walk away but thought again. He ratted the American's pockets, found some money, found a Bic lighter. Turned him over, patted the rear chino pockets, felt something in the right one, undid the tortoiseshell button and shoved his hand in. Garrison was still warm.

He came out with a piece of white paper. Golden Dragon Line letterhead. Three lines of numbers. Coordinates in nautical format.

Trousered it.

Then he sat down. Vomited.

CHAPTER 52

Mac staggered and fell, staggered and fell. Something wasn't right in his head. With his arms out he blundered through scrub and jungle, following the trail in the moonlight only to be plunged into blackness through stands of forest.

At one point he was so disoriented that he went over like a caber, smashed his face on a tree. He did the whole thing without the slightest sensation of falling.

Occasionally, the thromp of a helo would get louder and he'd get a flash of a big searchlight going round the top of a hill. Then it was gone.

At nine pm he gave himself a break, sitting on a log in a clearing and looking what he assumed was north over the Sulu Sea. Scores of tiny islands were dotted as far as he could see. Two ships steamed between them. US Navy or Chinese Navy? Maybe Philippine Navy.

Bats squabbled in the trees behind him, a macaque talking to itself.

He moved on, his head pulsing like his heart had decided to relocate. By the time the trail led him straight into the secret back entrance of the tunnel system, the agony in his head was subsiding, but the nausea was still there. It had taken an hour to cover the four miles.

There was a rusted hatchway door, larger than the ones they'd seen in the auxiliary tunnel. Mac grabbed the locking wheel, but he needn't have bothered. The thing swung open. There was a wooden ramp on the inside, obviously there for the bikes.

He could hear activity echoing and vehicles revving, the SIG held in front of him he walked down a long downward-sloping tunnel, bulbs on the ceiling spaced every thirty metres. Sabaya may have been out of the tunnels, but his MO included booby traps and surprise visits. Mac had no idea who was still running around down there.

The tunnel opened into a room. Mac smelled gasoline and two-stroke mixture. He followed a smaller corridor back from the room. It was low and tight, his shoulders rubbing both sides as he walked. Abruptly the tunnel came to a right-angle turn. Mac paused. Head-out, head-in, did it twice then looked around and saw a dead end three metres away.

He walked towards the sound of American voices. There was a steel frame and a steel panel inside it, a six-inch lever too. He pulled it up and the steel panel swung away from him.

He was in the command centre of the tunnel, in front of him a figure in a Level-A bio-hazard suit. They looked at each other and Mac lowered the SIG. Three other people in bio-hazards were doing something at the far wall.

'McQueen. Anyone got some water?' said Mac.

Mac briefed Don in person and Hatfield over the radio system. The US Army didn't like its generals wandering around in tango cave systems. Wasn't what they paid them for.

Mac pinpointed the VX bomb as best he could, told them they'd find Garrison there too. And no, he didn't do it.

Then he gave enough of a debrief so Don could do his paperwork. He'd grown to like the bloke, had come to realise the kind of stress these CBNRE blokes lived under. Stealing a CBNRE device might take some doing. But once you had it, the scale of destruction was huge compared with the resources required to use it.

Don wanted to run a tape, but Mac declined the offer so Don took notes. Mac sensed he was only double-checking Sawtell's account anyway.

After they'd finished Don led him through to the main tunnel. Sawtell's boys were slumped on and around the white LandCruiser. Mac heard someone say, *Shit, it's Chalks!*

The cab door opened and Sawtell stepped out, eyes red from the concrete dust. 'McQueen! Good to see you, my man,' he croaked.

They did a thumb-shake.

Sawtell shook his head. 'Man, we've been turning this place over like a crack-head looking for rock.'

'Sabaya and Garrison had me,' said Mac.

Sawtell's eyes widened. 'You're kidding?'

'I got knocked out on that bear trap in the office.'

Sawtell sniggered. 'Spikey slipped on that too.'

'Well shit – I didn't know,' came a voice from behind.

Mac turned, saw Spikey. They shook. Spikey pulled him in, touched chests. 'I mean, who puts a spring-loaded ramp in their floor?'

'Just what I was thinking,' said Mac.

Sawtell wanted the story. 'So, they let you go?'

Mac nodded. 'Sabaya shot Garrison.'

'No shit!' said Sawtell.

'Yep. Did it in front of me. Out the back here, out near the sea, on the other side. Some kind of dispute about those kids in the container.'

They stared at him in disbelief.

'Sabaya didn't know about it. He does now.'

'But he didn't shoot you?' asked Sawtell.

Mac looked away into the middle distance, thinking about it. Realised he was talking with veterans of that night in Sibuco Bay. 'You remember when we did the Sabaya thing in '02?'

They nodded.

'Remember how I wanted that tango's body pulled out of the water? Wanted him on deck?'

Sawtell snorted. 'Sure do.'

'Well word got back to that bloke's mum. She mentioned me at the funeral.'

They stared at him.

'Funny old world, huh?' said Mac.

* * *

421

Mac pulled himself onto the flat deck of the LandCruiser as Spikey fired it up. He shook with Fitzy and then looked down. Paul's body was lying there on his back, grey ovies, Hi-Tec Magnums. One of Sawtell's boys had draped their BDU jacket over his face, and the chest wound. The blue G-Shock on Paul's wrist was ticking over.

'Let's get you out of here, eh champ?' said Mac as the LandCruiser pulled out.

They motored in second, past the guys from the Twentieth in their bio-hazards, the DIA guys with their breather masks around their necks. Everything was being photographed and logged. Mac looked into eyes as they went past, his legs dangled over the side, Fitzy lounging beside him.

When they got to the first gold room they'd searched, the LandCruiser stopped. Sawtell got out and walked up to one of the DIA guys. 'Testing back at Andersen – Hatfield needs a sample,' he said.

Before the DIA bloke could do anything with his clipboard, Sawtell picked up a gold brick and walked back to the LandCruiser.

He came around Mac's side. Put the brick on the flat deck, between Paul's left arm and his body.

Looked at Mac, said, 'Pension. For his family.'

CHAPTER 53

The SEALs relieved the Green Berets. They couldn't wait to get a look inside that tunnel complex. As Mac and the Green Berets made for their Black Hawk they passed Hatfield's command Chinook. A middle-aged Anglo in a merchant marine white shirt was sipping from a soup cup at the base of the fold-down stairs. One of Don's sidekicks took notes while the man recounted his ordeal in a Canadian accent.

On the other side of the Chinook, and further down the road, Mac saw two Chinese military helicopters – an Mi-6 and an Mi-26. In front of the aircraft Wang remonstrated with a Filipino soldier; a bunch of Chinese Special Forces milled around, disarmed, while eight Filipino soldiers watched them like hawks. Wang yelled out to Mac as they got to their Black Hawk. Mac ignored him.

The clear-out flight from the island to Zam took thirteen minutes and Mac was given a room at Camp Enduring Freedom. Spikey lent him some clothes. It may have been the tail end of a terrorist incident, but it was Saturday night in Zam, and the Yanks wanted to party.

Mac got out of the Jeepnie behind Manz while Sawtell paid the driver. Spikey got out the other side. Behind them, another orange Jeepnie pulled up and more special forces guys piled out, everyone in jeans and T-shirts. They stood in front of Il Puesto, a bar that was rocking with live music. It was 11.10 pm.

Sawtell stood on the pavement and made sure everyone was there. In a white polo shirt, Levis and sneakers, he looked like a guy Rocky might fight.

The beers went down fast and cold. The band played ZZ Top and Rolling Stones, the female singer raunching it out like Linda Ronstadt. Sawtell ordered a bunch of pizzas. Other soldiers came over and there were thumb-shakes, chest-touches and loads of ribbing. The kind of thing Paul and Limo would have loved.

Mac noted the designated shooters. One was a large, heavily muscled Latino who looked a bit like Limo. The other was smaller but looked like a boxer. A Leb guy. The Leb stayed by the entrance, drank water. The Latino sat at Sawtell's table. They both wore black holster bags of the type Carl had worn during Mac's last supper with Diane.

Mac mentioned it to Spikey. 'Yeah man.' He pointed at the Leb. 'That's Arkie. A Muslim dude, so he's cool to carry when we go out.'

Mac nodded his head at the big Latino sitting opposite and Spikey laughed. 'That's Cheekie. He don't drink 'cos his momma won't let him!'

The table laughed. Cheekie raised his chin, put his hand out. 'Name's Chico.'

They shook, Mac feeling a bit silly. The biggest argument he'd ever had with Jenny had revolved around the problem of guns and grog. There'd been a strange and revealing surveillance gig concerning a Malaysian politician and a senior Indonesian bureaucrat. It turned out the blokes weren't swapping secrets, they were lovers. Mac and Garvs had started drinking early after they wrapped, had got on it something bad down at the Jakarta Golf Club.

By the time the evening had swung around, Mac reckoned he was ready to drop in on Jenny. Trouble was, he'd forgotten he was still carrying. He'd turned up at Jenny's apartment with some Carlsbergs, thought it was all going well. Then she'd felt the Heckler, hit the roof, yelling. She gave him a good clip over the ear then took the piece, shoved it in a drawer and told him to get the fuck out.

When it came to alcohol and firearms, Jenny was a lot like his father.

Mac realised Sawtell was that way too. No one carried unless they were off the booze. Mac had this feeling that maybe it was time to grow up.

Mac danced with an American girl from the navy, talked with a local bird, laughed with Spikey, who was hilarious. He asked after Hard-on and got ten different responses, all of which had something to do with either masturbation, nurses or penises. The attitude was that Hard-on was bludging while Alpha team ran around after tangos and nerve agent.

No one talked shop till it was one-thirty and the band was between sets. Sawtell turned to Mac, brought out an envelope, handed it over.

'Can you get this to Paul's momma?' he said.

All eyes looked at Mac. He had a peek inside. There must have been three thousand US in that envelope. Mac knew how much these people got paid, knew they weren't cashed up and he felt totally humbled. A bit overwhelmed. He'd spent years under the kind of stress that would buckle most people. He had methods for burying that. But an act of simple kindness was enough to bring him undone.

Mac looked away, looked at the ceiling, tried to keep the concrete where it was but he couldn't. He felt the bottom lip go, tasted tears. It was the first time he'd cried since he was nine years old and Frank had whacked him for mucking round with the Holden's handbrake in the driveway. After Frank had told him not to.

He nodded. He cried. Sawtell roughed his hair. Spikey put an arm round him, play-punched him in the jaw.

Sawtell raised his beer glass, said, 'To Paul.'

Everyone drank to Paul.

Mac pulled it together, wiped his eyes with the back of his hand, raised his glass, said, 'To Limo.'

They all drank to Limo as Spikey stood, put his hand on his hip and did a cruel mimic of Limo's deep, ghetto accent. 'Ain't made for running, motherfucker!'

The soldiers whooped and laughed. Someone said, 'Was made for eating, tho'. Got that right!'

Spikey stood again. Another mimic. 'I can't have thirds? What kind of army is this anyways?'

They squealed with laughter and Spikey got high-fives. The navy girl pouted at Spikey, said, 'Poor Limo!'

Spikey laughed at her, said, 'That boy could eat like a rabbit fucks!'

The evening ground on. They got boozed.

The owner kicked them out about a quarter to three, when Sawtell wanted to sing. The designated shooters left first. Stood on the pavement. Eyes up and down the streets of Zam. Hands hovering over holster bags as they got into the Jeepnies.

The navy girl kissed Mac on the cheek when it was her stop, said, 'You're sweet.'

Mac realised he didn't want to sleep with her.

That made him smile.

Mac passed through the security section of the British Embassy in Jakarta. They'd scanned the Cordura carry-all he'd grabbed at Camp Enduring Freedom but they couldn't find any crime with the contents. They showed him through to a large, open-plan waiting area in the public partition where Mac sat on a chocolate brown leather sofa.

He leaned back, easing his hangover into the day. It was early afternoon, maybe the last afternoon he'd ever spend in Jakkers, and then he was on the evening Qantas flight into Sydney. There'd be one stop after this, at the Aussie Embassy. Then a whole new life.

Three minutes later a middle-aged bloke came out. Pale blue cotton Oxford shirt, dark, expensive slacks and black lace-up shoes. He introduced himself as Martin Cottleswaine.

To Mac he'd always be Beefy.

'Told you I look better in my goldilocks, didn't I?' said Mac as they shook.

'I never had a doubt,' said the Brit, also smiling.

Mac thanked him for meeting him, gave him a vague rendition of what Paul and he had been up to with the Americans. Beefy raised his eyebrows and followed British protocol for discussing any countryman in a military or intelligence capacity. 'Didn't know one of ours was in that.'

Mac had tracked down Beefy from his recollection of the guy's name-tag. Mac had given 'cottage' and then 'cotton' to the switch woman, and the trail had led them to Beefy.

Mac leaned over, unzipped the carry-all, pulled the envelope out and showed Beefy the contents. Pushing the sides of the carry-all down, he also showed Beefy the gold brick. Away from other bricks of the same size, it now looked enormous.

Beefy's mouth dropped slightly. Years as a Customs guy, but some things still surprised. He looked at Mac. 'How can I help?'

'The Americans pitch in and send a fallen comrade home with what they call a pension.'

Beefy smiled. 'Tax-free, you mean?'

Mac shrugged. 'The tradition is that the body bag or the casket doesn't get opened until Mum or the wife opens it. Last perk left in American life.'

Mac watched Beefy take a deep breath. He was a Customs guy, an embassy guy, a guy totally with the program.

'Mate, this isn't for me,' said Mac. 'He's one of yours and he went down fighting.'

Mac looked away, the whole thing affecting him deeper than it should have. 'Good bloke too.'

'It's technically income,' said Beefy, looking at Mac, 'but only if he declares it. Right?'

They looked at each other.

'Ex-Army?' asked Mac.

'Fuck off.'

'The way you walked . . .'

'Royal Marines, squire,' said Beefy.

Mac smiled. 'Same here.'

'Where'd you train?' said Beefy, suspicious.

'Lympstone, mainly. Did Brunei with the SBS.'

'Ever see a feller mark a map?' said Beefy, squinting.

Mac laughed. 'Sure did.'

'What'd the instructors call him?'

Mac thought for a second, suddenly remembered. 'Cunt-hooks.'

'That's the one,' said Beefy, laughing.

They talked and laughed some more, then Beefy let out a hiss of air. Shook his head, leaned on his knees, looked away. Mac thought he heard him mumble *Fuck's sake* to himself.

Beefy turned back. 'Okay. I'll sort it.'

* * *

Mac still had valid credentials at the Aussie Embassy security section. The place had been battened down after the bombing in '04. Mac didn't have his security pass but Ollie – an APS bloke in the foyer – knew him and they had a temporary pass issued very quickly.

Mac didn't have much to clean out. He used shared office space in one of those hotel systems. He'd never been much of an office guy. All his reports were backed up on a hard drive somewhere and he didn't keep a diary, didn't have an appointment book.

His cover documents were mostly sitting in a make-believe office downtown, at Southern Scholastic. The corporate bunting of his forestry consulting cover was in an office park in north Jakarta. He assumed it had already been cleaned out, handed over to a new pretend-businessperson. Someone else would get to do their bit, take their shot.

He walked the stairs. Got to the fifth floor, turned left and made for the intelligence section.

The door was open. He paused, looked in, said, 'Can a bloke get a cup of tea round here?'

Anton Garvey looked up from his laptop, took off his half-glasses. He'd aged ten years since Mac saw him last, seemed to have lost his tan. A new kind of stress. The kind that takes your fire.

They made small talk in the kitchenette. Mac used his mug, the one with *Proserpine Brahmans JRLFC* and a picture of a bull. Every time Mac went back to Airlie to see his folks, Frank hit him with more Brahmans fundraising paraphernalia for the team he coached.

They got back to Garvs' office, which looked over the back of the embassy. Garvs shut the door, eased his charcoal suit into leather.

'So, Mr Macca. How'd you know?'

Mac shrugged.

'That Pommie bloke, Paul?'

Mac looked into his tea. 'Paul didn't make it.'

Garvs nodded. 'Heard a British national had been shot. Didn't know it was him.'

'Yep. Bought one in the chest from Sabaya's people. Those kevlar vests sure don't make you bullet-proof.'

Garvs snorted. Mac eyeballed him, realising Garvs' sole focus was his own ambitions.

'He was a good operator, mate. Brave as,' said Mac.

Garvs slurped tea, shrugged. 'So if it wasn't him, how'd you know?'

'You were too personal about the way I slipped that phone,' said Mac.

'Go on,' said Garvs, looking genuinely amused.

'The way you looked at me at the Lagerhaus that night you wanted me out of Jakkers. It wasn't about breaking the rules, it was someone who'd been personally inconvenienced. Maybe humiliated.'

Garvs looked at the ceiling like he was weighing something. Looked at Mac. 'Ah, yes. That's a fair reflection.'

'There was also the Bartook Special Mint wrappers.'

Garvs laughed. 'Damn, you're good!'

'Wasn't the wrappers as such, but the way you tear the main wrapper in a long thin spiral. Found that in the Palopo hotel and in the silver Accord.'

Garvs shut his eyes, chuckled, shook his head like *Macca is such a hard-case.*

'Something else,' said Mac, adopting his interrogation poker face. 'I found one of your wrappers up at the depot in Sabulu.'

Garvs sniggered, shrugged.

'So I guess you knew Judith Hannah was up there, huh? Becomes clear why you didn't want me talking to her.'

Garvs averted his eyes and made no comment. The hidden mics couldn't record what wasn't said.

'You know,' said Mac. 'You gonna be the bag-man for Urquhart, you'll have to decide if you're office guy or field guy. Know that, don't you?'

'Mate, let's not get catty,' said Garvs, hurt.

'That was the plan, though, wasn't it, Garvs? It's like, "Holy shit – Tobin's gone and fucked it all up. Brought Macca into this Judith Hannah shit. Right as Singapore is about to go down. Let's make sure he stays in Sulawesi for a while. Make it almost impossible to find Hannah. Keep him out of Singers."'

Garvs picked up a Parker pen, played with it end over end. Classic tell for a man who wanted to illustrate more control than he felt. 'Well, Macca, that's quite a story.'

'Yeah, silly old Tobin,' Mac continued. 'Labouring under this

429

delusion that he should be getting a missing Service girl back from Sulawesi. But Dave Urquhart has a whole other political mission, doesn't he, Garvs? And it's really, really serious stuff. Big-boy work. Not like Judith. And he needs his own bloke in the Service to do his dirty work, doesn't he, Garvs?'

Garvs had stopped smiling, stopped playing with the pen. He looked at a spot on the desk, his head shaking back and forth.

'Shit, Macca.'

'Garvs?'

'Mate, what happened? Huh? Why couldn't you just get old gracefully, get with the program, huh?'

Mac shrugged.

'I mean, why am I feeling bad about this? This is what happens to old spooks, Macca! Look at me!'

Garvs threw his hands out at the desk where there were files, an in box, an out box, and a big appointment diary.

'This is grown-up life, McQueen. Okay?'

Mac was silent, cold.

'So don't come in here with all this shit about people being *brave as*. Fuck's sake, Macca – you have no idea what's been just above your head all these years. I had no idea. You think a spy agency is about *brave*?! Oh, come on, mate!'

Mac shrugged.

'Well it's not. It's about politics, and that's who we answer to. They call the tune. You're in denial.'

'Just doing my job,' said Mac. 'That's what they pay me for.'

Garvs was through with it, and he waved a hand.

Mac got up, turning for the door.

'You know, Macca, I told Dave that trying to delay you in Sulawesi would backfire. Would just get your blood going,' said Garvs.

Mac felt sadder than he'd felt for a long time. One friend was dead before he got the chance to be a friend, now his old mate was discarding him like a toothpick. For what? A chance to suck up to a professional toadie like Urquhart.

Garvs shook his head, like he couldn't believe this whole thing. 'You know who you're like? It just occurred to me.'

'Who?'

'Your old man. That whole last-man-standing bullshit.'

Mac walked out, glowing with the compliment.

Mac watched the endless buildings fly past, looked through the brown smog of the late afternoon heat. Felt the cab swing onto the freeway to Soekarno-Hatta and watched the turquoise Java Sea chopping up to his right.

The chat with Garvs had gone about as bad as it could have. But it had clarified once and for all that he was firmly in the boy scout camp. In his twenties he'd tried to affect the cynical approach, thinking that the cynics had all the best jobs. But he couldn't make it work. He'd always be the guy trying to do the right thing, the last man standing, and he'd always skew towards others like him. People like Paul, like Sawtell.

People like Jenny.

He remembered being in the embassy in Manila one afternoon, catching up on paperwork. He'd come into one of the kitchenettes for a cup of tea and interrupted a conversation between a Customs intel bloke called Sammy Weston and a group of younger blokes.

Mac had made his cuppa while Sammy held forth about the possible sexual orientation of a woman Mac was just getting to know and like: Jenny Toohey.

Mac was going along with Jen's request for discretion about their new relationship, so he kept mum in the kitchenette while Sammy's round face sweated with the joy of his malicious bullshit.

Mac let him finish, and said, 'Sammy, she's not gay, mate.'

Sammy came back with some crap about how he had a mate who had a mate who had seen something in a washroom.

Mac hated that kind of rubbish. Sammy was the same bloke who referred to the Transnational Sexual Servitude Taskforce as 'the Dyke Squad', on account of the number of women working that detail and the fact that some of them lost their boyfriends because they'd gone off sex.

Mac tried to keep it light. 'She likes blokes, champ. Pretty simple.'

The younger blokes had stared at Sammy.

'Not what I hear, Macca. Bird's done nothing to show she's into blokes.'

Mac smiled at him. 'Thing about a girl like Jenny, mate. If she wants you to know, she'll let you know.'

Sammy's face went deep red. Mac heard laughter from the young blokes as he walked out.

Mac chuckled at the memory of that exchange and realised something: Jenny *wanted* him to know, and Jenny had *let* him know. And she'd been doing it for almost six years.

He leaned back, jammed hands in pockets. Checked he had his passport and cash. Pulled it out. Counted it. Found the piece of paper from Garrison's chinos. Looked at the nautical coordinates. Thought about it. Then he scrolled down his 'dialled calls' list in his Nokia. Hit the long number, with the Sulawesi prefix.

A man answered in two rings. Mac said, 'Mr B. It's McQueen.'

Cookie was in a good mood and Mac asked how Lastri was doing. Then told him a few of the basics of what he had for him. 'You were right, Mr B. Put Sabaya together with the Chinese and it equals money.'

Cookie asked where.

'You put a dive team together quick-smart?' said Mac.

'Bear read porn in the woods?' Cookie shot back.

'Got a pen?' said Mac.

He read him the coordinates. 'Don't know exactly where it is, but their final destination was an island in the Sulu chain, so it's around there somewhere.'

'There's a finder's fee, of course,' said Cookie.

'Give it to Lastri. School, uni, that shit,' said Mac.

'You ever want to set up in Indonesia, let me know,' said Cookie.

'Good as gold,' said Mac.

EPILOGUE

One year later

A light breeze blew across Surfers Paradise beach, powder-blue skies over the Pacific Ocean. It was almost eleven am, late November, three weeks before the tourist season. Mac pulled on his Proserpine Brahmans rugby league polo shirt – the one he'd bought from Frank to raise money for the club.

Closing the door gently, he made his way across the park at Broadbeach, through the trees and down onto the beach. He pulled his runners off as soon as he hit the sand, pushed them off with the opposite foot. Held the pair in one hand and walked up the beach to Surfers.

He went into a shopping mall off Cavill Avenue in the heart of Surfers Paradise and walked to the post office past milling Japanese tourists and Malaysian surfers. After doing the double back twice, he paused at the post office door, checked for eyes, checked for tails, half-hearted.

There were seven letters in the PO box. Mac scooped them and left.

He stopped on Cavill Avenue and bought a couple of blocks of Caramello chocolate and a banana and chocolate smoothie. Asked for extra malt and extra honey. Pausing at the newsagency, a puff across the top of the *Australian* caught his eye and he bought the paper.

He felt eyes, kept moving.

Sitting on a public bench at the Esplanade he watched youngsters surfing, oldies catching the sun. He followed the newspaper's puff to the international pages where the lead item was the talks between China and Singapore over closer military ties. Mac scanned the article, found the MSS-driven mention of a 'security relationship' between the two nations. It was followed – further down the story – by the opposition politician's comment about 'a secret deal to put Chinese warships in the Singapore Strait'. Which was a well-worn CIA talking point. He wanted to be interested, but the thought of Urquhart, Garrison and friends actually succeeding just made him feel jaded.

Tossing the paper aside, he sorted through the letters. The one from Sulawesi caught his eye. Bani was doing well at the Brothers' school in Makassar, seeing his family five or six times a year, preparing for university in Surabaya. English was going well, along with sciences, soccer and girls.

A photograph fell out and Mac picked it up. It showed a soccer team of teenage boys in red shirts, Bani one of them, kneeling on a paddock. In the front-centre was a black macaque monkey, wearing one of the red shirts and holding hands with the boys on either side. Mac flipped the photo and saw a message in Bani's hand: *Do you like our mascot? We call him 'Makka' – ha! ha!*

Mac threw his head back, laughed at the sky. 'You cheeky bugger! You'll keep.'

There was a knock at the door. Mac moved from the lounge room, down the hall. He'd rigged a CCTV system above the door, connected to a screen inside. Looking at the screen, he saw a blonde woman in jeans and a polo shirt.

Mac put the Glock back in the hall table drawer, took a deep breath and opened the door.

She was still beautiful – the smile, the teeth, big tan, and filling out a pair of jeans like Michelangelo might have carved it.

'How's it going, Diane?' he said.

There was silence, apprehension showing in her lack of gestures.

'That is your name, right?' said Mac.

'Yes, it is. They used to change my surname.'

Sounds flooded into the long pause, ocean roaring, kids yelling in the park.

'I miss you,' she said, exhaling.

Mac deadpanned.

'You have every right . . .' she said, trailing off.

Mac looked at her, impassive.

'Umm, look. Alan, right?'

Mac nodded.

'Yeah, it was a job,' she said, shaking her head, not looking at him. 'I had no idea I was going to meet someone like you.'

Silence hung between them.

Mac knew how much it had cost her to come here. In the spook world, to drop the shield and be a real person for even a few hours was tantamount to defeat. And once you'd dropped the shield, the effort to go back into character was too much. Which is why you didn't do it.

He didn't hate her. He could have been where she was standing, still running round in circles thinking that cheap diversions and ten-second charm were all that counted.

'I found happiness, mate. Hope you find yours,' he said finally.

She nodded and turned. Left before she cried.

Mac walked back into the apartment and sat down on the sofa. Turned and smiled and then lay down and put his head on Jen's tummy, listening for kicks.

'Who was that?' she asked, sipping on the smoothie and taking another piece of Caramello.

'Some girl,' mumbled Mac. 'Wrong bloke. Wrong number.'

Sneak preview of Mark Abernethy's thrilling sequel

SECOND STRIKE

CHAPTER 1

Flores, Indonesia, 12 October 2002

They sat like surfers waiting for a wave, the four of them dressed in thin black wetsuits facing south-west into the Indian Ocean. Huge blue-black and purple cloud formations loomed above as if declaring an end to the dry season and signalling the start of the monsoons. The swell lapped into Mac's rebreather harness as his eyes scanned the horizon for signs of the target through the salty humidity. Behind him the sounds of bird-life and monkeys occasionally drifted from the remote southern shores of Flores.

Alan McQueen looked at his G-Shock: just past 2.07 pm. Thirty-seven minutes past schedule for the start of Operation Handmaiden, and the crew were getting restless.

'Anything, Maddo?' asked Mac softly.

The man to his left shook his head, not taking his eyes off the horizon. 'Want me to call it in?' he mumbled, lips hardly moving.

'No,' said Mac. 'Sosa knows what he's doing. If the target's there, then we'll know about it.' Mac didn't mind incoming calls, but he wanted to avoid the potential locating beacon you put up every time you keyed the mic on a radio.

The Combat Diver Team providing Mac's escort was known as Team 4. All of them navy special forces based out of Western Australia, they'd flown in two days ago to perform a frogman snatch at sea. It was the most difficult naval commando mission, which suited Team 4 just fine. They sat astride a partially submerged inflatable vessel known in the Royal Australian Navy as a sled and as a skimmer by the British, each man strapped into his own seat. When the sled was fully submerged it became a battery-powered diver-propulsion vehicle capable of carrying five combat divers for about thirty kilometres though there were only three combat divers with Mac on this job. In the bow of the sled was a blond guy, Smithee, and to Mac's right was a huge Aussie-Leb they called Pharaoh, one of the largest combat divers Mac had ever seen. The divers were usually built like gymnasts or boxers, but Pharaoh looked more like The World's Strongest Man, as if he should be lifting balls of stone onto oil barrels. There was a large V-shaped object on Pharaoh's back, strapped over his rebreather pack and pointing over the level of his head.

Sitting in front of Mac was the team leader, Doug Madden, known simply as Maddo. He was a medium-height, dark-haired Kalgoorlie boy who, like most special forces blokes, conserved his energy until sudden outbursts of critical violence were required.

The spare seat was for a bloke named Ahmed al Akbar. A Saudi banker and accountant, Akbar used a legitimate trade finance program in South-East Asia to oversee Osama bin Laden's investments in Malaysia, the Philippines and Indonesia.

Following the September 11 bombings in New York and Washington, the Americans had hit back with an Allied invasion of Afghanistan that had broken the Taliban. But the invasion had also created a diaspora of senior al-Qaeda and Taliban figures who'd fled the al Farouq camp outside Kandahar and spread out through South-East Asia. Now, intelligence agencies like Israel's Mossad, MI6 and Mac's employer – the Australian Secret Intelligence Service – were focusing on what were known as deceptions and provocations. That is, getting the bad guys to go after one another, with a little help from your friendly neighbourhood spook.

Akbar was making his monthly tour of terror camps, and intelligence had him using a regular sea route that started in Surabaya, hooked under Bali and Flores before heading north for Sulawesi and then Mindanao. The point of Operation Handmaiden was to snatch the financier from the vessel he was in and feed a rumour back to the tango community that he'd fled his JI minders and cut a deal where he ratted out the Moro separatists. There were few organisations in the world that were game enough to go after OBL, but the Muslim gangs of the southern Philippines were up there with the White House, Downing Street and the PLA generals, as outfits with the stones to try and hit Osama where he lived. It was a simple plan that hinged on snatching Akbar without signs of a struggle.

Mac checked his gear for the twenty-third time: face mask, hoses, harness, handgun, knife, duct tape, a bag filled with goodies, a hard plastic syringe case and a foil of Xanax. Breathing deep, pain flared in his chest. He'd joined the combat divers only a day before, straight from the Bali Sevens, a seven-a-side rugby tournament held each year at Kuta Beach. In one of the group matches he'd been tackled ball-and-all by a big Yaapie mining foreman playing for a Malaysian team and could barely breathe after the hit. He'd backed up for another match against the Darwin Dreadnoughts an hour later, playing in agony. He suspected a cracked or bruised sternum but hadn't gone to Denpasar Hospital because his team, the Manila Marauders, had a no-piker policy: that is, you played and drank, played and drank for the whole week – no pikers.

The RAN rebreather rigs required deep and regular breathing by the divers, and Mac had no idea how he'd manage or how he might justify failure to Joe Imbruglia, the ASIS station chief in Manila who'd wanted Mac to flag the sevens and do the snatch. *Well, mate, at least I didn't pike on the boys, eh?* Wasn't likely to go down too well.

The call came from Sosa at 2.11 pm, saying he now had eyes on the target from his recon point on the headland. Maddo relayed the update to Team 4 and they fell silent as they waited for the ship.

Mac used the rising adrenaline to run through every last detail of the Akbar snatch in his mind. He visualised it, breaking it into pieces like scenes in a movie. He forced himself to imagine three different disaster scenarios and his exact response to each. The third contingency was a white flag – abandon the snatch and pull an 'escape and evade', an E&E, to a predetermined point.

This last option wasn't defeatist. During Mac's stint in the Royal Marines Commandos the chief instructor, Banger Jordan, had told them there was no such thing as a mission without an exit.

'In a professional outfit there're no heroes and no cowards, only alive guys and dead guys,' Banger had growled. 'The alive guy knows where the exits are.'

'Macca, your eleven o'clock,' called Smithee.

Mac saw it immediately. A faint plume of diesel exhaust signalled the arrival of their quarry. By the look of it, the small ship would be on them in five minutes. Mac looked at the others – the boys were ready.

'Your call Maddo,' said Mac. 'I'm good.'

Smithee locked in on the target and Pharaoh pulled his face mask up, winking at Mac. There was a small pause as they all breathed out and in and then Maddo called the mission.

Seating their masks they twisted their regulators to the settings Maddo called and did three tests on the mixture from the bottles on their backs. Mac tasted rubber, triggering a fleeting memory of using a rebreather for the first time, his heart going crazy, freaking out at the icy English water near Devon.

Maddo tested the comms and all three of them did thumbs-up. When Maddo was set he gave thumbs-up to Smithee. A whining sound accompanied the slow sinking of the sled as the motors sucked water ballast into the inflatable skin, using the weight of the batteries along the keel to pull it under. Mac controlled his breathing and felt the sea water filling up his kit, muting all sounds except for the rasp of his own breathing.

Settling at four metres under the surface, Maddo gave Smithee a heading. The whining sound began again and a pair of enclosed props started spinning on either ends of the bar that ran across the width of the sled's bow. Pharaoh and Mac lay down on their stomachs in the rear part of the sled, while Smithee knelt behind the driving controls at the front. Kneeling behind Smithee, Maddo called the heading from a compass built into the sled. The props angled slightly to the right – and upwards, to stabilise the running depth – and the sled built to its top speed of ten knots.

Mac concentrated on breathing solid and long, taking his rhythm from the sound of Maddo's breathing over the comms. Panters couldn't be trusted with rebreathing rigs because they couldn't properly utilise the carbon-dioxide scrubbers that gave you the four- and six-hour durations with a good military rig.

As they moved through the warm Flores waters, Maddo muttered at Smithee from time to time. Mac fought the panic urge – he hated full face masks and the sense of enclosure – and the pain building in his chest with every breath. After a few minutes of running Maddo whispered, 'Thar she blows, boys.'

Turning, Mac saw *Penang Princess* moving past them, looking like a whale, its darkness ominous in the tropical waters. About one hundred metres to their left, its single prop glinted in the reflected marine light, a trail of champagne bubbles spewing out behind it. Mac was glad he was working with Maddo's boys on this mission; the slightest miscalculation, a bit of bad driving, and that spinning brass disc would create what the naval world referred to as Prop Suey.

'Bring her round, Smithee,' said Maddo.

The sled tilted over into a big left-hand turn, the electric motors whining to keep the speed up as they came astern of the two-hundred-foot ship which was moving about eight knots faster. They held their course, waiting. If the arrangements they'd made were being followed, an Indonesian Navy patrol boat had motored out from Endeh and was about to RV with *Penang Princess*.

Mac had suggested the sharing deal between the firm and the Indonesian military intelligence organisation, BAIS. The boys from BAIS would provide the official decoy, the Service would do the snatch; BAIS could detain Ahmed al Akbar, but the Aussies would join the debrief – or interrogation, if Ahmed felt the warrior stir in him.

They followed and waited, the four frogmen's breathing now synchronised. The ship slowed visibly and Mac felt the sled lose power and then shut down. They were now drifting behind *Penang Princess*.

The single screw suddenly stopped and was still for three seconds. Mac watched it sitting there with water foaming past it. Then it started turning again, in reverse, slowly at first and then faster as the Indonesian Navy asked *Penang Princess* to stand-to.

The sled's power came up slightly and went off again and they closed further on *Penang Princess*, before *Penang Princess*'s prop stopped altogether.

Adrenaline always hit Mac doubly hard when frogging and he tried to keep his breaths long and deep as they closed on the ship. Pharaoh's voice came over the radio system, breaking into his concentration. 'Macca, watch for the loggie, mate.'

Mac was so focused on the ship, and doing what he had to do, that he didn't quite get it on the first go.

'Repeat?' he asked, looking over at Pharaoh, who was pointing at him, his eyes wide behind the glass plate of the mask.

Suddenly Mac sensed something and swivelled to his right to find a huge black eye in his face, a massive mouth opened at him.

'Fuck!' he yelped, whipping away from the thing, freaking at the safety belt holding him in place. He put his arms up to shield his head as a one-hundred-kilo loggerhead sea turtle – a lump of meat and shell the size of a dining room table – bore into his mask before diving down at his webbing. Mac flailed about, heart pounding, as the massive creature tore off one of his gear pockets with a whip of the head, and then swam away.

The sound of men in hysterics peeled through Mac's earpiece like church bells.

'Shit, Macca,' choked out Maddo, crying with laughter. 'She liked you, mate!'

'I thought she was going for a hug,' cried Pharaoh, 'then she tries to get the tongue in.'

As the elite of Australia's naval special forces shrieked with laughter, Mac tried to get his breathing back to regular – you couldn't stuff around with rebreathers.

The laughter died as Maddo spoke again.

'Target stationary, boys,' said the team leader over the radio system as they closed on the ship. 'Let's earn our money.'